AND THIS OUR LIFE

AND THIS OUR LIFE

Chronicles of the Darcy Family: Book 1

C. Allyn Pierson

iUniverse, Inc.

New York Bloomington Shanghai

And This Our Life
Chronicles of the Darcy Family: Book 1

iUniverse books may be ordered through booksellers or by contacting:

iUniverse
1663 Liberty Drive
Bloomington, IN 47403
www.iuniverse.com
1-800-Authors (1-800-288-4677)

Because of the dynamic nature of the Internet, any Web addresses or links contained in this book may have changed since publication and may no longer be valid.

This is a work of fiction. All of the characters, names, incidents, organizations, and dialogue in this novel are either the products of the author's imagination or are used fictitiously.

ISBN: 978-0-595-44844-9 (pbk)
ISBN: 978-0-595-70577-1 (cloth)
ISBN: 978-0-595-89165-8 (ebk)

Printed in the United States of America

This book is dedicated to my husband, Eric, who was most supportive of its creation and publication, and also to the eternal muse of love and marital politics, Jane Austen.

Special thanks to Agra Vinaude, Cherie Kristich, and Karine Grindberg for the cover art for this publication.

Prologue

Netherfield Park
19 October, 1813

Mr. Aloysius Burton
Ashbourne House, London

MY DEAR FRIEND,—

I have the great pleasure to inform you that Mr. Fitzwilliam Darcy is engaged to be married to Miss Elizabeth Bennet. As you know, we have gone through many trials over the course of the last year since our first visit to Hertfordshire, and since that fateful trip the master has endured many periods of lowness of spirits such as I have never seen in the seven years that I have been in his service. How many times have I regretted my frivolous complaint to you that our life was rather dull and routine and that I hoped that Netherfield Hall would provide some amusement in the observation of its inmates! Mr. Darcy's interactions with the very different temper of his friend Mr. Bingley and, especially, the machinations of Miss Bingley to attempt to gain the affections of our master did, indeed, provide amusement for a short while, but then the young ladies of the Bennet household turned our ordered world topsy-turvy! But now, at last, all is well. The master appears happier and more contented than I have ever seen him and, although his demeanour is, as always, quiet and refined, I am astonished at the change in his manner, as will you be when you see him again. Our master has always been just and fair in his dealings with others; he is now gracious and courteous to all he meets (not just those within his own circle) without, I may add, losing one iota of his natural dignity of person.

In spite of my earlier serious reservations with regard to Miss Elizabeth Bennet's family and the lack of sophistication of her upbringing, I am quite pleased with the future Mrs. Darcy, for she *continues quiet and elegant, but, by all reports, has an intelligence and wit that I believe will serve her well in the salons of London. If the Darcys are able to avoid much contact with Miss Bennet's less genteel relations (about whom I wrote you earlier), I truly believe that she will make Mr. Darcy very happy.*

Our master tells me that he plans to remain at Netherfield until the wedding takes place, unless he needs to make a brief visit to London beforehand. I do not yet know the exact date of the wedding (which they will share with Mr. Bingley and Miss Jane Bennet), or how soon they will go into Derbyshire, but I will inform you when I have any news, as always, and in a few short weeks I will join you in toasting the marriage of Mr. and Mrs. Darcy. My one regret at this time is that I will not be present when Mr. Bingley's sister receives the news of Mr. Darcy's engagement to Miss Bennet!—With most sincere regards,

PETER OLIVER

Chapter 1

Let me not to the marriage of true minds
Admit impediments.
William Shakespeare, Sonnet 116

Elizabeth briefly rested her head against the velvet upholstery of the Darcy carriage and permitted herself a tiny sigh of relief as she watched the darkening landscape rush heedlessly past the windows. The last four frantic weeks of preparation for her wedding were over and she was finally Mrs. Darcy. Who could have predicted a mere six months ago that she would now be married to the man of her dreams—if she had, indeed, ever dreamed that such a man truly existed. As she thought back over those last few weeks, and even months, she was amazed at the change in her prospects and in those of her sister Jane.

The season of courtship had been a difficult one for Elizabeth because of the vulgarity and lack of sense of so many of Elizabeth's and Jane's connections. In order to hold her head up without shame, Elizabeth spent much of her time with Darcy trying to avoid exposing him to the society of her more embarrassing relations. This was particularly true with regard to her mother and her aunt Phillips, whose gloating and gossiping over their good fortune in capturing two wealthy men for the eldest Bennet girls usually went far beyond the bounds of good taste. Fortunately, their awe of Darcy's fortune and status, and his rather dignified demeanour, kept them from becoming too familiar with him—unlike Jane's husband, Mr. Bingley, whose ease of temper did nothing to discourage their excesses but who was, fortunately for Jane, more able to close his eyes to their faults.

An annoyance of a different sort was the Bennets' cousin, Mr. Collins, who was a parson under the patronage of Darcy's aunt, Lady Catherine de Bourgh, and who was married to Elizabeth's friend Charlotte. Mr. Collins took every opportunity to fawn over his noble patroness's nephew, bowing and scraping and agreeing with his every word in a quite loathsome manner. Mr. Darcy, for his part, appeared to deal with these actions with equanimity, but agreed ruefully with Elizabeth when she said to him after one particularly trying evening:

"Mr. Collins is such a worm; I do not know how Charlotte and your aunt can bear his pompous ignorance."

Elizabeth closed her eyes for a moment to block out the pictures of her mother's greed and her cousin's groveling, then glanced quickly at her husband, whose face was slightly averted from her as he gazed out his window of the carriage. His dark curls and classic profile could have been drawn from an ancient Greek statue, but his lips, now curved in a complacent smile, were far too expressive to adorn a marble god. She smiled to herself and returned to her reflections.

A few days after Elizabeth's engagement had finally sealed the happiness of both sisters, Elizabeth's father, Mr. Bennet, had called her into his room.

"Lizzy, I know that you and Jane will be wanting to make plans for your wedding clothes, so I have written to your aunt Gardiner, and the two of you will be going up to London the day after tomorrow to spend a few days. I want my two eldest daughters to have clothes worthy of them and their husbands. Your mother tells me that a woman cannot feel her most confident if she does not have the proper wardrobe." He gave her a puckish grin.

Although acknowledging his attempted jest with a smile, Elizabeth's eyes were moist, for her father must truly approve of her marriage if he had exerted himself to make these arrangements. He had initially been appalled when he learned that Elizabeth had accepted Mr. Darcy's proposal of marriage after hearing so much about her dislike of Darcy during the first half year of their acquaintance, but had agreed with her choice after she had explained how completely her thinking had changed. She *had* been a little anxious about the wedding clothes since her engagement, because her father, although a gentleman with a modest estate, had little ready cash after supporting five daughters. Elizabeth knew that her introduction into London society would be difficult enough without the mortification of rustic or unfashionable clothing, and she could not bear to repay Darcy's affection (or his magnanimity in forgiving her previous rejection of him) with base coin. She kissed her father on the top of his head and thanked him for his efforts on their behalf, adding tentatively, "You will not distress yourself with the cost of a wedding for two of us at once, will you Papa?"

"Do not worry yourself, my love; this is the last time that I will have the chance to indulge my two favourite daughters. Let me enjoy it," he returned, his cheerful words belied by his wan smile. Elizabeth pretended not to see his sadness, but went up to her room for a quarter hour to wipe away a few tears and revive her spirits before rejoining the others in the drawing-room. As she entered, Mr. Darcy was just refolding a letter he had been reading. She sat next to him and told him about the proposed trip, and he surprised her with his response:

"I, too, have some preparations I must make for our marriage, including a visit to my tailor, among other things. I have been thinking about going to town for several days, but I have not wanted to leave you so soon. Perhaps your father would entrust you and Miss Bennet to my care, and Bingley and I could escort the two of you to town. Bingley will also have business there, I am sure."

Their plans were duly made, although Elizabeth and Jane were subjected to a brief period of horror when Mrs. Bennet insisted upon accompanying her daughters.

"I should enjoy an outing, and you will need my assistance in choosing your wedding clothes," she announced.

Fortunately for his daughters, Mr. Bennet was uncharacteristically firm, replying:

"No, Mrs. Bennet. The wedding is less than one month away; you are needed at Longbourn, and Mrs. Gardiner knows the London warehouses far better than you."

After many protests, Mrs. Bennet finally saw that her husband was not to be moved and ungraciously agreed to stay home; Jane and Elizabeth breathed again.

And so it was that the eldest Bennet sisters found themselves on the road to London. Darcy's reticence in regard to his business in town had piqued Elizabeth's curiosity, but he merely smiled when she asked him his plans and she was unable to tease him into answering her questions.

When they arrived just before noon and Darcy's coach took them to their uncle's house in Gracechurch Street, he stayed only long enough to exchange courtesies with the Gardiners before leaving. Elizabeth put on her most severe expression and chided him:

"So, you are abandoning us to the mercies of seamstresses and milliners while you disappear on your mysterious business?"

He merely replied, with his most dignified expression, "Do not worry, my dear Miss Elizabeth, your aunt Gardiner's kind invitation to dine tonight will ensure that I return promptly to your door. I have not the least doubt of my future wife's ability to subdue any rampageous bolts of silk." With a solemn bow he left with Mr. Bingley, who, unlike his friend, was unable to control his mirth, and Elizabeth heard him laugh as the door closed behind them.

Jane and Elizabeth spent the afternoon with their aunt, surrounded by silks and fine cottons, lace and satins, and placed some plentiful orders for their wedding gowns, day and evening gowns, and nightclothes. Elizabeth chose for her wedding dress a white, sheer silk gown with a satin underskirt and delicate silver embroidery bordering the skirt and bodice. A white, veiled bonnet with silver trim and white satin slippers would complete her outfit. Jane decided to have her gown done all in white: a fine cotton voile for the gown with white lace trim and matching bonnet and slippers.

In addition to these purchases, Mrs. Gardiner wished to give them each an elegant evening gown as a wedding present. They were a little reluctant to accept such an expensive gift, but their aunt convinced them, saying firmly:

"You will have no need for gifts from your friends to start your homes; please let me do this for you." And so they finally agreed.

Elizabeth eventually selected a sheer cream-coloured silk with a jacquard stripe and tiny puffed sleeves with a narrow Pomona sash at the waistline; the colours would contrast well with her dark, almost black, hair and eyes and would emphasise her fair skin. Jane chose a gown with a square neckline made of pale blue silk and Flemish lace that complemented her lighter colouring and delicate features. By the time they were finished with their shopping, the day was far advanced and it was time to return to the Gardiners' and prepare to greet the gentlemen when they arrived.

Darcy and Bingley were punctual for their engagement, both elegantly dressed for dinner, but Elizabeth and Jane were astonished to see Darcy's sister, Georgiana, arrive with them.

"Miss Darcy, this is such a surprise! I had no idea that you were in London," Elizabeth exclaimed.

Her future sister-in-law looked pleased at her reception but blushed and stammered a little when Elizabeth introduced her to Jane. She managed a shy smile when she greeted the Gardiners, whom she had met the previous summer, and said: "I am very happy to see you again, Mr. and Mrs. Gardiner. Please call me Georgiana. We will all soon be family, after all."

Elizabeth looked at Darcy archly and said:

"Now I understand all of your secrecy regarding your plans while in town." She turned back to Georgiana and took her arm confidingly. "Your brother has been keeping secrets from me, my dear, but I am very happy that you will be here to help us with some of the preparations for our wedding."

Georgiana thanked her, her gaze downcast and cheeks pink, but smiling. It was still a few minutes until dinner so they all went into the drawing-room and, now that the exclamations over Georgiana's surprise visit had ended, Elizabeth found that the gentlemen were willing to converse upon any subject except that concerning their activities of the afternoon.

"More mystery, Mr. Darcy and Mr. Bingley?" she asked, her lips pursed.

"My dear Miss Elizabeth," Mr. Bingley replied, an ingenuous look in his blue eyes, "gentlemen must sometimes have their secrets."

They all moved to the dining-room and the ladies had to content themselves with giving an account of their day, making the most of the difficulties of choosing colours and fabrics and discussing concerns about style, while Georgiana sat silently listening, a small smile playing over her lips. Elizabeth finally said:

"So, Mr. Darcy, have we now given you more information than you ever thought possible about ladies' dress?"

"Not at all, I am finding it a fascinating glimpse into an arcane branch of knowledge. I had not realised all the profound subtleties of the subject." He smiled at her impudent grin and continued with his meal.

After dinner, Elizabeth asked Georgiana if she would play for them, saying, "I never did have the pleasure of hearing you play last summer, my dear."

Georgiana nodded and sat down at the piano, her tense shoulders relaxing slightly as she became engrossed in the music. She had chosen an Italian love song and Elizabeth was touched by this selection of romantic music, but it told her more about her new sister than Georgiana could realise. While she exhibited formidable technical skill in her performance, Georgiana's very precision precluded expression of the deep emotions the words of the song conveyed. Elizabeth wondered whether this was merely a lack of experience and maturity or if her future sister was afraid of revealing too much of herself.

The gentlemen soon joined them in the drawing-room. Elizabeth sat next to Mr. Darcy on a sofa a little withdrawn from the others and they discussed their plans for their honeymoon.

"I suggest that we spend a week in London after the wedding, if that is agreeable to you," Darcy said. "We could then enjoy some of the amusements of town before traveling to Pemberley for the winter. There will not be many people in town during the hunting season, so it will be rather quiet, but we should still be able to find a play or a concert." He added ruefully, "I would prefer to give you a more elegant honeymoon in Paris or on the Riviera, but the war makes that plan a little too adventurous, I fear."

Elizabeth readily agreed with his suggestions.

"London will be delightful. I confess that wondering whether an army would come marching through town might put a serious check upon my enjoyment of a trip to the Continent," she said with a twinkle in her eye. "Hopefully, it will not be many more years before that situation changes."

"The newspapers suggest that the Coalition armies have Napoleon on the run, but so they have said many times before. Perhaps they will be correct one of these days," he returned dryly.

"We can only hope." Elizabeth smiled at him and added, "Will Georgiana return to Pemberley after the wedding?"

"Yes, Ashbourne House will be ours. I am sure that she will spend the week that we are gone impatiently planning for our return. Her letter to me on the subject of our marriage took all of four sides of paper to fully express her delight, and she was most eager to share in the excitement of the wedding preparations."

He looked over at his sister, who was across the room shyly talking with Jane by the fireplace, and his expression softened. Elizabeth's eyes followed his gaze. Georgiana's light brown hair glowed golden in the firelight and her eyes looked as green and limpid as water. They crinkled at the outer corners when she smiled, as she did now at something Jane was saying. Elizabeth had also received a letter from Georgiana upon her engagement to Darcy and, although brief, it had been eloquent in the affection it expressed for her future sister:

> MY DEAREST SISTER-TO-BE,—
>
> I cannot even begin to tell you how delighted I am to know that you are making my brother the happiest of men. I look forward with joy to the prospect of our relationship and hope that you will soon consider me a true sister and not merely a relation in law. All of the residents of Pemberley are completely distracted by their happiness that there will finally be a mistress to adorn and command Pemberley House, and Mrs. Reynolds has been extolling your beauty and grace to those who were not fortunate enough to see you when you visited all too briefly in the summer. I must make this note very short as I wish to send it to you, along with one to my brother, by return post, so I will put off further expressions of my delight until later and merely sign myself.—Your loving sister,
>
> GEORGIANA

"Georgiana is such a sweet, affectionate girl! I am very much looking forward to truly getting to know her before we are caught up in her presentation and first season," Elizabeth whispered, and then added, after a quick glance at the group around the fireplace, "I hope that we can help her overcome her self-consciousness before those events occur."

Darcy nodded, his brow slightly furrowed, and Elizabeth quietly put her hand on his arm. They had talked a great deal about Georgiana during the long walks they had taken daily in the countryside around Longbourn after their engagement. Darcy's sister was sixteen years old and would be seventeen soon, but Darcy had delayed her debut in society because of her shyness (as well as because of his romantic preoccupations of the past year). Her lack of confidence made it likely that these ritual appearances would be a miserable trial for her and would be an impediment to her ability to attract an appropriate husband. Her brother certainly did not want her to marry someone who was only interested in her fortune, but it would be very difficult for a stranger to break through her diffidence and find out what she was truly like. Her sheltered and parentless existence had probably been a rather lonely one, Elizabeth reflected to herself—quite unlike the tumult of the Bennet household.

The incident with Mr. Wickham more than a year and a half earlier had further eroded Georgiana's confidence in herself. Wickham had insinuated himself into the girl's life with the connivance of her then companion and convinced her to elope with him, hoping to obtain her considerable dowry. Fortunately, Darcy had arrived unexpectedly before the elopement took place and his sister had admitted everything to him, averting what would have been the death knell of her chances for happiness. Elizabeth had hopes that she could help her new sister emerge from her shell and become more comfortable in society, and was even now mentally working on a plan to accomplish this.

After a glance to make sure that the others had not noted their sudden quietness, Darcy cleared his throat and continued with his previous train of thought:

"We must have a ball at Pemberley after we arrive in the country so that our neighbours may meet you. We will follow it with one in the servants' hall so that all of our dependents may also celebrate our marriage. Perhaps we could have both balls around Christmas when your family will be visiting."

Elizabeth gave him a sceptical smile and he responded to her unspoken comment:

"Yes, I know what that look means, Miss Elizabeth. I have no greater love for balls now than I did a twelvemonth ago, but I will do my duty for my lovely bride, no matter how difficult it may be. And, I must confess, performing my social duties will be much more pleasant with her at my side." He smiled down at her. "What say you to these plans?"

She returned his smile and answered, "I say that your proposals sound wonderful, so let us do as you suggest. Shall we join the others at the hearth?"

As they moved towards the group around the fireplace, she gave some thought to the prospect of making her debut as Mr. Darcy's bride in London society. She had spent little time in the city, except for visits to the Gardiners in Cheapside—a very different neighbourhood than Mayfair where the Darcy house was located—and she felt a slight flutter in her stomach at the thought. She hoped that she would be able to blend quietly into society without embarrassing her husband with provincial manners or lack of sophistication.

At the conclusion of the evening, as the others were talking over a plan to attend a play the following night, Elizabeth took Georgiana's hand and asked her:

"Georgiana, my dear, you will join us for our shopping tomorrow, will you not?"

Georgiana glanced at her brother for approval.

"Of course you may go, dearest," he responded with an encouraging smile. "I will send you over in the carriage in the morning."

Elizabeth gently urged her, "Do come, my dear."

Georgiana nodded her silent assent with a sweet smile, and the ladies all agreed upon a time. Before they left, Darcy added, rather formally:

"I hope that you will all join us at Ashbourne House in the evening for a light dinner before we attend the theatre."

They all agreed to this proposal, and the two Darcys and Bingley said their farewells.

Chapter 2

The four ladies spent the day at the seamstress's and shopping for shoes and bonnets and other feminine details. When they arrived back at the house in Cheapside, Mrs. Gardiner urged her nieces to dress quickly for dinner, saying, "We are going to Park Street a little early and our shopping took longer than I anticipated, so hurry and change, girls. We will need to have Georgiana home in time to dress for dinner."

Surprised, Elizabeth and Jane willingly hurried with their *toilettes* and they all arrived at Ashbourne House at four o'clock. The butler, an elderly, grey-haired man of great dignity, admitted them with a deep bow and announced them as he preceded them into the drawing-room. Elizabeth was both diverted and nervous as she regarded the servant's perfect, impassive countenance, and was a little startled when she glanced up and thought that she caught a brief look of avid curiosity in his eyes. His expression was so quickly veiled that she was unsure whether she had truly seen it or not, but she gave him a slightly disconcerted smile to acknowledge his bow as she entered the room. After greeting the others, Georgiana went upstairs to change and Mr. Darcy whispered to Elizabeth, "Come with me, please, my love."

They left Bingley to play host and she followed Darcy into the adjoining room, which was lined with books and where a middle-aged gentleman in a sober suit of clothes was introduced to her as Mr. Bennington of the High Street Bank.

"I had Mr. Bennington bring over the Darcy jewels," Darcy said. "Some of them have been in the family for generations and are in rather outdated settings. They have not been worn in years and it is time that they were given new life."

Mr. Bennington removed the pieces one by one from the large case in which he had brought them and Darcy gave her the history of each piece or set as it appeared.

"My grandfather gave these to my grandmother when my father was born," he said as he picked up a velvet case containing a sapphire and diamond demi-parure. "They had waited for many years to have a child and my grandfather was very proud to have a son to carry on the family name."

"They are beautiful," Elizabeth said, touching one of the bracelets.

He picked up a heavy ruby choker.

"This one should be reset. The colour will look lovely on you, my dear, once they are in a better setting, but this one is far too heavy for your slender neck."

Elizabeth nodded silently, her eyes getting larger by the moment as the jewelry appeared.

"I do not know why I should be surprised that the Darcys have so many wonderful jewels, but I confess that I am quite overcome," she whispered to Darcy. He gave her an amused smile.

Mr. Bennington brought out a splendid emerald necklace and bracelet that particularly caught her eye. A simple rope chain of heavy gold formed the necklace. The clasp was a snarling dragon encrusted with emeralds, with ruby eyes and diamond flames flaring from its mouth. The bracelet was a smaller twist of gold fastened with a similar dragon clasp, but in the bracelet the dragon was sleeping, his head curled over his back. They would look wonderful with the simple style of the new gown that her aunt was giving her.

"Oh, these are lovely!" she exclaimed, leaning over them, "I have never seen anything like them."

The chains gleamed dully in the light as Darcy held the case and the stones forming the dragons had lost much of their sparkle, but they were splendid still.

"One of my ancestors was in the silk trade generations ago and brought this back from China for his wife," Darcy said, lifting the necklace. "It is probably close to one hundred years old and looks as if it should have a good cleaning."

He put it down and picked up a beautiful diamond necklace and eardrops in a modern setting.

"These belonged to my mother. I remember her wearing them whenever there was a ball at Pemberley. My father gave them to her as a wedding present."

"They are beautiful, but, my dear … don't you think that you should save them for Georgiana, when she marries?" Elizabeth exclaimed. "Surely she should have her mother's jewels."

"I suspected that you would say that," Darcy said quietly, giving her a slow smile, "It is a testament to your generous spirit."

Blushing at the intimacy of that smile, Elizabeth returned her attention to the jewels and Mr. Bennington, who was discreetly looking down at the items he was unpacking. She picked out a diamond necklace and eardrops and a rather ugly sapphire pendant, which were all in heavy, old-fashioned settings and would be improved by a lighter, more modern look. When Mr. Bennington left to replace the remaining jewels in the bank's vault, Darcy locked the jewelry they had selected in a wall safe, saying as he did so:

"Tomorrow we shall take these to Sheffield's shop in Bond Street and you may select the new settings."

He then went to the desk and brought out a velvet jeweler's case from the drawer and presented it to Elizabeth. He smiled a little self-consciously as he handed it to her.

"This is an early wedding gift. Bingley and I picked these out yesterday with Georgiana's assistance. She said, and I believe rightly, that a simple expression of affection would be more fitting than jewels and that it would be preferable to have something that you could wear every day, not just at a ball."

"Your sister is a very perceptive young woman," Elizabeth said as she opened the case and smiled. Inside was a narrow serpentine chain of gold. The clasp had a tiny cross hanging from it and on each side of the clasp, on the inside, was engraved the initials EB and FD: when the bracelet was fastened, their initials would be joined. He removed it from the case and started to clasp it around her right wrist, but paused.

"Once I fasten this chain you cannot escape," he said gravely.

She blushed and answered quietly, "I'll try not to struggle too much."

He secured it around her wrist and, his eyes still on hers, kissed her lightly on the fingertips. Elizabeth impulsively threw her arms around him and kissed him on the lips. He drew her close again for another more lingering kiss, and then they rejoined the others in the drawing-room, Elizabeth hoping her flushed complexion was not too apparent.

"I can see that a conspiracy has taken place in this house over the matter of these bracelets," Elizabeth commented to her aunt and uncle as they went into the dining-parlour, including Georgiana in her smile. "But I think Jane and I will probably try to forgive you." They all laughed and seated themselves at the table.

After dinner, they gathered their wraps and left for the theatre, an imposing building fronted with an arcade. The inside had been lavishly painted and decorated but was discoloured from the smoke of the many candles lighting the chandeliers, leaving to the elegantly dressed society gentlemen and ladies the task of providing colour and variety to the interior.

Elizabeth felt conspicuous as she made her way through the foyer of the theatre towards Darcy's box. She noted that Darcy was greeted with a slight nod by a few people, but most of those who took notice of their entrance merely stared, and Elizabeth was glad that Georgiana's eyes were modestly turned down so that she did not see them. Elizabeth was well aware that there were probably many mothers in the audience who had tried to capture Mr. Darcy for their daughters. She could not help but feel a little *frisson* of pleasure knowing that she, of all people, would be his wife after all the efforts of the society mammas had been in vain.

The first half of the entertainment was a series of arias sung by Signora Catalani, the undisputed prima donna of London opera, and the audience was entranced until the last note died. Georgiana seemed rapt, and Elizabeth needed to gently touch her arm to bring her back to earth when the interval arrived so that they could make their way to the refreshment room of the theatre.

"Angelica is certainly an appropriate name for a woman with such a voice," Elizabeth commented, to general agreement. She then added to Darcy, when Georgiana was out of earshot, "However, I am not sure that her private behaviour warrants that appellation." Darcy raised a brow and nodded in cynical agreement.

The second half was to be a series of *tableaux* from the recent productions of the company, and the diva would be joined by her fellow cast members to present them. While they were discussing the programme Elizabeth glanced around and noticed Darcy's cousin, Colonel Fitzwilliam, across the room, talking with an elegant older couple who had their backs to them. The colonel's curly brown hair looked almost russet in the candlelight and his face, which was not handsome but was pleasant and open in appearance, had a respectfully attentive expression as he leaned forward to catch the words of the woman. Elizabeth touched Darcy's arm and turned her eyes briefly in their direction. He squeezed her hand in acknowledgement and, when the attention of the others was absorbed in their conversation, said in her ear:

"Yes, they are my uncle and aunt, Lord and Lady Whitwell. Colonel Fitzwilliam wrote me a few days ago that his mother was very upset by Lady Catherine's letter about our marriage and fully expects that you will be a fishmonger's daughter, or some such ridiculous notion. Fitzwilliam says that he defended you as much as he could without, as he put it, imperiling his financially dependent status, but they will have to meet you to finally realise the truth, I suppose. Fitzwilliam's elder brother, Lord St. George, has stayed out of the fray as far as I know, but is not in the good graces of his parents himself at the moment. He has been banished to an estate of theirs in Scotland for the time being as there has been trouble over some recent debts of honour—which is just the sort of trouble St. George would fall prey to! My uncle is a reasonable man but he values his domestic felicity and will not oppose his wife's reading Lady Catherine's venom until things have calmed down somewhat."

"I am sorry that I am causing so much heartache in your family," Elizabeth said ruefully. She paused for a moment before continuing with a slight smile, "Not sorry enough to again refuse to marry you, but still sorry for the trouble you must go through."

"Actually," he returned in a conversational tone, "I am rather enjoying the unusual sensation of being the family black sheep after years of stolid attention to the business of running an estate. Perhaps my taking over this role will be of material assistance to my scapegrace cousin St. George by drawing attention from his misdeeds to my own."

Elizabeth put her fingers to her lips to hide her smile and glanced very briefly over at his aunt and uncle under the pretence of observing the crowd. There was no overt snub to cause comment, nor were there any surreptitious glances to see if Elizabeth and her relatives were aware that they were being ignored. She saw a few glances from the more discreet of the other theatregoers between their party and the Whitwells', and a great many avid stares from the less well-bred: the gossip-mongers watching for fodder.

The members of their party were finishing a lively discussion of the merits of several of the operas that would be featured in the second half of the programme. Georgiana was taking part in this conversation when she noticed the colonel and his parents.

"Fitzwilliam, there are my aunt and uncle," she exclaimed to her brother, "I should say hello before the programme begins again."

She started to turn away, but Darcy surreptitiously caught her arm. She looked back at him in surprise.

"Please do not go, Georgiana," he said very quietly.

"Why not, Fitzwilliam?" she asked, perplexed, her voice lowered to match his.

She suddenly seemed to become aware of the silence of the crowd around her and flushed a brilliant red. Elizabeth affectionately put her arm around Georgiana's shoulder and whispered in her ear:

"Do not be embarrassed, my dear; your aunt and uncle are upset with your brother because he is marrying me, so it would simply be better to not bring attention to the relationship at the moment. Everything will be fine in time, so do not be concerned."

Elizabeth hoped that her encouraging words were true. Georgiana nodded silently, her head hanging in mortification.

"I cannot believe that anyone could object to you, Elizabeth," she whispered. "Fitzwilliam should have told me."

"Thank you, my dear," Elizabeth returned with a smile. "You are right, you should have been told. You *could* do one thing to help me through this, if you would."

Georgiana's head came up.

"I will do anything that I can."

"Then pretend that none of this has happened, and we will return to our seats with our heads held high and ignore the vulgar gossips."

Georgiana gave the ghost of a smile, put her shoulders back with a visible effort, and twined her arm through Elizabeth's. As they turned towards the entrance to their box, the Whitwell group had just reached the doors to the auditorium. Before they disappeared through the door, Colonel Fitzwilliam glanced at Darcy and his right eyelid drooped in a slow wink. Darcy smiled and acknowledged his cousin with a minuscule nod, but Georgiana's smile was rigidly fixed. They returned to their seats and resolutely watched the remainder of the programme, but the joy had gone out of the evening for Elizabeth and, she suspected, for Georgiana as well.

The next day the lovers returned to Hertfordshire, leaving Georgiana and Mrs. Annesley in London where they would stay until the day before the wedding while Georgiana had some new gowns fitted. The next two weeks passed quickly, punctuated by only one minor incident. A week or so before the wedding, the Bennets found through a casual comment that Mr. Collins, who was still visiting his in-laws at Lucas Lodge, assumed that he was to perform the marriage service for the happy couples. Elizabeth and Jane had arranged to have the rites performed by Mr. Martin, who had been the vicar at Longbourn Church for most of their lives, but they were so taken aback by Mr. Collins's insistence that they were unable to immediately marshal a protest. Fortunately, his wife quickly stepped into the breach and said, in a shocked tone of voice:

"My dear husband, do you really think that you should perform the service? Lady Catherine will be most upset if she learns that you have attended the wedding, let alone performed the service."

Mr. Collins's resistance was quickly overcome by this reminder of his noble patroness's fury over Darcy's marriage, and he immediately gave way. Once this small crisis had passed, Elizabeth was amused by her friend's clever handling of her self-important husband.

The last piece of business before the wedding itself was the signing of the marriage articles by each couple. Darcy made over £30,000 to Elizabeth and Bingley settled £20,000 on Jane as their marriage portions. Darcy's estate, like Mr. Bennet's more modest one, was entailed and would be inherited upon his death by his closest male relative. If he had no son and another relative inherited, the marriage articles would provide for Elizabeth and any unmarried children. Bingley did not have an estate as yet, but planned to purchase one and had recently extended the lease on Netherfield Park for another year while he and Jane decided where to reside. Elizabeth found the day to be a sore trial as she tried to keep her mother from gloating aloud over her daughters' future wealth. Mrs. Bennet was, fortunately, not present at the actual signing of the articles, but her avid interest was evident all afternoon, until the exigencies of the wedding itself finally distracted her, and Elizabeth and Jane could breathe a mutual sigh of relief.

The two gentlemen and Georgiana came to Longbourn for dinner that evening but departed early, and Jane and Elizabeth retired soon after. Elizabeth lay sleepless in the dark next to Jane thinking about the changes in her life, and of Georgiana and *her* future. After some time she felt her sister move restlessly and she realised that Jane, too, was having difficulty sleeping.

"Are you awake, Jane?" she whispered.

"Yes, I am too nervous and excited to sleep."

"Just think of the happiness that your marriage will bring to Miss Bingley and Mrs. Hurst, and you will drift peacefully off," Elizabeth whispered in her ear.

"Lizzy!" Jane said in a shocked tone, which she then negated with a giggle.

Elizabeth took her sister's hand and patted it, and her efforts to soothe them both were eventually rewarded with Jane's regular breathing. But it was much longer before Elizabeth herself finally slept.

Their wedding day, when it at last arrived, went off beautifully. The day dawned cool and crisp, with a cloudless, pale blue autumn sky. Elizabeth saw that her sister looked rather wan, and commented, "I feel as if there is a lump of something large and hard caught in my throat. I hope that I do not faint or choke on the words of the ceremony this morning." She put on a rueful look that brought an answering smile to Jane's face, and then added seriously, "More important, I dare to hope that our mother will not embarrass us today."

Jane clasped both of her sister's hands reassuringly and said, "I am sure everything will be fine, my dear Lizzy."

When they were finally dressed and ready to leave for the church, the two sisters embraced each other for the last time as Bennets and entered the carriage for the short ride.

At Netherfield, Darcy and Bingley had stayed up long after Georgiana had retired the night before, keeping each other company with quiet talk of their hopes and expectations of the future over a last glass of brandy, and the morning of their wedding had arrived before they retired at quarter past twelve. At breakfast all were absorbed in their own thoughts until ten o'clock arrived and it was time to dress. The very last act of the gentlemen's valets was to offer their masters a small glass of wine with which to congratulate each other and afterwards the gentlemen solemnly shook hands before joining Georgiana and Mrs. Annesley in the carriage for the drive to the church.

Eleven o'clock finally arrived, and they were married in the tiny Longbourn Church with their families and a few close friends in attendance. When Elizabeth saw her bridegroom watching her come down the aisle on her father's arm, his face solemn but his eyes filled with happiness, she lost her nervousness and was able to meet his eyes with confidence, although with a faint blush adorning her cheeks. Bingley gazed at his bride with a frank grin as she came down the aisle, obviously delighting in his good fortune.

Colonel Fitzwilliam sat with Georgiana and her companion during the service and patted his cousin's hand as she dabbed her eyes with her handkerchief during her brother's vows. Georgiana was the first to embrace her brother and sister at Longbourn after the wedding, shedding a few more tears.

"This is supposed to be a happy occasion, little cousin," the colonel said afterwards.

"I *am* happy," Georgiana said with unconscious dignity. "I apologise if my tears on the day of my only brother's marriage are an embarrassment to you, Colonel Fitzwilliam."

"I am sorry, Georgiana," he said, chagrined. "I should not tease you."

"Indeed you should not," she returned with asperity.

When the newlyweds had greeted all of their guests at the wedding breakfast, Colonel Fitzwilliam gave Darcy a letter from the colonel's father:

> MY DEAR NEPHEW AND NIECE,—
> *I congratulate you upon your marriage and wish you great joy. I regret that we were not able to attend the ceremony, but hope that we may wait upon you this winter at Pemberley to give our compliments in person.—With our best wishes,*
>
> LORD AND LADY WHITWELL

"His lordship dared not risk the fury of Lady Catherine, it seems," the colonel commented to Darcy and Elizabeth. "Sad to have a father who is a coward," he said as he shook his head in mock sorrow.

"Would you face Lady Catherine's wrath?" Darcy queried with an ironic lift of his brows.

"I am a soldier, not an imbecile!" Fitzwilliam returned with a horror-stricken expression.

Darcy and Elizabeth laughed lightly but Elizabeth felt a twinge of sorrow that some of Darcy's closest relatives would not readily accept her. Georgiana silently entwined an arm in hers and Elizabeth was surprised and comforted by the girl's affectionate perception.

Darcy examined Elizabeth's features as they rode towards London after the wedding. He felt that he had neither seen her so clearly nor realised her beauty and grace so fully as he did now when they were irrevocably bound to each other. Her dark lashes curled lushly around her brown eyes below the elegant arch of her brow, and her full lips turned up slightly at the corners. Her slender figure was enveloped in her cloak against the chill, but he could see her heartbeat at the base of her pale throat and her breast rise with each breath. If he had ever doubted the existence of a benignant deity, he could no more. "*License my roving hands*"... but perhaps it was not wise to dwell upon Donne this early in the day, he thought, and spoke softly in Elizabeth's ear, interrupting her reverie:

"You are very quiet, my lady—I hope that you have not changed your mind about marriage to your most humble and grateful admirer."

She turned and gave him a smile of heart-wrenching sweetness. "I fear it is too late, sir, and I must make the best of it."

He slipped the glove off the slender left hand adorned with his ring, which rested upon his dark sleeve, and entwined his fingers with hers as they drove on through the early dusk.

Chapter 3

To save thy secret soul from nightly fears.
Thomas Gray, "The Bard, a Pindaric Ode"

Georgiana chewed her lower lip pensively as she and Mrs. Annesley rode north towards Derbyshire after the wedding. Her companion had dozed off, as she often did, from the rhythmic swaying of the carriage, and this had allowed Georgiana the freedom of her own thoughts. She knew that her brother would gently remind her not to chew her lip if he were here, and she also knew that it was childish and unladylike, but her nerves simply required that she take out her fears in *some* fashion.

Her new sister Elizabeth had been as lovely and kind in London and Hertfordshire as she had last summer in Derbyshire, but neither visit had given Georgiana enough time to really know her brother's wife, and the bustle before a wedding was hardly the proper time to learn someone's character. She trusted her brother's judgment implicitly, but *so* hoped that his wife would be a true sister to her. She knew that she was tongue-tied in company and unable to express herself well, but she prayed that Elizabeth would understand her and not judge her by her awkwardness. She must work hard to appear more relaxed and to speak in the company of others, not only to please her new sister but to be prepared for her own debut.

When she thought about her presentation and her first season, she shivered involuntarily and thanked heaven that her brother had not forced her to go through it last year. If only she could put it off another year altogether (which was, of course, impossible), she could rest easy for a while longer. Her mind veered away from thoughts of her coming-out as too horrific to even contemplate. She put her hand over her churning stomach and sat up straighter, forcing herself to look out the window at the countryside, and to engage her mind she resolutely counted the cattle in the fields and the carriages and waggons that passed.

As evening approached and they neared the inn that would be their first night's stop, Mrs. Annesley awoke and began gathering her belongings together. Georgiana smiled affectionately at the older woman, happy that her brother had found such an agreeable companion for her. She, too, gathered herself together, if only mentally, and told herself with determination that the new Mrs. Darcy would certainly be a lovely person. (Had their past interactions not shown her to be so? Was her brother not always correct in his judgments?) There was no point in worrying. She would put her worries into her private prayers tonight and give them to God; he was much more capable of handling them than she could ever be. This decided, she turned to Mrs. Annesley and said:

"When we return to Pemberley I should like to plan an appropriate welcome for the return of my brother and his bride from their honeymoon. Do you have any suggestions?"

Mrs. Annesley made a few comments and they discussed them until it was time for bed.

Chapter 4

My beloved is mine and I am his.
"Song of Solomon"

Upon the arrival of the coach at Ashbourne House, the Darcy servants gathered in the entry to greet their master and new mistress as they alighted from the carriage. As Darcy led Elizabeth through the door, Mr. and Mrs. Burton, the butler and housekeeper, stepped forward and bowed and curtseyed deeply.

"We are most happy to congratulate you on your marriage, Mr. and Mrs. Darcy," Burton said with a pleased smile.

Oliver, Mr. Darcy's valet, observed the smiles of his fellow servants complacently. Burton had been the head of the London household from the time of the previous Mr. Darcy, and remembered Mr. Fitzwilliam Darcy as a youngster. He had told Oliver that Mr. Darcy had always been a rather serious child; courteous and proper (almost) all of the time. The young master had done a great deal of reading and learned his lessons well—no larking about in the schoolroom, or tormenting the tutors.

Oliver, like his fellow servants, would have been horrified if Mr. Darcy had married a woman who was not of a suitably refined character. It would be terrible to have to take orders from a mistress of no breeding, and so embarrassing for the family! Nonetheless, he also knew from his years of observation that Mr. Darcy was different from the other young society men that he saw and heard about in London. His master would not be happy marrying simply for wealth and social status, without regard to the suitability of the temper of his wife. Mr. Darcy was not a young man who delighted in noise and parties. He preferred the domestic comforts of books and music to the riotous pastimes of many of his peers and a contented home life was essential to such a man. Since Mr. Darcy had passed his twenty-eighth birthday, Oliver had begun to think that he would never find a woman who was both beautiful enough to attract his eye and intelligent and charming enough to engage his heart.

Knowing that Mr. Darcy's fiancée was a young woman of no fortune, he had anxiously observed both of the Bennet sisters when they dined at Netherfield a few days after the engagement, and had been reassured by the manner of both

Miss Elizabeth Bennet and her sister, Miss Jane Bennet. He listened also to the paeans of the upstairs maids, who had attended the sisters when Miss Bennet had been ill and unable to return home for a few days at the beginning of their acquaintance with the residents of Netherfield. The Bennets were both praised as being as gentle and well bred as anyone could want, although he knew that neither of them fitted into the typical society appearance or manners. There was neither false dignity nor posing in any of their actions, just quiet elegance and courtesy. And now the newlyweds had arrived in London. Oliver shook himself out of his abstraction and hurried to the kitchen to make sure that hot water was on its way upstairs before he rushed up the back stairs himself.

The Darcy's were ceremoniously escorted to their rooms by Mrs. Burton, whose formal courtesy Elizabeth found a little chilling until the housekeeper allowed herself to smile approvingly upon the young couple before she curtseyed deeply and left them in their sitting-room. François, the new lady's maid who had been hired on condition of the mistress's approval, helped Mrs. Darcy remove her cloak and bonnet so that she could change out of her traveling clothes before she returned downstairs to join her husband for tea. By Mr. Darcy's instructions they would have an intimate supper at eight o'clock, but a cup of tea would refresh them in the meantime.

While François unpacked her gowns, Elizabeth looked around her room. It was of moderate size with light green walls and elegant, eighteenth-century French furniture. The curtains were light green damask that matched the walls and the hangings on the bed. The bed was large and spread with a coverlet in a floral print with leaves that echoed the colour of the walls and bed curtains. The remaining furniture in the room was in a mix of styles that, somehow, managed to fit together beautifully, with no single piece jarring the senses. Elizabeth felt very comfortable with the room as it was. She thought that she could see the same hand at work that had decorated Pemberley—refined and elegant, but not unnecessarily ornate—and thought of Darcy's mother, Lady Anne, who had died so long ago.

"Your dressing-room is through this door, *madame*," François said, interrupting her thoughts, "if you are ready to change now."

François opened the door and Elizabeth turned her attention to her new maid, examining her with interest as she led the way into the dressing-room. She was small and compact with a dark complexion, and of middle age. She had never been a beauty, but had that aura of confidence that is so effortless in French women, even in the servant class, and that makes them so desirable as maid and advisor to an English lady. She appeared very competent and Elizabeth was pleased with her on this first meeting. She hoped that François knew a great deal about London society, for she herself was a neophyte in the roiling cauldron of gossip and vice that made up that city's upper crust and a maid who was knowledgeable about style and manners would be of considerable assistance to her.

She thanked François after she finished helping her change into one of her new gowns, one of filmy silk in a light apricot colour with a white underskirt and delicate lace trim. She kept on the simple cross necklace and serpentine bracelet she had worn for the wedding, but added a long stole of the same apricot silk and went into the sitting-room that connected her bedroom to Darcy's. He was waiting for her, and rose when she entered the room with a smile of such pleasure that she was again reminded of how foolishly she had misjudged him when they first met.

She realised now that his appearance of pride and arrogance when she had first become acquainted with him was, in part, a reflection of the shyness that she had more easily recognised in Georgiana when they had met the previous summer. In his case, a family that had taught him to think meanly of the sense and worth of the world outside of his relations had done the rest. She could not really regret all of the pain and turmoil of their early relationship, for it had made great changes in both of them, and those changes had brought them, finally, to their current happy situation. She shrugged off these musings and returned his smile as she took his proffered arm and they slowly walked down the stairs to the drawing-room.

Tea arrived as soon as they had seated themselves on the sofa. The footman who brought it laid the tray out skillfully under Burton's eye and then disappeared with a bow, as did Burton.

They sat quietly sipping their tea for a few minutes; then Darcy set his teacup down and took Elizabeth's hand. "I cannot believe that we have finally arrived at this day, my dearest one."

She carefully placed her cup on the tray before saying quietly, her eyes downcast, "Nor can I. The last month has seemed an eternity."

As he brought her hand to his lips she raised her eyes and met his, and he said:

"I love you so much that even your glance causes an almost painful tug of my heart towards you. Rather an apt analogy for my emotions over the last year," he added with a smile. "Thank God, I no longer need fight that force."

He gathered her in his arms and, when she trembled slightly, tightened his embrace and rested his head on top of hers. After a moment, he echoed her earlier thoughts, saying:

"Dearest, loveliest Elizabeth. We have walked through the fire in the last year, my darling, burning away all the lies and misunderstanding, the anger and disappointment, and we have come out on the other side, I hope, finer and stronger, like the tempering of fine steel." He kissed her gently on the lips and added, "I love you more than I ever thought that I could love anyone." After a longer pause she could feel him smile as he rested his cheek on her head again, and he added lightly, "And I am sure that it is most improper to love one's wife so much."

Elizabeth chuckled and said, "Most improper, I am sure." She reflected that he had expressed her feelings very well indeed.

Their supper was ready promptly at eight o'clock, and they sat down at the table in the small dining-parlour. To Elizabeth the meal seemed very long as the servants silently served and removed the dishes. She was anticipating the end of the evening with nervous trepidation and her hands were shaking a little as she lifted her wine glass for a sip.

Darcy made desultory conversation or lapsed into silence and watched her across the table, his face appearing happy and relaxed. She could see no resemblance to the arrogant gentleman he had first appeared to be, displeased with the simple country society of Meryton—or even to the dignified, withdrawn man who had accompanied Bingley on their return to Netherfield for the start of the shooting season, wondering if he could ever make her love him. He seemed this evening to have gained all of the confidence that she had lost in the last few hours. His voice interrupted her musings:

"A penny for your thoughts, my lady."

"Not even for a pound," she managed with a faintly arch smile.

He did not pretend to misunderstand her, but arose from the table and put his hand out to her, whispering:

"It will be all right on the night, my love."

She blushed but took his hand, and he led her up to her room, where François awaited her. Her maid helped her into a beautiful cream silk nightgown and deftly removed her hairpins and brushed out her hair, leaving it to hang in an ebony curtain over her shoulders, then quickly tidied the room.

"Do you need anything else, *madame?*"

When Elizabeth shook her head and thanked her, the maid left her with a brief, "goodnight, *madame*" as she quietly closed the door.

Chapter 5

*Fain would I wed a fair young man that night and day
could please me.*
Thomas Campion, "Fain Would I Wed"

Elizabeth was awakened by the rustling of stealthy footsteps in the hall outside her door and, suddenly alert, she glanced over to the other side of the bed—empty. She was sitting propped demurely on her pillows by the time François answered her ring and entered with the tea tray. She set the tray on Elizabeth's bedside table and, with eyes averted from her mistress's blushing face, said:

"Good morning, *madame,* here is your tea."

"Thank you, François."

"Would you care for anything else with your tea, *madame?*"

"No, thank you, just tea is fine. I will be getting up as soon as I have finished."

"*Oui, madame.*"

François curtseyed and left the room. Elizabeth smiled to herself after the maid left, feeling an excitement about the day ahead, her first true day as Mrs. Darcy: a feeling of anticipation that she had rarely been able to feel about an ordinary day at home with her family. She had noticed that François, with great tact, had not asked her how she had slept, so as not to embarrass the new bride after her wedding night. Elizabeth blushed again, thinking about all of the servants in the house who were aware of that wedding night. She was accustomed to having servants in the house, and was aware that they frequently knew everything that occurred in the family (even family events that one would wish to hide, as she well recalled from the disaster involving her sister Lydia), but she had never really spared a thought about how many things they were privy to. The masters' and mistresses' wedding nights not being the least of them, she thought with chagrin as she rang for François to remove the tray.

When Elizabeth was dressed, she entered their sitting-room, finding it empty except for two places set for breakfast at the small table by the window. She was leaning dreamily against the frame of the window, absently watching the passersby, when her husband entered the room. He came quietly up behind her, put his arms around her and murmured in her ear:

"How does the day look, my lady?"

"It is beautiful, and the sun is shining. I wanted to check and see if London society had yet risen up against your shameful marriage." She smiled up at him with an ironic lift to her brow.

He peered over her shoulder at the street and said quietly, "Well, it appears to be safe, no mobs rioting in the street. Shall we call out the army to protect us, or shall we have our breakfast?"

"I think breakfast would be safe," she answered, and they turned from the window and took their places at the table as the footman entered with their food.

During breakfast, they decided to walk around the neighbourhood immediately afterwards so that Elizabeth could see Mayfair.

"If the weather is pleasant enough we could walk in Hyde Park; it is only a few steps away," Darcy suggested, "and maybe we should visit Bond Street this afternoon and see if there is anything else that you will need before we leave for Derbyshire for the winter. You will, naturally, find a much greater selection here than in Lambton, or even Derby."

"Thank you, King Copetua," Elizabeth said primly, causing him to laugh. "I might need a few things, if I give it some thought."

Darcy looked at her, his eyes kindling, and said:

"We could stay home today, if you prefer."

The colour rushed to Elizabeth's face and it was a moment before she could overcome her embarrassment and say with creditable calmness, "As you wish, Mr. Darcy; I will leave it to you to give the servants the day off."

He laughed at her discomposure and, kissing her hand, said:

"I can think of nothing that I would like better than to send the servants off and have you all to myself until the end of time; however, I do not want you to waste away from inanition, so perhaps we should keep the cook."

She shook her head sternly at his levity, and they finished their breakfast.

When they were ready to leave for their walk, the footman brought their coats. Mr. Darcy's was the same overcoat he had worn the day before, but instead of Elizabeth's cloak he brought her a beautiful, dark russet pelisse of fine cashmere and trimmed with fur.

"I must not let my wife get too cold when she is walking," Darcy said as the footman opened the door for them. "I know, after all, that she is an avid walker."

"It is just beautiful. Thank you, my dear!" she said sweetly, while glaring at him behind the footman's back for this sly reference to one of their early encounters.

They left Ashbourne House arm in arm. The Darcy residence was a large stone edifice on a corner of Park Street, the entrance facing the small, quiet, cobble-stoned street and with a walled garden on the side facing noisier Grosvenor Street. The garden wall was high enough to muffle slightly the sounds of the traffic passing by outside and created an intimate little Eden into which the salon and dining-parlour faced.

As they strolled around the neighbourhood, she saw many large homes along the streets, and surrounding nearby Grosvenor Square. The houses were all made of brick or stone, with three or more floors and tiny flowerbeds along the slate-paved paths to the front doors. They were surrounded by low wrought iron fences, which enclosed the beds and the areas leading down into the kitchens. Similar fences surrounded the square itself: a small park with graveled paths and benches for those who would sit and enjoy the sun, or for nursemaids who would bring their charges out to play on the lawn.

The houses around the square were just beginning to show their daytime faces to the world, their front steps freshly swept and the curtains pulled back. Tradesmen's carts rumbled quietly through the streets to disappear down the alleys where the trade entrances were hidden. Few of the householders who were still in residence in town were about at this time of the morning and the Darcys were able to enjoy their walk together without much need to speak with anyone but each other. As they meandered down the streets they planned the rest of their day, and decided to attend the theatre that night as a new production of *Romeo and Juliet* was being presented at the Covent Garden Theatre.

"I'm not sure a romantic tragedy sets the proper tone for a new marriage," Darcy said with a smile, "but I do enjoy Shakespeare."

Elizabeth agreed readily, but commented, "I have never seen *Romeo and Juliet* on the stage, but I have always thought that the young lovers behaved extremely foolishly. If they had just waited long enough to make sure their messages were received, neither would have died … not that I should be quibbling with lack of proper communication in romantic affairs," she added in sudden embarrassment, remembering the tangled web of misunderstanding which had caused them so much grief in their early relationship. Darcy chuckled over her blush.

They continued their walk down Park Lane until they could enter one of the walks into Hyde Park. There were very few riders out that day in Rotten Row, and the chill in the air had discouraged walkers on the footpaths. They wandered slowly along a graveled path and found a small bench at the end where they could sit, the remaining fall leaves swirling around them like a golden and crimson blizzard as they were teased by the light gusts of a breeze freed from the enclosing buildings of the city. Elizabeth watched the dancing leaves, her hand through her husband's arm, and felt something rigid inside her relax. All of the tension of the past year melted in the cool autumn air and she was left feeling warm and light. She gave a small, contented sigh and Darcy turned his head towards her and smiled.

"Happy, my love?"

"Blissful—I suddenly feel as if I have been translated onto an entirely new Earth from the one on which I had been living, everything bright and new around me."

As he opened his lips to respond, a pair of urchins suddenly appeared with a ragged mongrel in tow to chase the squirrels around the trees before running off on some mysterious business of their own, but not before giving cheeky grins at the couple sitting, arms entwined, on the bench. Elizabeth laughed as the ungainly dog lolloped after the children.

"Well, perhaps not everything is bright and new!" she said, thinking of the difficulties with various in-laws that interrupted her serenity like the urchins invading the Park. "However, I do feel that I have an entirely new outlook on life and on the people I know or meet. I remember a conversation I had with Jane not so many months ago, wherein I expressed to her my dissatisfaction with the human race and how inconsistent were the characters of so many of the people that I knew. This was after my friend Charlotte became engaged to Mr. Collins, which shocked me greatly. I had not thought that she would disregard every better feeling merely to obtain a comfortable home."

"This was also, I presume, after Bingley had left Netherfield so suddenly."

She gave him a rueful smile and nodded. "Yes, indeed it was."

"And to what do you attribute your more charitable frame of mind?" he asked.

"I am not sure that I should say," she said, raising one brow. "It could be detrimental to your character."

"I will try to not let it go to my head."

"Well then, it was finding a man whose character not only proved to be invariably honest and good in spite of all of my ungenerous acts and assumptions, but who was willing to reassess all that he had believed in and admit that he had been wrong. How could I do less? Even if you are, as I believe, unique among men, you still give me hope for the future of humanity."

Darcy bowed his head. After a minute he cleared his throat and looked at her, saying quietly:

"You humble me, my dearest Elizabeth. I do not deserve you."

They sat silently, hand in hand, for a few moments. Then she said teasingly, "Possibly not, but I am afraid that this ring has chained you to me forever." She added reluctantly, "It is getting a little cool—I suppose that we should walk home."

"If you wish—we would probably draw unwanted attention if we sat here until nightfall," Darcy returned with a soft smile as he rose and turned towards Park Street.

After a cup of coffee to warm them, they took the carriage to the shopping district and spent the remaining afternoon hours walking through the milling crowds, peering at the displays in shop windows and doing some desultory shopping. Elizabeth purchased a beautiful cream-coloured Belgian lace fichu for Georgiana, and they stopped at a bookshop and looked over the new publications. Elizabeth picked up a slim volume of poetry and showed it to Darcy.

"Here is the new poem by Lord Byron. Does Georgiana enjoy poetry?"

"She does. What is the title?"

"It is *The Giaour*," she said, stumbling over the title. "I am not sure of the pronunciation."

"Let us get it. She spent hours over *Childe Harold's Pilgrimage*, although I hope that she did not understand all of the allusions contained in it!"

They purchased the book and turned their steps towards Sheffield's Jewelry.

"These should let Georgiana know that we were thinking of her," Elizabeth said. "I want her to know that I care for her."

Darcy squeezed her hand, which rested lightly on his arm, and they entered the shop. Mr. Sheffield waited upon them himself and assured them respectfully that the jewels were ready for their inspection.

"Oh, they are lovely!" Elizabeth exclaimed when she saw them. "I cannot wait to wear them! They are simply works of art, Mr. Sheffield. And the Chinese dragons are truly wonderful now that they are cleaned. Thank you so much for your care."

The proprietor beamed at her.

"I thank you, Mrs. Darcy, for your kind words. I hope that you enjoy wearing them. If you would like, I will have them delivered to you this afternoon."

They agreed and turned to go, but as they were leaving Elizabeth stopped by a small case near the door. In it was a single strand of perfectly matched seed pearls with a tiny gold cross hanging from it, a seed pearl embedded at the tip of each of the arms. She was entranced.

"Do you think that we could get this for Georgiana for Christmas?" she asked. "It would look wonderful on her."

Darcy had the jeweler remove the necklace from its case and carefully examined it with the jeweler's glass. After much discussion and further examination, he turned to Elizabeth.

"The pearls are lovely—are you sure that you do not want it for yourself?" he asked, smiling.

"Thank you, but I have a few jewels which need to be worn before I think about new ones—although I do love this, and so, I hope, will Georgiana."

"Then she shall have it," he replied.

The theatre was only partially full that evening, in contrast to their last evening there the month before, but the turnout was good for the end of the little season. The Darcys were greeted coolly by a few couples as they entered the lobby of the theatre and ignored by several mothers who were there with their as yet unmarried daughters, for Mr. Darcy was no longer an object. Elizabeth quietly returned the greetings of those few who deigned to acknowledge Darcy and were then introduced to her. She again refused to allow the speculative looks of society gossips to disconcert her and she followed Darcy with outward serenity to their box, but she noticed that Darcy looked rather grim by the time they sat down.

"Smile, my love," she whispered in his ear, "you do not want the gossips to think that we are fighting already, do you?"

He looked down at her with a half smile as she affectionately put her arm through his and they both resolutely turned their attention to the stage as the curtain rose.

In spite of the whispers and stares of the audience and her previous comments about the characters in the play, Elizabeth enjoyed it and even shed a few tears when the lovers breathed their last, drawing a gentle smile from Darcy as she dabbed at the drops with her dainty handkerchief. They had stayed in their seats during the interlude, quietly talking, but their departure was a repetition of their entrance: a few nods, a brief introduction or two, and then they were in the carriage and on their way home.

The evening was slightly chilly, but pleasant, so they spent a few minutes in the garden before retiring. With Darcy beside her, Elizabeth wandered the pathways, looking at the ghostly forms of the leafless trees and shrubbery in the moonlight, turning her face up to the breeze to cool her warm cheeks.

"I am sorry that you had to face that this evening, my love," Darcy said hesitantly.

"Do not worry, my dear," she said firmly, "it was no more than I expected. They will come around. I just hope that you do not lose any friends that you truly esteem over our marriage."

"If I *do* lose them then they do not qualify as friends, do they?" he said with asperity.

"I suppose not."

He embraced her, holding her tightly to his breast for a moment.

"I find it very difficult to keep a pleasant and open countenance when people who have not a fraction of your worth openly snub you, but I know that glowering will only make me look defensive and will not help you."

She reached up and gently put her hand on his cheek.

"You must try to see the humour in the situation, my love. The ridiculous behaviour of society people *should* provide us with a great deal of entertainment." She exerted herself to give him a cheerful smile, and his expression softened.

"Shall we go inside?" she suggested.

He nodded and they walked quietly upstairs.

Chapter 6

The rarest of all women.
William Shakespeare, "The Winter's Tale"

The Darcys spent most of their week in London together, with a small number of hours spent apart: Darcy conducted a very few short but necessary meetings with his man of business before he retired to the country for the winter, and Elizabeth had fittings for some new frocks. To Elizabeth's surprise, Darcy had offered to accompany her to the seamstress's shop to help choose the fabric and trims for her gowns. When she expressed her astonishment, he said:

"You forget, my love, that I have been buying these fripperies for Georgiana for the past five years, so I am not completely ignorant. I do admit, however, that it is the pleasure of your company that induces me to join you."

Elizabeth accepted his companionship, but with a few internal reservations. She was concerned that she would be rather inhibited having a gentleman with her, as her father would have died rather than consenting to accompany his wife and daughters in shopping, but she found that Darcy was quite fluent in the language of ladies' fashion and he joined in the search for the perfect fabric with zeal. He was, in fact, the one who found the silk she ultimately decided to use for one of the gowns, a beautiful lemon-coloured satin and a translucent silk of a changeable, iridescent sheen for an overlay. She would probably never have looked at such expensive material on her own, not yet being accustomed to the benefits of the wealth into which she had married.

They did a little more shopping after leaving the seamstress's. Derbyshire was farther north than Hertfordshire and would be colder, so she added a fine Kashmir shawl in cream trimmed with Venetian lace, and a short, quilted spencer of burgundy-coloured velveteen to her purchases, and Darcy ordered a pair of top boots from his boot maker. When they finally returned to Ashbourne House there was a letter awaiting them from Georgiana. She did not have much news, but expressed her eagerness to have them at Pemberley and hoped that their week in London was enjoyable.

Darcy read it and looked gravely at Elizabeth as she gathered her writing materials.

"You may thank my sister and assure her that parts of it are excellent."

Elizabeth gave him a repressive look as the footman brought in the tea tray, and then she sat down and wrote Georgiana a short note while she and Darcy drank their tea. She included in it regards from both of them and assured her that they would be in Derbyshire very soon, naming a day five days hence for their arrival.

Their evenings during their week in London had been most commonly spent at home, where they talked or Elizabeth played the beautiful pianoforte in the drawing-room for Darcy. Even with the many hours they had spent together in the month before their marriage, they found no shortage of topics for conversation. When they did not have personal subjects about which to talk, the progress of the war in Europe and in America could always provide food for a lively discussion, and there was plenty of news in London as well. After each day they retired early to their rooms and sent the servants off, and Elizabeth had soon stopped being self-conscious about her time alone with her husband. He stayed with her most of each night, returning to his room only when morning arrived and the servants were called.

He had begun bringing tea into her room himself in the mornings, dismissing the startled servant who brought the tray, so that they could have more time together while they drank it, an unconventionality Elizabeth was sure would cause talk in the servants' hall, but which she enjoyed. She took pleasure in the few hours each day when they were alone, and when they could show their affection for each other without wondering if a servant would disturb them. It would not do to embarrass the servants, as they both well knew—although on the other hand, she noticed that all of the older servants seemed to be walking around in a frank state of euphoria since the master's marriage, and would most likely not have blinked an eye (much) if Darcy and Elizabeth had been caught kissing passionately on the main staircase. She chuckled to herself at the thought of the impassive Burton's face in that event, and then sighed as she put the thought away. The proprieties must be preserved.

The next day, they received an invitation by the morning post for dinner at the home of Lord Cranton. Darcy considered the invitation while they sipped their tea. After a few minutes, he tapped the card and reflected:

"Cranton was at Cambridge at the same time as I, but he was a few years older and we were not close friends. He was always insatiably curious about other people's affairs, so I suspect that he wants to be among the first to meet you, Elizabeth. I also seem to recall that he and my cousin St. George had a bit of a falling-out last year over an affair of honour, so he probably also wants to spite St. George a little by welcoming me, the family outcast." His final remark was a trifle acerbic.

"Well, we do not need to go in that case, do we?" Elizabeth queried as she refilled his cup.

"Well, it is not required, certainly, but Cranton was not a bad sort—at least he was not when we were in University together. I don't really know if he has changed," Darcy mused. "He was always rather like a puppy who was eager to be friends with everyone: like Bingley in some ways, now that I come to think of it. That wasn't a quality I truly appreciated at the time, but I think that I might be more tolerant of it now." He smiled down at her. "He and his wife are known for their frequent dinner parties, which are small but select … They try to put together an assortment of interesting people: not just those who are socially prominent, but people who are accomplished in their fields. I think, on consideration, that we should go. I want you to be accepted wherever you choose to go in society, and Lord and Lady Cranton's parties have the reputation of being stimulating without pandering to the dissipated element of the *haut ton*. In addition, I could probably use the experience to further my transformation into a full-fledged human being; a process which was started a year ago by a young lady in Hertfordshire."

"All right, if you wish, dear," she said warmly, and twined her arms around his neck. "However, I think that you are fairly human already—of course, one can never practice too much, as Lady Catherine kindly pointed out to me several times while I was playing the pianoforte at Rosings."

He smiled at her and then kissed her brow and added, "And don't be nervous about appearing in society. I am sure they will be enchanted with you—although I hope not as much as I."

She laughed with an air of unconcern and kissed him back, but spent some minutes with François that afternoon planning her *toilette*. She had discussed her difficulties with her maid as she became more acquainted with her, and had expressed her desire to slip easily into society and uphold her husband's confidence in her without appearing overeager or awkward. François, in turn, had told her a little of her *histoire* as she helped her dress and did her hair.

"I was a lady's maid to a young lady of noble family who died in childbirth a year ago. I took my time choosing my next situation and lived with my sister and her family while I was unemployed and assisted them with the care of their children while I searched."

"Whatever made you choose to accept this position? We will be living very quietly, except when my young sister-in-law has her first season, and really do not provide you with scope for your talents, much as I appreciate them!"

"*Madame* is too kind," François said, bobbing a small curtsey. She paused a moment to consider and then continued, "To be frank, I chose to apply for this position because of *Monsieur* Darcy's reputation as an honourable gentleman of excellent character, and I heard that he had married for love rather than to increase his lands or to fill his pocketbook. *Pardon, madame,* for my candour, but my last post was with a couple who married for social consequence and fortune at the will of their parents, and they were but poorly suited in temper. There were many scenes and much unhappiness that was impossible for a lady's maid to avoid. But to return to the question of your gown, *madame,* I would suggest the cream silk with the green sash. It is *au courant,* but not too assertive for a first dinner party. It is also of a simple style that will make a lovely background for your emeralds," she added with a brief, rather sardonic, smile.

Elizabeth agreed to her suggestions with a chuckle and was able to face the rest of the afternoon without anxiety.

When their carriage pulled up in front of Lord and Lady Cranton's town house, the Darcys alighted and were admitted by a footman. Lord Cranton was a rather heavy, dark-haired man in his early thirties in age, with thinning hair and a slight paunch, who greeted them enthusiastically and introduced his wife. Lady Cranton, in contrast to her husband, was a tall, elegant woman dressed in the height of fashion. She greeted them politely, but rather coolly, and examined Elizabeth speculatively.

"I am pleased to meet you, Mrs. Darcy; your fame precedes you," she said courteously.

"And how is that Lady Cranton? I did not realise that my activities were of sufficient note to constitute fame," Elizabeth returned irrepressibly.

Lord Cranton interjected with a guffaw, "Your cousin, Colonel Fitzwilliam, has been singing your praises for weeks, I assure you."

"My cousin does me too much honour," Elizabeth returned politely.

"If you will enter the salon, you may thank him yourself, as he is one of our guests tonight," Lady Cranton said with a flicker of amusement in her eyes. "He must be commended for his judgment," she added as she slipped her arm through Elizabeth's and led her into the salon to meet the other guests. Elizabeth felt that she had passed the first hurdle.

Most of the men seemed to be "Lords" or "Sirs" and were generally known to Darcy, and they seemed uniformly eager to make Elizabeth's acquaintance. The ladies in the room were, at least superficially, courteous to her, but there were a few that Elizabeth thought looked rather rapacious, watching her with suspicious, predatory eyes as the gentlemen gathered round to be introduced. Colonel Fitzwilliam excused himself from the group he was in and greeted his cousins warmly.

"It is good to see the both of you," he said, "I hope everyone is well at the Darcy household."

Elizabeth assured him that they were quite well and he asked how her family was coping with the loss of two daughters at once.

"My father will find it very difficult to have us out of the home circle," Elizabeth said, "but the Bingleys reside only a few miles from Longbourn, which must be of some consolation to him."

Darcy interjected smoothly, "How is your family, Fitzwilliam?"

"My parents are very well and are back at Whitwell Abbey," he said, his eyes twinkling with mischief. "I am sure you will be hearing from them soon. It is such a shame that they were unable to join me at your wedding."

"Indeed, I hope that we will see them soon," Darcy returned, with a touch of dryness that only his wife and cousin would detect.

When dinner was announced Elizabeth, to her surprise, was expected to lead the way into the dining parlour with Lord Cranton. She realised that it was customary for a new bride to be so honoured, but she felt uncomfortably conspicuous taking the lead in front of all the women of much greater status. Their jealous looks bored into her back like daggers, and she wondered briefly whether Lord Cranton was purposely trying to make her unpopular. A glance at his face assured her that his straightforward nature was unfeigned and he was simply unaware of their looks. She accepted Lord Cranton's arm with a graceful inclination of her head and was seated at his right at the dinner table. On her right was a slightly built but boldly handsome and rather dissolute-appearing young man with dark auburn hair and intense grey eyes. She had noticed him talking to several of the young women in the drawing-room but she had not met him before dinner was served. Lord Cranton introduced him to her as Lord Byron. She was intrigued to meet the notorious poet, whose unsavoury reputation had reached even to the wilds of Hertfordshire.

"I am delighted to meet you Mrs. Darcy. I understand that you and Darcy were married only a few days ago."

"Yes, my lord, only five days ago."

"I congratulate you. I am desolated, however, that I have never met you in the years that I have been in London. I thought that I had met all of the beautiful young ladies here."

Elizabeth examined his face to see if he was patronising her, but saw only intense interest.

"My family lives very retired in Hertfordshire, my lord," she said simply.

"A shame, but I am very pleased that I am now able to make your acquaintance. How did you and Darcy meet?"

She gave him a very short (and much edited) version of their courtship, which seemed to amuse her dinner partner.

"I do not know Darcy well, but I can see that I have underestimated his fire and audacity, Mrs. Darcy. I would have guessed that he would make a much more—shall we say?—*conventional* alliance with one of the belles of the *haut ton* that are trotted out each week to be shown at the local balls."

"I think perhaps, my lord, that many people underestimate the depth and breadth of my husband's mind," Elizabeth said firmly.

"I certainly did!" Lord Cranton interjected with a laugh. "And I have known Darcy since we were at Cambridge! He always took top honours, but no imagination at all!"

Elizabeth could not resist saying, with a knowing look at her host:

"From what I have heard of undergraduates, my lord, perhaps imagination is something that should be discouraged on a university campus."

The gentlemen both laughed good-naturedly as the soup was served, and Elizabeth had a moment to gather her thoughts and look around.

Darcy was seated across from her and part way down the table with an attractive young woman in a very low-cut sapphire gown to his right and an older woman dressed in elaborate purple satin on his other side. The older woman had introduced herself to Elizabeth before dinner as Mrs. Hatfield. She was polite enough to her dinner partners but seemed to have only partial attention to give them, spending most of her time attempting to watch an older gentleman down the table who was talking animatedly with the young woman seated between him and Darcy. The young woman, who had been one of those hovering around Lord Byron earlier, seemed far more interested in Darcy than in her other neighbour. She turned often from her more loquacious partner to ask his opinion, gazing into Darcy's face while he answered politely but with a touch of the sardonic in his smile.

After talking to Lord Cranton during the soup, Elizabeth turned back to Lord Byron during the fish course, as courtesy dictated. He had an almost magnetic gaze, which he now turned eagerly back upon her.

"I must ask you, Mrs. Darcy, from whence your remarkable jewels came. I have never seen anything like them."

"They have been in the Darcy family for generations, my lord, and came originally from China."

"They are magnificent."

"I thank you, my lord."

"And so, Mrs. Darcy, how do you find London? Have you been here before?"

"Yes, my lord, but only to visit my aunt and uncle and take in the occasional concert or play. I have not spent any great time here."

He was eager to hear what she had seen and, as she told him, she felt as if his large eyes were boring into her soul. She tried to ignore her discomposure at the intensity of his gaze, and mentioned that they had attended *Romeo and Juliet* that week.

"It is not one of my favourites among Shakespeare's works," he said, "I would recommend *Hamlet* for the person of discriminating taste. Shakespeare's portrayal of the edges of madness rings very true to my ear. Have you seen it?

"No, my lord, but I have read it. I found that *Romeo and Juliet* seemed much more credible on the stage than it had in my reading. It is difficult to really appreciate the passions driving the characters when you are merely reading dialogue, particularly dialogue in archaic English." He leaned towards her and appeared to be even more intent on her words as she spoke of passions. She hurried on. "I prefer his comedies; *Much Ado About Nothing* is my favourite, I believe. I am of rather a cynical temperament, I confess, but I nonetheless prefer my entertainment to have a happy ending. Perhaps also I identify myself overmuch with Beatrice." She smiled, and Lord Byron seemed charmed.

"I am positive that you could have very little in common with Beatrice, Mrs. Darcy," he said gallantly. "Besides having no resemblance to 'my lady disdain,' I have difficulty picturing you threatening of one who had done a family member wrong to 'eat his heart in the marketplace.'"

Elizabeth smiled again, thinking of Wickham, and Lord Byron adroitly interpreted her look, asking, "But perhaps I am wrong and *Mrs.* Darcy also has more fire in her temperament than is visible to the eye." He looked at her questioningly with a slight, expectant smile on his face.

Elizabeth decided that it would be prudent to draw back a little and answered noncommittally, "Who does not have someone in their past who sparks their ire?"

"Very true. You are a wise woman, Mrs. Darcy," he said with an intimate smile.

Elizabeth gave him a vague smile in return and was relieved when Lord Cranton claimed her attention, allowing her to turn away from Lord Byron's dangerous notice. He was certainly most interesting to talk to, and made her feel that she was the most fascinating woman in the world, but his intense conversation teetered upon the edges of propriety. She felt that she must carefully modulate her every response so that her interest in the discussion did not overstep the bounds and she found the verbal fencing enervating. She could not, however, completely suppress her amusement at the awkward situation, and several times she glanced over to find Darcy looking at her, mirroring her enjoyment in his smile before turning back to one of his dinner partners.

Several more times during dinner, she could feel Lord Byron's eyes upon her and would occasionally pretend not to notice. At other times she would speak politely, but only when courtesy dictated. She could now understand some of the gossip about his romantic exploits. It would be very easy for a woman who was lonely or discontented to fall under his spell, in spite of his unprepossessing physical presence, and then find herself in a compromising situation.

All in all, Elizabeth found her first foray into society to be rather an unsettling experience, although she had exerted herself to behave in a relaxed fashion and felt that she had not committed any egregious missteps.

As they drove home, Darcy was able to explain some of the undercurrents that Elizabeth had noted in the room.

"Mrs. Hatfield was watching her husband down the table. He has a reputation as a lady's man, and, well, let me just say that I wouldn't want my wife or my sister to be left alone in his company. His wife is obviously aware of this, and he was not behaving very discreetly tonight with Miss Bainbridge, whom I had not met before. I noted that there were a few older women there who had very clear designs on my fortune for their daughters in the last couple of years and who did not seem terribly happy to see us. I was relieved that I was not seated between them as poor Fitzwilliam was. He probably considers himself lucky at this moment to *not* have an inheritance or he would have had an uncomfortable evening with his dinner partners—rather like a nice plump cow swimming in a school of piranhas."

Elizabeth laughed and commented archly, "Miss Bainbridge seemed happy enough with *one* of her dinner partners."

"Did she? I fear that I did not notice. I was more interested in observing my wife's dinner partner to make sure that he behaved with decorum. I would hate to have to call him out on your first appearance in society."

He smiled slyly and Elizabeth responded with a genteel snort.

"Cranton told me, when we had a moment alone tonight, that he was amazed at how much I had changed since university. He was happy to see that I had the sense to recognise a woman of quality, even if she did not have an inheritance to sweeten the pot. He also expressed the sentiment that the coming season would be improved by your presence, so you have obviously made a conquest. I assured him that I fully appreciated my good fortune." He smiled smugly down at her. "By the way, you have not yet said how you got along with the notorious Lord Byron."

She explained her discomfiture at being his dinner partner and added, "He is a talented poet, but he would be very uncomfortable to be around very much. Those gimlet eyes of his are quite disconcerting. I was rather surprised at how small he is—I somehow expected a roué such as him to have a more impressive figure."

"The man is a menace to society in spite of his small stature and clubfoot; or, possibly, it is *because* of those characteristics. I am not surprised that you found him dismaying."

"I have met other menaces to society; in fact I am now related to one, as you know. The main difference between the two of them is that Lord Byron has a title and money to buy his way out of trouble, while Wickham has nothing," she said with a sniff, which caused Darcy to chuckle as they climbed the stairs to their room.

They had invited the Gardiners to dine the last evening they were in town and Elizabeth enjoyed seeing her aunt and uncle very much. They in turn expressed their pleasure at seeing their niece happy and contented, presiding over her own table with grace and assurance. They felt a warm concern for the well-being of their niece and new nephew, as their trip with Elizabeth to Derbyshire was the event that had finally brought them together.

All of the Gardiners would be coming to Pemberley for Christmas, so Elizabeth would not be separated from them for long, but she was happy to see them before she and Darcy left town. Elizabeth and Jane had discussed the holiday season before their marriages and worked out a plan with Mr. Bennet and the Gardiners, which their fiancés had approved. The Gardiners would come to Pemberley for Christmas and Jane and Bingley would stay in Hertfordshire with the Bennets. Shortly after Christmas, the Gardiners would travel to Longbourn and stay a day or two there on their way home to London. When they left Longbourn, the Gardiners would take Mrs. Bennet and her two remaining unmarried daughters with them for a visit in town, and the Bingleys and Mr. Bennet would come to Pemberley for a fortnight. They were pleased with their plan, as this would allow them to see each other without exposing Georgiana to the peculiarities of the Bennet family and, hopefully, without Mrs. Bennet feeling herself ill-used. When they concluded their planning, Elizabeth had commented to her father:

"If I am able to carry off this complicated maneuver I should offer my services to the army as a tactician. I regret that the plan does not allow me to see Charlotte when she is home, but I have seen enough of Charlotte's husband in the past weeks and am happy to think him in Kent, consoling Lady Catherine for the terrible shock of her nephew's marriage."

He father had replied, with a brief grin, "It is the duty of a commander to maximize gains compared to losses, not to completely avoid the battle."

She had grinned back at him and kissed his cheek. "Thank you, Papa, for your assistance."

He had patted her cheek affectionately and gone back to his library.

Chapter 7

Where'er I roam, whatever realms to see,
My heart untravelled fondly turns to thee;
Oliver Goldsmith, "The Traveller"

As they rode in the carriage on the long highway that curved northward towards Derbyshire, bundled into cloaks and gloves and their feet warmed by heated bricks, Elizabeth thought about Pemberley. Once they had settled in, she would have to begin learning to be the Lady of the Manor (she could not avoid thinking of it with capital letters). She and her sister Jane both had some experience in managing a household; the incapacity of their mother to control her emotions and her frequent vapours over various perceived difficulties had forced a great deal of responsibility upon them. But up until now she had never had the superintendence of a large household of servants, and she found the prospect rather daunting.

She knew that Mrs. Reynolds, the housekeeper, was very loyal to the Darcy family and very competent at running the household, as she had done so during the many years that Pemberley was without a mistress. Elizabeth hoped that Reynolds's very high regard for her master and the Darcy family would not make her look down upon his new wife and her less than exalted, although gentle, upbringing. She recalled her saying, as she had shown Elizabeth and the Gardiners the public areas of the manor house the previous summer, that she would like to have the master married so that he would spend more time at Pemberley, but had commented, "I do not know who would be good enough for him." The Burtons, at least, had seemed to accept her as mistress during their stay at Ashbourne House, and she had Georgiana's assurances that Mrs. Reynolds had expressed pleasure at the news of Elizabeth's engagement to her employer.

When she had been gazing pensively out the carriage window for some time, mulling over these thoughts, her husband interrupted to ask her what she was thinking about so gravely. She told him her concerns.

"You will have many things to learn, I grant you," he replied, "but I think Mrs. Reynolds will turn out to be your greatest friend in that process. I have a suspicion that Burton has been sending Smithfield reports all along, and it is clear that you have won him over. If it weren't for his high regard for the dignity of his office, I am sure he would have been clucking like a proud hen over her chicks this entire week."

Elizabeth sat back, somewhat reassured by Darcy's confidence in both her and his servants. It was clear that she would have no problems being accepted by Georgiana, and that was the *most* important point.

When they finally reached Pemberley after three days of driving, Elizabeth was ready to remove from the carriage. Even with the unhurried pace and the almost voluptuous comfort of the Darcy carriage, the journey had begun to take a toll after those three days. When she had last been through Derbyshire it had been full summer and the fields and woods had been cloaked in green. Now, the verdant trees were transformed into barren skeletons and the chill of coming winter was in the air. Still, it was beautiful, rugged country with jagged peaks looming over the deep valleys, which were adorned with fields and pastures.

As the carriage began to slow and turn past the lodge and onto the drive into Pemberley, the lodge keeper and his wife popped out of their door and bowed and curtseyed, big, beaming smiles on their faces. Darcy acknowledged them with a nod and a lifted hand and Elizabeth with a smile. After they had driven about a mile, Elizabeth began watching for the moment when the manor house would appear. The demesne was ten miles around and forested over much of its extent, and the road wandered through the trees for nearly a mile farther before they reached the top of a ridge and a vista opened, revealing Pemberley House, an enormous Palladian edifice of pleasing proportions fronted by a graveled sweep.

The lawn and trees surrounding the house ran down to a stream edged with paths and traversed by the occasional rustic bridge. There was a small folly, like a tiny Grecian temple, crowning a low rise towards the rear of the manor house and shaded by several willow trees which were scattered around it, now bare of leaves. The entire appearance was of natural beauty unmarred by too much refinement or an awkward taste, and Elizabeth felt that her memories of the beauties of Pemberley had not been distorted by the passage of time or the many miles of distance she had traveled since her last view of it.

They pulled up to the front and Smithfield and Reynolds appeared to greet them with a crowd of servants behind them, all smiling in welcome of their master and mistress. Mr. Darcy smiled at Elizabeth and whispered "Welcome home, Mrs. Darcy," as he handed her out of the coach. At Reynolds urging, a little girl came shyly forward with a bouquet of asters and chrysanthemums, and the housekeeper curtseyed and said:

"We are most happy to greet you, Mr. and Mrs. Darcy, and may we wish you joy upon your marriage."

Elizabeth thanked the child, who gave her a brilliant smile and ran back into the throng of retainers, and turned to Reynolds, saying:

"Thank you, we are delighted to be home."

Smithfield bowed and said a few words of his own, which were almost drowned by the clapping of the other servants after they had curtseyed and tugged their forelocks. The Darcys smiled on them before ascending the steps to the main hall. Georgiana was awaiting them in the entry, as befit a lady, a huge black dog with a massive head sitting tranquilly beside her. She could not maintain her regal air once they were in the door, however, and she met them with shy hugs and kisses while the dog stood and sedately waved his plumed tail.

"My dear sister, I am so happy to see you again!" Elizabeth said warmly; she then looked over at Georgiana's companion. "My goodness; that is the largest dog I have ever seen!"

Darcy answered her. "This is Pilot; he was my father's dog and as you can see is beginning to get a bit grey around the muzzle. He is, fortunately, of a very placid disposition."

"I would hope so! I did not meet Pilot last summer," Elizabeth returned while patting Pilot on the head, finding it rather disconcerting that she needed to raise her hand above her waist to do so.

"No, we keep him in his kennel when there are visitors touring. We don't want to cause swooning or apoplexy when he appears." Darcy scratched Pilot behind the ears as he talked about him, the dog accepting the attention with dignity.

After refreshing themselves and changing out of their travel clothes they went down to the drawing-room, where Georgiana and Mrs. Annesley were waiting. Elizabeth sat next to her new sister and a footman entered with a tea tray almost immediately.

"I thought you might need some refreshment after the long drive, so I ordered tea when we saw the carriage arriving," said Georgiana diffidently.

"Bless you, my child," said Elizabeth with a warm smile, "you may have saved my life, for I am indeed ready for tea!"

Georgiana giggled and then blushed. Elizabeth was pleased to hear that laugh; it showed that Georgiana was already becoming comfortable enough with her to let down her guard a bit. She was still planning how to help her sister-in-law come out of the shell her shyness had built around her and she was sure that Mrs. Annesley would assist her. However, although Mrs. Annesley was kind and well bred, she was a great deal older than Georgiana, and Elizabeth hoped that having a woman close to her age to spend time with would benefit her new sister's confidence and poise.

She began her campaign that night when the four of them had supper together by first making sure that the dining table was made as small as possible, so that they could easily talk, and by lightly complimenting Georgiana on how well she looked in her new fichu.

"I just knew that it would suit you, my dear. I am so glad that we saw it while we were in town."

"Thank you, Mrs. Darcy, it is beautiful, and I love the poetry book. I have wanted to read it since I heard news of its publication," she said, then added softly, "You are too good to me."

Elizabeth kissed her on the cheek and they walked in to dinner together, one on each of Darcy's arms. During dinner Elizabeth talked to Mrs. Annesley about London and the amusements and parties they had attended there. She gradually extended more of her attention to Georgiana, including her in the conversation without requiring that she speak. By the end of dinner, Georgiana was occasionally making a quiet contribution to the discussion, and as they finished Elizabeth asked:

"Georgiana, dear, would you be willing to show me around Pemberley tomorrow morning? Mr. Darcy needs to meet with his steward and I am much too impatient to wait for him." She gave him a grin and turned back to her sister.

Georgiana blushed and looked down, but nodded with a brief smile. Elizabeth thought that this was a good start in breaking down her reticence; she and Darcy went upstairs early, tired after the long journey.

Chapter 8

An unlessoned girl, unschooled, unpractisèd,
Happy in this, she is not yet so old
But she may learn.
William Shakespeare, "The Merchant of Venice"

Elizabeth planned to spend the next few days learning everything she could about Pemberley and her responsibilities there, and rose early in anticipation. Her reception from Mrs. Reynolds had at least partially allayed her fears, but she would need to show herself capable if she was to win the respect of the household servants, and she was eager to start. She arranged to meet with Reynolds immediately after she and Darcy had finished eating in the small breakfast-room downstairs. When she had visited Pemberley in the summer with her aunt and uncle, they had been shown a small chamber at the back of the house that looked out on the folly and that had been used by Darcy's mother as a morning room. Elizabeth thought it would suit her very well.

The room was small and intimate and was very comfortably furnished in a feminine style. It contained an exquisite, finely carved rosewood desk of beautiful proportions, perfect for a lady's correspondence and other business. She made herself comfortable, slightly rearranging the items on the desk to suit her taste, and started a letter to Jane. She had written her a short letter when they reached London to let her know that they had arrived safely, and told her that she would write more when they reached Pemberley.

> MY DEAREST JANE,—
> We have arrived at Pemberley after a very long three-day ride. Somehow it did not seem so far last summer when I traveled here with our aunt and uncle, but of course we were sightseeing and stopping frequently. Mr. Darcy says that he has, on occasion, covered the same road in one and a half days! Must I already begin to question the veracity of my dear husband? His assertion simply does not seem possible! In addition to assuring you of our safe arrival, I would like to ask your advice on how I may help Georgiana gain confidence in

herself and become more comfortable in society. She is such a dear girl—I should like to do my best for her. Now that you have spent a few days with her, I am in hopes that you will have some counsel for me. If you do not feel that you know Georgiana well enough yet to advise me you may at least be able to observe her at Christmas and offer some suggestions. I know that I may count on your discretion and good sense in this matter. I do not want Georgiana to know that she is being managed, even with the best of intentions. Give Mr. Bingley my best regards and know that I am:—Your Loving Sister, etc.

When Reynolds arrived at her door, she invited her in. They reviewed the menus for the week and Elizabeth approved them. Reynolds also gave her a list of all the household and outdoor servants and reviewed it with her as well. As they finished Elizabeth said:

"Thank you Reynolds, I believe that will be everything, except that I would like to ask you to show me the picture gallery one day and tell me the history of the paintings. I know little of the art of painting, but I am interested in the family history.

"I will do so with pleasure, Mrs. Darcy, whenever you wish. As Mr. Darcy has perhaps mentioned, I have a great interest in the family history."

"He has indeed. Thank you, Mrs. Reynolds."

Reynolds curtseyed and departed, and Elizabeth went in search of Georgiana. The sound of the pianoforte led her to the music room and she watched her sister for a moment while she finished her piece. When Georgiana played the final crescendo of the concerto she looked up and saw Elizabeth in the doorway. She jumped up immediately and closed the instrument before hurrying over.

"Are you ready for your tour, Mrs. Darcy?" she said, a little breathless.

"Yes, please, Georgiana, and do call me Elizabeth, I beg you, or I shall feel very old and matronly. Shall we go down and start in the entry hall and then work our way upstairs?"

Georgiana nodded her agreement with a brief smile and they went to the front of the house. They started at the door and saw all the rooms on the ground floor, most of which Elizabeth had seen the previous summer but which she wanted to see again so that she could orient herself. The rooms were arranged around the four sides of a pleasant courtyard with a formal garden that provided an attractive view from the inside rooms. Georgiana's manner was constrained when she started the tour, merely naming the rooms and opening the doors so that Elizabeth could see them. After Elizabeth had asked her a few gentle questions she began to open up and was soon adding comments on the history of the manor house and the family.

"This is the ballroom. We have not had a ball here within my memory. My brother, as I am sure you know, does not like balls." She risked a quick smile at Elizabeth, revealing a charming dimple in her right cheek.

Elizabeth laughed and said, "Indeed, I do know. The ballroom will be used next month, however, as we are planning to hold a ball when the Bingleys are visiting. It is a beautiful room—we could probably fit a hundred couples in here if we wished to."

Georgiana smiled and walked on to the next door. It opened on a chapel, which made a small wing off the back of the house; the windows were of stained glass, and filtered multicoloured light over the Darcy tombs in the back. Gold chrysanthemums decorated the altar and it was very quiet, separated as it was from the routine bustle of the rest of the house. After a moment's silence, Georgiana quietly said:

"My parents are in that tomb in the near corner."

Elizabeth took her hand and they walked over to it. It merely said "Darcy" over the stone lintel, but there were small plaques on the wall beside the tomb listing the Darcys who were interred there, and their dates of birth and death, including "Alexander Richard George Darcy" and "Lady Anne Winslow Darcy."

"My father used to come here every morning and sit for a few minutes, and Mrs. Reynolds still makes sure that there are fresh flowers on the altar every day. The chapel has not been used for regular services in years, only the occasional funeral."

Elizabeth heard the loneliness in her young sister's voice and put an arm around her. Then she silently led her back to the main hallway and they continued their circuit of the house, a little more subdued than before. When they reached the picture gallery along the back of the house they merely walked through, stopping only at the portraits of Darcy and Georgiana and one of their parents, all of which had been painted by Sir Thomas Lawrence. The paintings were arranged chronologically and it was interesting to see the changes in clothing styles over the centuries and the Darcy features appearing in various forms, but they did not linger.

They eventually returned to the entry hall and ascended the main staircase, a large, gracefully curved sweep of white marble, to reach the family quarters on the first floor. In addition to the master suite, which consisted of a corner sitting-room with one bedroom and dressing-room along each side of the northwest corner of the house, there were twenty bedrooms on this floor. Georgiana had a suite of rooms on the opposite front corner and Mrs. Annesley had a bedroom and sitting-room next to her, both of them facing the tree-covered ridge that filled the view from the east side of the manor.

The other sixteen rooms on the first floor were furnished as guest rooms, providing plenty of space for large parties. All of the rooms were elegantly and comfortably furnished, although the furniture in the less-used bedrooms at the back of the house was covered with dust cloths, giving it a ghostly appearance that was at odds with the morning sunlight streaming around the edges of the draperies. Elizabeth was pleased to note that even those rooms that had been disused for several years were still free of dust and dampness, a compliment to Reynolds's abilities as housekeeper. As they toured the bedrooms they passed several housemaids who curtseyed to them before continuing their morning work, peeking at them from the corners of their eyes as they did so.

The second floor held the servants' quarters—small, simple, but comfortable rooms—and the nursery and schoolroom, as well as quarters for a governess, which were all empty now. Elizabeth was interested to see the schoolroom where generations of Darcys had learned their lessons. There were well-worn schoolbooks neatly arranged on the bookshelves and appearing rather forlorn. She pulled out a tattered copy of *Gulliver's Travels*.

"This was one of my favourite books when I was young. Of course, I thought that Lilliput and Brobdingnag and all of the other countries in the book were real places."

Georgiana smiled. "I did too. I actually enjoyed it more before I understood that it is a satire."

"So did I."

They smiled at each other rather shamefacedly and Elizabeth moved on to a drawing that was hanging forsaken upon the wall, signed by Georgiana in a childish hand.

"I drew that when I was seven," she said with a nervous laugh.

"It is quite good for a seven-year-old, but I am sure that you can do better now. Do you have a portfolio of your drawings?"

Georgiana nodded.

"You must show them to me sometime, Georgiana."

She blushed and nodded. "If you like."

They returned to the ground floor and Georgiana took her into the conservatory at the back of the house, which they had neglected earlier. It was a large glass addition with beds containing ornamental trees arranged with flowering plants at their feet. A few of the trees were covered with shiny dark-green leaves and had fruit on them—oranges and lemons, Elizabeth saw. In the centre of the conservatory was an open space with a slate floor, furnished with wicker chairs and *chaises-longues* and scattered with small tables. It was the most informal room Elizabeth had yet seen and the faint fragrance of the fruit scented the air, which gave it the feel of a summer's day in the midst of autumn's cold winds. Elizabeth was delighted with it.

"This is lovely, Georgiana! Shall we have our morning coffee here?"

"I should like to, Elizabeth." She tried the name out tentatively, and then added with a smile, "I am glad that you like the conservatory—it is one of my favourite places at Pemberley."

Over their coffee Elizabeth delicately tried to draw out her sister-in-law about herself: her likes and dislikes and her passions.

"I know that you are very fond of music, my dear. How long have you been studying the pianoforte?"

"I started when I was five or six; I do not recall exactly. I had a governess who was very interested in the arts: she could play, and draw and paint beautifully, and it was her influence that made me also love them."

"I believe I heard mention that you are also learning to play the harp?"

"Yes, but I am just a beginner. I have a master who comes once a week from Lambton to teach me."

"You are fortunate to have a teacher available so far from the city."

"Yes. He is a retired schoolmaster, but he is willing to give me lessons. He also helps me with the pianoforte. He is very fond of etudes and scales," she added dryly.

Elizabeth laughed with her.

"I am sure that I will meet him one day. What else do you do with your days?"

"Well, I do some needlework, but I am not very fond of it. I like to read and Fitzwilliam's library has an endless supply of books. Thank you again, by the way, for *The Giaour;* I have wanted to read it since I heard of its publication. I wish that he could have given it an easier title, however."

"I would certainly agree with that! What else do you like to read?"

"Oh, everything. I suppose that I enjoy history the most."

Pilot appeared at the French doors that led back into the house, and Georgiana rose to let him in. He flopped at their feet, his forepaws crossed and his head up, gazing at them.

"He is a beautiful beast—quite a noble brow," Elizabeth commented.

"Yes, he is. I adore him, but he is such a monster—I have learned to step aside when he walks by so that I am not covered with drool."

They smiled at each other, and Elizabeth added, "I suppose a huge, slavering Newfoundland dog, no matter how benign, is not the most appropriate pet for a lady."

"Perhaps not," Georgiana said, looking at Pilot wistfully.

A few days later, Elizabeth received a letter from Jane:

> DEAREST LIZZY,—
>
> *I must reject any claim to extraordinary abilities when it comes to advising you about Georgiana, but I will give you all the assistance in my power. Georgiana is indeed a sweet girl and I would like to help her. I do not feel that I know her well yet, but my first piece of advice would be to make sure that she has plenty of social contacts among familiar people, and to gradually give her more responsibilities for greeting and offering invitations. I believe that if you give her these small parts to play in society, she may increase her confidence and it may make the more complicated interactions eventually less onerous for her. We have certainly seen from our time with her that she is a very lively conversationalist when she can forget herself. I will do all I can for her while we are visiting after Christmas. Bingley sends his love.—Your loving sister, etc.*

As the days passed, Georgiana became more relaxed around Elizabeth, who quickly found herself becoming very fond of her young sister. She showed remarkable good sense and maturity in her thoughts and feelings, in spite of her outward self-consciousness. Georgiana confided to her one sunny day, as they took a walk on the grounds accompanied by Pilot, that she had never felt comfortable around Mr. Bingley's sisters, with their ill-natured criticisms behind the backs of their so-called "friends."

"I confess that I was rather fearful that my brother would marry Miss Bingley since she expended a great deal of time and attention on him. I was not quite sure what his thoughts were about *her*, since he was invariably courteous, so I was very happy when I found out about his high regard for you, even before I met you! I should have known that he would not be led to make a mistake … he never does." Elizabeth smiled to herself and then patted her sister's hand and thanked her for her regard as they continued their walk.

Chapter 9

And this our life ...
William Shakespeare, "As You Like It"

The three Darcys gradually made the rounds of their neighbours, introducing Elizabeth to the local gentry. Darcy had, without question, the largest estate in the neighbourhood, but there were a number of pleasant manors nearby and they visited them all.

First they made an early afternoon call on Sir Andrew Ffoulkes, whose manor, Kympton Hall, was a mile from the village of the same name and about four miles from Pemberley. The Ffoulkes' were an old Derbyshire family and had lived at Kympton Hall for about ten years, having previously lived in the south of the county on a lesser manor. The new manor house was a large, square red-brick building with smaller wings at each end and with large paned windows flanked by green shutters. Sir Andrew was a bluff man, somewhat stout and pompous, with the look of the stereotypical English country gentleman: blue eyes and ruddy cheeks and about fifty years of age. His looks suggested that he spent a great deal of time out-of-doors and his conversation was mainly concerned with the state of his pheasants and whether the weather would be fine enough to hunt at Christmastime.

Lady Ffoulkes was rather a surprise. She appeared to be much younger than her husband, had dark, Gallic good looks, and spoke English with a distinct French accent. Elizabeth wondered how she came to be married to this most prosaic of English gentlemen. The Ffoulkes' had seven children, and Sir Andrew also had two unmarried sisters who lived with them, both in their late thirties in age and in appearance much like their brother. Both women spent the visit fussing over their nieces and nephews and scrutinizing their visitors in a way that Elizabeth found rather unnerving, especially with the sisters' too prominent eyes and pale lashes.

During the visit, Sir Andrew mentioned that Lady Ffoulkes's widowed brother, the Comte de Tournay, was expected for Christmas and would stay a fortnight, and he expressed his hope that the three Darcys would join them for dinner while the comte was visiting. They indicated their willingness and made their farewells.

On the way home, Elizabeth asked, a little hesitantly as she did not want to be uncharitable:

"Do Sir Andrew's sisters always stare in that way?"

Darcy laughed and answered, "Not always. Perhaps they find you an interesting study, or maybe they have not seen the latest London fashions."

Georgiana interjected, "I have always thought that they looked rather like a pair of geese flanking a swan when they sit on either side of Lady Ffoulkes, as they did today." She faded into silence and a flush crept up her neck as she neared the end of her comment, but she joined Darcy and Elizabeth weakly when they chuckled at her apt description.

Lady Ffoulkes and her sisters-in-law returned their call very soon and Elizabeth found Joanna and Emily Ffoulkes a little more personable when their nieces and nephews were not distracting their attention, but neither had much to say. Lady Ffoulkes was very pleasant and, while Georgiana was struggling through a conversation with the two sisters, she quietly told Elizabeth a bit more of her history.

"My father, the late Comte de Tournay, had a large estate in the south of France, but was well known at court. He advised the king to be more moderate in his dealings with his subjects but His Majesty, as usual, refused to be guided by his advisors' opinions. When the Revolution came and the Bastille was breached, my father took all of us back to the chateau for safety, but the Terror did not leave any of the aristocracy untouched, and eventually we were arrested and imprisoned. We were saved on the very brink of death on the guillotine by a courageous group of English gentlemen who spirited us across the English Channel to safety. My husband was one of those gentlemen, and that is how we first met." She smiled softly, her eyes looking across the years to a past more dangerous and exciting than Elizabeth could have imagined.

"What a terribly tragic story, my lady," she responded quietly. "You were fortunate to survive. How soon after that were you married?"

"We waited about two years. I was only fifteen, you see, when we met, but my husband was twenty-four, and had already inherited his estate. So although the horrifying events in France delayed our marriage, when I reached age seventeen I insisted that my parents agree to our engagement. I loved Sir Andrew and I believe that I saw much more clearly than my parents did that we would not be returning to our previous life in France. My father liked Sir Andrew, but he kept hoping that the world would change back to the way it had been before 1792. I knew that it could not be." She smiled at Elizabeth, a touch of sadness deep in her dark eyes. Elizabeth gave her arm a quick pat of sympathy, and Lady Ffoulkes steered the conversation into less emotional channels, talking about her eldest daughter, who would be coming out the following year.

"Will you be coming to London for the season this spring?" Elizabeth asked her.

"*Mais non*, London is too expensive to keep a suitable house when you have such a large family as we do, and we prefer the country life. We will wait until Jeannette comes out and is presented at court."

After Elizabeth had asked about her other children, Lady Ffoulkes terminated their visit with expressions of regard, which were echoed by her two sisters-in-law.

Later, Elizabeth asked Darcy:

"Did you know of the Ffoulkes' history—that he helped rescue her family from the guillotine twenty-five years ago and brought her to England?"

"I heard something about it when I was a boy, but it was long after the event and the gentlemen involved kept their identities very secret. I was not really aware that it involved people that I knew."

Elizabeth smiled at her husband's casual acceptance of his neighbour's gallant past, and wondered whether he would have joined the small band of saviours in their rescue of the French aristocracy if he had been old enough. She suspected that the answer would be yes, for she knew that Darcy had a noble and romantic heart beating in his dignified breast. She could easily picture him living a quietly heroic life while covering his deeds with a façade of commonplace ease and pleasure.

The day after the Ffoulkes' call, Georgiana and Mrs. Annesley had plans to go to town in the early afternoon to buy some supplies for their needlework, leaving Elizabeth and Darcy to their own devices. Darcy had planned to see his steward, but he appeared at the door of the music room while she was looking over Georgiana's music.

"Are you busy, Elizabeth?"

She smiled at him. "Not at all, my dear. I am just looking to see if Georgiana has any music that is not too difficult for me to play."

"The weather is quite warm today for the time of year and there is little wind, so I wondered if you would like to take a picnic and go for a walk in the woods. I thought that I could show you some more of Pemberley."

"Are you not meeting with Mr. Johnston?"

"I have put him off until later this afternoon."

"Then I should be delighted to go. Just give me a moment to change my shoes and put on my bonnet."

They set out just after noon, walking slowly and stopping frequently to look at the beauty of the changing views. He took her up a path that led in easy stages over the ridge in back of the main house, following the stream until they lost it into a curve of the hills. The graveled path was wide and smooth, but the way was ever upward, requiring that Elizabeth stop often to catch her breath. When they came to the top of the ridge, she could see down into a little glen adorned with a small, rocky stream that formed a pool below a tiny waterfall. In the summer the glen would be very shady, but now the trees were bare and the forest was carpeted with dead leaves, the drab brown interspersed with flashes of gold and red, which made a shushing sound as they wound their way down through them.

There was a small clearing next to the stream that was flat and dry and would make a fine place to sit and eat. Darcy had brought a blanket, which he laid on the ground, and Elizabeth knelt down and looked into the basket to see what the cook had sent them to eat. There was a loaf of new bread, sliced thin, cheese and apples, a bottle of wine, and tiny fruit tarts for dessert. As they ate, Elizabeth commented:

"I feel very decadent sitting here eating in the woods. I fear that Zeus will send down his thunderbolts from Mount Olympus to punish us for our audacity in having a picnic next to his sacred pool. There is definitely something uncanny about these woods—or perhaps it is the unusual sensation of the two of us being totally alone."

"So, I take it that you want to go back to the house?" He pretended to start to his feet.

"I think not yet, sir," she said with a laugh.

They finished eating, and Darcy settled himself against the bole of a tree at the edge of the glade, patting the blanket next to him. Elizabeth took off her bonnet and curled up beside him in the crook of his arm, resting her head on his shoulder. The woods were very quiet except for a flock of goldfinches that flitted from tree to tree, twittering and singing snatches of song and seeming delighted with the reprieve from the autumn cold. As the flock drifted farther away, silence enveloped the two of them, broken only by the occasional rattle of the dead oak leaves that still clung to the trees. They might have been a hundred miles from the nearest habitation instead of a mere quarter mile. A light gust swept by, bringing with it the remembrance of late fall, and Elizabeth shivered a little at its frigid touch.

"Cold, my love?"

"Just a little."

He wrapped his cloak around both of them and tightened his arms around her and they resumed their contemplation of the water and the birds.

After a few minutes, Darcy said, "This spot does not remind me of Zeus so much as Shakespeare. I had almost forgotten until now.

"And this our life, exempt from public haunt,
Finds tongues in trees, books in the running brooks,
Sermons in stones, and good in everything."

"That is quite appropriate; this could be the Forest of Arden. 'Are not these woods more free from peril than the envious court?'"

She lifted her face to smile at him and reached up to run her fingers through his wind-tousled hair. He kissed her on the forehead, moving slowly down to linger on her lips. Eventually, they somewhat breathlessly resumed their enjoyment of the autumn scene and listened to the quiet chuckling of the water as it trickled over the rocks and into the pool. When they had been sitting in this manner for quite some time, Elizabeth lifted her head from his shoulder and asked:

"My love, what was your mother like? I have heard much about your father, but I do not feel that I know your mother at all, excepting, of course, her appearance in her portrait."

"Well, I will see if I can capture her personality for you. I have given much thought to my parents and who they were in the past twelve months of my life, so I can probably sketch her more adequately than I would have been able to before you and I met." He paused to smile down at her, and then continued, "She was very much like my aunt, Lady Whitwell, in looks, as you will see when you meet her and can compare her to my mother's portrait. They were very close in age, only eleven months apart, while Lady Catherine was almost ten years older. Their father was the Earl of Winslow. The family was very small and he had no male relatives, so the title would die with him—to his great distress.

"I remember my mother as very cool and elegant. She had a calm demeanour like your sister Jane, but without Jane's warmth of personality. My father loved her very much and put her on a pedestal like a goddess, and she seemed happy to remain there. I feel, thinking back with the advantage of maturity, that she was rather—I suppose 'detached' would be the best word—from life. I do not remember ever seeing her passionate about anything, but then she died when I was thirteen years old, so my memories are quite possibly imperfect.

"As you would guess from the difference in our ages, Georgiana was born when my mother was past her youth and I believe from what I gathered at the time, even as sheltered as I was, that the birth was a very difficult one. My mother was never in good health after that, and she died when Georgiana was less than two years old.

"My father carried on his duties after her death, as he had always done, but his heart was not quite with us. One of the penalties of being in love with your wife, I suppose." He smiled at her again, his gaze slowly traveling over her features as if etching them in his memory, until she blushed and lowered her eyes. He toyed with a stray curl at the side of her hair and wound it around his fingers before going on. "Like most children of our background, we were both raised by nurses and governesses, and I cannot but feel that Georgiana would have benefited by having parents to serve as an example, advise her and oversee her upbringing, as I did for most of my youth."

Elizabeth frowned down at her hands. "I see—Poor Georgiana. It is not surprising that she does not have confidence in herself when she really never knew her mother, and her father was grieving for most of her life." After a few moments quiet contemplation she added, "I will be interested to meet Lady Whitwell. She sounds quite different from Lady Catherine, which, I must add, is a blessing."

Darcy laughed. "Indeed it is!"

After about an hour, Darcy sighed and said, "I suppose that we should gather up the remains of our *alfresco* party and make our way back to the real world."

"It will probably not be warm enough again this winter to come back here, but let us return to this spot in the spring; I should like to see it again. It will be even lovelier, if that is possible, when the trees leaf out. And it is wonderful to be alone with you, even if only for a few minutes."

Darcy raised his brows in mock surprise. "You admit to preferring the company of your husband to the gaieties of society? I am quite shocked."

"To such depths have I fallen," she admitted with a rueful expression.

"Well, in that case I must make sure that we return to this idyllic spot as soon as possible. We will do so on the first really nice day of spring."

He helped her up and they repacked the hamper. Hand in hand, they made the climb up the ridge and stopped for a moment at the crest to look down at Pemberley House. They saw the carriage far down the graveled drive, returning Georgiana and Mrs. Annesley from town, and started slowly down the path. By the time they emerged from the woods the two ladies had unpacked their shopping and were in the drawing-room having a cup of tea and discussing their purchases, so Darcy and Elizabeth joined them until it was necessary for Darcy to withdraw for his delayed meeting with his steward.

The afternoon post brought Elizabeth a letter from her sister Lydia, the first she had received since their wedding:

> MY DEAREST SISTER AND BROTHER,—
> *Congratulations on your marriage. I hope that you are as happy as are my dear Wickham and I, and I wish that I could have been at the wedding, but we are very lively here in Newcastle and I could not be spared. I hope that Pemberley suits you very well, Lizzy, and that*

you find Miss Darcy very agreeable. We are currently searching for new living quarters as the ones we are now in are far too expensive to leave us money for food and clothes at the end of the month. I assume that you will be spending the season in London at Mr. Darcy's town house this spring. If you find yourself in need of company, write me and I would be happy to join you.—Etc.

Elizabeth shuddered at the thought of Lydia's uncontrolled behaviour being associated with the Darcy name and tainting Georgiana's first season. Lady Catherine's predictions of social ostracism would be swiftly validated were Lydia to join them. Most importantly, Georgiana must be saved from contact with Lydia's shocking example. Elizabeth admitted to herself that a great deal of her concern was to avoid allowing Georgiana to see *all* of the weaknesses of the Bennet family. Elizabeth's *amour propre* demanded it. She would need to write to her sister and make it politely but firmly clear that an invitation would not be forthcoming; diplomacy would be wasted upon Lydia. At any rate, she might possibly be able to spare a few pounds from her pin money to assist with the Wickhams' expenses, as she had no difficulty at all believing that the finances of two such heedless people were in a shambles.

Chapter 10

But war's a game, which, were their subjects wise,
Kings should not play at.
William Cowper, "The Winter Morning Walk"

Soon after Darcy and Elizabeth had arrived at Pemberley, Darcy had called on a new neighbour, Sir Robert Blake, at Coldstream Manor. Sir Robert had turned out to be a young man of around Darcy's age who had inherited a large fortune two years previously, and who had recently fulfilled his father's dying wish by purchasing the estate. He had taken possession while Darcy and Elizabeth were preparing for their wedding in Hertfordshire, so Darcy had not previously had an opportunity to call upon him, but he had been favourably impressed and returned home from his call with an invitation to dinner. After telling Elizabeth of his visit while they awaited tea in the drawing-room, he added:

"I think that we will find Sir Robert a most agreeable neighbour. I suppose that I will be considered a traitor to my class, but I must say that since I have tried to moderate my prejudices and choose my friends for their merit rather than just their birth, I have been a much happier man. I blush to think that a year ago I would not have called upon the Blakes because of their association with trade. I must count the pleasure of Sir Robert's acquaintance as one more benefit of meeting my dearest Elizabeth."

"I am glad that there *are* benefits, my love," she answered with a smile.

"There are many, but I will not enumerate the others until later, Mrs. Darcy."

Georgiana came in then, so Elizabeth contented herself with merely raising a brow at him before pouring the tea.

During the ride to Coldstream Manor a few days later, Darcy told Elizabeth and Georgiana of what he knew about the Blakes:

"From what I have heard, Sir Robert's father was a mercer and accumulated a great fortune providing uniforms for the military in the wars with both Napoleon and the Americans. He was elevated to the baronetcy after giving some sort of assistance to the crown and had intended to purchase an estate consummate with his wealth and importance, but died suddenly of a fever before fulfilling his ambitions. Sir Robert inherited the family business as well as the family fortune, with instructions in his father's will to provide for his brothers and sister. His middle brother serves as his agent and factotum in the family business in Leeds, where their factories are located. The youngest brother, Edward, is twenty-two years old and still living at home while his nineteen-year-old sister, Emily, keeps house for Sir Robert at the manor, and will have a fortune of £20,000 when she marries. I believe that you will find Sir Robert very pleasant and I have hopes that his brothers and sister will be likewise agreeable."

Sir Robert retained no traces of his modest lineage, and was very much the gentleman in appearance. He was above average height, although not so tall as Mr. Darcy, and fair-haired, his eyes the colour of cornflowers but with dark lashes and brows surrounding them. He greeted them cordially:

"I am most delighted to meet you Mrs. Darcy, and Miss Darcy," he said, bowing to each of them in turn. "May I please introduce my sister, Emily, and my youngest brother, Edward."

Miss Blake was fair in colouring like her brother, but had eyes of a tawny golden brown. She was elegantly dressed and had a tall, graceful figure that was emphasised by her upswept hair. Although not a beauty, she was attractive and her gentle manners were pleasing. Her voice, however, was rather at odds with her appearance: high pitched and childish-sounding. She was gracious to her guests and Elizabeth felt very comfortable with her, and even Georgiana was able to relax a little and join in the conversation without much hesitation. Their discussion, when the ladies withdrew to the salon, was pleasant but of the most banal type: Miss Blake talking about what she had done while in Leeds on a recent visit to her other brother, a subject that might have had some interest but which the speaker did not imbue with any vivacity or piquancy.

When the gentlemen finally rejoined them Elizabeth had more of an opportunity to assess the youngest of the Blake brothers than had been possible earlier in the evening. Edward Blake was a young man of middle height, of modest good looks and somewhat shy manners, who greeted them quietly and spent most of the evening listening to the conversation, only joining in when asked a question. Elizabeth, attempting to set him at ease, asked him what his plans were for the future.

"Are you going into the family business as well, Mr. Blake, or do you have other plans?" she enquired.

"I am not really interested in the business, I am afraid," he replied with a brief laugh. "Rather than helping my brothers I am hoping for a military career. My eldest brother has kindly offered to purchase a lieutenant's commission for me once I determine the regiment that I would prefer."

Elizabeth smiled at him. "Well, not everyone is the same, and with the war going on the military offers many opportunities for advancement, I would guess."

"I believe that it does, Mrs. Darcy," he answered. "I confess that my dreams are more of the heroic stamp than could be answered for by a career in trade, although I *am* hoping to obtain a discounted price on my uniforms from my brothers."

Elizabeth laughed with him and the conversation moved on to other topics.

In the quiet of the carriage on the way home, the Darcys discussed the evening. During his interval with the gentlemen after dinner, Darcy had found the two Blake men to be well informed about the state of the war and other current affairs and he had had a very lively discussion with them about the future prospects for the conflict. The Blakes' business interests had given them some insights into the conduct of the war, and had stimulated them to follow the news closely. He had enjoyed himself very much, sparring pleasantly with them over their port and cigars about what the future would hold against Napoleon.

"I find myself looking forward to our next engagement," he said, "if you will forgive the play on words."

"I am not sure we should associate with them if they are going to have such an unfortunate effect on your vocabulary," Elizabeth teased him.

Georgiana watched them with eyes wide in surprise as their badinage went back and forth. Elizabeth noted her sister's surprise at her saucy repartee and smiled reassuringly at her in the dim light as they drew up to the front entrance of Pemberley House.

The next morning Elizabeth was alone at the breakfast table when Georgiana came down. After greeting her, Elizabeth cleared her throat and said:

"Georgiana, I wanted to talk to you about something."

"Yes?" she said absently as she sat down with her plate.

"I noticed that you looked rather shocked last night when I was teasing your brother."

"Yes, I was rather surprised, at first," she said indistinctly, looking down at her hands.

Elizabeth gently continued, "I do not want you to be uncomfortable, but I want you to realise that it is much different being married to a man than it is being his much younger sister. A wife may tease her husband when he might not tolerate such conduct from someone to whom he stands as a father."

Georgiana looked up briefly and said slowly, "Yes, I did realise that after I thought about it for a while. I suppose that it had never occurred to me before. My mother died when I was so young that I have no recall of my parents together, and I have no young relatives who are married. My brother, for all of his affection for me, has always been rather serious and dignified. I believe that it is because our father's untimely death put him in a position where he was required to take up all of the family responsibilities at an early age, including the responsibility for an eleven-year-old sister." She glanced at Elizabeth with a shy smile. "I am happy that he has married someone who is able to help him take off the yoke of duty for a while. He has changed a great deal since he met you, Elizabeth; his heart seems much lighter." She took Elizabeth's hand and gave it a quick squeeze. "So, do not worry about me, my dear sister. I am pleased and delighted to see the two of you together."

Elizabeth smiled at her and said, "You are a very wise young woman, Miss Georgiana," just as the footman came in to check the serving dishes, and they amicably continued their breakfast.

That afternoon, they called on the squire of Lambton, who was an elderly gentleman named William Walker, rather portly in appearance but with an open countenance and blunt, friendly, but unrefined manners.

The Walkers were a family of landowners who had been the leading citizens of the village of Lambton for over a century, and had been known by the Darcy family for all those years. Their house, The Yews, was located at the edge of the village and was of moderate size: a brick, half-timbered manor house of Tudor ancestry, almost disappearing behind mounds of ancient yews that scented the air with their bitter aroma. Squire Walker welcomed them heartily to his parlour and introduced Elizabeth to his wife, Beatrice, a little, cheerful woman some years younger than her husband, who reminded Elizabeth of a wren as she tilted her head alertly while she followed the conversation.

While they drank tea, Mrs. Walker told Elizabeth about their two daughters and their families, who lived near Derby. Their son Jonathan, much the youngest of their children, was twenty-one years old and lived at home, running the family estate while his father devoted himself to his duties as Justice of the Peace.

Jonathan Walker entered the parlour halfway through their visit and greeted them courteously, seating himself between Georgiana and Elizabeth and making himself agreeable during the proffered tea. He was slightly built and dark complexioned, almost swarthy, with dark hair, hazel eyes and attractive features; although with a mouth and jaw line somewhat softer than could be considered the ideal of masculine beauty. He entertained them with amusing and slightly malicious portraits of the local gentry.

During the visit Master Jonathan asked Georgiana questions about her recent activities. The questions themselves were benign, but when she responded with eyes downcast and monosyllabic answers, he pressed her for a reply.

"Did you go to the theatre when you were in London, Miss Darcy?"

"No, sir."

"What did you do while you were there?"

"I was helping my sister-in-law prepare for the wedding."

He looked at her intently, and Georgiana fidgeted with her gloves.

"Ah. Did you enjoy it?"

"Yes."

He gave her an intimate smile when she glanced up, and she reddened and looked back down at her hands.

He persisted. "How long were you there, Miss Darcy?"

"Several weeks."

Elizabeth interjected a few comments about the opera night they had attended to divert Master Walker from his demanding questions, and Georgiana looked relieved. After similar impertinences from Master Jonathan had again occurred, Darcy rose and they left with protestations of friendship and invitations to return from Squire Walker.

Later, Elizabeth asked her husband about young Master Walker.

"He seemed most insistent about making Georgiana speak. I thought it was very rude of him."

"He has shown an interest in Georgiana several times before, but she quite obviously does not like him. I do not really know him well since there are seven years between our ages, but I have some concerns about his respectability. For one thing, I do not like the way he treats his dogs or his servants, which I have usually found is often a good indicator of a man's character. I do know that he attended Oxford for about a year and then suddenly reappeared back at Lambton, where he has been ever since, barring the occasional trip to London. Even though Georgiana does not seem attracted to him, I think that I should check on his background if we are going to be visiting the Walkers with her."

"How will you find out more about him?" Elizabeth inquired.

"I think I will enlist Oliver to assist me," he said, tapping his finger thoughtfully on his chin. "He has a friendly way with him and can probably pick up some information discreetly in the servants' hall when the Walkers next visit."

A few days later he broached the subject again while they were having morning tea in their sitting-room.

"I heard back from Oliver about Mr. Jonathan Walker, and I am afraid that my suspicions seem justified. Oliver enlisted James, one of the footmen, to strike up an acquaintance with the Walker coachman when they visited the other day. They apparently met for a pint at one of the local pubs and the Walker servant was not at all reticent about his master. He is evidently in debt up to his ears and there have been a number of callers that the coachman describes as appearing to be 'of the financial persuasion.' Master Walker has told his parents that they are 'business associates,' but all of the servants know what they are. He makes frequent visits to London on some unknown business, but always returns in a foul mood. He is also, apparently, skimping on the upkeep of the estate and the servants' wages are always late."

"What will you do, my dear?" Elizabeth asked.

"I believe that further investigation is warranted. I will write to someone I know in London who can discreetly check on Master Walker's activities there."

Chapter 11

Heap on more wood!—the wind is chill;
But let it whistle as it will,
We'll keep our Christmas merry still.
Sir Walter Scott, "Marmion"

The day finally came for the Gardiners' arrival for the Christmas holiday. Elizabeth had been looking out at the cloudy, gusty rain off and on all afternoon, hoping to see their carriage, but to no avail. Just as she was finally sitting down for a cup of tea with Darcy and Georgiana, Smithfield came in and announced that the carriage had appeared. Elizabeth quickly rose and met their guests in the hall, the others at her heels. She greeted her aunt and uncle affectionately and kissed her nieces and nephews. Georgiana curtseyed and smiled silently as her brother welcomed them, and the Gardiners introduced her to the children. She turned to the little ones with a kind smile and spoke to them for several minutes, learning their names and ages and laughing when one of the younger boys did a little caper of excitement. While Georgiana was thus occupied, Mrs. Gardiner, her eyes twinkling, whispered to Elizabeth and Darcy that she had brought the package that they had requested.

"Where is he?" Elizabeth asked quietly.

"In a basket on the floor of the carriage," she replied. "The children will be wild to see him. We thought it best that they not play with him during the journey, as I feared that the enthusiastic attentions of four children would be overwhelming for the poor little creature."

"You are probably right about that," Elizabeth returned with a conspiratorial smile.

Reynolds arrived at that moment to take the Gardiners upstairs to change out of their travel clothes and to refresh themselves before rejoining the Darcys in the drawing-room for tea. Georgiana went upstairs with them, holding the hands of the two youngest children, who were boys aged four and five years, respectively. When they were gone, Elizabeth and Darcy went to the footmen who were unloading the carriage and had them bring in the basket. They opened the lid and peeked in. Curled up on a scrap of blanket was a tiny white puppy, small enough to fit in the palm of a hand. He opened his eyes sleepily and wagged his whip-like little tail, which curled in a near circle over his back.

"He is adorable—Georgiana will love him!" Elizabeth said excitedly, "When shall we give him to her?"

"We will not be able to hide him easily and the children may inadvertently give the secret away, so I would suggest that we do it immediately when she comes downstairs," Darcy said.

At that moment Georgiana came down the sweeping staircase, pausing in the middle of the flight and looking perplexed when she saw them bending over the basket.

"Come down, Georgiana, dear, we need to give you your Christmas present early!" Elizabeth exclaimed.

Georgiana tripped lightly down the remaining stairs and hurried over. When she saw the puppy, she put her hands to her cheeks and exclaimed:

"A puppy! He is just adorable! Is he really for me?"

She reached gently into the basket and picked him up, cradling him against her and stroking him. He wagged his tail and licked her fingers, then started whimpering. Darcy gently took him from her with a smile and gave him to one of the footmen, saying:

"He probably needs to go outside for a moment; he has had rather a long ride today."

While this was taking place Georgiana hugged and kissed her brother and sister with tears in her eyes, thanking them for the gift.

"I have wanted a dog since I was a little girl!"

"You should thank Elizabeth," Darcy said, kissing her affectionately on the forehead, "it was her idea and she arranged it with the Gardiners. They got him from a breeder near London."

"What kind of dog is he?" she asked.

Elizabeth answered, "He is a Maltese. I knew someone once who had one and he was very sweet—the dog, I mean." She laughed with them, and then added, "Do you know what you want to name him?"

"I must think about it—this is such a surprise that I am quite overwhelmed."

The Gardiners came down the stairs and Georgiana ran to them, embracing them and sweetly thanking them for their part in bringing her gift. The children, meanwhile, were crowding around the footman who had returned with the puppy. Georgiana took the little dog and held out her hand to the smallest of the children, saying,

"Let us take him into the drawing-room, shall we?"

They trailed after her happily, and they all sat on the floor in a circle while the now wide-awake puppy gamboled around them. The older adults sat outside the circle and had their tea, amused by the antics of the puppy and the children. The elder of the two boys said suddenly:

"You are so lucky to have a puppy, Miss Darcy!"

Georgiana's head came up and she said, "That is a perfect name for him! I shall call him Lucky!" And so, Lucky he became.

The next day they took Lucky into town so he could be fitted with a little collar and leash. They took all of the children as well, since Georgiana wanted them to help her pick the items out. They also got dishes for his food and water, and a tiny brush so they could groom his hair, as well as a piece of rawhide for him to chew on. Georgiana herself appeared a little haggard that day, as she had insisted that Lucky and his basket be kept in her room and she was kept awake much of the night by his whimpering.

"I am sure he will be better soon," Elizabeth said reassuringly, "after all, this is the first time he has been away from his mamma."

The children all looked very sad at that idea but started laughing when Lucky stuck his head over Georgiana's arm, where he was nestled, and looked at them with his bright black button eyes. The tiny tip of his tail was visible, curled over his back and vibrating furiously in excitement.

That afternoon they introduced Lucky to Pilot, who generally spent his day sleeping in the library near his master's desk. Darcy watched Pilot with apprehension as Lucky waddled up to him, alert for any signs of aggression toward the tiny dog. Pilot, however, waved his tail majestically while he sniffed the newcomer over carefully, his muzzle as large as the entire puppy. When he was done with his examination he licked him with his huge tongue, knocking him off his unsteady little paws. Lucky returned the compliment, giving the great nose in front of him two quick licks and waving his feet in the air, his tail wagging.

"It seems that Pilot is going to accept him," Darcy said with relief, and Georgiana picked up Lucky and went back into the drawing-room, patting Pilot as she went by.

The day passed quickly, but by dinnertime Elizabeth was exhausted, tired out by enjoyment and by the new responsibilities that came with being the hostess for her guests. Bessie, one of the younger housemaids, had been given the task of entertaining the children while they had their dinners upstairs in the nursery and the adults ate theirs in the dining-room. Lucky was taken outside, and then Georgiana reluctantly put him in his basket in her room while they ate. Her eyes sparkled with happiness and she was able to converse with Mrs. Gardiner without visible embarrassment or self-consciousness during dinner and afterwards in the drawing-room while they had tea and coffee. Mrs. Gardiner had met Georgiana when she had visited Derbyshire the previous summer with Elizabeth, and was amazed at the change in her.

"Georgiana has acquired much more equanimity since we last met," she whispered to her niece while Georgiana went upstairs to check on Lucky.

Elizabeth had also seen her sister's ease in the company of the Gardiners with pleasure and reflected to her aunt, "Dogs and children break down a great many barriers."

Her aunt nodded in agreement, smiling as she watched Georgiana disappear.

Elizabeth received a letter the next day from Jane, wishing them a happy Christmas, and then continuing:

> *I must tell you, dearest Lizzy, that Caroline has joined us unexpectedly for Christmas. She was to spend it with the Hursts, but she and Louisa had a disagreement (which Bingley attributes to bad temper resulting from Darcy's marrying you, but which I would not like to think of my sister-in-law) and she left town and came to Netherfield. If it is not convenient for you to have an additional and unexpected guest, I fear that we must stay here, for I do not feel that it would be correct to leave her. I will say that she has been very courteous to me since our marriage, and has been a charming guest since her arrival. I believe that Kitty would also like to join us, if you approve. She has been hinting that she would like to see Pemberley, and I think that it would be nice for her to meet Georgiana, do not you? Please write me as soon as possible and let me know what you wish me to do.—With our dearest love, etc.*

Elizabeth wrote back immediately to cordially invite Miss Bingley and Kitty to come with Charles and Jane to Pemberley, but commented to Darcy:

"I can think of few people whom I would not prefer to Miss Bingley as a guest, knowing that she tried so hard to capture your heart, and her jealousy added to our mutual dislike to make her insufferable to be around in all of our previous encounters." She sighed and, with a chagrined smile, added, "I suppose that I should try to repress my feelings about her. I have erred in the past in my evaluation of character. Perhaps I will be proven wrong in her case as well."

Darcy gave her a sly smile and returned, "You must take consolation, at least, in the fact that you were the victor in the contest for my heart (even though you did not know at the time that you were competing), and realise that it must be even more embarrassing for her to be your guest than for you to be her hostess."

Elizabeth agreed, but warned Georgiana that Miss Bingley was coming, much to Georgiana's dismay.

"Oh dear," she exclaimed, "I hope her manners have improved since the last time I saw her! I was quite disgusted with her nasty comments about you last summer, and I took great pleasure when my brother was finally driven to set her down about it."

"Was he now?" Elizabeth commented, surprised by Georgiana's unusual vehemence. "Well, we must try to forgive her for her past jealousy. She will probably be more amiable now, since she will want to continue to visit Pemberley."

"No doubt," she replied tartly.

The rest of the week before Christmas passed quickly away and Christmas day arrived with just a dusting of snow to make everything sparkle in the pale sunlight. There was ice on the stream and icicles hung from the eaves of Pemberley. When Elizabeth entered the sitting-room for her morning tea, she found a small wrapped package at her place. She placed her gift for Darcy at his place and contemplated her own.

"Well ... open it, my love."

Elizabeth started and turned. Darcy was leaning casually against the doorway of his room. She removed the wrapping from the parcel and saw a small volume with a faded cover, which she opened to the title page. It said:

SHAKE-SPEARE'S
SONNETS

Never Before Imprinted

Published
At London
By *Thomas Thorpe*
1609

She gave a quiet gasp and stared at him. "It is the most wonderful gift I have ever received, my dear husband!" She silently shook her head in astonishment, then ran over and kissed him.

She clung to him and whispered, "You are so wonderful to me, my darling. I love you so much that it hurts."

"I did not intend to cause pain, my love," he said, his voice muffled by her hair.

She looked up at him seriously. "I could hope to have this pain every day of the rest of my life."

He smiled at her. "'For well thou know'st to my dear doting heart, Thou art the fairest and most precious jewel.'"

They heard the footman's steps approaching with their tea and reluctantly separated, but they were both smiling as they came downstairs together.

Several small packages were piled at each place at the table when the rest of the family gathered in the small dining-parlour for breakfast, and the children could hardly eat because of their excitement over the presents, and over the unusual treat of eating with the adults. When they had finally finished their breakfasts and opened their packages, Bessie took them off to the schoolroom to play with their toys and the adults finished eating in peace. Afterwards, they opened their gifts and Georgiana gasped at her pearl necklace.

"This must surely be the most beautiful present I have ever received," she said, then looked down at her lap where Lucky was sitting and added, "Other than you, Lucky!"

She once again hugged and kissed her brother and sister for their kindness, as well as the Gardiners for the beautiful embroidered Indian shawl they had given her, then came over and sat next to Elizabeth and whispered in her ear:

"Did you open your present from Fitzwilliam yet?"

Elizabeth nodded at her and smiled. "Yes, I did. I take it that you knew about it beforehand?"

"Oh yes! I helped Fitzwilliam search for it in London when we were all there."

Elizabeth put her arm around her young sister and looked over at her husband. He gazed at her silently, his lips turned up slightly at the corners, and she suddenly felt the room start to tilt. I really must stop this, she thought with a blush—we have been married more than a month and I can still be completely undone by one look. How preposterous!

The Gardiners were talking politely with Georgiana while this went on, but Elizabeth noticed that her aunt and uncle wore rather complacent smiles, as if her happiness was by their arrangement—which, in a sense, it was.

A footman entered and quietly spoke to Mr. Darcy.

"You have not received your final gift, Mrs. Darcy," said her husband, rising from the sofa and taking Elizabeth's hand.

"Another gift! You must be joking!" she asked in surprise. "Where are we going?"

"Only to the front door, my dear."

The footman reappeared with the heavy cloaks and, thus prepared, the Darcys and the Gardiners stepped out the door. They heard the rumbling of wheels and around the corner drove a low-slung phaeton, just wide enough for two slender passengers on the seat, and with a small seat behind where another rider or a groom could sit. It was painted glossy black with a narrow line of gold trim outlining the body, and the wheels were yellow with black rims, while the upholstery was soft velvet the colour of early spring leaves. Hitched to this splendid equipage was a matched pair of tiny horses that looked like miniature coach horses, dappled gray with arched necks and braided and beribboned manes and tails, standing proudly in their black, belled harnesses. One of the pair shook his head, making the bells tinkle, and looked proudly around, the red plume on his forehead waving gently in the slight breeze.

"Oh, my dear," Elizabeth breathed, "they are beautiful! Thank you so much!" She slipped her arm through his. "Aunt Gardiner, you will get your ride around the park—today if the weather allows us!"

Mrs. Gardiner had expressed a wish the previous summer for a ride around the ten-mile circumference of Pemberley Park, but Elizabeth had not expected to be able to indulge her aunt so soon, nor so elegantly. The children appeared with Bessie and capered around the terrace with excitement. "Who gets to take the first ride?" was heard several times before their mother quieted them with:

"Mr. and Mrs. Darcy should get the first ride, don't you think?"

"Oh, yes, yes they should!"

Darcy helped Elizabeth into the carriage, and then took the reins from the groom and drove them down the drive a short way and back up to the house.

"We shall now let the children have a ride," Elizabeth declared, "and then, my dear aunt, we shall go inside for a while before we go on our longed-for drive around the park. The weather is lovely for December, but it should be a bit warmer in the afternoon."

The children stared in wide-eyed wonder at the tiny horses and their beautiful, jingling harnesses, to the exclusion of the scenery around them, as they each took their turn riding with the groom, then were bustled back into the warm house.

The ride around the park in the afternoon was enjoyable, but still cold. Elizabeth drove her aunt through dense woods, open meadows, and rocky hills as they made their way, with many stops to enjoy the view, on a neat, graveled path, which occasionally intersected the main estate road. They abbreviated the ride because of the cold temperatures, but had a satisfying jaunt nonetheless, and saw enough of the terrain of the estate to satisfy Mrs. Gardiner until she could enjoy the full circuit in the summer. Elizabeth was a little nervous about driving the unfamiliar horses, and took a groom with them in case she should have difficulties, but the horses were very well trained and their behaviour was as beautiful as their appearance. They spent two hours in this agreeable way and returned to the manor house with rosy cheeks and sparkling eyes, ready to shed their cloaks and warm their hands at the fire before it was time to change for dinner.

Christmas dinner was a sumptuous feast of roast turkey and venison, Yorkshire pudding and buttery roast potatoes, and plum pudding and trifle for dessert. The children were again allowed to join the adults in the dining-parlour for this special occasion, seated at a small table just for them, with Bessie supervising and helping the littlest ones cut their food. They were overawed by the sparkling chandeliers and the footmen silently attending the table, but managed to eat some of their meal. Georgiana sat at the main table with the adults, and her eyes sparkled in the candlelight as she ate and talked and watched the children solemnly doing their best to behave correctly. By the time dinner was over, the children were drooping from exhaustion and Bessie took them up to bed, their feet dragging even as they protested that they were not at all tired.

The ladies adjourned to the drawing-room while the gentlemen had their port in the dining-parlour, but they did not stay up long after they rejoined the ladies, for everyone was very tired after the excitement of the day.

When they went upstairs, Elizabeth said to Darcy, "My nieces and nephews are dear children, but they *are* exhausting!"

Darcy laughed and returned, "I think it is easier when you do not suddenly acquire four at one time, especially at Christmas."

"Very true. But Georgiana is obviously having a lovely time with the children and Bessie has done very well caring for them."

Darcy put his arms around her and looked at her with one brow cocked. "Perhaps one day we shall have to promote Bessie to nursery maid."

Elizabeth blushed slightly, but merely said with a smile, "Perhaps we shall."

The next day was Boxing Day and Darcy and Elizabeth were up early to supervise the distribution of the Christmas boxes to the Pemberley dependents. After the boxes were given out, the family had a quiet breakfast and enjoyed their last day together, for tomorrow the Gardiners would leave for Hertfordshire. They were expecting Colonel Fitzwilliam to arrive that afternoon after spending Christmas day with his family, so they would not be totally bereft of guests until the Bingleys and Bennets arrived.

The colonel arrived in good time on the lightly snowing afternoon, and the Gardiners were interested to meet him, for Elizabeth had told them how pleasant the colonel was after she had first met him in Kent when she was visiting her friend Charlotte. Georgiana and Elizabeth welcomed him to Pemberley and he kissed their hands gallantly before Elizabeth introduced him to the Gardiners. He greeted them and they talked easily as they moved into the drawing-room. He was a welcome addition to the dinner table that evening, entertaining them with (hopefully embellished) stories about his life since they had last seen him. He finished a tale involving some new recruits and some errant buckshot and Georgiana commented sardonically:

"I hope that this story is not entirely true, Colonel. I would hate to think that the safety of the monarchy is in such inept hands."

"I swear to you, little cousin, that the tale is entirely, or at least mostly, true."

His audience laughed and Georgiana rolled her eyes. Elizabeth noted that Georgiana seemed not at all reticent with the colonel, which was, she supposed, not surprising since she had known him her entire life, and he was her guardian along with her brother. When they finished eating, Georgiana went upstairs and brought Lucky down to meet him.

"This is Lucky, our new watchdog, Cousin," she said sternly. "Beware if you decide to sneak downstairs for a glass of ale or a bite of cheese during the night. He is especially fierce about cheese."

"I am sure he will be a welcome addition to the pack when we go hunting tomorrow, little cousin," he teased. "He will likely be the first to flush the birds, although those short legs may have some difficulty getting over the stiles."

"Lucky is far too intelligent to spend his morning running around in the mud and the cold as you will be doing, dear cousin," she replied, giving him an impudent grin.

The Darcys and the colonel excused themselves after dinner and made their required appearance at the servants' party. Elizabeth and Darcy led the first dance, followed by Georgiana and the colonel. They then bowed and wished everyone a happy Christmas and returned to their guests. The adults stayed up rather later than usual talking that last evening of their visit, but the Gardiners were up and ready to leave by nine o'clock the next morning. After the bustle of packing and loading the carriage they all said farewell, Elizabeth with a few tears, for she would miss her favourite aunt and uncle. As the carriage started forward, the colonel offered his arm to Georgiana and they went inside. Elizabeth's last glimpse of her aunt and uncle, as she stood on the terrace with Darcy's arm around her shoulders, was when the carriage rounded a curve of the drive, then disappeared between the hills.

Chapter 12

All the world's a stage,
And all the men and women merely players.
William Shakespeare, "As You Like It"

Pemberley was quiet that day after the loss of their friends, but Elizabeth felt that there was an air of expectancy in the house as they waited for the arrival of the Bingleys and her father and younger sister, who were to arrive in a few days. Mrs. Reynolds was bustling cheerfully about, making sure that everything in the house was perfect for the next round of guests. Darcy and the colonel spent the morning out with their dogs and the kennel master since the weather permitted, hoping to flush some pheasants but mostly attempting to train a couple of young dogs. Georgiana went up to the music room and Elizabeth followed her a quarter hour later, surprised that she did not hear the pianoforte. When she entered the room, she caught Georgiana gazing pensively out the window in the direction that the men had gone.

"Is there something wrong, Georgiana?" she inquired gently.

The girl straightened her shoulders and smiled.

"Not at all. I was watching the dogs as the men walked them down to the field. The two young ones are very amusing. They gambol along with their ears flapping and their tongues hanging out, obviously having great fun until they commit some egregious error and the older dogs snap at them. The elders are clearly not amused by their callow brethren."

Elizabeth looked out and laughed. "You are right; the older dogs could not express disgust more clearly if they could speak. Well, if you are going to practice, I believe I will spend some time in the picture gallery with Mrs. Reynolds."

"I will join you, if you do not mind. I always enjoy hearing about the history of my ancestors, particularly some of those who made rather bad ends. It is interesting to see if you can see their history painted into their portrait faces."

"I had not thought of looking at it that way. I have heard of occasions, although I do not know if it is true, when subjects were unhappy with their portraits because the artist revealed too much about their true character in the work. Apparently, in some cases, the sitter actually paid extra to compensate the artist for not allowing him to display his work at the Academy, took the painting, and it was never seen again."

"It would be very interesting to see those paintings, would it not?"

"Indeed it would."

They sent a footman for Reynolds and spent about an hour in the gallery. Elizabeth had decided after her first session with the housekeeper that she would record the histories of the paintings, so afterwards Georgiana sat down with her and she wrote as much information as they could recall in a bound journal.

"Well, my dear, I think that we had better quit for today. My brain is full of as many facts as it will safely hold. Thank you for your patience, Georgiana."

"It was my pleasure, my dear sister."

They busied themselves later in the morning with making preparations for the ball that they would hold to coincide with the Bingleys' and the Bennets' visit. After they had decided on the many details with Reynolds, Elizabeth suggested a walk to Georgiana since the day was fine, although cold. She accepted and they bundled up in their warmest pelisses and gloves, setting out along one of the paths beside the trout stream with Lucky on his lead.

They meandered along the paths, keeping fairly close to the house since it was too cold to walk far, and talked about the ball. All of the local gentry had been invited, as well as some from farther away who were old acquaintances of the Darcy family, and who would stay the night at Pemberley after the ball. They would have ten of their guest rooms filled, and Georgiana was both excited and apprehensive because she had never been to a ball, nor seen so many guests at Pemberley.

"I am always so fearful of saying the wrong thing, or not doing what I am supposed to, Elizabeth. I don't know how to stop feeling so nervous," she said quietly, fidgeting with Lucky's lead.

Elizabeth reassured her that experience would help her feel more confident, but Georgiana still had a small crease between her brows.

"Perhaps I could help you," Elizabeth finally said. "We could pretend various situations and you could practice your responses so that they will eventually come naturally to your lips." She gave the girl a wry look. "I know that I hate it when I think of something witty to say after the opportunity has passed!"

Georgiana laughed in spite of herself and said, "I doubt if I will ever be witty, my dear sister, but it would be nice to not feel so awkward."

They agreed to try Elizabeth's plan when they could be alone, and made their way slowly back to the house.

In the meantime, the gentlemen were watching the kennel master put the dogs through their paces.

"Darcy," started the colonel, hesitantly, "I want to congratulate you again on your marriage. Elizabeth is a wonderful woman and I am very jealous of your good fortune in marrying her." He smiled, looking a little chagrined. "If I had been an eldest son, I might have been tempted to woo her myself."

Darcy looked at him quizzically, for it was not like his easygoing cousin to be dissatisfied with his lot in life.

"I know that I am very fortunate, Fitzwilliam, and I cannot believe it myself," he said quietly. He then added in a lighter tone, "I will just have to annoy you as I did when we were lads and quote the Bard to you: 'Get thee a wife,' Cousin."

"I would like to marry," the colonel said soberly. "I am ready to settle down, but finding the right woman is the obstacle. After so many years at court, I am afraid that I have developed rather a jaundiced eye for society women—they all seem to be rather shrill and brainless, not to even mention the moral standards of those who gather round the prince regent. That, of course, includes the exceedingly small number who would even consider marrying a penniless younger son." He paused for a moment, slapping his gloves against his hands absently, and then continued, "Did I tell you that Lady Catherine has been very attentive, writing me weekly and hoping that I will return for a visit again soon? I think that I am the next sacrificial victim selected to marry our poor cousin Anne." He grimaced. "I need a wife with money, but I am not willing to sacrifice every other comfort to marry for it. My father has been gently hinting to me that I should marry Anne; I think he feels that he will have done his duty by his younger son if he can marry him to the de Bourgh money and keep it all in the family. I do not believe, however, that he has seen Anne in several years, since he is not fond of his sister-in-law's domineering nature and prefers to be amiable from a distance, and so probably does not realise how ill Anne truly is. I know that Lady Catherine always sends glowing reports of how much better some new treatment is working." He shrugged off his unaccustomed seriousness, pulling his gloves on briskly and adding, "Still, there is always hope! Thank you for listening to my whining, Cousin."

"I am happy to give you a shoulder to cry on, Fitzwilliam," Darcy said, clapping him on the back, "Perhaps we can find some pleasant ladies at the ball next week who have not been jaded by too much time at court.

They both laughed easily and turned back to the dogs and the kennel master, who were returning from the end of the field.

The gentlemen rejoined the ladies for tea in the afternoon and Darcy asked: "How was your morning, ladies?"

Elizabeth and Georgiana told of their plans for the ball and about their walk (excluding only their plans for Georgiana's "lessons") while they poured the tea.

"I hope, little cousin, that you are planning on giving your old guardian the first dance at the ball."

Georgiana looked at her hands, suddenly shy, but said calmly enough, "Of course, Colonel."

"Good, it is settled then. We must show the local youths how it is done."

Georgiana just smiled down at her hands and the conversation flowed around her. Soon afterwards, the gentlemen retired to the billiard-room and the two ladies went upstairs to Georgiana's room. Mrs. Annesley was visiting her family for the holidays, so they would be undisturbed while they practised the social graces. Elizabeth played various parts and coached Georgiana when she was at a loss, which was frequently.

"Let us try, again, my dear. Let us try a situation that will soon occur. I will be my sister Jane and I am arriving at Pemberley with my husband, my sister, and my father. You must greet them and then introduce them to Colonel Fitzwilliam. I will play all the other parts, as well. All right?"

Georgiana nodded, her face grimly intent.

"My dear Miss Darcy, it is delightful to see you again." Elizabeth embraced her and gracefully turned. "I am sure you remember my husband, Mr. Bingley?"

"Of course I do. Welcome to Pemberley, Mr. Bingley. May I introduce my cousin, Colonel Fitzwilliam?"

In a deep voice Elizabeth answered, "Delighted, Colonel. We met briefly at the wedding a few weeks ago."

As Jane she said, "Miss Darcy, Colonel, may I introduce my father, Mr. Bennet, and my sister, Miss Catherine Bennet?"

"How do you do, Mr. Bennet, Miss Bennet." Georgiana sketched a graceful curtsey and then paused, frozen.

Elizabeth looked at her expectantly, and finally Georgiana threw up her hands in despair.

"Now what should I do?"

"You could invite them to follow Mrs. Reynolds upstairs to refresh themselves. If they had come just a short way, you could invite them into the drawing-room, or wherever you were planning to entertain them, and then order refreshments."

Georgiana sighed.

"I just seem to freeze. I wish you would instead ask me to conjugate a French verb, or recite a passage from a history text—as long as I did not need to do it in front of other people. I wish I could be witty and playful like you are, Elizabeth."

"My dear sister," Elizabeth said gently, "please do not try to be someone else—you want to be yourself. The main purpose of this playacting is not to make you into someone you are not, but to make you able to show your lovely, true self without being uncomfortable and shy."

"How can someone like me compete with all the beautiful, elegant young ladies like you?"

"I thank you, Georgiana, for the compliment, but you are an attractive and intelligent young woman, so do not wish to trade places with someone else," Elizabeth said bracingly. "Now, let us try to go back to the beginning and go step by step through greetings; perhaps we are going too fast."

They struggled on for another quarter hour; and Georgiana sighed, "I do not think that I am a good actress."

Elizabeth laughed. "Your brother would probably be happy to know that; he would be horrified if you really *were* an actress! You must realise, dearest, that we are all actors, every moment that we are in the society of another person. Every time we are courteous to someone we do not like, or feign an interest in the conversation of someone who is a bore, we are acting. Even with those we love we are acting when we cover up a bad mood or pretend more interest in our friends' activities than we actually feel in order to avoid hurting their feelings."

"I never thought of it that way," Georgiana said slowly.

"The other thing that you must realise," Elizabeth added," is that you have the felicity to be able to choose your marriage partner without having to worry about fortune causing difficulties. When you are in society you will often have the superior status, so you need not be embarrassed or worried about what others will think of you; they will be more concerned with gaining your favour than in criticising your behaviour."

"I know that," Georgiana said, hanging her head, "I sometimes feel like a prize heifer at auction … Elizabeth, there is something I want to tell you. I don't know what my brother has told you, but about a year and a half ago I was convinced by a young man of our acquaintance to elope. I thought that he loved me, but he was only trying to punish my brother for not giving him money, and he wanted my dowry. Fortunately, my brother found out and saved me from a terrible mistake, but since that time I feel that I cannot trust others. I feel that all of the young men that I meet are interested only in my wealth and family connections and I cannot believe their protestations of regard. I cannot believe that they are truly interested in a girl without beauty or grace, whose only charm is a large fortune."

Elizabeth gently embraced her sister and said, "You are very wrong if you think that you are either of those things, my dear sister. You are very attractive, and I have seen you dance, so do not tell me that you are graceless. Your beauty, though, is a quiet beauty—it is like the lady's slippers in the woods. They hide under the foliage of the other plants, but when you look for them and find them they are exquisite. Enough, I do not want to swell your head—I prefer it as it is. And … I know far more about Mr. Wickham than you can possibly imagine, since, as you know, he is married to my youngest sister.

"I … I do not want to criticise your brother-in-law …"

"Do not be concerned; I have no great love for him. During the early months of our acquaintance he told innumerable lies about the entire Darcy family, which I believed implicitly until I became better acquainted with your brother and learned the truth. It was humiliating to learn how easily I could be taken in about someone's character. I thought that I was so clever at assessing people's true nature. I know too, dear Georgiana, that *you* were the one who told your brother what Wickham was planning, so you saved yourself by your honesty with him. You need not be ashamed that you could not detect the insincerity of such a practised rogue, and you also need not be worried about discussing him with me. I know that your brother does not like to remind you of that time and he is very modest about his own good qualities, so perhaps you do not realise that my sister eloped with Wickham, but he had no intention of marrying a girl without a dowry. Only your brother's intervention saved my sister's reputation and, at the same time, my entire family's good name. No, you need not be concerned about blackening Wickham's name with me. I am only too happy to be out of his company."

Georgiana embraced her and sighed, "I feel much better now that we have this understanding between us. I did not like feeling that I was hiding something from you that might make you think less of me."

They embraced again and then went to their rooms to change for dinner, each meditating on the conversation.

That night in the privacy of her room she told Darcy of her afternoon with Georgiana. He chuckled a little at the thought of the two of them playacting upstairs but became serious when she told him of their conversation about Wickham:

"I am glad that she told you herself about Wickham; now that she knows that there are no secrets between you and that you can be trusted with her confidence she may be more relaxed. Wickham has much to answer for."

"Do not worry," said Elizabeth grimly. "By being married to my sister Lydia, he is in a way to pay back his iniquities for the rest of his life."

"I am just happy that his machinations did not succeed in keeping us apart," he returned. He held her tightly to his chest and kissed her gently on the forehead. "I had actually almost forgotten Wickham in the last two months. I seem to have had more interesting things to think about," he murmured as his lips made their way slowly down to her mouth.

Chapter 13

And tune thy jolly voice to my fresh pipe,
And all the daughters of the year shall dance!
William Blake, *Poetical Sketches*, "To Autumn"

The Bingleys and the Bennets arrived the next afternoon. The footman announced the appearance of the carriage to the ladies as they sat in the music room, Georgiana playing the harp while Elizabeth listened and fitfully worked on her needlepoint. They went downstairs and met Darcy and the colonel in the hall as they came from the book room. Georgiana had hesitantly agreed to Elizabeth's suggestion that morning that she introduce the colonel to everyone, but Elizabeth saw that she looked strained, her fingers white as they gripped her handkerchief. Elizabeth felt strange waiting in the hall with Darcy and the others as the carriage pulled up; it emphasised to her how much had changed in the last few months.

Miss Bingley entered first and greeted them, her face wreathed in smiles.

"Mrs. Darcy, Mr. Darcy," she said effusively to Elizabeth and Darcy as she curtseyed. Then she embraced Georgiana fervently and exclaimed, "And of course, my dear Georgiana! How wonderful it is to see you!"

"Welcome to Pemberley, Miss Bingley," Georgiana replied with a stiff smile. "May I please introduce you to my cousin, Colonel Fitzwilliam."

Miss Bingley's eyes had already found the colonel, and she curtseyed gracefully. "I am very happy to meet any relation of the Darcys, Colonel. I was desolated that I did not have the chance to meet you at my brother's wedding."

The colonel bowed and murmured, "*Enchanté, mademoiselle.*"

Elizabeth saw Georgiana look sharply at him, but his face was a picture of bland courtesy and Miss Bingley did not seem to notice the dryness in his tone. Jane and Bingley appeared and Elizabeth embraced and kissed them both.

"Welcome, my dear sister and brother. And of course you know Georgiana." Jane embraced Georgiana and Bingley shook her hand cordially.

"My dear sister. It is so good to see you again," Jane said to her and smiled her gentle and irresistible smile. Georgiana's face relaxed and, after a moment, she seemed to recall herself, saying smoothly, "Mr. and Mrs. Bingley, I would like to introduce you to my cousin, Colonel Fitzwilliam. Perhaps you met briefly at the wedding?"

"We did, but very briefly," Bingley said, bowing and then offering the colonel his hand. "I am delighted to make your acquaintance again."

Mr. Bennet and Kitty had come in behind the others. Mr. Bennet embraced Elizabeth tenderly and whispered in her ear, "I am very happy to see you, my dear. I have missed you exceedingly, as I am sure you know."

He greeted the others while Kitty embraced Elizabeth and shyly curtseyed to Darcy and the introduction to the colonel was duly made. Elizabeth noted that Georgiana looked relieved now that the colonel had taken over the conversation and she could listen from the background.

After the visitors had changed out of their travel clothes and refreshed themselves upstairs, they all met in the drawing-room. Georgiana seemed to have a recurrence of her shyness, but she made an effort to be especially kind to Kitty, who seemed to be a little awed by her surroundings. After they had talked for a few minutes Georgiana took her upstairs and they brought Lucky down to meet everyone. Kitty was enraptured by the puppy and soon the two young women were at ease, playing with Lucky and—Elizabeth was pleased to see—talking without embarrassment to each other while the rest of the conversation ranged freely around the room.

"Darcy, I would like to discuss a couple of things about Netherfield with you when we have a chance," Bingley said. "I would like to increase the bird population, but I do not want to take too much of the land out of production."

"Perhaps we could sit down and talk about it tomorrow morning?"

"Splendid. I brought the maps so you can see more clearly what I am talking about, but you fortunately are familiar with the land around there."

Mr. Bennet sat with Jane and Elizabeth. They caught up on all the news of Longbourn and Meryton and Elizabeth told her sister about the ball she and Georgiana had planned. Miss Bingley managed to seat herself next to Colonel Fitzwilliam and appeared to Elizabeth to be quite satisfied with her companion as she claimed his attention with as much determination as she ever had Mr. Darcy's a year ago.

After dinner when the gentlemen had rejoined them, Elizabeth, at the colonel's request, played the pianoforte and sang, and then she and Georgiana played a duet they had been practising for the occasion while their guests enjoyed their coffee and tea. Colonel Fitzwilliam sat next to Kitty during the performance and asked her if she played, but Kitty had never learned and seemed rather embarrassed by her lack of accomplishments, a reaction her sisters had never before seen from her. After they had finished playing, as the guests circulated around the room, Elizabeth found herself standing next to the colonel, a little apart from the others.

"I have not had the chance to speak with you much since my arrival," the colonel said quietly. "I wanted to thank you for all that you have done for Georgiana. I can see that she is already a little more comfortable in company, and Darcy tells me that you have taken her under your wing like a true sister. She is still very young, even for her age, and it is reassuring that she will have you to advise and guide her—it is very difficult for two old men like Darcy and me to take care of the needs of a sixteen-year-old girl without a woman's advice. Mrs. Annesley, of course, has been very good for her, but a sister just a little older than she is will understand her far better than we can."

"You do not need to thank me, Colonel," Elizabeth said in some embarrassment, "Georgiana is a delightful young woman and I love her dearly already."

"Well, I won't mention it again, but I just wanted you to know that I appreciate your efforts." The colonel murmured absently as he looked over at his ward, who was giggling with Kitty at some of Lucky's antics.

The days passed quickly. The Friday of the ball soon arrived and the house was filled with the bustle of preparations. Elizabeth and Georgiana met with Reynolds immediately after breakfast, but dealing with the many details of the ball took them most of the morning. When they were finished, they returned to their guests and found that the younger gentlemen had gone for a ride, while Mr. Bennet was reading in the library. The ladies spent the rest of the morning talking and working on their needlework as it was too cold for a walk. Georgiana had shown Kitty the conservatory, and they enjoyed playing with Lucky among the tropical foliage. He was already learning to fetch a ball on command, although he was still clumsy and often tumbled head over heels trying to chase it, landing on his nose with a very surprised look on his face, to the amusement of the girls.

They had an earlier and larger repast than usual that afternoon, not quite dinner but more than tea, for they would need time to prepare for the ball and supper would not be until midnight. Elizabeth sat next to Kitty with her tea and a cucumber sandwich and made sure that her sister ate, for she seemed to be rather agitated; not surprising since she had never been to a ball as grand as this. Kitty seemed to have lost much of the forwardness that she had exhibited around her sister Lydia. Perhaps, Elizabeth reflected, Lydia's disgrace had shown her how improper their behaviour had been, for she seemed to be in a much more subdued state of mind. Kitty had always been the follower in her relationship with her younger sister, so there was hope for her amendment if she was kept from Lydia's company.

Jane was talking quietly with Georgiana, who also looked very nervous. Elizabeth saw that she was relaxing a little under Jane's ministrations and eating some from the lavish trays of sandwiches and cakes Mrs. Reynolds had offered with their tea. When they went upstairs to change, Jane walked up with Elizabeth and commented *sotto voce*:

"Georgiana is such a sweet girl. I hope that she can find a husband someday who will appreciate her."

Elizabeth agreed and quietly returned, "The biggest difficulty, of course, will be deciding which one loves *her* and not just her money."

"Yes," Jane replied, smiling, as they reached the top of the staircase, "she will have a much different problem than we did, but hopefully she will end up as happily married as are we."

Upstairs, everything was in a state of hushed pandemonium as the ladies' maids and valets rushed to and from their masters' and mistresses' rooms on urgent errands, to touch up the ironing of a cravat or find a needle and thread for a repair. François told Elizabeth, with a twinkle in her eye, that she and Oliver had agreed that the master and mistress should be especially dazzling tonight.

"I have been planning a new hairstyle for you, *Madame* Darcy, which I saw while we were in London and have been waiting for an occasion to try. I think that it will be *très chic, madame,* and will be *magnifique* with your new gown. Oliver has selected, pending *monsieur's* approval *naturellement,* a black waistcoat which has a very thin, pale yellow stripe in the pattern, which will thus pick up ze *couleur* of *madame's* gown: nothing blatant *vous comprenez*, but just a leetle hint to ze other ladies that *Monsieur* Darcy belongs with *madame.*"

"Very well, François," Elizabeth said in amusement as François's accent became more and more pronounced in her excitement. "I put myself entirely in your hands."

With an air of supreme satisfaction, François began her work.

When she looked down over the balustrade and saw everyone gathered downstairs for the ball, Elizabeth felt that they were all transformed. Jane was a vision in a pale pink gown of silk and with pearls woven into her hair. Miss Bingley had on a vibrant russet silk, with many yards of lace, and a turban with matching marabou feather trim. Kitty had blossomed out in a new gown that Jane and Elizabeth had together given her for Christmas, in a gray-blue colour that accented her fair skin and blue eyes. Her hair was a creation of plaits and curls that was very feminine and suited her very well.

Elizabeth had on her lemon-coloured gown, which was in a simple style, and the translucent overskirt shimmered with iridescence when she moved and gave glimpses of the yellow satin from under a scalloped border. Her hair was swept up with several plaits looping down from her chignon, and a yellow aigrette at one side was adorned with a flirtatious white ostrich feather. She wore the Darcy diamonds, which had been reset: eardrops with a tiny cluster of diamonds on the earlobe and a teardrop-shaped diamond pendant from each of them, and a "chain" of small diamonds with a similar but larger pendant diamond resting just at the top of her *décolletage.*

She had just begun to look around for Georgiana when she appeared behind her, gowned in cream silk with a modest neckline, her new pearl necklace around her neck and ribbons in her hair.

"My dear, you look wonderful!"

Georgiana smiled ruefully. "Thank you. I just wish that my gown was a little more stylish. The one part of my debut that I am looking forward to is that I will be allowed to wear lower-cut bodices on my gowns."

"Well, you look very well anyway." Elizabeth took her arm and they walked down the stairs together.

"You ladies all look splendid," Elizabeth said as she kissed Jane and Kitty and smiled at Miss Bingley.

The gentlemen soon joined them, and the company began arriving for the ball. The Darcys were kept busy greeting their guests and introducing them to the Bingleys and the Bennets. Elizabeth had felt that the ball itself would be quite challenging enough for Georgiana, and so had placed the girl between herself and Darcy. Georgiana had merely to say "good evening" and curtsey and the responsibilities of greeting and introducing would be left to her brother and sister.

The orchestra had begun playing as soon as the first carriage rolled up to the door, and when the guests had all arrived Elizabeth and Darcy led the first dance, followed down the line by Georgiana and Colonel Fitzwilliam and Jane and Bingley. Kitty had Jonathan Walker as a partner and followed the Bingleys, her face showing her pleasure in being asked for the first pair of dances.

Elizabeth was kept busy during the evening making the acquaintance of all their guests but she kept one eye upon Georgiana and Kitty. The two young women stayed together when they were not dancing, which was good policy on Kitty's part since all the unmarried men were gathered around Georgiana and she was assured of plenty of dancing partners. Georgiana held up well during the early evening but began to look a trifle harried as the ball wore on. Elizabeth rescued her from the crowds of admirers and made sure that she was seated with herself and Darcy for supper, leaving Kitty, who had a stronger constitution, to sit with Jonathan Walker and Sir Robert Blake's middle brother, James.

Elizabeth confirmed during the evening that she liked Sir Robert Blake very much; he was unpretentious and easy to talk to, and very much the gentleman.

He was quietly attentive to Georgiana and asked her to dance two pairs of dances, but did not push himself forward. He was quite a bit older than Georgiana, but not excessively so, and Elizabeth watched them closely. She hoped that Georgiana might show some interest in him but was unable to draw any conclusions from the girl's expression.

Elizabeth also studied the Comte de Tournay keenly. He had arrived at his sister's for Christmas, as expected, and tonight was the first time Elizabeth had met him. The Darcys had been invited to Kympton Hall for dinner two days after the ball, so they would have a better opportunity to learn his tastes and temper then, but this, Elizabeth's first glimpse of him, was intriguing. He was somewhat over forty years old, and handsome in a dark, brooding way, but looked rather dissipated, his lower lids pouched and deep creases marking the line between his nose and mouth.

In spite of having lived in England for more than twenty years, he was consciously French, with Continental manners. He was trying to make himself agreeable to Georgiana, but he was, Elizabeth thought, far too experienced for a naïve young English girl. Georgiana looked at him with her eyes wide, rather as if he was some sort of exotic wildlife, and possibly dangerous. Elizabeth took great pleasure in introducing him to Miss Bingley, after a subtle hint about Miss Bingley's agreeable financial status. He seemed to be quite pleased to dance with her and Caroline was entranced to meet a comte.

Elizabeth was not so well satisfied, however, with Jonathan Walker, who seemed to be always hovering near Georgiana. She saw him talking to her, leaning towards her in an intimate manner, while Georgiana tried to surreptitiously move away from him. Perhaps it was time to intervene. She walked over and heard Master Walker say:

"Please say you will, Miss Darcy. I am counting on you."

Elizabeth interjected mildly, "For what Mr. Walker?"

He started, but quickly recovered himself.

"I am trying to convince Miss Darcy to allow me to escort her to church this Sunday, Mrs. Darcy."

"I am sorry, but I am afraid that Georgiana will have responsibilities with our guests on Sunday, Mr. Walker," she responded coolly.

"Ah. Perhaps another time then," he said smoothly, then bowed and moved off.

Elizabeth watched him for a moment as he asked Miss Blake to dance, and then turned to Georgiana, who looked at her in relief.

"Are you all right, my dear?" Elizabeth whispered.

"I am now. Thank you, Elizabeth. You are my friend forever," she answered with a brief smile.

Elizabeth returned her grin and went back to Darcy's side, relieved that Georgiana still had a spark of spirit remaining. Darcy had noticed her defection from his side.

"How is Georgiana doing?"

"She seems to be fine, but I thought that I needed to give her a little assistance in detaching Master Walker. He rather reminds me of a limpet."

Darcy chuckled but had a wary look in his eye as he watched Mr. Walker dance with Miss Blake. "A very apt comparison, but if we must, we will use a knife to disengage him and throw him back into the sea."

Elizabeth nodded. "Indeed we will," she said, and turned to talk with some guests who were approaching. She was having a very good time at the ball on the whole, and saw with pleasure Jane and Bingley dancing together all night; they were clearly very happy. Jane had a beautiful glow about her, beyond even her usual beauty, that made Elizabeth smile to see her, and Bingley obviously still loved to dance. She also noted that Darcy was making a real effort to be the perfect host, in spite of his general dislike for balls and dancing. She watched him with a complacent smile as he talked to everyone, clearly charming them. Colonel Fitzwilliam stopped at her side after finishing a set with Miss Blake and commented on the change in his cousin.

"I have never seen Darcy so relaxed and happy at a ball," he said, "You are a miracle worker, Mrs. Darcy." He gave her a courtly bow.

She smiled archly and thanked him, but commented, "You just keep your eye on Georgiana, my dear cousin; I do not want her to be overwhelmed with all these young men. They are insistent enough to give her a 'cauld grue', as the Scottish would say."

He looked over at his ward and said, "You are right, Cousin, and Jonathan Walker is the most importunate of them all. I believe that I will go break up the group and ask her to dance again; I think an old cousin can have a second dance without causing undue comment."

He strolled over and neatly captured her from the mass in a manoeuvre that did credit to his military training and Elizabeth saw a look of relief and pleasure on Georgiana's face. Elizabeth watched them dance and was reassured to see her young sister relax a little. When Georgiana felt sure of herself she was a very graceful dancer and Elizabeth noted that some of the young men watched them also, and somewhat speculatively; the colonel's soldierly carriage stood out from the civilians, even when not adorned with a red coat. Georgiana herself had a pleasant, open countenance and attractive, if not classically handsome, features, particularly her large grey-green eyes and dark lashes. With these added to her tall, elegantly formed figure, she was quite striking. If she could appear relaxed and happy, as she was at this moment with her cousin, she would undoubtedly cause a ripple among the young men in London in the coming season.

Kitty was dancing every dance, as was Georgiana, and had partnered with Edward Blake, the youngest of the Blakes, at least twice that Elizabeth had seen. They made a pleasing couple as they went through the figures of the dance and Kitty's face was flushed with heat and gratification. Darcy had commented to Elizabeth, after he had hunted with the Blakes a couple of times, that the youngest brother seemed to be a young man of intelligence and quality just as the elder brothers were, so she was content to let Kitty dance with him and merely kept an eye on them to make sure that her sister behaved with decorum and did not embarrass her family.

She saw her father come into the ballroom and went to join him. "What have you been doing, Papa?" She smiled, and took his arm. "I haven't seen you all evening."

"I have been enjoying your library, my love; as you well know balls are not to my taste, but," he said as he patted her hand, "I thought that I should see how all my girls are doing and show my appreciation for your skills as a hostess."

"Thank you, Papa, we are having a lovely time—at least I am, and I think that our guests are, too," she returned. "I think even my poor husband, who likes balls almost as much as you do, is having an agreeable time."

They both looked at Darcy, who was talking with Bingley and Jane and had a pleased smile on his face.

"And how is Kitty conducting herself, Lizzy?" her father asked.

"She is doing very well," Elizabeth answered. "I think that the short time she has been separated from Lydia has already made a great difference in her sense of propriety. How has she behaved at Netherfield? Jane said that she was acquitting herself with decorum, but about who has dearest Jane ever said anything ill?" she said with an ironic smile and shake of her head.

Mr. Bennet laughed and answered, "Very true, my dear Lizzy, your sister Jane is unfailingly charitable in her assessments of people's character. But in this case I believe she is correct, for I have not seen Kitty do anything improper or immoderate, although she is still occasionally a little peevish. That, too, I think is improving."

After a few minutes Mr. Bennet returned to the library and Elizabeth joined Colonel Fitzwilliam and Georgiana, who were talking with Miss Blake. Elizabeth and the colonel forwarded the conversation between the two younger women, but, Elizabeth reflected to herself, Miss Blake, pleasant as she was, was rather insipid and silly. Still, her manners were excellent, and it was nice for Georgiana to have a wider circle of young women with whom to spend her time. Elizabeth noted that Miss Blake seemed to be rather taken with the colonel, smiling at him attentively whenever he entered the conversation, which was often with his charming and well-spoken manner. Georgiana seemed to discern Miss Blake's attentions to the colonel as well, and coolly examined the two of them while they talked to each other, her face impassive.

A short while later, Georgiana pulled her sister aside and whispered, "It is almost two o'clock, Elizabeth, and I am exhausted. Would it be discourteous for me to go upstairs now?"

"No, of course not, my dear. It is very late for you, and you do look ready to collapse. I am sorry that I did not notice before." She put her arm around the girl.

"It came upon me rather suddenly," Georgiana said with a feeble smile.

With a pat on the hand, Elizabeth sent her up to her room. Kitty was apparently still full of energy, for she was still dancing. Elizabeth did not worry about her overtiring herself, since she knew that her younger sister loved to dance and could continue all night if need be. The ball continued until almost three o'clock, when the orchestra finished with "Sir Roger de Coverley." The guests all said good night, and those that were going home made their way to the entry hall, where they took their leave of their host and hostess. The guests who were staying the night straggled up the stairs to their rooms, and by half past three the house was quiet.

Chapter 14

Love looks not with the eyes, but with the mind.
William Shakespeare, "A Midsummer-Night's Dream"

The next morning Elizabeth and Darcy discussed the ball while they had their morning tea. Elizabeth thought the evening had gone well and was pleased with the fortitude with which Georgiana had withstood the onslaught of all the single men.

"I am not best pleased with Jonathan Walker, however," she said tartly. "He is too exigent and I think he makes Georgiana uncomfortable."

Darcy agreed, and was about to say more when a footman entered with the morning post.

"Ah," he commented, looking at a letter, "this may be the information I requested on just that subject. Please pardon me, my love, while I read this."

She watched his face as he read, eager to know what information his agents had been able to find, and she saw his brow lower.

"Good God," he cried, tossing the letter onto the table. "Walker is worse than I suspected. He was sent down from Oxford over some unpaid debts of honour and went to London with some 'friends' that he had made at school. They proceeded to drink and gamble their way through the money his father had sent with him for school and ran up considerable debts. When he no longer had enough money to be entertaining to them, his so-called friends abandoned him and he came home. His father must not realise the extent of his financial difficulties, or else he is blinding himself to his son's true nature, or he would surely not give him authority over his estate. Walker has somehow managed to mortgage the entire estate, and his creditors are becoming rather hopeless. He is evidently desperate to find a rich wife to bail him out of his troubles, and makes periodic visits to London to try the marriage market, but only succeeds in increasing his losses while he is there."

"We had better warn Georgiana," Elizabeth said in some alarm, "I doubt that she has any interest in Mr. Walker, but she should certainly know what kind of man he is."

"She undoubtedly should know," Darcy agreed grimly. "Do you want to tell her? I am afraid that if I tell her it will remind her too much of the Wickham incident, which I do not particularly want to bring to her mind again."

"I will most certainly tell her as soon as our guests leave," Elizabeth agreed.

Their guests from the ball made their departures in the early afternoon, and the Darcys spent the rest of the day with their remaining friends. The Bingleys and the Bennets would be leaving on the morrow, so everyone was a little subdued that last day. Elizabeth spent some time with Jane in her little morning room before the girls were up, and her sister's eyes filled with tears when she was talking to Elizabeth about leaving, but she dashed them away quickly saying:

"I am sorry, Lizzy, I do not know what has come over me. I seem to be very emotional the last couple of weeks. I do not want you to think that I am unhappy, because I am most definitely not, but I do confess that I miss you daily. Still," she said, forcing a smile, "we will see you in town for the season, so it will not be long before we meet again for a more extended visit."

Elizabeth embraced her sister affectionately, and by unspoken consent they steered the conversation into a less emotional channel.

"I am concerned about Kitty," Elizabeth said. "Miss Bingley seems to be fixed with you for the indefinite future as it does not sound, from what she has said, as if she and Louisa will make up their differences anytime soon. Miss Bingley barely tolerates Kitty; I have heard her make sarcastic comments to her several times and then turn around and praise Georgiana to the skies in front of her. That is not good for either of the girls. Miss Bingley is very foolish if she thinks that Georgiana does not see through her attempts to humiliate Kitty. Georgiana is very perceptive, and she is not impressed by being fawned over, particularly when the fawning is primarily done to spite another person."

"I hate to admit that Caroline could be so unjust," Jane said with a sigh, "but I must agree that she does not seem to like Kitty and is unable to behave toward her with tolerance."

"Perhaps I should speak with Mr. Darcy and see if he would agree to let Kitty stay with us for a while," Elizabeth said, tapping her fingers on the desk as she mused. "It would probably be nice for Georgiana to have another young girl around and Kitty would most likely benefit from Georgiana's example."

"That is a very good thought, Lizzy. Please do ask Mr. Darcy if he would approve."

Elizabeth found Darcy alone in his library that afternoon while he was looking for a book he and Mr. Bennet had been discussing, and broached the subject of Kitty staying with them. He immediately agreed, saying:

"I have been somewhat concerned over Miss Bingley's behaviour to her while they have been here. It is not good for Kitty to be stepped on all the time, particularly since she has behaved very circumspectly while she has been here; much better, in fact, than has Miss Bingley."

When she thanked him he kissed her affectionately on the top of her head and she hurried off to speak with her father, who willingly gave his approval to the idea. After searching in the drawing-room and the music room, she found Georgiana in the conservatory, gazing meditatively at the snowflakes that were slowly drifting onto the roof.

"There you are, my dear!"

Georgiana looked up with a start and blushed slightly. "I am sorry, were you looking for me?"

"Yes. I have been talking to my family and Mr. Darcy about the possibility of Kitty staying a while longer. I wondered if you, too, would like her to stay."

"Oh, my dear sister," she said, straightening abruptly in her chair. "I would very much enjoy having Kitty spend more time here." She smiled. "I feel very fortunate having acquired five sisters at one time and I would like to know Kitty better."

Elizabeth finally found Kitty and made her proposal to her. Kitty clapped her hands and danced around her sister, saying:

"I would love to stay here, Lizzy, thank you *so* much!"

They spent the remainder of the day in quiet relaxation. Elizabeth noted that Miss Bingley was exceedingly attentive to both Mr. Darcy and the colonel until Sir Andrew Ffoulkes and the Comte de Tournay rode over so that the comte could make his farewells to his new acquaintances.

"And where is your estate, *Monsieur le Comte?*" Miss Bingley asked casually as they all drank tea in the drawing-room.

"It is about twenty miles from Windsor, *mademoiselle,*" he replied. "It is a small estate but, unfortunately, virtually all of our land was lost during the Terror, and the current *régime* is not pervious to the demands of the former aristocracy to be reinstated to their property. I am resigned." He shrugged eloquently.

"It must be very difficult to be living in exile from your homeland, *Monsieur le Comte,*" she purred.

He eyed Miss Bingley speculatively for a moment, then put on a sad but noble face. "*Oui mademoiselle,* it is a very sad thing, but we must make the best of it. We are fortunate to have had the assistance of our English friends to help us escape from the Terror with our lives."

Miss Bingley sighed and said, "Will you be visiting London during the upcoming season, *Monsieur le Comte?*"

"*Bien sûr*. I always try to spend part of the season with friends in London. You understand that I am unable to afford an establishment of my own in town; however I am fortunate enough to have friends who are willing to oblige with an invitation."

"Possibly we will see you there, then, my lord, as my brother and his wife are spending the season in town and have kindly invited me to join them. My elder sister and her husband also live in London and have extended me an invitation as well."

"That would be delightful, *Mademoiselle* Bingley."

Both the comte and Miss Bingley seemed gratified by this conversation and Elizabeth was highly entertained, especially as she noted the sardonic glint in the comte's eye when Miss Bingley turned her attention to his brother, Sir Andrew.

While Sir Andrew and the comte were still visiting, the three Blakes arrived on the same errand: to say farewell to the Darcy's guests. Miss Blake seemed charmed to see all of the gentlemen together, but spent most of her time vying for the colonel's attention, which he seemed happy to give. Elizabeth noted that Georgiana was again watching them while she listened to Elizabeth and Darcy talk to Sir Robert. Mr. Edward Blake sat next to Kitty. Elizabeth could not hear them, but both seemed to be well satisfied with their conversation, and parted with mutual smiles. In half an hour both sets of visitors left, after bidding farewell to the Bingleys and the Bennets.

Early the next morning all of their guests departed: the Bingleys and the Bennets to return to Hertfordshire and the colonel to return to his duties at the Court of St. James. The air was cold and crisp and the horses' breath made wreaths of steam around their muzzles as they stamped and shook their heads. The footmen had loaded the luggage and the servants were waiting in the second carriage when the four passengers said their farewells and climbed into Bingley's barouche. Elizabeth watched the carriages sadly as the wheels swirled them quickly down the long drive towards the highway. After Georgiana and Kitty had turned back to the house, Elizabeth continued to watch until both carriages disappeared into the trees, her eyes filled with unshed tears. Darcy said quietly:

"Shall we go inside, my love?"

She nodded and turned towards the house, her arm through his. She forced herself to smile and said:

"Well, Mr. Darcy, now that the holidays are over we shall be very busy getting Georgiana ready for her debut. In a couple of weeks we will probably look back on these last weeks with nostalgia for the relative quiet and calm of the Christmas season."

He smiled ruefully and said, "I suspect that you are right, my love" as they entered the house.

Now that their guests were gone, Georgiana and Elizabeth resumed their practise sessions. They did their practising early in the morning before breakfast, while Kitty was still asleep and Darcy was busy with estate business. At their next meeting, Elizabeth told her of Walker's disgraceful behaviour.

"I am not in the least surprised," she sniffed, "he is most forward."

Elizabeth was curious to find out what Georgiana thought of the young men of the neighbourhood, so soon after they had restarted their lessons she asked her. She was shocked by Georgiana's response. A flush of red rushed up to the girl's face and she averted her eyes.

"I am sorry, Georgiana, I did not mean to embarrass you!" Elizabeth said quickly, her eyes wide with surprise.

"No, no ... I ... I should like to tell you," Georgiana whispered, as her eyes filled and a teardrop fell on her clenched hands. "I like the gentlemen in the neighbourhood well enough, excepting only Mr. Walker. Sir Robert is especially nice and very handsome, and I like his brothers and sister, too. The problem is that ... well," she paused for a moment, took a deep breath, and plunged on: "My heart is already taken."

Wickham appeared immediately in Elizabeth's mind, in all his deceitful charm. She breathed in slowly and said with as much calmness as she could feign, "You are in love with someone already?"

Staring at her hands as they twisted her handkerchief, Georgiana whispered, "I have been in love with Colonel Fitzwilliam since I was a little girl."

Elizabeth gave a silent sigh of relief, her breath returning.

Georgiana continued, unaware of her sister's sudden fear, "I remember when I was six years old and I was afraid to ride my pony. He spent the two weeks he was here teaching me to ride. He was so patient, and he never made fun of me for being frightened, in spite of his being a grown twenty-year-old who was afraid of nothing.

"I always worshipped him as a child and thought of him as almost another brother, but it was not until my stupidity with Wickham that I realised that I had let a foolish, romantic tale almost make me do something that would ruin my life, as well as the lives of my relations. Colonel Fitzwilliam came to see me afterwards and he had not one word of blame for me; his only concern was for my well-being. My brother was of course the same, but he is my brother, not a cousin who has been saddled with the guardianship of a stupid young girl. I think that was the moment when I realised that I had always loved him, and not merely as a brother!"

Elizabeth took her hand gently. "Well, dearest, there is no reason that you cannot marry Colonel Fitzwilliam. I will speak with your brother ..."

"No!" she cried, clutching Elizabeth's hand so hard that it was painful. She released it immediately and said, "I am so sorry, Elizabeth, but please promise me you will not talk to Fitzwilliam about this!"

"But, why not, Georgiana? He could talk to the colonel ..."

"No! That is exactly what I *do not* want!"

"But, dearest ..." Elizabeth said insistently.

Georgiana riveted her eyes upon Elizabeth's with an intensity that Elizabeth had never before seen in her sister. "Do you not see? I do not want the colonel to feel *obligated* to marry me. I do not want him to marry me only for duty to his family—I want him to marry me because he loves me. I want the kind of love and respect that you and my brother have for each other, not a cool, logical arrangement for the benefit of the family."

"I begin to see the problem, my dear," Elizabeth said, rather helplessly, "but what can we do about it?"

"He thinks that I am a child; when he visits he kisses me dutifully and pats me on the head and rescues me at the ball if the young men get too importunate, but he does it as a duty to a child. He even calls me 'little cousin'—sometimes I could just slap him for that!" she said passionately.

"Yes, I noticed him doing that," Elizabeth said absently. "So ... what do you want me to do, Georgiana?"

"I do not know. I just do not know what to do to get his attention," she sobbed, "I will be seventeen years old next month and am no longer a child, but how do I make him see that, and how do I find out if he cares for me without risking awkwardness and humiliation for both of us? It would be mortifying if he found out that I love him and he does not feel the same towards me."

Elizabeth embraced her and Georgiana clung to her like a small child. Elizabeth stroked her hair and said, "Well, Georgiana, my dear, the only answer I can give you now is that I will give this problem some thought and we will see what we can do. As far as I know, the colonel does not have a particular young woman that he is interested in, so I think that he is safe for the moment—although he might have a dozen young women courting him in London and I would not know it!"

"Heaven forbid!" Georgiana said, smiling wanly through her tears.

"Now, dry your eyes, my dear, and we will see what we can do."

Georgiana carefully blotted her eyes, and, after sitting quietly for a few minutes with their arms around each other to compose themselves, they each went to their own room. Elizabeth felt herself distracted most of that day, although she tried to exert herself to behave normally. She was relieved that Darcy did not ask her what was wrong. Hopefully he would attribute her lack of spirits to the recent loss of their family and friends. She hoped that the colonel's duties would keep him busy and away from the young society women for the next few weeks—Georgiana would be in town in less than two months. That evening, while Georgiana was attempting to teach Kitty a duet, Elizabeth suddenly remembered her earlier thoughts about her sister's playing. Well, she thought wryly to herself, I think that I can discount the notion that Georgiana does not yet feel the passion of the music she plays!

Chapter 15

Oh what a tangled web we weave,
When first we practise to deceive!
Sir Walter Scott, "Marmion"

One rainy day in early March, a few weeks after all of their guests had departed, Elizabeth was crossing the entry hall and was surprised to see, through one of the tall windows, Colonel Fitzwilliam ride up. When Smithfield opened the door she greeted him warmly:

"Colonel! I did not expect to see you again so soon. You are most welcome! Have you come for Georgiana's birthday today?"

"My dear Cousin Elizabeth, I am, unfortunately, here on business, and it is very important that I speak to Darcy immediately; however, I did bring Georgiana her present," he said gravely, handing a small silver-wrapped box to Elizabeth.

"Of course, Colonel," she said, her eyes widening. "I believe he is in his library. Smithfield, would you please announce the colonel?"

"Yes, madam."

Elizabeth stood with Georgiana's gift in her hands, looking after the colonel quizzically as the heavy mahogany door of the library closed behind him. She had never seen the colonel look so serious.

Later, Darcy came to find her in the drawing-room, where she was absently watching Georgiana and Kitty play with Lucky, part of her mind still in the library with the two men. She wondered what had happened to make the colonel look so grim, and felt a little anxious. Darcy put his head in the door without speaking and caught her eye. He made a small motion with his head to draw her out of the room.

"Come to the library, my love, I need to talk to you," he said quietly as she came to the door. His mouth was compressed in a thin line as he led her into the library and carefully shut the door.

"Where is the colonel?" she asked as she sat down, watching him pace in front of his desk for a moment before he spoke.

"He is on his way back to London, as I will be tomorrow morning, and then most likely I will travel to the Continent."

"The Continent!" she exclaimed. "What do you mean?"

Darcy clasped his hands behind his back and stopped in front of her. "The colonel came here with the express purpose of giving me a message. It is of an extremely sensitive nature, but I know that you are perfectly discreet and I do not feel that I can leave without giving you some explanation, for you will have to cover my absence while I am gone. I am 'requested,'" he said in a voice heavy with sarcasm, "to go to London and meet with the prince regent, who has a favour that he has 'requested' that I do, which may involve traveling to Paris."

"The prince regent!" she said with astonishment.

"Yes. As you know, I do not associate with the fast set that makes London its home and of which the prince is the leader. His behaviour is scandalous and irresponsible in many ways and, as you might guess, I do not approve of it. It has always been my impression that the prince regent does not approve of me, either, considering me, I am sure, to be rather like Banquo's ghost at the feast," he said dryly. "Be that as it may, he apparently wants me to do something which he feels, and which, just as importantly to me, the colonel feels, only I can do. I do not yet know what that errand is. The prince is no fool, in spite of his reckless behaviour, and I suppose he feels that the sycophants that surround him are not trustworthy when it comes to discretion—a feeling that is probably quite correct.

"You know that the colonel is a member of the Horse Guards, which are charged with protecting the royal family, but what you may not know is that his primary charge is to protect the safety of the prince regent himself. How Fitzwilliam can spend so much time working intimately around the prince and his cronies and avoid the corruption that springs up around them, I do not know, but he seems to be able to manage it, and the prince regent places a great deal of trust in him.

"In spite of his glib tongue and easy manner, Fitzwilliam can be extremely reticent when it is necessary. In fact, much of this information on his role at St. James I have gradually accumulated over the twelve years he has been in the Horse Guards, mostly from what other people have told me. At any rate, I will be leaving in the morning and I must be finished with this 'errand', whatever it may be, by the time Georgiana is presented. It would look too suspicious were I not there, even if I would consider missing it."

"I see," Elizabeth said, perplexed. "… At least, I do not see, but I understand what you have told me so far. What am I to do about Georgiana's presentation?"

He sat down next to her and took her hand. "Well, the one bit of good news Fitzwilliam brought is that his parents will be coming to Pemberley—they will probably arrive in a couple of days—and my aunt will take responsibility for all of the details and help Georgiana ready herself. Unfortunately, I will be gone when they arrive, so you will have to meet them for the first time with Georgiana alone to support you. I do not know what they think of our marriage at this time, but at least Georgiana's need for my aunt's experience and social standing during her first season will give them an excuse to meet you that even Lady Catherine would not gainsay.

"Actually," he added, "I think that you will like them; they think rather too much of their position in society (a charge which I am hardly in a situation to criticise, considering past events), but they are not bad sorts, and I think that they will like you when they know you. I suspect that they have stayed away thus far because they did not want to deal with the conniptions of Lady Catherine over our marriage, but I am not surprised that their sense of family responsibility for Georgiana has overcome their hesitation in that matter. You must tell anyone who asks that I was called away to London on business, and that you will be joining me there soon."

"And what if you have not returned by the time we arrive in London?"

"Then you must tell inquirers that I had to return to Pemberley unexpectedly to finish some business so that I will be free for the season, and that I will rejoin you in London before Georgiana's presentation."

"What do I tell your aunt and uncle?"

"Apparently, they have been told enough by the colonel to let them know that I will not be here. They are fortunately not indiscreet. I do not think that they will ask questions."

When Elizabeth returned to the drawing-room, Georgiana asked her, "Where is the colonel; is he going to stay for my birthday?"

"He had to return to London after he concluded his business with your brother, but he brought your birthday present," Elizabeth said, exerting herself to be off-hand. Georgiana looked rather surprised but did not question her further.

That evening they celebrated Georgiana's birthday with a family party. Cook made Georgiana's favourite dinner and outdid herself on a lovely cake filled with raisins and nuts. Georgiana seemed a little subdued, but managed to smile and exclaim when she opened her presents. Darcy gave her a pair of pearl earrings to match the necklace they had purchased in London and some new music, and Kitty had netted her a reticule that matched her best pelisse. Elizabeth had purchased a new spring bonnet for her to wear during the season and knitted a warm scarf and mittens for her, with a matching coat for Lucky. Georgiana laughed when she saw the coat and told Lucky, who was sitting on her lap, that they would wear them for their walk the next day. The colonel's offering was the last to be opened and she gave a brief smile when she saw the delicate gold bracelet cradled in the velvet-lined box. She silently clasped it on her wrist, leaving her hand around it for a moment before taking the knife to cut the cake.

The next morning just after dawn Darcy left with his valet in the coach-and-four, taking all of the clothes he would need for the coming season in case he was not able to return to Pemberley beforehand. Elizabeth clung to him for a moment before he left their sitting-room, but sent him off with as brave a face as she could.

"Please hurry back, my love," she whispered.

Darcy did not speak as he held her for a moment in his arms, his head bowed and his eyes closed. Then he was gone. She shivered involuntarily as she watched the coach race down the drive from her window, then she took herself in hand and spoke firmly to the empty room:

"Are you nervous for your husband, or for yourself sitting here waiting for the unknown in-laws, you stupid girl?" She turned from the window, marched into her bedroom, and called François to dress her.

When she entered the breakfast room, rather earlier than usual, she found Georgiana before her.

"Georgiana, why are you up so early!" Elizabeth exclaimed in surprise.

"I could not sleep, so I thought that maybe we could put in some extra practise time today."

Elizabeth glanced at the door where the footman would reappear and said softly, "Are you upset because the colonel did not stay?"

Georgiana nodded her head silently, her eyes on her plate.

"I am sorry, my sweet. He had some urgent business with your brother and it required that he return immediately to London."

The girl sighed. "I know. I just wish that he had spoken to me before he left."

"I understand." Elizabeth drew herself up and said with a cheerfulness that sounded false even to her ears, "Kitty is not up yet, I assume?"

"I have not seen her."

"Let us eat then, and we will start our practise."

By the end of two hours, Elizabeth was ready to take a break. Georgiana looked grimly exhausted, tendrils of hair hanging limply around her face. But, Elizabeth thought, we have made a great deal of progress today. Georgiana was finding it easier and easier to assume a calm mien and take part in a variety of conversations without stumbling or losing her countenance. Elizabeth had, finally, instructed her to pretend that she was a princess royal who was kind and gracious to those below her, but who had a certain reserve that added mystery to her air. This seemed to suit Georgiana very well, allowing her to be her warm-hearted, thoughtful self, but also permitting her to merely smile enigmatically if she did not know what to say in a conversation. Her performances had immediately begun to improve.

After giving thought to Georgiana's problem with the colonel, Elizabeth had decided to discreetly consult François and ask her advice on how to make him realise that his cousin was an adult. François had suggested a complete change of hair and dress to alter her appearance, and especially to make her appear older, because, she said:

"The gentlemen, they do not respond to subtlety, *Madame* Darcy; while Cupid's little arrows sound lovely and romantic, he would be much more effective with ze truncheon."

Although she laughed at this assessment of love, Elizabeth had agreed with her, especially as Georgiana must fight against brotherly feelings in the colonel that had developed over seventeen years. So they had devised their schemes, and Elizabeth had sought out Georgiana in the music room where she was playing a mournful Albinoni *Adagio*.

"My dear, I have talked to François and we have come up with a plan."

Georgiana looked startled. "What is it?"

"We are going to have a ball gown made, something completely different from your usual style and quite *au courant*." Elizabeth tapped her chin as she thought out the details of her plan. "I think that we will try to find some sea-foam green satin. That will look lovely with your eyes. When we arrive in London we will have most of your gowns made in white or cream—I want them to be beautiful, but similar in colour. When we decide the time is ripe and it will make the most impact, we will have you appear in the new gown. François is already planning your hair; she wants something dramatically different from your usual style. I think we can trust her to come up with something wonderful. We want to gain the attention of as many gentlemen as possible—in some cases competition can spark an indifferent lover and make him want to vie for the prize that he has previously taken for granted."

Georgiana covered her mouth with her fingertips to stifle a nervous giggle. "Do you really think it will work, Elizabeth?"

Elizabeth put her arms around her. "I think that we have nothing to lose. It will take an earthquake to bring the colonel out of his complacence, and I, for one, am going to do my best to bring about that earthquake."

"I will do my part, too, if it kills me," Georgiana said, her face grimly determined.

Elizabeth gave her an encouraging squeeze. "Excellent. As you know, I sent for the seamstress a few days ago so that we could start her on your presentation gown, and she wrote that she will arrive today, if possible."

Later in the morning, Elizabeth and the two younger women decided to take a short walk with Lucky and Pilot, as the day was sunny and windless. They bundled up in their heaviest cloaks and warm bonnets and gloves and put Lucky in his new sweater, then walked quickly down to the stream, where they turned up a path that was partially sheltered from the brisk air by rocks and shrubbery. They had walked about a half mile and had just turned back when Lucky tugged on his leash, stiffening and growling as he stared towards the woods. At the same time, they were hailed.

"Mrs. Darcy, Miss Darcy, Miss Bennet, I am very glad to see you," Jonathan Walker called cheerfully as he broke out of the trees and swaggered towards them. Behind him appeared two retainers carrying fowling pieces. Seeing their startled faces he added, "I apologise for surprising you, but we were hunting and lost our way. We apparently wandered onto Pemberley land inadvertently and I am happy to now know where we are. I saw Darcy drive by this morning, apparently on his way to town, so I was afraid that we would not find succour in our distress." He smiled ingratiatingly.

Elizabeth felt an icy trickle down her spine when she saw the guns and Walker's arrogant attitude, but responded coolly, "Indeed, sir, you must have wandered a great way."

"Yes, I am afraid we have," he said engagingly. Elizabeth noted that his smile did not reach his eyes, which studied her with chilly composure. He paused, and Elizabeth could hear the wind rustling the dead leaves in the profound silence of the woods. He continued, a little less surely, "May I escort you ladies back to the house, or were you going to walk further?" He looked meaningfully at Georgiana.

Georgiana spoke up, looking at him unsmilingly, "I am afraid we must turn back, sir. We have already walked farther than we should and it would be very rude to be late for our guests."

Elizabeth added quickly, "Indeed, it is late. We had better hurry back before a search party is organised."

"Oh, you have guests? We will just walk with you as far as the drive, then, where we can cross to the main road." He offered Georgiana his arm and Pilot, who had been sitting quietly behind Elizabeth with his eyes glued upon the unwanted guests, growled deep in his throat, like the rumble of thunder.

"You are too kind, sir," Georgiana responded, ignoring his proffered arm to pat Pilot on the head and put the dog between herself and Walker.

After the three men left them at the drive, Kitty whispered to Elizabeth, "What is going on?"

Elizabeth touched her finger to her lips and shook her head slightly, hurrying them towards the house. Georgiana picked up Lucky, who continued growling under his breath as he peeked at the men from over her shoulder. They went quickly up the stairs and into the house while Pilot stayed behind on the terrace, silently watching the intruders walk down the drive. The ladies stared at each other while they caught their breath in the hall and a footman assisted them in removing their wraps.

"I think, perhaps, that we would all like some hot tea to warm us up. What do you think, ladies?" Elizabeth said, in an attempt to be calm.

The others nodded silently and went to the drawing-room while Elizabeth gave the orders for their tea.

"Well?" Georgiana asked when she had closed the door of the drawing-room.

"I don't know exactly what Mr. Walker's game is, but he is beginning to make me very uneasy," Elizabeth said slowly. "His claim to have accidentally wandered onto Pemberley land is patently false. It is a full six miles to the nearest boundary of the Walker property and they would have crossed several roads on the way. He also knew that Mr. Darcy was gone." She paused, not wanting to frighten the girls unduly, and then said carefully, "I am afraid that Mr. Walker might feel that Georgiana's fortune might be the solution to his financial difficulties and wishes to press his suit however he can. At any rate, I strongly recommend that we do not walk alone, even near the house, and we will take a couple of footmen with us when we do go. I find it interesting that Pilot and Lucky are as suspicious of him as I am. I think they must be good judges of character." She attempted to smile reassuringly, but Georgiana looked very pale and Kitty pressed her hand to her lips as they nodded their agreement. Elizabeth added, with as much pertness as she could summon:

"Georgiana, you handled him very well, my dear. A queen could not have been more deadly courteous."

Georgiana smiled tightly, and when Elizabeth saw the flinty look in the girl's eyes she suddenly realised that it was anger and not fear that blanched her face.

"I hope that your aunt and uncle will be here very soon, my dear—I expect them in the next day or two. I will feel much safer with their support."

At that moment the tea tray arrived and broke their tense conclave. Elizabeth changed the subject, and gradually took their minds off the strange incident, but they were all rather thoughtful as they drank their tea.

The seamstress arrived just after noon and Mrs. Reynolds settled her in the old governess's room. Elizabeth and Georgiana left Kitty working on her embroidery and spent several hours with the modiste, discussing the style and fabric of the dress that Elizabeth envisioned to launch Georgiana's dream of capturing the colonel's heart. By late afternoon they had made their selections and were back downstairs in the drawing-room with Kitty, having a cup of tea. Elizabeth felt a flood of relief when, at a few minutes before five o'clock, a fine carriage with four horses and liveried coachman and footmen pulled up the gravel drive. The reinforcements had arrived.

The three women rose when the visitors were announced.

"Lord and Lady Whitwell, madam."

Georgiana advanced to greet her aunt and uncle.

"It is lovely to see you my lord and lady," she said smoothly, giving them each a kiss. "I would like to introduce you to my new sisters, Mrs. Darcy and Miss Catherine Bennet."

Their visitors smiled and kissed Georgiana and greeted Elizabeth and Kitty courteously, if not warmly. Lord Whitwell was a slim, grizzled man of about fifty years, of medium height and with blue eyes and a rather weathered complexion. Lady Whitwell was tall and slender, almost as tall as her husband, and had light brown hair liberally mixed with silver and with streaks of pure silver in front. She wore her hair in a simple style that enhanced its striking colour, and her gown of blue emphasised the light blue of her eyes. Although both had rather reserved faces at rest, the lines around their eyes indicated that they were not without good humour, and were more accustomed to smiling than frowning. Elizabeth and Kitty returned their courtesies, Kitty somewhat shyly.

"I have heard so much about you, and I am happy to finally meet you," Lord Whitwell said formally. He paused and his cheeks blushed slightly as he appeared to realise the mischievous interpretation she might make of this commonplace formula.

Elizabeth returned his greetings calmly, but could not repress a smile; she was quite sure that he had heard a *great* deal about her from Lady Catherine. She ordered tea for her guests, and the familiar ritual of pouring and serving allowed everyone to recover from the awkwardness of the introductions. Once Lord and Lady Whitwell had told Georgiana the family news and given her the birthday present they had brought for her (a pair of fine doeskin gloves), the atmosphere became somewhat more relaxed and the time passed quickly until dinner.

The next morning Elizabeth rose early, in hopes that she could speak with Lord Whitwell about Jonathan Walker before the others arose. She was fortunate and found him breakfasting alone in the small breakfast-parlour.

"My lord, may I speak to you for a few moments before the others join us?" she asked.

"Of course, Mrs. Darcy," he answered, his brows tilted quizzically. "How may I serve you?"

"I wanted to apprise you of a situation which has arisen since my husband left for London and to ask for your advice, but I do not wish to further alarm my sisters," she said diffidently. "One of the young gentlemen of the neighbourhood has been rather importunate towards Georgiana, and my husband made inquiries into some questions he had about his past behaviour. He found that he is not at all a respectable young man, but we did not feel that we could avoid his society entirely as his father's ancestors have been the squires of Lambton for many generations and are long family acquaintances." She then proceeded to tell him of the incident of the previous day and the measures she had adopted.

"You feel that the young man is a threat to Georgiana?" Lord Whitwell asked, a little scepticism in his voice.

"I feel, at least, that we should be excessively cautious to ensure Georgiana's safety," Elizabeth returned, suppressing the little sting of irritation she felt at his doubt. "I am not a fancier of Gothic romances, my lord," she said dryly. "The young man is deeply in debt and might feel that a forced marriage to Georgiana might answer where his charm did not. At the very least, he has accosted us on Pemberley property and lied about his reasons for being here."

"You are certainly correct about Georgiana's safety being paramount," he said, drumming his fingers nervously on the table. "Well, we will adopt your measures, and possibly we should leave for London a little sooner than we had originally planned."

"Thank you, my lord." Her voice was cool.

They were not able to leave very soon, however. The orders for Georgiana's presentation gown and ball gowns for the season needed to be made, as well as for a few gowns for Elizabeth and Kitty, so the ladies spent most of the day looking at patterns and fabric samples. Georgiana's spirits seemed improved now that she and Elizabeth had a plan for her makeover and she had her aunt and uncle for support. When they were discussing dresses with Lady Whitwell the morning after she arrived, Georgiana earnestly insisted to her aunt that her ball gowns be cut lower in the bodice than what Lady Whitwell was suggesting she wear.

"My dear aunt, I am an adult now, and you do not want me to look like a child for my first season, do you? I am not asking to appear in an unseemly way, but I would like to be as fashionable as is consistent with propriety."

Lady Whitwell appeared rather taken aback at Georgiana's firmness of will, but finally agreed that a lower neckline would be acceptable:

"I suppose we must show you off to best advantage, my dear, and you do have a lovely figure," she said as she eyed Georgiana appraisingly. "I do not have any daughters, so I am not experienced in these things, but you are correct; the current fashion is for a lower-cut bodice."

Georgiana merely smiled.

Their time with the seamstress was interrupted in the early afternoon when Jonathan Walker came to call. Elizabeth introduced him to Lord and Lady Whitwell in the entry hall and ordered refreshments for their guest as they accompanied him to the drawing-room. His avowed reason for calling was to apologise again for disturbing their walk the day before and to ask if the ladies would consider taking one with his escort later. He did so while keeping an eye on Pilot, who was standing at the foot of the stairs watching him in an intent silence that Mr. Walker seemed to find more intimidating than the previous day's growling. Elizabeth reflected to herself in amusement that it would take a strong constitution to face the entire Darcy clan if Mr. Walker did not behave properly.

"I am so sorry, Mr. Walker," Elizabeth said, answering his question without much warmth, "we are just now preparing to go to London with Lord and Lady Whitwell. We will be gone for the season, so we are simply overwhelmed with business that must be concluded before we can leave. Unfortunately, I doubt that we will have time for walks, even if the weather is conducive."

"Of course," he said politely, looking coolly into her eyes, "in that case I would, of course, not want to take up any more of your time." He turned to Georgiana as they made their goodbyes and made a deep bow. "I trust that you find the season delightful, Miss Darcy, and hope that you will not forget your friends in the North."

"I never forget my friends, Mr. Walker," Georgiana replied, her eyes meeting his with chilly courtesy. "Good day to you, sir."

Georgiana and her aunt went back upstairs to the schoolroom, where the seamstress was holding court, but Lord Whitwell detained Elizabeth for a moment with a touch on her arm as she turned to follow them.

"I apologise for my doubts earlier this morning, Mrs. Darcy. I agree with you that Mr. Walker is a man of whom to beware. He has a cold eye that belies the courtesies that come from his mouth. I think I will have the forester and some of his men casually check the woods during the day and make sure that he does not become 'lost' again."

"Thank you, my Lord; I appreciate your assistance," Elizabeth answered. "I am sure Georgiana will feel better knowing that Mr. Walker cannot disturb us."

He returned her warm smile and went back to the library, where he had been reading before Mr. Walker had arrived, while she followed the others upstairs.

Chapter 16

Utrumque enim vitium est, et omnibus credere et nulli.
(It is equally unsound to trust everyone and to trust no one.)
Seneca, "Epistulae"

While Elizabeth was returning upstairs to rejoin her sisters and Lady Whitwell, Darcy was recovering from a brutal ride to London. They had changed carriage horses at posting inns along the way and ridden from dawn to dusk to dawn, arriving at Ashbourne House on the morning of the second day. Darcy had written Burton that he was coming to do some business, and he greeted his master without surprise at the unorthodox time of his arrival. Darcy arranged for breakfast to be served in an hour and hurried upstairs, where Oliver had already arranged a hot bath and clean clothes. He tried to relax and enjoy the hot water as it soaked away the aches and stiffness from the trip, but without much success. He had not told Oliver anything of his business in London and he debated with himself whether he should or not. His valet had been with him since Darcy was twenty-one years old, and he was prepared to trust him with (almost) anything; however, this was not his secret and he had no idea, as yet, whether this business was of importance to the government or merely a personal matter that the prince regent wished to keep quiet from his courtiers. He sighed as he reached for the soap Oliver had placed on a small table next to the bath. Clearly, he must postpone a decision on this matter until he met with the prince regent and had some information on which to base his plans, but he chafed at the uncertainty.

Colonel Fitzwilliam arrived promptly at eight o'clock the next morning in full dress uniform to breakfast with Darcy before escorting him to the palace. Darcy wore his finest coat, waistcoat, and knee breeches, all black, for his appointment, and they left in his carriage as soon as he and the colonel had finished eating. On the ride to the palace, the colonel told him that they would enter by the main entrance to avoid any suspicions; it would not do to have them seen sneaking around the back entrance like conspirators.

"The prince regent does not usually rise until afternoon," said the colonel, "but he wants to speak with you before his courtiers begin flocking around. His rising at nine o'clock in the morning will be regarded as unusual, but fortunately,

His Majesty keeps irregular enough hours that the staff will probably not think much about it. He is most insistent that this be handled confidentially."

"Have you any idea yet why he wants to see me?" Darcy asked.

The colonel shook his head. "No, he has not dropped a syllable beyond what I told you at Pemberley."

The carriage pulled up at the entrance of St. James Palace and they alighted and walked up to the door, which had been opened by the majordomo by the time they had reached the top step.

"Good morning, Colonel Fitzwilliam, how may I serve you this morning?"

"My cousin, Mr. Fitzwilliam Darcy, has an appointment with His Majesty the Prince Regent, Childes."

"Yes sir, I will ascertain if His Majesty has arrived from Carlton House and is ready to see you. Please wait here."

"Thank you, Childes."

Childes returned immediately (causing Darcy to lift a brow in surprise), bowed them into an adjoining chamber dominated by a massive mahogany desk, and then shut the door behind himself as he left.

The prince regent entered quietly through an inner door. "Well, Darcy," he said coldly, "I see that you are punctual, as usual."

"Yes, Your Majesty. I pray, Your Majesty, tell me how I may serve you." Darcy returned his bow with one as frigidly correct, and stared levelly at his monarch.

The prince regent was a large man and his features were not unhandsome, but his looks were marred by his obesity and now, in his late middle age, he had a debauched appearance, with bloodshot eyes and sagging jowls.

"I have an errand that needs to be performed, of a most confidential nature," the prince said as he paced the carpet, his hands clasped behind his back. "This errand requires someone who speaks French fluently and who is familiar with the court; characteristics which are available in abundance among my courtiers. However, it also requires someone who can think quickly and keep his own council when he needs to; and these characteristics are *not* found in great measure at the palace. The person performing this errand should also be someone whose absence will not be immediately commented upon, and so must be someone who is not a regular in court circles. The colonel has suggested that you would be the best man for this errand."

"The colonel does me too much honour," Darcy said, unsmiling.

"Darcy," the prince said impatiently, "as you know, I have always considered you to be a prig, always disapproving of the enjoyments of others and too unimaginative to step out of the mould your father formed for you. I hear, however, that you were recently married, and that your bride is a gentlewoman of no family name or pretensions, nor of any fortune."

Darcy glanced at the colonel, his brows furrowed.

"No, no, I did not hear it from the ever-discreet colonel; it is a matter that I heard mentioned briefly in court gossip. Frankly, it was a matter of some chagrin to a number of predacious mammas." He smiled slightly. "Now that you are married, however, they have gone on to other, juicier topics of conversation. The incident has, however, made me wonder if I have misjudged you over the years since you have inherited your estate. I wonder if, perhaps, there is more to you than meets the eye if you have the audacity to risk the displeasure of your formidable aunt, Lady Catherine de Bourgh, in order to marry as you wish." The prince regent eyed Darcy speculatively, then sighed. "I would prefer to turn this problem over to someone who is considerably more silver-tongued than you, Darcy, but all the silver-tongued courtiers I have seem unable to *hold* their tongues when a juicy piece of gossip comes along, and discretion is more important than diplomacy and eloquence to me right now."

"If you have decided that I am the one who must perform this act, perhaps you will give me more details of what it is," Darcy said, careful to not let his impatience show.

The prince sighed again, rubbing his well-shaven chin uncomfortably. "I would just as lief avoid the entire topic, but ignoring it will not make the problem easier. So … about two months ago a new ambassador from the Austrian court arrived with his wife and household. His wife is French, a ravishing little creature who is about twenty years younger than her husband. We became friendly, and one thing led to another, but after a couple of weeks, I tired of her attentions and wished to move on to … greener pastures, shall we say?" He looked at the ceiling and clasped his hands behind his back again, his movements uncharacteristically awkward, as Darcy gazed at him stonily. "She, however, with Gallic passion and tenacity, was not ready to fade into obscurity with the gifts and favours of a prince to remember, but had taken, as insurance against such an eventuality, something from my room. I need to have that item back."

"What is the item, Your Majesty," Darcy asked, his jaws clenching, "that is so important that you are willing to risk a scandal to obtain its return?"

The prince regent sat behind the desk and irritably turned a paper knife over and over in his hands. "It is a packet of letters. The letters are from a lady who has been a friend for many years. They are quite indiscreet. I do not know how *Frau Klein* found them and spirited them from my room, but they are gone."

"How can you be sure that they were stolen by the ambassador's wife?" Darcy asked.

"She left London not long before I discovered the loss; sent home by the ambassador because of her scandalous behaviour, presumably. I received a letter from her a few days after, written from Paris, demanding what was, literally, a king's ransom for the letters and threatening to send them to my wife if I did not pay her: a consequence that I need not say would be most undesirable." He shivered slightly in horror, dabbing his lips with his lace-edged handkerchief. "The difficulty is that I do not have that kind of money, my income being totally inadequate to cover my expenses, as you are probably aware—which is why Parliament must periodically, and most grudgingly, give me grants to pay my debts. I most certainly do not have the money to pay off blackmailing females."

Darcy sighed. "Just how sensitive are these letters, Your Majesty?"

"Sensitive enough to affect the succession to the throne," the prince said simply, finally looking Darcy in the eye.

"Good Lord, Your Majesty," Darcy said weakly, "how many letters are there, all told?"

"There are about twenty of them; I do not know the exact number, but they were tied in a packet with a pink ribbon when they were stolen. Of course, I cannot know whether they have been separated since the theft."

"Are there any other political issues at stake that you know of, Your Majesty," Darcy asked, "such as a foreign head of state who wishes to embarrass you or some such thing?"

"Not that I know of," replied the prince hesitantly, "I haven't heard any murmurs of that sort since this started, but it would certainly be to Napoleon's advantage if the British monarchy were in jeopardy and the country in turmoil; and the lady is undeniably in Paris, not in her husband's native country."

"If we could summarise the problem, then, Your Majesty: you wish me to travel to Paris while Napoleon is crouching near there with his army, under pressure from the armies of the Sixth Coalition, find these letters, and return without allowing them to fall into the hands of either Napoleon *or* the Coalition on the way. Is this correct?"

"Quite correct, Mr. Darcy," said the prince regent, lifting his chin pugnaciously.

"How do you propose that I get the letters from the lady, and how can I be sure that I have them all, Your Majesty?"

"You could get them back the same way she obtained them in the first place," the prince said; a smug smile on his face.

"I am sorry, Your Majesty, I am not willing to go that far to assist you."

"No, Darcy, I assumed you would not be," he returned dryly.

"Where can I find this *femme fatale,* Your Majesty?" Darcy asked pointedly.

"I will send that information with the colonel later this afternoon, along with a letter of passage in case you get into difficulties with the army over there. Needless to say, you will not use it except in the most dire of circumstances. You must be ready to leave tonight; the lady is expecting an answer within the next few days. I am sure you can find a ship willing to take you to Calais, for a consideration," the prince said briskly. He stood up and started for the door, but paused for a moment at the threshold, his hand on the doorknob, and turned his head towards Darcy. "The colonel tells me that your sister is to be presented at the Drawing Room in four weeks, so you must be back before that day. You will present your charming wife at the same time."

"Yes, Your Majesty," Darcy said in resignation, bowing as the door clicked shut. He had hoped to avoid putting Elizabeth through the ordeal of the formal presentation at court, since he had no intention of attending any court functions with either his wife or his sister, but there would now be no alternative. He and the colonel made their way back out to the entrance in silence, where his carriage appeared, summoned by some unseen lackey.

"Well, this is a delightful situation that you have dropped me into, Fitzwilliam," Darcy whispered bitterly, "I have not the first idea of how to accomplish this 'errand' and the fate of the crown may hang upon its success. Thank you so much, my dear cousin."

"I am sorry, Darcy," the colonel said, shifting uncomfortably in his seat, "but I cannot think of anyone more capable than yourself to do this discreetly. I would have undertaken it myself if I could have absented myself without causing gossip, but there are several official events that I am expected to attend with my regiment in the next two weeks and there is not an excuse in the world that would allow me to disappear, short of my sire's death, without a major flap. I cannot even give you any information about the lady as I was out of town when this all occurred. On the positive side, this is an opportunity for you to improve your standing with the prince, which may be of benefit to both Mrs. Darcy and Georgiana."

"Well, it is done now, and I have agreed to attempt the thing. I will contact you when I return, as it is unlikely that I will be able to safely do so until I am back on English soil. What do you think the Coalition is planning over the next few weeks?"

"I do not know all of their plans, but I know, as you do, that Napoleon is somewhere in France, where he has been driven by the Coalition forces from Eastern Europe. The British forces are moving up from the south towards Paris. My sources do not know exactly where Napoleon is at the moment; he could conceivably be in Paris by the time you arrive there. If you must escape quickly, it would be better to try to leave from the south of Paris and meet up with the

English forces, or, better yet, from the west and avoid the armies entirely. Darcy," the colonel said seriously, "be careful, Cousin, I am not ready to lose you and I had no idea what this errand was going to involve."

"Believe me, I will be as careful as I can; I have a good many reasons to want to return unscathed."

The two men shook hands solemnly before the colonel alighted, and Darcy saw him staring after the carriage before it rounded the corner and he was blocked from view.

When he reached Ashbourne House, Darcy went to his bedroom and found Oliver arranging clothes in the dressing-room.

"Oliver, I need to speak with you."

"Yes, sir. Let me help you with your coat, sir."

"That can wait. I must take a trip to Paris and I am leaving tonight."

Oliver's eyes widened and he opened his mouth to speak, but Darcy held up his hand.

"Hear me out before you say anything. I am quite aware of the risks of traveling to a city that may very well be under siege by the time I get there, so you do not need to speak about it. What I wish to talk about is *you*."

"Me, sir?" Oliver looked confused.

"You. I am going to Paris on an errand for an important person. It is a matter of great delicacy. I ask you if you will accompany me." Darcy held up his hand again before Oliver could speak. "I am going over incognito as a businessman. It would assist my appearance to have a secretary with me, and your fluent command of the French language could be helpful. I can also think of many circumstances where it would be of benefit for me to have a trustworthy man to assist me. I would appreciate your assistance; however, I do not feel that it would be fair to order you to accompany me into a potential war zone. If you do not feel that you can accompany me for *any* reason, I will not hold it against you, and your employment will not be affected. In that case, I will send you to visit your family for the duration of my travels, as it would cause undue comment if I left you in London without me."

"Yes, sir, I understand," Oliver said quietly, "but what will you do for an assistant if I choose not to go?"

Darcy gave his man a wry smile. "I will go alone and hope that I do not need help. I am of two minds about taking you with me as it is; the more people who know about this jaunt, the higher the risk of exposure of my task; however, I trust your discretion implicitly."

"I will be happy to assist you in any way that I can, sir, as always."

"Thank you, Oliver." Darcy put his hand briefly on his valet's shoulder.

"I will pack our things immediately, sir. Will we be leaving before or after dinner, sir?"

"After. The colonel is joining me for dinner. Pack clothes that are conservative and not too rich, but respectable."

"Yes, sir. I understand."

The colonel brought the information and the letter of passage under the pretext of dining with his cousin at five o'clock. By six o'clock Darcy was ready, with a small bag packed with fine but nondescript clothing. At half past six Darcy and Oliver left the house in a cab, which he instructed to drive to an inn where they could catch the coach line to Dover. Burton had been given instructions to tell any callers that he was out of town but would be back within three weeks. As they drove away from Ashbourne House, Darcy suddenly realised the date and grimaced to himself. It was the Ides of March. He hoped they were more fortunate for him than they had been for Caesar.

Chapter 17

Qui desiderat pacem, praeparat bellum.
(Let him who desires peace prepare for war.)
Flavius Vegetius Renatus. "Epitoma Rei Militaris"

Darcy spent the six-hour ride to Dover on the coach trying to form a plan of action that would allow him to perform his task without undue danger or delay. It had been a number of years since he was last in Paris, and he hoped that his knowledge of the city would be adequate for their purposes. His previous visit had been just after he had turned twenty-two, and it had been the first stop on his grand tour of the Continent during a brief period of dubious peace in Europe. Unfortunately, he had been called home by the illness of his father before he had progressed beyond that great city. After his father's death some months later, he had taken up the duties left to him with determination, if not joy, and put aside any thought of trying again that frivolous jaunt of noble youth. And, of course, there had been Georgiana, who had been only eleven when she was left to his and to the colonel's care.

The two men rode in a silence imposed by the presence of the other passengers on the coach until they reached the inn at Dover. Darcy sent Oliver up to their room and made for the harbour as soon as the coach stopped. The wind had come up and was blustering through the trees and scudding dark clouds across the stars. There were a number of fishing boats bobbing at their moorings, but only two ships large enough to make the crossing to Calais. After a quick examination, he hired a dockside fisherman to row him out to the older of the two in his dinghy, and then hailed a crewman. He hoped that the poorer ship would have a captain who would be more willing to risk the crossing without questioning the *bona fides* of his employer, as long as his fee was paid beforehand.

He was allowed to board the ship and was taken to the captain's quarters by the crewman, noting as they went that the ship was clean and trim in spite of the aged appearance of the fittings. The captain was of middle age, but weathered and battered by his years on the sea. He had a shifty eye that gave Darcy pause, but, after a moment's reflection, he decided that the man for his purpose was unlikely to be of an open and honest countenance, so he sat down in the indicated chair and said:

"Captain, I am looking for a ship to take me and my man to Calais on some business."

"When are you wanting to travel, sir?" the captain asked indifferently.

"As soon as possible."

The captain gave him an appraising look, and then named an outrageous fee. Darcy, reassured that this venal start indicated that the captain could be persuaded, named a much lower fee. The captain gave him a shocked and injured look.

"Sir, the crossing is risky at this time of year, and I must pay my crew. I cannot afford to make the trip for no profit."

He named a fee that was much higher than the probable cost of the trip, but within what Darcy thought acceptable—high enough to get the captain's agreement, but not so high that it would arouse suspicion and curiosity—and so he agreed to the figure. The captain smiled and offered his hand on the deal.

"We will be ready to depart at dawn. The tide will be favourable soon after that, so do not be late or you must wait another twenty-four hours."

"We will be here."

Darcy repaired to the inn, and he and Oliver soon retired for the night. They were up well before the first faint blush of dawn in the sky and arrived at the dock with their few bags before the sun appeared. At Oliver's sceptical stare at their transport, Darcy said, with a brief, ironic grin:

"I know that it does not meet your standards, Oliver, but I was more interested in secrecy than beauty when I selected her."

"As you say, sir," he returned between compressed lips.

The mainsails were soon unfurled and the ship left Dover, sailing across the gusty northerly winds towards the coast of France. The ship proved to be seaworthy in spite of its battered appearance, and in just a few hours they made shore. Darcy had the captain row them in the ship's dinghy to a beach just north of Calais, and they walked quietly into town. After questioning a few natives, all of whom peered suspiciously at them before answering, they obtained directions to a hostelry where they were able to stay for the night and to catch the post chaise for the trip to Paris the next day.

The post chaise left at dawn filled with travelers, and only the fact that they were wedged tightly in their seats kept them from flying around the interior of the coach as the ill-fitting wheels clattered over the highway with abandon. After an endless day of riding, with only minimal pauses to stretch or grab a meal of bread and cheese while the horses were changed at a posting inn, they finally began to rumble over paved streets. Large warehouses gave way to smaller businesses, all closed for the night, and then, finally, the post chaise pulled up to an inn and stopped. The coachman opened the door, calling out: "*Paris du Nord.*"

Darcy looked around while Oliver claimed their baggage. It was too late to take a hackney nearer to their destination tonight, he thought. Better to take a room at the coaching inn and finish their journey in the morning.

They spent an uncomfortable night in a small, stuffy room at the back of the inn; all that was available at that late hour. At the first faint glimpse of dawn through the tiny window of the room, they finally gave up on sleep and rose. They were fortunately able to find a battered hackney carriage to take them to the Montparnasse district, where they found a modest lodging house from which they would be able to come and go quietly and without notice.

As soon as they were settled in their rooms and the slatternly *concierge* had left them, they went out and took a turn around the block and, finally, stopped briefly at Frau Klein's address. It was a three-storey block of *appartements* that had oriel windows and attractive stonework on the front. Over the front entrance was carved "*Auberge du Printemps.*"

"Whatever Frau Klein's motivations, she does not appear to be short of money," Darcy murmured to himself.

"Pardon, sir?" Oliver asked.

"Nothing, Oliver. Please disregard my mutterings."

"Yes, sir."

Darcy saw a café a few steps from the entrance to the flats, and indicated to Oliver with a nod that they would dine there. He placed the valet with his back to the building and sat where he could see the entrance. As they awaited their dinner, Darcy cautiously tried to fill in enough of the details of the situation for Oliver so that his man could assist him, without giving away the prince regent's secrets.

He steepled his fingers in front of him, and said quietly, "Our task while we are here is to contact a lady who has a *pied-à-terre* in that building, in order to obtain the return of something valuable which she has stolen and which cannot be reclaimed by legal means. She is attempting to blackmail the owner into ransoming the item."

Oliver's eyebrows climbed his forehead, but Darcy shook his head.

"No, it is nothing to do with me, except that I have been requested to perform this task very quietly and expeditiously. Unfortunately, the ransom demanded cannot be paid, and once the lady discovers this she may try to abscond again with the packet and sell it elsewhere."

"I see, sir. I presume that we need to watch the building carefully to prevent her from escaping with the item?"

"*Exactement.* You have hit the nail on the head, Oliver, with your usual perspicacity."

Oliver looked cautiously pleased. "Can you give me any idea, sir, what this item is, or what it looks like?"

Darcy hesitated, wondering how much he should risk, but decided that Oliver would not be able to help if he could not recognise the letters.

"It is a packet of letters, which were tied with a pink ribbon at the time they were taken—about twenty letters in all. You understand, Oliver, that if you should happen upon the letters you are not to open them."

"Yes sir, I understand perfectly, Mr. Darcy." Oliver ate his dinner silently, obviously mulling over the problem that they were undertaking. Darcy kept a surreptitious eye on the entrance to the apartment building while he ate, but did not see anyone coming or going from it. There must be a back entrance for the servants, he thought. After they finished their coffee and left the café, Darcy led the way around the building to the alley at the back and they contemplated the entryway. They could see that it was frequently used and Darcy noted that there was another café across the side street that barred the end of the alley.

"We clearly must watch both exits. My information includes the lady's apartment number. Since you can move about less conspicuously than I can, I want you to find apartment number five. I am guessing from the size of the building that it will be on the second storey."

Oliver nodded and immediately disappeared through the back entrance. He was gone only about five minutes before he returned with the information.

"The flat is on the second floor, in the front, sir."

As they walked back around to the front of the building, Darcy said:

"Well done, Oliver. I am going to send my card upstairs and request an interview with the lady. She is expecting a messenger from the owner with the ransom for the letters. I am guessing that she has only one servant, most likely a maid, as she is probably not planning to stay long enough to establish an entire household. If I cannot convince the lady or her maid to give up the letters we may be forced to take them by stealth."

"Do you mean theft, sir?" Oliver said in surprise.

"I do. I am hoping that it will not come to that. I have no experience with breaking and entering and am not eager to learn." Darcy looked grimly at his valet, who looked back at him with eyes like saucers, but nodded. "Very well. Conceal yourself where you can observe the foyer. When the servant comes down you will see her and be able to identify her later."

Oliver nodded and started across the street, disappearing casually into a clump of shrubbery in the garden next to the café. When Darcy sent up his card via the *concierge*, Frau Klein sent her maid down with a message. She waited until the *concierge* went grumbling back into his cubbyhole, and then said in passable English:

"*Monsieur* Darcy, *madame* would be pleased if you would return at nine o'clock this evening. She is indisposed to see visitors at the moment."

"Of course. Please inform *madame* that I will return at nine." He bowed and left.

The two men met at the corner, out of sight of the *Auberge du Printemps*.

"Did you obtain a good look at the maid?"

"Yes, sir."

"The lady will see me at nine. We will conceal ourselves and watch until then, although I doubt if the lady will try to smuggle them out before she has met with me. Still a little excess of caution will not hurt."

Darcy went back to the café across the street, had a leisurely cup of coffee, and pretended to read a newspaper that he picked up from a chair while Oliver went to find a niche in the alleyway where he could watch the back door discreetly. While he sipped his coffee, Darcy listened to the conversation of his fellow diners. He noted what he had not earlier: that many of the patrons of the café looked sullen and there was some grumbling amongst them, although they often glanced at him to make sure that their words were not being attended to. This was clearly not a crowd of carefree diners.

The talk that he *could* hear seemed to be about the emperor, and the populace was apparently not satisfied with the current political situation. The murmurs that Darcy could decipher included "feeding us to the Russian wolves," "got out of Paris when he had the chance," and "drained the blood out of France;" all suggestive enough statements for him to interpret the tenor of their thoughts. Paris was not happy. As he scanned the newspaper, the situation appeared even more alarming. The lurid headlines were a jumble of contradictory "facts" and opinion, often juxtaposed on the same page. Battles won, battles lost, French soldiers killed, French soldiers triumphant, Napoleon fighting valiantly, Napoleon scurrying away like *un rat*.

When the appointed hour approached, Darcy rose and paid his bill, then walked slowly around the *Auberge* to the alley. As he paused, peering into the darkness, Oliver spoke suddenly at his elbow:

"Sir."

Darcy jumped slightly. "Oliver you have a remarkable facility for this cloak and dagger nonsense."

Oliver looked a little affronted. "Thank you sir. A good servant knows how to do his work unobtrusively, sir."

Darcy stared at him for a moment.

"You are quite right, Oliver, he does. It never occurred to me that a well-trained servant has the perfect credentials for espionage. To get back to the issue at hand; has anyone come out this door?"

"No, sir, it has been very quiet."

"Very well. I am going upstairs. Wait at the café at the end of the alley."

"Yes, sir."

He melted again into the darkness, and Darcy entered the building and mounted the stairs to the second floor. Apartment five was only a few steps from the head of the stairs. He tapped upon the door and it was opened immediately by the maid, who curtseyed and said:

"Please come in, *monsieur*."

She showed him into a salon that was lavishly furnished in gold and white. A woman was sitting upon the sofa and she rose to greet him as he was ushered in. He almost smiled when he saw her, but recovered himself and solemnly bowed. It was not surprising that the lady had decided to accept his visit in the gentle candlelight of evening rather than in the harsh daylight. The prince regent's "ravishing young thing" was an attractive woman of early middle age and of Junoesque proportions. The prince's taste ran true to form.

"Welcome, *monsieur*. Do you have news from our mutual friend in England?"

"Yes, *madame*. Our friend has need of the letters you possess, as they contain business of which he has need. I should like to see the letters, if you please, so that I can assure myself of their safety."

She nodded her head slightly and went to the adjoining room, returning with a packet of letters tied with pink ribbon. Darcy held out his hand for them, but she replied serenely, "You may examine the letters more closely when you have met my terms, *monsieur*; they are clear enough."

"Very clear, *madame*, however our friend is unable to comply with the terms. He is in a difficult position at this time, neither man nor boy, and his income is determined by others. He has many debts and no chance of relief through his relations due to the unfortunate illness of the head of the family."

Frau Klein glowered briefly before regaining her calm mask.

"I see. *Monsieur* Darcy, I will ponder this information. Perhaps you could return tomorrow evening at the same time and we will talk again. If I am unable to satisfy my conscience about returning the letters I must find another use for them." She paused a moment, then said in a flirtatious tone, "I do not recall meeting you when I was in London, *monsieur*. I look forward to knowing you better. *Bon soir*."

Darcy suppressed the shudder that her final look induced, bowed, and left the apartment, smiling warmly at the maid as she gave him his beaver. He went to the café, where Oliver was waiting with a cup of coffee in front of him, and sat at the table. The valet looked at him quizzically but did not venture any questions. Darcy accepted a cup of coffee from the waiter and they both drank in silence. The patrons at this café were as sullen as those of the other, with the exception of a few hotheads who waved their hands and whispered urgently to their companions. As soon as they were finished with their coffee, the two men left the café and Darcy briefly summarised the conversation for Oliver.

"I am afraid that we must watch the exits to the lady's apartments tonight, Oliver. If she has accepted my statements and concluded that her blackmail will not work, she may try to escape with the letters during the hours of darkness. She is evidently a woman of quick decisions."

They each found a post from which to watch; Darcy took the niche in the alley in which Oliver had been so well concealed earlier and sent Oliver to the front of the building.

Chapter 18

... and they shall beat their swords into plowshares
Isaiah 2:4

Darcy fidgeted restlessly over his *café au lait* as he sat at the tiny table in his room at the lodging house. It was now the end of March, more than two weeks after they had left Pemberley, and, he thought with dissatisfaction, they had accomplished nothing. Oliver had managed to enlist the assistance of the *concierge* at the *Auberge* (for a consideration) in noting the movements of the denizens of apartment five so that he and Darcy could sleep occasionally. Oliver's accomplice was to watch and signal if either the lady or her maid left through the back door, and either Darcy or Oliver would watch the front while the other slept. The maid had occasionally appeared; she would leave for a few minutes to perform the shopping or run errands, but never carried a bag or reticule in which she could have hidden the letters. She could, of course, have secreted them in her petticoats and they would have been none the wiser. Frau Klein had not appeared even once.

Oliver had contrived to make the acquaintance of the maid by the expedient of delivering a note from Darcy, and was cultivating that acquaintance very cheerfully with flowers and the occasional walk in a nearby park. Darcy envied him his part, for the flirtation at least gave Oliver something definite to do.

Each evening Darcy had been invited to visit Frau Klein, and they had politely discussed her demands. The lady had become increasingly friendly as the week went on but had not bent in her demand for the full price of the letters. Her heavily made-up face frequently contorted with avarice and any attractiveness that Darcy had detected on their first meeting was gone. Her persistent and escalating flirtation merely served to enhance his pain over leaving Elizabeth, and he was having difficulty keeping his mind on his job during the interminable waiting outside the *Auberge*. Whatever Darcy did, it must be soon, for he was running out of both time and patience with the lady.

He sighed and left the tawdry room to take over the spying duties from Oliver.

"Are you meeting the *mademoiselle* this morning?" he asked his valet after relieving him from his watch.

"Yes, sir."

"It is time to finish this charade. Do you think that she has sufficient confidence in you to enable you to convince her to steal the letters and turn them over to us?"

Oliver considered. "I believe so. She knows, of course, that I am in your employ, and has gone so far as to say that she is not fond of her mistress. She finds her grasping and suspicious. Apparently *mademoiselle* is not trusted with the contents of *madame's* jewel case, and she believes that the letters are kept there."

"Convince her to give *madame* a sleeping draught in her evening tea, and to find the letters. You can wait outside the service door of the apartment and she can hand them to you. Do you think that you will be able to manage that?"

"I think so," Oliver said slowly, staring up at the building as he reviewed the possibilities. "I will do my best."

"Good man."

When Oliver found Darcy in the early afternoon at his post, they both slipped deeper into the shadows.

"Well?"

"It is all arranged, sir." Oliver looked a little sheepish and Darcy gave him a questioning look.

"What is the matter, Oliver?"

"Well, sir. I took the liberty of promising the young lady that I would take her with me back to England."

"Oliver!"

"I have thought it out, sir. She is not interested in a bribe, I could easily see that. I believe she has enjoyed the adventure of flouting her not-very-well-loved mistress by sneaking off to meet me and sharing her mistress's secrets, but what she truly wants is to go back to England with us. I am hoping, sir, that we will be able to give her some monetary recompense that would allow her to do so on her own.... Sir," he finished awkwardly, his stance stiff as a new recruit under inspection.

Darcy looked at him and grinned. "All actions for breach of contract will be covered by the management, Oliver."

"Thank you, sir," Oliver said with relief.

As they waited out the afternoon at the watch post, they suddenly heard a deep booming sound and a few distant explosions. They looked at each other for a moment and then walked cautiously out into the street. The sound had come from the south and they could see several columns of smoke rising from that direction.

"Cannons," Darcy said.

Oliver nodded silently, his face pale. After a moment, he cleared his throat and asked:

"Do you think that the Coalition will try to destroy the city, sir?"

"I rather suspect that it depends on whether Napoleon is in Paris, and, if so, whether he puts up a fight. The cannonballs do not seem to be coming this far north, so I think we had better return to our post. You return to the alley where you hid the first evening. The confusion of the cannon fire could be a good time for Frau Klein to smuggle the letters out."

As the day slowly advanced, the cannon fire sputtered to a stop. The city had an air of expectancy that was oppressive to the point of suffocation. The streets were silent, but Darcy could see dark forms behind the lace curtains; eyes were watching.

Oliver reappeared at five o'clock to take the next shift. Darcy was about to leave, when suddenly the cannons began firing again; and much closer. Before they could run for cover they heard a whistling sound and a cannonball struck the *Auberge* just above apartment five, damaging it and the parapet above. Both men gasped and started towards the building, pushing their way through the crowd that was fleeing the destruction. Frau Klein was not amongst them, that Darcy saw. He looked up as they reached the entrance and saw a wisp of smoke coming from the window of number five.

"Oliver, stay here and watch for the lady or her maid. I am going to see what is happening upstairs."

"But, sir ..."

"I will be cautious, but we must see what is going on," Darcy said impatiently, and ran for the stairs.

The building was eerily quiet now that its denizens had fled, and Darcy hurried up the stairs unimpeded. The service door to the apartment was open—the maid must have escaped past them unseen. He rushed through and, as he burst into the salon, he saw Frau Klein reach into a dark opening in the wall. She whirled around when she heard him, a packet of letters in her hand. She grimaced at the sight of him and reached down to draw a small pistol from the reticule on the table beside her. There was a thin trickle of blood running down the side of her face from a small cut on her forehead, but the steely glint in her eyes was intact. She spoke first:

"So, you have arrived for the letters, *monsieur*. I had planned to take your employer's money and turn the letters over to the emperor, but I find that I must now make other arrangements. However, they will be safe with me for the time being."

He moved into the room, keeping his distance from the gun in her hand. A sudden noise from the doorway he had just left caused her to swing the gun around. Darcy, without looking towards the door, sprang for her and knocked the gun out of her hand. Oliver, who had entered by the same service door as had Darcy, retrieved it before Frau Klein could recover. She turned towards Darcy with a mocking look, then shrugged and said:

"The letters are yours; enjoy them in good health, *monsieur*. I would, however, not recommend that you read them here, in spite of their fascinating subject matter."

Darcy followed her eyes to the doorway where the men had entered. There was smoke billowing through the door and he could see the flicker of fire.

"I will take your excellent advice, *madame*," Darcy answered as he counted the letters. There were twenty-two of them. "Is this all of them?"

"Would you trust my answer to that question, *monsieur*?" she returned acidly.

"Of course not, *madame*; consider the question withdrawn."

Darcy bowed formally to her and the two men left the apartment, hurrying towards their lodgings. Fortunately, Darcy thought, our room has a fireplace. The cannon fire had convinced him that it would be fatal to his purpose to attempt to carry the letters through the streets of the city while the Coalition armies were invading Paris. No, the letters must be destroyed.

Oliver deftly kindled a small fire in the grate as Darcy looked over the letters.

"Dear God," he whispered as he read them.

"Are you all right, sir?" Oliver asked diffidently.

Darcy shuffled the letters back together and said, "They are the letters we were seeking, fortunately."

He shook his head and, one by one, tossed the letters onto the grate, pushing them into the flames with the poker and then breaking up the ashes. It was now late in the day and the light was beginning to dim. Silently, they gathered up their bags and crept down the stairs and out into the dusk.

Chapter 19

Sturm und Drang.
(Storm and Stress.)
Christoph Kaufmann

During Darcy's sojourn in Paris his family had arrived in London and Georgiana was preparing for her presentation. Her gowns had all been decided upon before they left Pemberley and the seamstress dispatched back to London to start work on them. The Whitwells and their charges had departed soon after, having seen no more of Jonathan Walker. Two long days of travel had brought them to London and the younger ladies had settled into Ashbourne House while Lord and Lady Whitwell had gone on to their own town house, Longford House. They had spent the subsequent week having the gowns fitted, and when they were not entangled in pins and tapes, Lady Whitwell had instructed Georgiana in court protocol and the curtsey. Overall, Elizabeth looked back upon the past two weeks with *some* satisfaction, although her uneasiness over Darcy's continued absence was continually at the back of her mind, and growing in intensity. Lady Whitwell's crisp voice broke through her reverie:

"Let us try again, ladies. You must place your train over your arm and when you are called by the lord chamberlain you will walk to the door and into the Presence Chamber. You will gracefully put down your train, one of the lords-in-waiting will spread it out behind you, and then you will move forward until you are facing the throne. You will then curtsey to the prince regent and to any other members of the royal family who are present—and you must not let the feathers fall out of your hair! Let us again practice your curtseys, my dears, and how to back out of the chamber afterward; you must not turn your back on your monarch!"

"Mrs. Darcy," Lady Whitwell said suddenly, "have you ordered your court gown?"

Elizabeth winced delicately, "No, my lady, I had not thought about being presented. I certainly do not want to be presented on the same day as Georgiana—that should be her day.

"Well, I suppose you are right; Georgiana's day should be exclusively hers. But you must be presented as soon after as possible. Perhaps we can have her court dress altered for your presentation. You certainly will not want a dress with a mantua for any other use and I very much doubt if they will ever come back into style."

Elizabeth laughed, "I would hope not, my lady."

Lady Whitwell smiled and her austere face lighted up. Elizabeth had seen some physical resemblances to Lady Catherine in Lady Whitwell during the last two weeks, but she could not imagine that august and peremptory lady smiling with such warmth. Georgiana, who had blanched at the discussion of what was required of her for her presentation, relaxed a little and smiled at her aunt and her sister as well.

Kitty had joined Georgiana and Elizabeth in their practices. Her sister might someday have a chance to be presented, and Elizabeth had thought that the presence of others trying to do the same court curtsey might help to keep Georgiana from feeling quite as awkward as she might have done as she practised. The deep curtsey was very difficult, and to do it, rise gracefully (without wobbling), and then back out while controlling the three-yard-long train had seemed almost impossible at first. Under Lady Whitwell's strict tutelage, they had all pinned tablecloths to their shoulders to practise and they had repeated their curtseys and retreats over and over, until Elizabeth was ready to scream and even Georgiana's calm temper was beginning to fray. Finally, at the end of their first week in London, Lady Whitwell declared that they were doing well and assured them that Georgiana would be ready when the time came for her presentation.

"We have only a few small items that we must still finish," she stated with satisfaction.

In spite of Lady Whitwell's confident assertion, the ensuing days continued in a similar tediously busy fashion and Elizabeth tried to hide her increasing discomposure as each day marched on with no sign of Darcy's return. Lady Whitwell was planning a ball in Georgiana's honour later in the season, and she and Georgiana were kept busy with this, as well as with all of the other preparations, for which Elizabeth was grateful. However, now that the big day was less than a week away, Georgiana appeared in Elizabeth's sitting-room, where she was finishing her morning tea.

"I haven't wanted to worry you about it, but do you know when Fitzwilliam will be returning?" she asked anxiously, her fingers clutching the back of a chair. "I am concerned that he will not be back for my presentation."

"I do not know when his business will be concluded," Elizabeth said, trying to speak with calm assurance, "but I am certain that he will be back in time. Do not worry, my dear; there is no business that is as important as your presentation."

She hoped that her reassuring words were true. Unfortunately, she was unable to dissemble to herself when she was alone in her room, and sleep seemed farther away each night. Her face was beginning to appear strained when she examined herself in the mirror: an appearance that she hoped would be attributed by others to the stress of Georgiana's presentation. It took all of her powers to continue to appear collected and cheerful during the day. When she finally fell asleep at night, it was to be visited by fantastic dreams filled with unseen perils and vague fears, which merely left her more exhausted when she awoke than she had been before retiring.

They dined at Longford House five days before the presentation, and Colonel Fitzwilliam was in attendance. Elizabeth noticed that he appeared rather *distrait* as well. His serious mien caused her stomach to clench. If the ever-cheerful colonel was this distracted, the business Darcy was on must be even more difficult than she had thought. She watched his careless courtesy with Georgiana and was not encouraged for her sister's chances of igniting his interest in her, but hoped that if—no, when—Darcy returned that the colonel would have more attention to spare for his young cousin. She found herself a little irritated that he continued to treat Georgiana as he would a child—indulgent, but somewhat offhand and even a little patronising in his preoccupation—but she suppressed her feelings, knowing that her prickly mood was a reflection of her worries. Georgiana, she was pleased to see, appeared quite collected, listening to her uncle and her cousin courteously and occasionally making a comment. Elizabeth was quite sure that, with her keen perception, her sister felt all of the tensions in the room, and her composure encouraged Elizabeth to make a greater effort to take part in the conversation and keep it flowing smoothly.

The next day was Sunday, and the entire family went to church together, sitting in the Darcy and Whitwell pews. Elizabeth heard hardly a word of the sermon, occupied as she was with saying several prayers: for Darcy's return, for the success of Georgiana's presentation, and for her new sister's future happiness. By the time the hour-long service ended, Elizabeth felt as if her legs were leaden and she was afraid that she would not be able to rise in her exhausted state. The colonel noticed her pallor as he passed and offered her his arm.

"Are you well, Mrs. Darcy?" he asked quietly, his face a polite mask, but his eyes worried. "Do you need to sit down again for a moment, or should I bring the carriage up?"

"No, I am well, I thank you, Colonel," she replied, barely above a whisper. "I am merely a little tired. The strain of the last few weeks is beginning to catch up with me." She tried to smile reassuringly, but the effort was rather weak.

"I will escort you and Georgiana home," he said, "Perhaps you are too tired to come to Longford House for dinner tonight?" He looked at her questioningly.

"I will rest a little this afternoon and then I am sure I will be fine by evening. Do not worry about me, Colonel."

They caught up with the others and Elizabeth made a supreme effort to appear as usual, but she was very relieved to arrive at Ashbourne House. They were met at the door by Burton, who smiled happily and said:

"You will be pleased, madam, to know that the master arrived not thirty minutes ago. He is upstairs in his room, changing."

Elizabeth thanked him breathlessly, left Georgiana to make her farewells to the colonel, and hurried upstairs. She arrived at their sitting-room just as Darcy, hearing her footsteps, came out of his dressing-room, fastening the cuffs of a fresh shirt.

"Elizabeth!"

He caught her up and clutched her tightly against his breast, his face buried in her hair, completely disregarding the presence of his valet, who quietly let himself out the other door. She felt tears of relief stinging her eyes as she clung to him. Then, suddenly, the room began spinning and she heard, as from a long way off, Darcy's voice say again, "Elizabeth!"—this time in concern and agitation.

When she opened her eyes, she saw that she was lying on her own bed and felt Darcy holding her hand. "Elizabeth," he said in a worried voice, "are you ill, my darling? Should I have Burton call the doctor?" He glanced over to the door where Burton was peeking in, a worried look on his face.

She struggled to a sitting position, saying, "No! I am well; I am just—rather tired. I'm sorry to worry you. What happened?"

Darcy nodded to Burton, who silently closed the door.

"When I was holding you, you went limp in my arms," he said with relief, "I did not know what to think ... you were so pale and thin. I am afraid that the last few weeks have been too much for you."

"I cannot believe it—I have never fainted in my life! Of course, I have never had so much reason to be out of countenance." She smiled wanly up at him, tears welling up in her eyes, to her great embarrassment. "You are really home and safe? I was beginning to think that I would never see you again—I suppose that sounds rather melodramatic, but the last three weeks have felt more like three centuries," she said as she clung to him, struggling to control her tears. She looked into his face. "You don't look well, yourself, my love. You look as if you have not eaten or slept in days. Are you exhausted?"

"Yes, I am, but I will be fine now that I am home to stay." He smiled and looked at her tenderly. "Every minute I was gone I thought of you." He tightened his arms around her and they sat silently, both thanking God for his return.

After a few minutes, Elizabeth remembered Colonel Fitzwilliam and Georgiana. "Perhaps you should go and see if the colonel is still here; you will need to talk to him, I am sure. I ... I think I will stay here for a short while."

Darcy went slowly downstairs after he finished dressing. Georgiana was in the drawing-room alone.

"Fitzwilliam!" she cried when she saw him, "I am so glad you are home! Is Elizabeth all right? She looked very pale after church today." She kissed him affectionately and then Darcy stepped back and held her at arms length, looking at her.

"I believe she is well. She has been overexerting herself these last few weeks and is very tired. She is resting now. You have changed, Georgiana, even in the short time I was gone." He smiled at her.

"Well, I have been very busy with my aunt and I am ready to have this presentation over so that I can enjoy the season."

"It won't be long now."

"I thank heaven for that!" she said with a roll of her eyes.

He laughed.

That evening Darcy sent Georgiana and Kitty off to Longford House and he and Elizabeth had a quiet dinner in their sitting-room. Elizabeth felt as if a great weight had lifted from her shoulders, a weight of which she had not been fully aware until it was gone.

"Georgiana's presentation is on Wednesday, as you know, and I believe that she is ready. Lady Whitwell has been a tower of strength through the entire time and really has done everything. She is giving a ball for Georgiana in early June and I think she has invited about three hundred people." She smiled. "I am glad that her secretary and Mrs. Annesley have had to write the invitations, and not I." She gave a small chuckle and then added, "I believe François has found a lady's maid for Georgiana. She is someone that François knew when she lived in London previously, and who has experience as a housemaid, but François feels that she would be an excellent lady's maid. She says that her character is unimpeachable."

"Has Georgiana met her yet?"

"No, I was waiting for you to approve her first."

"Very well, I will interview her tomorrow."

In such ordinary conversation their dinner passed quickly. Elizabeth retired early at Darcy's insistence, and she immediately fell into a deep, dreamless sleep, awakening only when the sun was high in the sky the next day.

Chapter 20

Lord, what fools these mortals be!
William Shakespeare, "A Midsummer Night's Dream"

Elizabeth awoke feeling quite refreshed for the first time in weeks. When she opened her eyes she found Darcy, fully dressed, sitting on a chair next to her bed, drinking a cup of coffee; it was the aroma of the coffee that had roused her. He offered to bring her a cup from the coffee pot in the sitting-room, but she insisted upon rising and joining him there.

He smiled when she appeared in her morning dress. "How are you feeling, my love?"

"Much better, thank you my dear husband," she said, giving him an ardent kiss, "No tea this morning?"

"No, I felt that I needed a heartier brew to start the day today. Colonel Fitzwilliam will be here soon to take me to the palace. He brought Georgiana and Kitty home himself last night, and we were able to exchange a few words."

Burton tapped on the door of the sitting-room and opened it when Darcy said:

"Come."

"Colonel Fitzwilliam is below, sir, and wonders if you are ready."

"I am, and I will be down immediately."

"Very good, sir."

When Darcy descended the stairs his cousin was awaiting him in the entry hall and they left in Darcy's carriage. During their ride to the palace the colonel said uneasily:

"Darcy, you are as thin as a rake. Did you eat at all while you were gone?"

"Fear not, Cousin, I am well enough; and I will be more so when I finish my report today."

"So, you were successful?"

"In a manner of speaking."

"What does that mean, Darcy?"

"Wait just a few minutes, Cousin, and you will hear all."

"All right, all right, I will be patient."

They rode the rest of the way in silence, Darcy with his eyes closed and the colonel watching him in concern. A few minutes from their destination, Darcy roused himself to say:

"Oh ... I *will* tell you one thing, Fitzwilliam, which might amuse you. His Majesty's nubile young French woman is at least thirty-five years old and of rather—shall we say?—ample proportions."

The colonel laughed heartily, and commented, "I am not at all surprised!"

When they reached the palace they were ushered into the prince regent's presence immediately. When the door had closed behind the majordomo, the prince eyed Darcy with some apprehension and said:

"Well?"

"Well, Your Majesty, I can report some success with my errand, although I was not able to finish it precisely as you requested."

"What the devil does that mean, Darcy?"

"I will tell you the entire tale, Your Majesty, if you will give me leave." He paused briefly for the prince's nod of assent. "I went to Dover, and managed to find a ship that was willing to sail to Calais in the morning ..."

He briefly summarised the two weeks that he had been in France. When he had completed his tale of Frau Klein's perfidious scheme, and of his final success in obtaining the letters, he finished with:

"I looked at the addresses on the letters to confirm that they were truly the ones for which we had been sent, and then burned them in the grate at my lodgings before we crept out of Paris. So, Your Majesty, I am unable to return the letters to you; however, they have been destroyed and so should no longer worry you."

"How do I know that they have all been destroyed if I do not see them first?" the prince said peevishly.

Both Darcy and Colonel Fitzwilliam merely looked at him. Finally, Darcy said very quietly, "The reason you chose me, Your Majesty, for your 'errand' was because you trusted me to do it and to keep quiet about it, and the circumstances of the recovery suggest that all of the letters were together."

"Of course, of course," the prince said, looking from one to the other nervously and then walking to the window and staring out. "I do, of course, trust you. I just meant that I hoped the lady had not separated any of the letters from the packet earlier."

"Please accept my best wishes, Your Majesty," Darcy said, "for your continued health. Do we have your permission to withdraw?"

"Yes, of course. You may go," the prince said as he stood at the window, his voice tinged with relief.

They withdrew to the anteroom and left the palace.

"Darcy," the colonel said quickly, as soon as the carriage door was shut, "thank you for not losing your temper. You have been sorely tried, but I should like to keep my job for a while longer." He looked at his cousin in mute appeal. Darcy stared at him for a moment, his brows still lowered, and then his face relaxed and he laughed at his cousin's worried look.

"The last time I saw you with an expression like that, you were about ten years old. You had stolen a whole sack full of apples from the Pemberley orchard and our fathers were demanding to know who had done it. You were afraid that I would give you away. Well, Cousin, I knew enough to hold my tongue then, and I know enough now. If your job depends only upon me holding my temper and my tongue, it is safe enough."

The colonel grinned at him and said, "I am glad to hear it, Cousin, because I have not yet found a rich and beautiful wife who is willing to marry a penniless younger son so that I can retire to the country."

They both laughed, but after a moment Darcy turned serious again. "Fitzwilliam, I did not tell His Majesty the entire truth in there."

"What do you mean?" the colonel said in surprise.

"I did not just look at the salutations of the letters. I felt that I needed to truly make sure that they were the letters we needed, so I read them."

Colonel Fitzwilliam merely looked at him inquiringly, one brow raised.

"They were from Mrs. Fitzherbert and addressed His Majesty as 'my dearest husband.'"

"Good Lord," the colonel exclaimed quietly, "so he really did marry her. Were the letters dated before his marriage to the Princess of Wales?"

"Yes."

"Then it was no exaggeration to say that they could affect the succession, was it?"

"No. Although the marriage was not legitimate in the eyes of the government since it was not legally sanctioned by the king, it could be legitimate in the eyes of the Church, which would make the prince regent a bigamist."

"I think you were very wise to destroy them, Darcy."

"Once I saw them I knew that, even without the threat of exposure by the Coalition armies, they must be destroyed. He was a fool to keep them."

"I am appalled," the colonel said in a resigned tone, "I cannot believe that His Majesty would be so blind as to think that it was safe to keep them. As we have already seen, it is an open invitation to blackmail. Imagine if she had succeeded in delivering them to Napoleon." He shivered.

"Well, it is over now. They are ashes and cannot come back to haunt the royal family. Pray God he has no other incriminating items that he is keeping secreted in his rooms."

"Amen, Cousin."

Chapter 21

Fashion, though Folly's child, and guide of fools,
Rules e'en the wisest, and in learning rules.
George Crabbe, "The Library"

The day went by in a fog for Elizabeth as she and Lady Whitwell helped Georgiana in the final preparations for her presentation. Georgiana had come to Elizabeth after Darcy left for St. James Palace and, after talking with her for a few minutes, said:

"Elizabeth ... I think that I will move to Longford House until my presentation, if that is all right with you."

"Why of course, if you want, my dear."

"I thought that I would take Kitty with me so that you and my brother may have some time alone." She blushed slightly in embarrassment.

Elizabeth squeezed her hand and thanked her with a quiet smile:

"You are very sweet, Miss Georgiana Darcy."

"Just promise me that you will come to Longford House every day to help me, my dear sister," she added in an anxious tone. "I am relying on you."

"An easy promise to make—I would not miss it for the world."

Elizabeth and Darcy had dinner together again that night. Elizabeth looked at herself in the mirror as she was changing clothes beforehand and saw a quite different person from the one she had seen two days before, when she did not know where her husband was or if he would return in time for Georgiana's big day. Instead of a pale, strained face with eyes like burnt holes, she saw a countenance that was happy and eager and looked at the world with anticipation. She noticed at dinner that Darcy, too, was already losing his gaunt look and beginning to appear more his normal self, although his clothes still fitted rather loosely on his spare frame.

After dinner they sat in the garden for a half hour and enjoyed the cool spring breeze that gently teased the soft new foliage of the trees, bringing with it the scent of the lilacs planted along the wall. Darcy sighed in contentment and drew her close.

My love," Elizabeth said quietly, "can you tell me where you have been all this time, or is the need for secrecy too great?"

"I can tell you most of the story, but you may not mention it to anyone else, my dear."

"Of course," she said with a brief smile and then folded her hands in her lap like a schoolgirl learning her lessons. "I am all anticipation."

He then proceeded to tell her of his first meeting with the prince regent and of his trip to France, excluding only the details of the letters' contents that he had shared with the colonel.

When he finished describing the capture of the letters, Elizabeth asked, "How did you then get home, my love? The armies must have been very close."

"They were. We walked west through the outlying suburbs of the city during the night, ducking into doorways when we heard patrols, and headed for the *Bois de Boulogne,* thinking that it would be easier to conceal ourselves there than in the city proper. By dawn we had left the villages just to the west of the *Bois* behind. We rested for a short while behind a convenient haystack until it was late enough in the morning to hail a farmer who was driving into the next village, and who was willing to give us a ride. From there we were able to catch the post chaise to Calais."

"I am quite certain that you have left out many difficulties, my dear." She gave an involuntary shiver. "It gives me a chill just to think about it. I'm so glad that you are home safely."

He wrapped his arms around her and kissed her. "So am I, my love, so am I. Are you ready to retire, *mon ange?*"

She nodded silently and smiled up at him as he rose, took her hand, and led her upstairs.

The next morning while they drank their tea, Darcy went through the large stack of mail that had accumulated while he was gone, much of it invitations to various social events.

"It is brought home to me while reading the mail how much has changed in my life in the last year," he commented.

"Why is that, my love? Are there fewer invitations than in the past?" Elizabeth asked in surprise.

"Not at all, in fact there might possibly be more; however, last year most of the invitations were from families who had unmarried daughters while this year they are from families with unmarried *sons.*"

Elizabeth laughed with him and refilled his cup, as it appeared that the mail would take him some considerable time. His secretary had sorted it so that he could deal with the business letters and the invitations in order of importance. Most of the invitations Darcy tossed aside for his secretary to send regrets, but a small pile of them he kept. While he was finishing his mail Elizabeth sorted her own notes and calling cards and decided where she and Georgiana and Kitty would be making morning calls. When they were done, they both retired to their rooms to dress before going down for breakfast, for Elizabeth would be leaving for Longford House soon after.

Later, as Elizabeth watched the final fitting of Georgiana's court dress, her sister appeared flushed and excited. Her shyness and discomfort seemed to be a thing of the past. When Elizabeth had a few moments alone with her while Lady Whitwell was downstairs, Georgiana confided that she was less nervous about her presentation than about Lady Whitwell's ball.

"My aunt is planning to invite a huge number of people and everyone will be there. Both of my cousins will attend, as well as all of the eligible young men that she can find."

"I have heard very little about the colonel's brother," Elizabeth said in surprise, "what is he like?"

"In looks he is rather similar to the colonel—fairly tall with curly reddish-brown hair and blue eyes—but in temper he is quite different." Her voice became tart. "His name is George Lewis Winslow Fitzwilliam, Viscount St. George, and he is aware of that title, *and* of the fact that he will inherit the earldom from his father, every minute of the day, I do assure you."

"It doesn't sound as if you like him very much, Georgiana," Elizabeth said, startled.

"I do not and have not liked him since I was a little girl, and neither does my brother, truth be told, which is probably why you have heard virtually nothing about him. My brother would not malign his relations, but he treats St. George with deadly courtesy to his face and ignores his existence when he is out of sight. St. George has been in Scotland for the last six months in exile at one of my uncle's estates because of his gambling and carousing and running up of large debts." She paused and sighed. "From all that I have seen and heard, particularly from my friend Catherine who lives around the corner from Ashbourne House, most of the young men in London are the same: gambling and racing and boxing are all they think about. They sound like very dull company."

Elizabeth laughed. "Most girls would find those characteristics exciting, my dear, but I am glad that you do not! But then, you have always been a Darcy, and the Darcys do not waste their time on such foolish things. Which is probably why the Darcys continue to have a healthy estate to pass on to their heirs," she finished dryly. "How do you know all this about your cousin? I am sure your brother never told you these things."

"I have my sources of information, Mrs. Darcy," she said primly, then changed the subject abruptly. "You *will* help me dress for my aunt's ball, won't you, Elizabeth?"

"Of course, dearest. Lady Whitwell will be busy with the ball, and François and I will help you dress. Your dress is lovely; they delivered it this morning and I had forgotten about it until now. I have it at the house, ready for you. You will have your own maid very soon, but François and I will be there to assist."

"My gown for the ball will, I hope, be much better than this presentation gown," she said as she looked down in dismay at her dress. The wide hoops of the skirt, so old-fashioned, did indeed look rather silly, but the seamstress had done her job well and it fitted Georgiana perfectly. The bodice was low cut and off the shoulder, as required for court dress, and set off Georgiana's creamy skin and long slender neck. The sleeves were a mere suggestion of a wisp of gauzy silk and the train, fastened to the gown just behind the shoulders with silk rosettes, was of soft white silk that flowed behind her like cream when she moved. The rest of her gown was encrusted with seed pearls and embroidery, all in white, and just the tip of her satin slippers peeped out from under the stiff hem. The tall white ostrich-feather plume for her head was tightly sewn onto a small brooch, which they would pin securely to the back of her upswept hair. Georgiana sank into her deep curtsey and rose in one fluid motion, and then Elizabeth lifted her train and spread it gracefully over her left arm so that she could back out of the room. She was ready.

The next morning Darcy and Elizabeth were at Longford House very early. They had a leisurely breakfast, which Georgiana could barely touch. Lady Whitwell encouraged her to eat something:

"We would not want you to faint from hunger while you are awaiting your turn, my dear," she said gently. "We may have to wait hours at the palace."

"I know," Georgiana sighed. "Perhaps I can get a piece of toast down. Where is Colonel Fitzwilliam? I thought he was going to come over this morning so he could see my dress."

"I am sure he will be here soon," her aunt said kindly. "Now eat your breakfast, dear girl."

Georgiana's face was pale but she appeared resolute, and she forced herself to eat the toast and drink a cup of chocolate. The ladies retired to Georgiana's room upstairs to help her dress while the gentlemen tried to relax over their tea and read the morning newspapers.

The footman had just poured them each a second cup of tea, not long after the ladies had disappeared, when the colonel entered hurriedly. Both men looked up at him in surprise. He was slightly out of breath and threw himself down in a chair without ceremony, barely managing to keep the scabbard of his sword from hitting the chair as he did so.

"I apologise for my tardiness and lack of courtesy, Father, but the news from the Continent has thrown the palace into a commotion. Napoleon has finally abdicated!"

His two companions exclaimed at his words and threw their papers down, demanding more details. He gave them what news he had, and then rose.

"I am sorry, but I must get back to the palace. Tell Georgiana I was here to give my moral support and wish her the best."

Both agreed and he left. A moment later, Elizabeth came into the breakfast-parlour.

"I saw the colonel riding off. Is there something wrong?" she asked in confusion.

They explained his precipitous departure and her eyes widened.

"So the war with Napoleon is definitely over. I can hardly believe it is true. I will tell Lady Whitwell and Georgiana."

Before she could leave, Lord Whitwell interjected, "Are you sure that you should tell Georgiana? I would not want her composure to be strained on such an important day."

Elizabeth smiled and gently said, "My lord, Georgiana is not a child and she is not a simpleton. You cannot hide a piece of news such as this, and she will not thank you if you try."

"I suppose that you are right, my dear; I am being an old fool. She must know sometime and will wonder why there is so much activity at the palace."

Elizabeth walked over and patted his hand, her eyes twinkling. "'Old' and 'fool' are the last words that I would think of associating with you, my lord."

He lifted her hand and kissed it and she ran back upstairs, her errand downstairs forgotten for the moment. Darcy stared at his uncle in surprise at his gallantry, and his lordship cleared his throat and turned back to his newspaper. Darcy picked up his paper and hid a smile behind its pages.

Georgiana was disappointed that the colonel could not stay, but said, "He was, of course, needed more at the palace! So the war is finally over." Her eyes were bright as she continued to dress, her ordeal ahead less daunting with the news to think about. "My presentation is hardly of the magnitude of importance of

Napoleon's final defeat, although it will be an interesting story to tell my children someday," she said with a sparkle in her eye.

They finished their preparations and she swept downstairs to show her costume to her uncle and her brother, curtseying to them both. Then she and her aunt left for the palace, Georgiana's hoop skirt barely fitting into the carriage. The day was, fortunately, sunny and fairly warm, so she would not be too chilly after leaving her cloak in the carriage and entering the palace.

Elizabeth and Darcy returned to Ashbourne House and spent the rest of the day discussing the news and awaiting Georgiana's return. Kitty sat with them for a while but Darcy's tension made her nervous as she was still rather in awe of him, and eventually, with a glance at her brother-in-law, she excused herself and escaped upstairs. Darcy was ultimately reduced to pacing the floor of the drawing-room after abandoning all attempts to divert himself. Georgiana finally arrived home at about four o'clock, looking exhausted and relieved. Elizabeth and Darcy both kissed her affectionately when they met her in the hall.

"I don't need to ask how it went," Elizabeth said, "I can see that it went well."

Georgiana sighed and sat carefully down on the sofa in her hooped skirt. "It went perfectly fine, but I feel like a limp piece of rag. What a day! There were more than a hundred women and girls to be presented and they kept interrupting the line when messengers came for the prince regent ... Well, it is done and I survived without tripping on my hem or falling over during my curtsey, or having my plume fall out of my hair." She smiled in exhausted contentment.

"Why don't you go find Kitty and tell her about it," Elizabeth suggested. "She has been waiting eagerly for your return."

Georgiana nodded and took herself upstairs. Elizabeth heard Kitty meet her on the way through the hall and smiled at their laughter as they went up together. Darcy sat on the sofa with his head resting on the back, gave a sigh of relief, and commented:

"I feel as though I have been through a battle—and lost!"

Elizabeth smiled and said, "My poor, dear husband! Now that Georgiana's presentation is over you can relax. I have no doubt now that her first season will be a success."

"I thank heaven for that!"

Darcy had accepted an invitation to dinner that evening from some distant relatives. They were elderly and the evening would be early, so Georgiana would be able to retire in good time to recover from the stressful presentation day. Tomorrow, the round of parties and balls that made up the season, and which were such important opportunities for young women to meet suitable husbands, would begin. Georgiana and Kitty were both rather keyed up in anticipation when they got home from dinner but went to their rooms quietly, determined to try to sleep. Elizabeth and Darcy followed them more slowly up the stairs.

Elizabeth was helped into her nightclothes by François, and after dismissing her maid sat down on a low stool by the dying fire to brush out her hair. The nightly ritual of letting down her hair and brushing it until it glistened always relaxed her, and she would sit dreamily by the dying embers until she was warm and ready for bed. The weeks of Darcy's absence had been punctuated each night when she finished her brushing and climbed alone into her bed, warmed only by the warming pan filled with embers that François placed between the sheets. Tonight she looked up from the fire to find Darcy watching her from the doorway, as he often had in the past. He always seemed fascinated by the dark curtain of hair falling to her waist and he walked over and ran his fingers through it, letting the shining strands slide over his hands as the fire sparked red and gold into the ebony. Letting the hair tumble down over her shoulders, he gently turned her toward him and helped her to her feet, folding her in his arms and resting his cheek upon her head. She said, with gentle mockery:

"It is good to have my lord and master home."

He chuckled into her hair.

"You, my wife, are about as humble and retiring as the Queen of Sheba. May your lowly slave carry you to your opulent bed curtained with gold and silk, Your Most Gracious Majesty?"

"Yes, please," she whispered.

She awoke early the next morning feeling ready for the day, more so it seemed than her sister-in-law, who appeared rather pale: a reaction to the tension of the last few weeks, Elizabeth suspected. She insisted that Georgiana rest a little in the afternoon, and was rewarded by seeing her look a little more in spirits by tea time.

That night they attended a ball given by an acquaintance of Lady Whitwell's. When they arrived they were introduced to the young man of the house, a gangly youth who appeared younger than his twenty-five years and, unfortunately, had rather large ears that stuck out from his head. He was not at all intimidating, and Elizabeth saw that Georgiana was not going to have a recurrence of her shyness, for she appeared very calm and gracious to the eyes of her sister-in-law, although a glint of what looked suspiciously like amusement flickered in her eyes when she was introduced to the young man.

This was Elizabeth's first look at the new crop of debutantes and she was overwhelmed with the number of them; there appeared to be more than fifty girls at the ball. Georgiana introduced Elizabeth and Kitty to one who was a particular friend of hers:

"My dear sisters, I would like you to meet my friend Catherine Freemont. We have known each other for many years, and the Freemont house is on Green Street, just around the corner from our house. We used to play together when we were little girls, and Catherine was also presented yesterday. Catherine, these are my sisters, Mrs. Darcy and Miss Catherine Bennet," she finished triumphantly.

Catherine Freemont was a petite young woman with very dark hair and bright blue eyes, and she had a low-pitched, musical voice with a somewhat unusual inflection in her speech. Although not a classic beauty, her appearance was very striking, and she seemed a very pleasant and elegant young woman.

The ladies exchanged courtesies and the four talked for a few minutes before Elizabeth said with a smile:

"You young ladies should go mingle with the others. You do not want to miss the dancing."

They agreed and, after parting curtseys, went off to join the other debutantes and the young men dancing attendance on them. Darcy soon rejoined her after speaking to some of the other gentlemen, and they watched the dancing. Elizabeth, when she had a chance, asked Darcy where Miss Freemont was from.

"The Freemonts have been neighbours of ours in London for generations. They have an estate in the far west of Shropshire, near Shrewsbury, and, as you can see by Miss Freemont's looks and hear in her accent, her mother is Welsh."

"She and Georgiana seem to be good friends."

"Yes, they played together for many years. They were the only two young girls on our block when Georgiana was growing up and they always got on very well. Her father is the younger son of his family and a judge in the king's court. Miss Freemont's parents are likely to be here somewhere. I will introduce you if I see them, although this is such a crush that we may not survive the evening, let alone meet anyone!"

Elizabeth laughed and they gradually made their way to the refreshment tables, nodding to acquaintances along the way. Elizabeth was pleased to find that there were some people who wished to be introduced to her, and she greeted and curtseyed her way gradually across the room with Darcy. They did not see the Freemonts, and the ball was too noisy to converse much, but they finally found an isolated corner where they could sit down. They joined in the dancing a few times during the evening, and enjoyed themselves as much as they could in the crowded room, but it was a relief when the ball was over.

Georgiana was in high spirits when they went home. She chattered about whom she had danced with, and who her friend Catherine had danced with, and seemed very pleased with the evening. Kitty had also danced a few times, but she did not appear to Elizabeth to be as satisfied as Georgiana was with the ball. When they arrived at Ashbourne House, Georgiana floated up the stairs to her room ahead of the others and to her bed, and Elizabeth stayed behind and talked with Kitty for a few minutes.

"I was asked to dance only four times the entire evening!" Kitty said, her lip trembling.

"Dearest," she said very gently, "you must realise that you are moving in a very different society than that in Hertfordshire. The parents of these young men probably know to a penny how much our father is worth, and they are not going to allow their sons to dance with someone who cannot bring them a dowry for fear that they will fall for you—and those with daughters do not want the competition.

"In addition, they are most likely surprised at Mr. Darcy's marriage to me, a woman of no standing in society, and are waiting to see if I will be accepted or if I will be branded a shameless fortune huntress who will drag my husband's good name in the mud with my behaviour. I am sorry Kitty, my dear, but those are the facts of life. You must just be pleasant and enjoy the dances that you get, and when people know both of us better they may allow their sons to dance with you more. I think that you already know that if you were not with Georgiana, you would not have been asked to the ball at all; and nor would I if I was not married to Mr. Darcy."

Kitty's eyes filled with tears at this recital of facts, but she hung her head and said:

"I am sorry Lizzy, I did not quite realise the position you are in. I will try to enjoy myself, but I must say that the militia in Hertfordshire was much more pleasant than London society."

Elizabeth embraced her sister and they walked slowly upstairs together. She related this conversation to Darcy, who shook his head.

"I am sorry that she has had to face this. It did not occur to me that this problem would appear, although I suppose that it should have. I will talk to Georgiana now that she has survived the presentation and her first ball, and I am sure that she will be able to assist in some way."

"Thank you my love; that will probably help. I do not want to push that responsibility onto Georgiana when she has so many other things to think about, but if she realises how Kitty is feeling I have no doubt that she will do what she can. She always tries to be kind to others."

Elizabeth kissed him gratefully and they retired.

Chapter 22

No cord nor cable can so forcibly draw, or hold so fast, as
Love can do with a twined thread.
Robert Burton, "Anatomy of a Melancholy"

The day finally neared for the Bingleys' arrival in London; they were due the next day at about noon and would come to call on the Darcy household after they settled into the house they had leased near Berkeley Square for the season. Elizabeth wondered where Miss Bingley would stay during the season: with her sister, Mrs. Hurst, or with her brother Charles and Jane. Caroline and Mrs. Hurst had made up after the differences that had separated them at Christmas, and they both enjoyed the pleasures of ridiculing all of their "friends" in private after meeting them at social events. But on the other hand, their brother had a much better fortune than Mr. Hurst, and so could afford more of the expensive pleasures of London. Elizabeth hoped that Caroline had chosen to stay with the Hursts so that Jane would not have to listen to her unkind chatter.

Elizabeth and Jane met affectionately at Ashbourne House on the afternoon of her arrival, and Georgiana and Kitty seemed almost as delighted to see Jane as was Elizabeth. They had planned an enjoyable afternoon visiting together while Darcy and Bingley went out to their club, and Elizabeth was happy to see that Jane looked in as excellent health as she had at Christmas, in spite of looking a little tired after the move of their household. She seemed a bit flustered as they caught up on the news from Hertfordshire, fidgeting with her handkerchief and teacup. Elizabeth did not comment to her about it in front of the others, assuming that the move had discomposed her—unusual though that was for her sister, whose calm demeanour rarely failed. When the two girls went upstairs for a few minutes and left Jane and Elizabeth alone in the drawing-room, Jane, her cheeks slightly flushed, said:

"My dear sister, I have something that I want to tell you. I have suspected for several weeks, but I wanted to be sure … and to tell you in person … so I did not mention it in my letters. You are going to be an aunt, Lizzy."

Elizabeth exclaimed in surprise and embraced her sister. "I am so happy for you, my dearest sister! I should have known from just looking at you; you look even more lovely than usual! I cannot believe that you could keep this a secret! Do our parents know?"

"I have not told them yet. I wanted you to be the first among our relations to know ..." She hesitated for a moment and then added with a sigh, "I have one other piece of family news to relate, Lizzy. Our mother received a letter from our sister Lydia before our departure from Netherfield. She, too, is expecting a child. Our mother's transports of delight were quite overwhelming, so Mr. Bingley and I decided to tell them about our happy news in a letter while we are here."

Elizabeth laughed at the expression of chagrin on Jane's face as she said this and agreed that her plan was sound, but shook her head over their sister Lydia's condition. Lydia was in no way mature enough to care for a child, and the Wickhams would fall even further into debt with the additional expenses.

When the girls came back downstairs Jane told them her news and briefly mentioned Lydia's, and they spent the afternoon in happy chatter about the baby linens Jane was having made and about how soon the baby was due to arrive. Jane expected her confinement to be around mid-September, and now that she had told them she relaxed and enjoyed the visit.

That evening the Bingleys were to dine with them, and Elizabeth could see when the men returned from the club to dress that Bingley had given Darcy the news. Bingley was more cheerful than ever, and treated his wife with a gentleness and affection that was very charming. She did not have time to speak with Darcy before dressing for dinner, but she could see that he had a pleased smile for his friend. Darcy and Elizabeth had avoided any outside social engagements this one night so that they could spend the evening with the Bingleys before they continued the round of parties. The evening was one of quiet pleasure, which Elizabeth thought would be salutary for any first season nerves that Georgiana might still have.

The next evening, they attended a large party given by another acquaintance of Lady Whitwell's, Mrs. Dalrymple, for her daughter Justina. There were many young men at the party for the family was an ancient and respected one and the daughter would have a good fortune to offer her husband.

Justina Dalrymple was a small, pretty, and vivacious girl of eighteen years who was entering her second season and who possessed a tart wit that amused the gentlemen—and, judging from her confident air, she had a rather a good opinion of herself. Georgiana was slightly acquainted with her and she whispered to Elizabeth that Justina was very pretty but her tongue was rather sharp.

"In fact, she reminds me a little of Miss Bingley, who, by the bye, has just arrived," she said in a dry tone.

Elizabeth looked up and saw Caroline Bingley posed in the doorway, Bingley and Jane following quietly behind her. One of the gentlemen separated from the group that was milling around the debutantes and approached the arriving trio; Elizabeth suddenly realised that it was the Comte de Tournay. He was dressed in the latest fashion, and was a fine figure of a man in spite of his forty-plus years. He must be making the rounds of the parties to find another wealthy wife, she thought cynically. One would think that he would look for a wealthy widow closer to his own age rather than one of these young innocents, but perhaps a widow would not be youthful enough for his discerning tastes—and might come with additional encumbrances, such as children. Elizabeth could not picture the suave aristocrat as a doting father to someone else's children.

She smiled and greeted Caroline and the comte when they came over. They watched Georgiana dancing with a handsome young man who had been introduced to Elizabeth as the eldest son of the host family, while Kitty danced with the young man with the protruding ears whom they had met at the previous ball. As they watched, the dance ended and Georgiana and Kitty exchanged partners; Elizabeth wondered to herself how Georgiana had arranged the manoeuvre.

When there was a break in the dancing, Elizabeth thanked Georgiana quietly for her kindness to Kitty and asked her if she had arranged the exchange of partners. Georgiana blushed and admitted that she had, saying:

"I did not realise that you would notice. You are far too acute, Elizabeth! I told George Dalrymple that I would only dance with him if he would ask Kitty for the next two."

"That was very kind of you, dearest."

"Not at all. I have no interest in Mr. Dalrymple, as you know, so why should I not direct him towards Kitty?"

Elizabeth smiled and shooed Georgiana back to the debutantes.

The evening passed uneventfully and Elizabeth could see that her sister-in-law was well liked by her contemporaries. Kitty did not dance every dance, but she was engaged for enough of them to keep a smile on her face. Caroline Bingley, on the other hand, ignored the younger men and women, giving virtually all of her attention to the comte. Darcy also watched Georgiana's progress around the room, and Elizabeth could tell that he was a little apprehensive for his sister.

"She will be fine, my love," Elizabeth said in his ear when they were alone for a moment. "You must relax, or you will make Georgiana anxious as well; your sister is a very perceptive young woman, you know."

"You are right ... was I being that obvious?" he asked in chagrin as he worked to smooth his brow and appear unconcerned.

"Only to me; I am sure Georgiana did not notice," she whispered back, with a smile.

About an hour after the ball began, Colonel Fitzwilliam arrived, handsomely outfitted in a beautifully cut black coat and breeches and snowy stockings. Elizabeth was standing by Georgiana when he greeted his cousin.

"I am pleased to see you, my dear little cousin. I am sorry that I missed you yesterday morning, but I hear that your curtsey was flawless," he said, bowing to her.

Georgiana flicked a glance at Elizabeth and then returned the colonel's courtesies. She moved off when an impeccably dressed young gentleman with a pleasantly ugly face came to claim his dances with her. The colonel bowed to Elizabeth and asked her if she would like to dance.

"I know that my cousin does not like to dance and I would not want a handsome young lady such as you to not be allowed to enjoy the ball." He smirked at Darcy, who just shook his head and rolled his eyes.

As they danced, Elizabeth teased the colonel about his own matrimonial ambitions. "You will never find a wife, Colonel, if you spend your time dancing with the married women."

"Very true, but I like to do a tactical analysis before plunging into the maelstrom of battle," he said, his eyes alight with mischief. "It is a very difficult problem when the loveliest ladies are already taken," he added with a courtly bow.

"I thank you, sir, for the compliment; however, I suspect that there are probably plenty of pretty young ladies who would be happy to dance with you and with whom you could find ample consolation."

"It is not the dancing, but the predatory mammas that frighten me," he said with a straight face.

Elizabeth laughed and they continued their dance. After a moment the colonel added, still with a light tone:

"Seriously however, the mammas who are interested in the younger son of an earl are those with no breeding and plenty of lucre; they wish to get their foot in the door of the nobility and their daughters have not the beauty or charms to attract an eldest son. It is quite frustrating."

They finished their dance in silence, and when the colonel went off to ask the daughter of the house to dance, Elizabeth stood again with Darcy and watched the dancers. Elizabeth noticed that Georgiana kept a surreptitious eye on her cousin as he made the rounds of the room, while at the same time she appeared to listen attentively to her partners. The evening went well, and Elizabeth quietly congratulated her sister afterwards on her success.

"Thank you, my dear sister, I enjoyed myself moderately well," she responded, and added, "It is much easier to be gracious when I am only doing it for practise and I do not really care about whether the young men notice me or not. Actually, it is quite liberating."

She smiled briefly as she made this last statement, but her eyes belied her casual tone. On the way home in the carriage, however, she threw off her serious mood and chattered about the ball with Kitty, who seemed to have had a better time than at the previous one, and the two girls went upstairs giggling together. Darcy and Elizabeth made their way sedately up in their wake and Elizabeth sighed in relief at the success of the beginning of Georgiana's season.

The next night they attended a party given by Sir Robert Blake, who was down from Derbyshire with his sister. Elizabeth was surprised to see Jonathan Walker among the guests. Edward Blake was also there, wearing the uniform of the Horse Guards; Colonel Fitzwilliam, at Darcy's suggestion, had helped arrange a commission for him as a lieutenant in his regiment and he was required to be on duty at the palace later in the evening. The colonel clearly liked the young man, and Elizabeth overheard him comment quietly to Darcy:

"I wish that all of my lieutenants shaped up as well; most of them are worthless pups that I wouldn't trust to guard the safety of the royal hounds, let alone the royal family, and who are only interested in using their regimentals to cut an impressive figure in society." To Edward Blake he said, "Well, young sir, you make a good showing in that uniform."

Blake blushed slightly at the compliment but responded with a bow and "I thank you sir, I am proud to wear it."

Sir Robert smiled at the colonel gratefully and thanked him for his kindness to his brother. When the guests were assembled in the drawing-room Sir Robert stood and held out his hand to his sister and to Jonathan Walker.

"I welcome you all to our party and would like to announce that we have good reason to celebrate this evening. Before we left Derbyshire my sister became engaged to Mr. Jonathan Walker, whom I believe many of you know.

There was a pause, and then Elizabeth began clapping hesitantly, soon followed by the others. Congratulations came from around the room and the awkward moment passed. Elizabeth did not look at her family but the room was unusually quiet until a middle-aged cousin of Sir Robert's began playing a country dance and the young people began pairing up for the set. Elizabeth and Darcy went over to Miss Blake and Mr. Walker and Elizabeth said:

"I hope that you are both very happy. How soon do you plan to marry?"

"Quite soon." Miss Blake giggled. "My dear Jonathan is very impatient."

Walker grinned at her affectionately and Elizabeth gave them a perfunctory smile. Darcy bowed before moving off to allow other well-wishers to speak to them.

Later in the coach, the Darcy party all stared at each other in silence, until Elizabeth said:

"What should we do? Sir Robert evidently does not know his prospective brother-in-law's character."

Darcy answered slowly, "I do not know Sir Robert well enough to bring up this subject unsolicited, so I think that we have no choice but to pretend to congratulate Miss Blake."

"I do not have an alternative to propose, either, but I shudder to think of any young woman marrying him."

They all lapsed into silence for the remainder of the trip home.

Chapter 23

This wondrous miracle did Love devise,
For dancing is love's proper exercise.
Sir John Davies, "Orchestra, or a Poem of Dancing"

The next day Darcy went to his club, but was home in time to have tea with Elizabeth and Georgiana while Kitty was out shopping with Jane. He sat and listened to them talk about their day but there was a crease between his brows. Finally, Elizabeth said:

"Is there something the matter, dear?"

He did not answer for a moment, but then he said, "I ran into Sir Robert Blake at my club today. He took me aside and quizzed me about Jonathan Walker. He saw our surprise last night when he announced his sister's engagement and was concerned."

"What did you tell him?" Georgiana asked with a worried look.

"I hemmed and hawed a little but he insisted that it would be better to know the worst now, when she might drop the engagement if necessary. I finally told him about the reports that I received on his gambling and his debts. I did not report Walker's effrontery or persistence with regard to Georgiana."

Elizabeth asked, "And what did he say?"

"He was rather taken aback to find out about Walker's dissipations but, finally, he decided to wait and see what happened. His sister has been out for several years and is eager to be married. They have lived very quietly in Derbyshire and there are not many suitable young gentlemen in the area. That was one of the reasons that he planned to bring her to town this season, but of course their engagement occurred immediately before they left for London."

"I hope, for her sake, that Mr. Walker really does care about her," Georgiana said softly.

They all sipped their tea thoughtfully, but did not discuss the subject further.

The next two weeks flew by. They continued to have engagements every night and Georgiana seemed to be enjoying herself but, although they saw the colonel frequently, Elizabeth did not see any signs of his awareness of Georgiana beyond the indulgent notice he had always given his cousin. Georgiana was becoming frustrated with him, and complained (with a petulance that was very unusual for her) to Elizabeth when they were alone:

"The colonel is still oblivious to me. How can men be so unaware of what is going on around them? I wonder if I must knock him over, or do other violence to him before he notices that I am alive."

Elizabeth smiled a little. "You must forgive them, my dear sister, for men do not like change any more than the rest of us, and ignore it for as long as possible. The colonel undoubtedly still sees a twelve-year-old girl when he looks at you, instead of a young woman of seventeen years."

"He has been paying a lot of attention to Justina Dalrymple lately; he has danced with her more than once at several of the balls. You don't suppose that he is considering making her an offer, do you?" she said with a frown.

"I certainly hope not; I have seen her speak rather sharply to her mother a couple of times in public—I would not be easy about his chances of happiness with her, even were there no other considerations. However, I agree that he is spending far too much time with her. I had originally planned to have you make your *true* debut at your aunt's party, but I think, everything considered, that we should not wait to unveil the new Georgiana."

"Really?" Do you really think so?" Georgiana said, putting her hand nervously to her throat.

"I do. Tomorrow night is the Elliots' ball. You shall make your 'appearance' there."

The next evening, the ladies went upstairs earlier than usual to prepare for the ball. Elizabeth hurried through her *toilette* with François, quickly donning her cream silk dress with the green sash and her emeralds, and then they went to Georgiana's room where her new maid, Bernard, had all of the clothing ready. As they had planned, Georgiana had been wearing white and cream-coloured dresses thus far in the season, so her new gown would be a splash of colour to vividly contrast with the others, as well as being the last word in decorous sophistication with its *décolleté* design.

François swept up Georgiana's light-brown hair into two shining wings on either side of her head and into a confection of curls on her crown, emphasising her height. She then helped her into her shift and stays, tightening the stays to enhance her bust line. Next, she and Bernard brought out white silk stockings and a white cotton batiste petticoat that ended just above her ankles. The gown was next, a sea-foam green satin bodice and skirt, which was reflected in the colour of her eyes. The skirt of the gown was split from the waist to the hem to show an underskirt of finely pleated white silk that swept almost to the floor, peeping out below the green. At the shoulder began the barest suggestion of a puffed sleeve, in green satin to match the bodice, and the low, scooped neckline was enhanced with a sweep of stiff, finely pleated white silk that stood up from the front of the shoulders and around the back, gently cupping the back of her long, slender neck and framing her face.

Bernard helped her mistress don her white satin dancing slippers and then, when François reached for Georgiana's pearl necklace, Elizabeth stepped in and shook her head. She brought out a jeweler's case she had been holding and opened it. She fastened the diamonds that had belonged to Lady Anne, obtained from the bank that afternoon, around Georgiana's neck and fastened the eardrops onto her earlobes. She stepped back, and she and the two maids examined their charge. The diamonds in their delicate setting sparkled in the candlelight and the dress picked up the colour of her eyes beautifully. After a moment of intense consideration as they walked around Georgiana, looking at all sides of her costume, François smiled and nodded, and Elizabeth said:

"Yes. You are ready, Georgiana."

Georgiana examined herself in the mirror and smiled slowly at Elizabeth.

"Yes, my dear sister, I believe I am."

They covered her gown with a white satin cloak, careful to not crush the pleats around the neckline of her dress. By the time Darcy had appeared from the drawing-room Elizabeth had her cloak on as well, and they left as soon as Kitty appeared a moment later. Darcy commented in the carriage that the ladies looked very well. Georgiana and Elizabeth smiled at each other and at Kitty as they thanked him.

When they arrived at the ball, which was given in a large ballroom at the rear of their host's home, Elizabeth ushered Georgiana and Kitty into a dressing-room to make sure that their costumes were perfect before they went into the ballroom. Darcy had gone ahead and was standing with the colonel and another gentleman who, Elizabeth guessed from his resemblance to Colonel Fitzwilliam, was Viscount St. George. They all three turned when the ladies entered, and both of Georgiana's cousins and her brother stared for a moment in surprise at Georgiana. Elizabeth wanted to laugh at the astonishment on their faces. The viscount recovered first and stepped forward to take Georgiana's hand, bowing over it and saying:

"My dear cousin Georgiana, how lovely you look tonight! I hope you will give me the pleasure of your hand for the first dances."

"Of course, Cousin," she answered gravely.

The colonel watched them as his brother led her to the dance floor and joined the lines facing each other, then walked over to Justina Dalrymple and asked her to dance. Darcy looked quizzically at Elizabeth and she said brightly:

"Doesn't Georgiana look well tonight, Mr. Darcy?"

"She does indeed," he answered, turning his gaze to follow his sister speculatively as she danced. "She looks like a queen. Is there some reason for this dramatic change in hair style and ornamentation?"

"We are merely increasing the stakes in the matrimonial game—sometimes men need to be hit over the head before they notice the obvious."

He looked at her perplexedly. "And who might she be trying to 'hit over the head' tonight?" he asked as he watched Georgiana dance, her eyes glancing over at Colonel Fitzwilliam several times. He looked at the colonel, who was watching Georgiana rather to the neglect of his own partner, who looked piqued. Before Elizabeth could answer, Darcy's face took on a look of surprised awareness:

"Surely, not Fitzwilliam?"

Elizabeth smiled briefly. "Would you have any objections if it *were* the colonel?"

"None at all; my cousin is a fine man. I am just—surprised—I did not expect it. How long has this been going on?"

Elizabeth temporised, since Georgiana had not yet given her permission to tell Darcy. "Georgiana finds it very frustrating that he treats her like a child. She is not a child any more."

"No, much as I hate to admit it, she is definitely no longer a child," he replied, lifting a brow at Elizabeth's avoidance of his question. She looked out over the dancers and pretended not to see.

They were watching as the pair of dances ended and a crowd of young men surrounded Georgiana. The colonel observed the swirl of activity from across the room until his cousin accepted a partner, and then approached an unattached young lady and obtained her hand for the next dances. After they finished, Georgiana was again besieged by several young men and Colonel Fitzwilliam joined Darcy at the side of the room. Elizabeth was talking to Jane, who had arrived not long before, but she overheard the colonel comment to Darcy:

"I hope that all these young bucks don't overwhelm Georgiana, Darcy. Perhaps I should rescue her from them."

She glanced over to see her husband's response. Darcy looked his cousin in the eye, his face expressionless, and said very quietly, "Oh, I don't think she needs to be rescued anymore. She's not a child, Fitzwilliam." The colonel stared at him for a long, frozen moment, his brows raised in surprise, and then he looked back towards Georgiana.

"I believe you are right, Darcy," he said slowly, "but I think I may ask her to dance anyway."

Without another word, he walked toward his cousin as she stood with a couple of other girls in the cluster of admirers. Lord St. George appeared on the opposite side of the group, but before he could catch Georgiana's eye Colonel Fitzwilliam neatly manoeuvred between the others and took Georgiana's hand, cutting off one of the younger men before he could finish asking her to dance. Georgiana nodded to her cousin, her eyes downcast as he led her to the floor. As she rose from her first curtsey to start the figure her eyes came up and met his squarely, her right brow lifting slightly. Elizabeth saw the colonel stiffen. He covered his discomposure quickly and began the dance, but he appeared bemused as he danced the figures, his neck flushing slightly each time the dance returned him to his partner. Georgiana, for her part, kept her eyes modestly averted as she moved down the line, but raised them to meet his briefly each time they faced each other, the challenge in hers offering a counterpoint to the small, serene smile on her lips.

When they finished their dances, the colonel led Georgiana back to her friends and made his way to the refreshment table, where he slowly drank a cup of punch while he watched his cousin dance the next dances.

Later in the evening, Viscount St. George again asked for her hand for a pair of dances, and Georgiana accepted him, but she seemed rather distracted during the dance. Elizabeth noted as she looked on that the colonel was watching them as well, with a serious intensity that was unusual for him. She hoped that he would ask Georgiana to dance again, but he kept his distance, maintaining his observation post and ignoring the other young women.

Georgiana looked exhausted as they rode home from the ball. Elizabeth felt very tired also, and reflected to herself that chaperoning was far more tiring than the dancing she had done before her marriage—particularly on this occasion, where both she and Georgiana had such intense hopes for the evening. Elizabeth did not know quite what to think about it; the colonel seemed to finally be aware that Georgiana was a young woman, but he appeared to be content to merely observe while she danced and talked, rather than engaging her attention himself.

When they arrived home, Georgiana and Kitty went immediately upstairs, but Darcy held Elizabeth back and gestured towards the drawing-room, closing the door behind them.

"Did you know that Georgiana was interested in the colonel before tonight?"

Elizabeth paused, but could see no way to avoid the direct question, "Yes."

"Why did you not tell me?"

"Georgiana told me in confidence and asked me not to tell you, so I felt I could not betray her trust."

"Why did she not want me to know? I could have spoken to Fitzwilliam …" His brows knitted in irritation.

Elizabeth stared at him. "That is exactly what she does *not* want!"

"I don't understand: why would my sister not want me to know her feelings when it concerns her entire future?" he exclaimed, his voice momentarily rising before he forced it back down to a whisper.

"She is in love with him and wants him to marry her because he loves her, not because he feels a family obligation," she said crisply. "If you talk to him about her feelings for him, it is tantamount to asking him to marry her. He probably will agree because he feels a responsibility towards her and the match is very eligible for the both of them. She, however, does not want to spend the rest of her life with a guardian; she wants to spend it with a husband—and it is entirely your fault that she feels that way, my love!" She stopped, a little shocked at her own vehemence.

"My fault! What do you mean?" he asked with some asperity.

"Your sister, my dear husband, wants a marriage with the love, affection, and, I hope, trust," she said dryly, "between husband and wife that you have achieved." Then she added with a slight blush, "… albeit through months of agony and uncertainty beforehand, of which she has probably only the slightest comprehension."

They stared at each other.

"I am sorry, my love," Darcy said finally and slumped down onto the sofa, rubbing his brow. "I am being a mutton-headed dolt. I cannot blame Georgiana for not wanting a neat and polite marriage arranged by family members when she could have a 'marriage of true minds' as her brother and sister have. Particularly after I turned down a similar arrangement myself." He finally smiled at her and she felt a rush of relief that he was not annoyed because she had not shared Georgiana's confessions with him earlier.

She returned, quietly, "*Comprends-tu la situation maintenant, mon amour?*"

"*Oui, je comprends parfaitement. Mais, mon Dieu, quelle probleme!*"

"*Oui, c'est vrai.*"

They slowly mounted the stairs, both musing over what she had told him. As Elizabeth turned to go to her room, Darcy stopped her again and whispered:

"Is there nothing we can do to help this situation?"

"I think that we have done every thing we can do; it is up to Georgiana now," she said, her confidence returning.

He nodded in reluctant agreement then turned to his dressing-room, shaking his head as he went.

Later, when Elizabeth was asleep, Darcy stared up into the darkness and reviewed the discussion in the drawing-room without satisfaction. The question of his sister's feelings for her cousin, and his for her, was of only peripheral importance to his current reflections. His thoughts and actions in the beginning of that conversation struck him as unpleasantly similar to those of the person that he had been eighteen months ago, the ghost of an affronted, arrogant man rising like the miasma from a crypt to assault his intellect and emotions. He had managed to suppress that Darcy this evening, but it was disconcerting to know that he lurked in a dim corner of his mind, waiting to appear at the slightest provocation. Elizabeth's ironic comment about trust had, fortunately, struck home, bringing him abruptly to his senses.

He had always wanted Elizabeth to be Georgiana's sister, and it was only fair that she should keep her sister's confidences, just as he knew she would keep his. His insufferable pride that had caused all of the emotional pain he had endured during their courtship was clearly not excised, merely dormant. He must make sure to keep that phantom of the past in the deepest dungeons of his mind. He smiled to himself. No doubt Elizabeth would point out his error, as she did tonight, should he stray towards overweening arrogance again.

Another question rose in his mind. What should he do about Georgiana and Fitzwilliam? He had already taken a small step towards enlightening his cousin about Georgiana's regard for him when he opened Fitzwilliam's eyes to the fact that she was no longer the gangly little girl who had followed them adoringly, barred from joining their pursuits by both her youth and her gender. Even he, who had provided her with all of the accoutrements of a young lady for the past five years, had been rattled tonight when he had seen her in the ballroom. He had, for a fraction of a second, not recognised the elegant woman before him as the same girl who had kissed him on the cheek this morning when she came down to breakfast. He had felt a sense of loss as she glided off for her dances with her cousin St. George, foreshadowing her inevitable loss to adulthood and marriage. That Georgiana was ready for the change was unarguable after tonight, and the answer to his question was clear. She did not want him to influence the colonel's decision. As Elizabeth had said, it was up to Georgiana now.

He turned on his side, his musing finished, and finally drifted off to sleep.

Elizabeth had fallen asleep immediately when she had curled up next to her husband, and slept a dreamless sleep. She awakened only when Darcy brought her a cup of tea at eight o'clock the next morning. As usual, he was fully dressed for the day and appeared to have been up for hours.

"How do you manage to keep your regular morning hours with these late nights?" she asked with a sigh as she sipped her tea.

"Merely habit," he returned with a flicker of a smile, "I have been getting up before six o'clock since I was ten years old."

"You are simply much more virtuous than I am, I suppose," she returned primly.

He laughed then, and said, "I must be virtuous, for I cannot imagine how else I managed to convince the most beautiful woman in England to marry me."

"An excellent answer, sir," she said, her eyes belying the solemnity of her countenance.

She set aside her tea, took his face between her hands, and kissed him, his freshly shaved skin smooth under her fingers. She smiled and said regretfully:

"I suppose that I should get up and dressed for the day. François is probably pacing outside my door, wanting to hear about the ball last night. She arranged Georgiana's hair, and so could be said to have a personal stake in her success."

With a heartfelt sigh, Darcy stood up and went downstairs, leaving her to François's ministrations.

Elizabeth was surprised to see Georgiana in the breakfast-parlour when she came down.

"Why are you up so early, my love? You need your sleep if you are going to attend all of the parties for which you are engaged," she exclaimed.

"I awakened early and could not fall back to sleep," she said with a serious countenance.

Darcy glanced at Elizabeth and rose, saying, "Well, I had better go; I am expecting to meet Bingley at the club soon and I would not want to keep him waiting."

He quickly left the room.

Elizabeth turned back to Georgiana and watched her pick at her food, her mouth drooping.

"What is bothering you, dearest?"

Georgiana sighed, her lip quivering slightly.

"I was disappointed that the colonel did not dance with me again last night. I am probably being unreasonable, but I hoped that after all of the preparations we did before the ball he would respond more." She stopped and smiled ruefully. "I guess that I expected him to fall at my feet in a swoon when I appeared in the room."

Elizabeth quickly reassured her. "You must give him a little time. I believe from my observations last night that he now realises that you are a woman, not a little girl. You must now make him also realise that he loves you."

Georgiana sighed and said, "You are correct, of course, but it is so difficult to be patient. I am afraid that he will make an offer to someone else before I can convince him to look at me, especially since you and my brother have given him such a model of domestic felicity to strive for. While my brother was still unwed and I was not yet out in society, I felt as if I had all the time in the world, but now

I feel as if time is careening away like a runaway horse while I am plodding behind in the dust. I hope that I have not grown up too late. If you will excuse me, I think I will play the pianoforte; it will probably soothe my fevered brow." She made a determined effort to smile and left the room.

When Darcy returned in the early afternoon he sought out Elizabeth in the drawing-room while the two girls were upstairs playing with Lucky, and asked her how Georgiana was.

"I thought it best that I leave this morning so that she could talk to you confidentially, but I am concerned about her. I have never seen her so out of spirits before. She has always been very even-tempered."

"Trust me, I have previously lived with three younger sisters and this is not abnormal. She is a bit overwrought about the season and marriage, and everything that is changing in her life. She will be herself again when the suspense of this year is over, whether she is engaged by that time or not, unless of course the colonel becomes engaged to someone else during that time."

"I hope you are right, my love. I feel as if I have aged several years in the last month." He rubbed his hands wearily over his face.

"I feel the same. I am afraid that I am going to collapse before the season is over. Between watching over Georgiana and Kitty, both, I think that I am wearing down to a mere shadow of my former self."

"You do look tired, my love," he said with a worried frown. "Why don't you rest this afternoon?"

"I believe I will, if I can."

She took his advice and rested for two hours in her room that afternoon. She felt much better afterwards and decided to ask Jane if she would invite Kitty to stay with her for a few weeks. Jane called in the afternoon, soon after she arose from her rest, saying:

"I sent a note earlier, but Mr. Darcy said that you were resting. Are you feeling quite well?"

"I am well; just a little tired after all the parties and balls for Georgiana."

"Perhaps I should ask Kitty to stay with us until you are feeling better," Jane said immediately.

Elizabeth laughed, shaking her head in surprise, "I was going to ask if you would invite her, but you have anticipated me, as you usually do."

It was soon settled that Kitty would spend the next two weeks with the Bingleys and help Jane with a party she was planning. She went happily to Berkeley Square the next day, and the Darcys were left to their own devices.

Chapter 24

The course of true love never did run smooth.
William Shakespeare, "A Midsummer Night's Dream"

Elizabeth had expected to see the colonel in their drawing-room very soon, but three days went by and they saw nothing of him, not even at the parties they attended. Viscount St. George, on the other hand, was a daily visitor, stopping for short visits during each late afternoon to talk with Elizabeth and to be charming to Georgiana. Elizabeth wished to know this relative of Darcy's better, since Darcy rarely mentioned him—which, along with Georgiana's comments, had aroused her curiosity. His social graces were formidable and he was able to converse on a variety of topics in an interesting fashion. His easy manners rivaled those of his brother, but Elizabeth found him rather too interested in his own self. She noticed that when he passed a mirror he always checked his appearance in it and stopped to rearrange a fold of his cravat or the curl tumbling artfully over one brow. He was courteous to Elizabeth in a condescending way which clearly demonstrated that he knew of her rather humble origins.

She hoped that Georgiana, in her frustration over Colonel Fitzwilliam's indifference, would not be taken in by Lord St. George's fine looks and be drawn into a situation that would cause her regret—or worse yet, lose her head and try to play the two brothers off each other to make the colonel jealous. Georgiana herself was invariably gracious and appeared to be happy to see him, but she made no mention of him when he was not there, which reassured her sister. Elizabeth tried to keep her composure and appear unconcerned for Georgiana's sake, but she knew that the younger woman was distressed by the colonel's seeming lack of interest in her.

Georgiana was evidently nettled by St. George's patronising attitude towards Elizabeth as well. On the third day after the Elliots' ball, Lord St. George was telling them a piece of gossip, which included familiarly dropping the names of several peers in the prince regent's circle. He stopped part way through the story and said to Elizabeth, with a deprecating smile:

"I am sorry, my dear cousin, I should not bore you with stories about people with whom you are not acquainted."

Georgiana interjected austerely, "Indeed not, Cousin, it would be abominably rude of you to do so."

She smiled sweetly at him and he had the grace to look a little ashamed. He turned the conversation to another topic and left after a few minutes, scrupulously polite to both ladies in his farewells.

The set-down did not keep Lord St. George from their door the next day, however, and he was still with them when the colonel, resplendent in his regimentals, finally came to call in the afternoon.

"I apologise for neglecting you, Cousin Georgiana," he said after he had greeted both ladies, "but I was needed at the palace and was not able to absent myself." He turned to his brother and added in a cooler tone, "What a surprise to see you here, Brother."

"Yes, I have been enjoying making the acquaintance of my new cousin and renewing my acquaintance with Georgiana while you have been playing soldier," Viscount St. George drawled, with just the faintest hint of condescension in his voice.

"How thoughtful of you, my dear brother," the colonel said smoothly. "I am surprised that your busy schedule allows you to pay afternoon calls."

"Well," he remarked with a quick smile at Georgiana, "one must not neglect one's family, especially not such attractive family."

Elizabeth saw the colonel bridle slightly, but he quickly brought himself under control, although his face was far from having its usual pleasant expression. He appeared to Elizabeth … she struggled for the apt description: stiff and uncomfortable, and possibly, deep down, resentful of his brother. The viscount left after a few minutes and the colonel followed soon thereafter. Georgiana tried to keep him longer by saying:

"Must you leave so soon, Colonel? You just arrived."

"I am truly sorry, my dear cousin, but duty calls me. I wanted to stop in and let you know that I have not forgotten you, however," he said rather hesitantly, then bowed and left abruptly.

Georgiana stared after him for several moments after he left.

"Well," Elizabeth ventured after a pause, "at least he did not call you 'little cousin.'"

Georgiana finally found her voice and said:

"Please excuse me, Elizabeth, I am going to have a fit of hysterics and I don't wish you to witness it, so I will go to my room."

She walked stiffly out of the drawing-room and up the stairs, although greeting Burton courteously when they passed in the hall. Elizabeth could not help smiling to herself, in spite of her worries over Georgiana. Having a sister who went calmly upstairs to "have hysterics" was a considerable change from the Bennet family, where every passion was inflicted upon all of the relations. She sighed at the perversity of mankind and went to her room to rest. She could not help Georgiana keep her spirits up if she was so exhausted that she was in a state of collapse.

After lying down for an hour, unable to fall asleep, Elizabeth rose and dressed. She went down the stairs from her room and heard the sound of the pianoforte coming from the drawing-room. She entered and approached Georgiana as she finished a funereal Handel *Largo* in a whisper of chords.

"How are you doing, my sweet?" she said quietly as she brushed a few hairs back from the girl's brow. "Are you feeling calmer now that you have had your hysterics?"

Georgiana gave a weak smile. "Yes, I am—I am sorry to be so out of spirits lately."

"Compared to some of my sisters, you are a model of serenity, my dear." Elizabeth smiled reassuringly. "Sometimes I feel that it is a shame we women cannot relieve our emotions by participating in some of the more violent sports," she reflected aloud. "There have been times in my life when I have felt that a few rounds in a boxing ring would be just the thing to restore my happiness."

Georgiana laughed until she had to wipe the tears from her eyes. "My dear Mrs. Darcy, you never cease to surprise me. I wonder if I will ever be able to predict what you will say next."

They both laughed then, and Elizabeth, for one, felt better as she went upstairs to dress for dinner. They were to dine at the Whitwells' before going on to a party at a friend's. The dinner was to be a family party only and the colonel was expected to be there, as was Lord St. George. Lady Whitwell told Elizabeth, when she extended the invitation:

"We will have a nice quiet family dinner. Georgiana probably needs to recoup her energy after her first round of parties."

Elizabeth agreed that a quiet dinner would be a good idea, although privately wondering whether Georgiana would get one with the two sons of the house present.

When dinner was served, Lord Whitwell led Elizabeth into the dining-room, followed by Viscount St. George and Georgiana, and Darcy and Lady Whitwell. Colonel Fitzwilliam brought up the rear of the procession with Mrs. Appleton, a very elderly cousin of Lord Whitwell's, on his arm. Elizabeth noted sardonically to herself that this was a rather apt demonstration of the status of the younger son of a noble house.

Georgiana was seated between Lord Whitwell and Lord St. George and she divided her time between the two, listening quietly to them and nodding occasionally as the conversation demanded but not saying much in return. Elizabeth saw her glance down the table towards the colonel, who was talking abstractedly to Mrs. Appleton. Elizabeth was between Lord St. George and the colonel and found herself given little attention by the former, who seemed absorbed by his conversation with Georgiana. She saw Lord and Lady Whitwell give each other a significant glance when their son and their niece were not looking, as, from the other side of the colonel, Elizabeth's ears caught the querulous tones of Mrs. Appleton asking him:

"When are you two young men going to get married? It is time that you both did your duty to the family."

The colonel smiled wanly but managed to deflect the attack, agreeing with her that it would be a desirable action on his part, but that he would not want be precipitous.

"A little more precipitance would perhaps be advisable in the case of yourself and your brother. Neither of you is getting any younger, you know," she returned tartly. Then with a wizened smile that took the sting from her words she added, "However, you must forgive an opinionated old lady for prying into your affairs. Marriages and deaths are meat and drink to someone as old as I." She chuckled at his expression and patted his arm. "You must take some pointers from your cousin," she said, nodding towards Darcy, "and find yourself a pretty young woman before they are all married off."

The colonel chuckled half-heartedly, glancing at his brother and Georgiana. His mother turned the conversation in another direction and the colonel seconded her efforts with relief.

The ladies soon rose and adjourned to the drawing-room, where Mrs. Appleton engaged Georgiana's attention with a lively account of her own coming-out many years earlier. They were well entertained until the gentlemen rejoined them and they poured out the tea and coffee. Lord St. George requested a song from the ladies, bowing to Elizabeth and Georgiana. When Elizabeth demurred Georgiana rose and went to the pianoforte, where she selected a sonata and began playing. Lord St. George turned the pages for her and seemed rapt in the music—or at least in the musician.

The colonel joined them at the instrument and stationed himself where he could see Georgiana's face, and where she could, in turn, see him when she glanced up from her music. During one glance upward her gaze caught his and she stumbled over a note before she could look down again and find her place. Lord St. George gave his brother a sardonic look and drawled, again in that patronising tone:

"Brother, you should find another place from which to enjoy the music. You disconcert our cousin hanging over her like a carrion bird."

Georgiana gave him a piercing look and said, with just a hint of astringency, "I know of no one who resembles a vulture less than your brother, Lord St. George, and if I was disconcerted by being watched while I played, then you would be at fault as well."

He chuckled gently and murmured, "I would not want to do anything that would make you uncomfortable, my dear cousin."

She looked away and continued playing until it was time to leave for their party.

Before she could leave the pianoforte, Lord St. George took her hand and said:

"I hope that you will allow me the first pair of dances again this evening, my dearest cousin."

She bowed her head slightly in assent and glanced at Colonel Fitzwilliam. Intercepting her look, Lord St. George added to his brother, "If you want a dance with our lovely cousin, Brother, you should speak now, for I will be keeping her quite busy this evening."

The colonel bowed and said, very formally, "I, of course, wish to dance with you as well, Miss Darcy. Perhaps I could have the second pair of dances?"

Georgiana bowed her head again, this time a smile playing at the corners of her mouth. The colonel smiled in return and the group left the drawing-room for the party.

The entertainment that evening was at the home of another of the debutantes, this one a rather plain girl who was the eldest daughter of a baronet and a friend of Georgiana's. The family was a large one and of only moderate fortune, so they made sure that they hosted several parties to attract the eligible young men.

Jane and Bingley had decided to remain at home this evening, so the Darcys chaperoned Miss Bingley (who had decided to spend the first half of the season at her brother's house) and Kitty, as well as Georgiana. The baronet had kindly invited all of them, in spite of the additional competition they provided for his daughter, because the presence of Georgiana would ensure that the wealthier young men would attend as well. The house was of moderate size but furnished in an elegant style, and the refreshments were lavish.

Georgiana left her family to dance the first dance with Lord St. George. She danced well, with little conversation, merely answering her partner's comments with a small smile or brief comment of her own and then gazing remotely over his shoulder. When he escorted her off the dance floor, she curtseyed briefly before moving off with some other young women.

The colonel immediately claimed her for his two dances. She put her gloved hand gently on his offered arm and glanced up at him, her cheeks flushing slightly as she briefly met his gaze. During the dance she smiled and gazed steadily at him when they were facing each other, still not speaking much but obviously very aware of him. Elizabeth could see that he was flustered by her regard and soon his easy conversation died and they danced in silence.

Elizabeth saw that Edward Blake had come with Colonel Fitzwilliam and was happily dancing with all of the young ladies, but when he was free he came back to talk to Kitty and danced two sets with her during the evening. Sir Robert Blake came late to the party and Georgiana, who was talking to Elizabeth at that moment, said impishly:

"You know, I think that I will introduce Sir Robert to Catherine Freemont. They would make a lovely couple."

She went to find her friend and proceeded to take her over to Sir Robert and introduce them. Sir Robert bowed courteously and talked with them for a few moments. A young man came to claim Georgiana for a promised dance and Sir Robert apparently asked for Miss Freemont's hand for the next set, for they moved onto the dance floor at the same time as Georgiana and her partner. Elizabeth thought it amusing, but very endearing, that Georgiana could think of match-making when her own prospects were still so indefinite.

The Comte de Tournay was not present that night, and so Elizabeth introduced Miss Bingley and Viscount St. George when he came over between dances. Caroline was charmed and danced and talked with him with evident enjoyment through a set, and then she and Georgiana both accepted refreshments from him. Lord St. George preened himself before the two ladies, Georgiana looking on indifferently and Miss Bingley hanging upon his every word.

The evening slowly ran its course while Elizabeth and Darcy watched the formal movement of gentlemen and ladies as they met off the dance floor, bowing and curtseying, telling a small joke or anecdote, smiling, sometimes with their mouths alone, sometimes with their eyes as well. It was an endless parade of young men and women showing their looks and their grace, displaying their wealth by their elegant and fashionable clothing and caught in an elaborate dance as formal as any taking place on the dance floor. Elizabeth suddenly realised that she was extremely fatigued, and she asked Darcy if they could sit for a while.

"Of course, my dear," he said, noticing that she was rather pale, "shall we sit over here by the window where you can get some air?"

"Thank you; that would be lovely."

"Are you sure you are well?" he asked with concern. "Do we need to go home?"

"I will be fine in a moment, I thank you. The fresh air revives me wonderfully." She put her hand reassuringly through his arm and turned her attention back to Georgiana and Kitty. Both seemed to be enjoying themselves and had not, she was happy to see, noticed her indisposition. The evening eventually wound to its close, and they were on their way home by one o'clock, the two younger women sagging like wilted flowers in the carriage.

Chapter 25

But still the great have kindness in reserve.
Alexander Pope, "An epistle to Dr. Arbuthnot"

Finally the day came for Elizabeth's and Jane's presentations at court. Although she was nervous about making a *faux pas* in front of the court, Elizabeth confessed to Jane that she was eager to see the prince regent, about whom she had heard so many scandalous tales.

"I realise that I am showing a rather prurient interest in his activities, but he seems to be a man who inspires many different emotions in those around him and I long to make my own judgment in the case."

Jane laughed nervously. Elizabeth knew that she was somewhat overwhelmed by the many rules of etiquette and protocol, so she reassured her:

"Do not distress yourself, my dear sister. With your beauty and grace you will charm the court. I, on the other hand, hope that I do not humiliate myself by laughing inappropriately at all of the pomp and ceremony."

Jane smiled more easily at her and kissed her on the cheek. "Dear Lizzy, you always make me feel better."

Lady Whitwell arrived and checked their costumes to see if they were perfectly correct, and then had them demonstrate their curtseys in front of herself and Georgiana. She would be Elizabeth's sponsor and a friend of hers, Lady Southaven, would be Jane's, since court protocol forbade Lady Whitwell from presenting both of them herself on the same day. Georgiana kissed them both, as did their husbands, and wished them luck before sending them off with her aunt.

The carriage ride to St. James Palace seemed far too short to Elizabeth. The day was a little cool and threatened rain but they were able to leave their wraps in the carriage and enter the foyer of the palace without mishap, their trains draped gracefully over their arms. Lady Southaven awaited them in the entry, and after greeting her they made their way to the anteroom of the reception area. There, the lords-in-waiting lined up all those who would be presented in order of their rank. Elizabeth and Jane were separated since Darcy, although untitled, had a much more ancient name and fortune than Bingley, whose wealth went no further back than a grandfather, who had been in trade (a fact that Miss Bingley conveniently forgot when she was being superior).

Elizabeth prepared herself for an interminable wait since the line was long, but she consoled herself with the knowledge that it was, fortunately, an ordeal that need only occur once. Lady Whitwell stood with her and they occasionally exchanged remarks, but mostly they waited in silence, for the room was too noisy with the nervous chattering of the debutantes being presented to make conversation easy.

After they had been waiting a good while and the din had quieted somewhat, Lady Whitwell turned to her and said in a low voice:

"While we have the opportunity of being relatively unremarked, I must thank you for all you have done for Georgiana." Elizabeth blushed and started to shake her head, but her sponsor continued, "Do not try to modestly deny it, my dear. I have seen a most remarkable change in Georgiana's poise and maturity since you and Darcy married. Although he and Edward have done their best as her guardians, two men more than ten years older than she is are much better suited to manage her financial affairs than they are to manage her development into a graceful young woman.

"Unfortunately for Georgiana, although her brother loves her dearly she has had no female relatives, until now, to help guide her and provide a model from which she could learn. I myself have several times regretted that I could not spend more time with her, but having only sons I am not sure that I would have been able to do nearly as well as you. I confess that a year ago I was doubtful whether she would be able to face presentation and the season. She has always been an intelligent and courteous child, prevented only by her excessive shyness from shining in the company of others. But she has now blossomed into a confident woman, and I thank you."

She patted Elizabeth's hand as she said these last words. Elizabeth glanced up at her and said diffidently:

"If I have been in any small way able to help Georgiana in the last few months, she has amply repaid my efforts with her kindness and affection. I am delighted to claim her as a sister and I do not look forward to her marrying and leaving home with any anticipation. I will miss her dreadfully."

Lady Whitwell smiled warmly at her, changing her entire countenance from one of serene austerity to one much more approachable and even lovely. Elizabeth could now see the patrician beauty that had attracted Lord Whitwell and which had been passed through her sister, Lady Anne, to Darcy and Georgiana.

Their further conversation was interrupted as the line moved forward, and they arrived at the front more quickly than Elizabeth had expected. Lady Whitwell gave Elizabeth's card to the lord chamberlain and in a few too-brief moments he opened the chamber doors for her and bowed her in. One of the lords-in-waiting spread her train out behind her and she approached the throne.

The prince regent, when her name was read, sat up a bit straighter and observed her closely as she walked sedately up to the throne and curtseyed deeply to him and to his mother, Queen Charlotte, who was also in attendance. The prince regent nodded in his turn and, after the lord-in-waiting draped her train back over her arm, she backed out of the room, unable to keep her amusement at the solemn ritual from showing in her eyes above her studiously serious mien. She thought that she saw a small answering smile play over the prince regent's face, but it was gone in an instant and she was sure that she must have been mistaken.

When she had managed to back out of the room without mishap, she looked at Lady Whitwell and gave a small sigh of relief. Her sponsor's eyes crinkled in amusement as she led her to a bench in the anteroom where they could relax and wait for Jane to finish her presentation.

Eventually the ordeal was over and, after thanking Lady Southaven for her sponsorship of Jane, they returned to their carriage—not forgetting to turn sideways at the carriage door to get their hooped skirts inside.

At Ashbourne House, Darcy, Georgiana, Kitty, and Bingley were all waiting in some anxiety. Georgiana had just begun to pour tea when they heard the carriage arrive, and they jumped up to congratulate Elizabeth and Jane on their presumed success.

Georgiana, after they had all given their congratulations, put on a solemn face and said:

"I am so proud that you have both succeeded in this most important milestone in your life."

This provoked all the laughter she was seeking and Elizabeth and Jane entered the drawing-room with lighter hearts than when they had departed in the morning. After the footman had taken their wraps and Burton had congratulated them, they were more than ready for tea, but first they would change out of their court dresses and into their ordinary gowns for, as Elizabeth pointed out:

"If we sit down in these gowns, there will be no place for anyone else to be seated. Whoever created this style must have had investments in the furniture industry and planned to make a vast fortune enlarging all of the furniture in the country so that more than one lady could sit on the sofa."

Bingley choked on the tea he had just sipped and, while Darcy was pounding on his back, she and Jane swept grandly upstairs to change.

The rest of the day passed in a much more restful fashion than had the morning and they dined at the Bingleys' house that evening. They had not accepted any invitations for later in the evening: they would need an early night tonight, for tomorrow was Lady Whitwell's ball.

Chapter 26

The best-laid schemes o' Mice an' Men
Gang aft a-gley.
Robert Burns, "To A Mouse"

They had no special plans during the next day, and spent it relaxing. Georgiana went to the music room and worked on a new Beethoven sonata, which her brother had given her on her birthday and which she had not had a great deal of time to practise since. After she had worn herself out with the new piece, she played another piece at double speed and then stopped, a little breathless. Elizabeth, who was sitting with her and doing some desultory work on her embroidery, smiled at her choice of composers.

"Feeling in a Beethoven mood are you, Georgiana?" she queried.

"Yes, Mozart or Handel would simply not express my feelings properly, although perhaps the *Rondo Alla Turca* would be quite good," she said, smiling sheepishly.

"You are fortunate to have a pianoforte on which to express yourself; the harp would probably not be sufficient, but on the pianoforte you can pound without fear of alarming the servants."

They both laughed, and Georgiana took out "Le Coucou" and played it *molto vivace* before covering the keys and taking up her needlepoint.

The day dragged slowly by until Lord St. George visited in the early afternoon. Georgiana acknowledged his bow politely when he entered, and rang for tea. She sat down next to Elizabeth in a chair facing St. George and he settled on the sofa, where she had been sitting before his entrance. He began the conversation by discussing his mother's ball that night, and by again engaging Georgiana for the first pair of dances.

"Although," he said with a charming smile, "I don't suppose my mamma will give either of us much choice in the matter, since she will expect us to open the ball." He smiled at her winningly and continued: "Still, I would like for it to be a matter of choice rather than merely a duty."

Georgiana smiled slightly and nodded her acceptance of the engagement, then turned the conversation to the happenings around town, about which he

170

knew a great deal, and he was happily occupied with retailing various bits of news until the door of the drawing-room opened and Darcy appeared with Colonel Fitzwilliam. They greeted the ladies and Lord St. George, and joined them for tea. St. George finished the story he had started before their appearance, and then gracefully made his excuses and departed.

"What did my esteemed brother want today, Georgiana?" Colonel Fitzwilliam asked, looking at the door where his brother had just disappeared.

"He wanted to engage me for the first two dances tonight, although he pointed out that my aunt would force us to open the ball anyway, so I did not seem to have much choice in the matter," she said with a spark in her eye.

"I very much doubt whether he worded his request in quite that fashion," the colonel said with an amused smile, "since, for all his faults, his manners are generally quite acceptable."

She smiled impudently and acknowledged the truth of his statement, and they finished their tea companionably. When the colonel made his *adieux* Darcy saw him out, and by the time he returned to the drawing-room Georgiana had gone upstairs. He sat down next to Elizabeth and asked her how she was feeling.

"I am well. However, I feel like a spring is wound up tight inside me, waiting to explode. I cannot but be influenced by Georgiana's tension, although she covers it very well. Perhaps too well. I sometimes think that if she would scream and cry and get it over with, as some of my younger sisters would do, it would be like a storm passing, leaving fresh air in its wake—however, that is not the Darcy way." She smiled at him, her eyes twinkling. "So she has had to resort to Beethoven, which I believe has been somewhat efficacious."

"Yes, I could hear her battle with the pianoforte from my library this morning. Perhaps we should contact Herr Beethoven and commission a work: 'For the Reduction of Tension in Young Ladies During Their First Season'—but possibly we could find a more romantic title."

Elizabeth laughed, kissed him, and tugged on the hair tumbling over his brow, then went upstairs to rest until she needed to dress for the ball—while attempting to reassure herself that all would be well with Georgiana.

Elizabeth and François went through the same routine they had used during the earlier ball, with the older maid taking charge of Georgiana's hair while Bernard watched attentively. Georgiana's maid was young and inexperienced but she and Georgiana had already developed a bond of trust, and Elizabeth thought that she would do very well. She seemed eager to learn from her mentor, François.

Since Georgiana had worn her sea-green gown to the earlier ball, Elizabeth had helped her select material for another to wear to her aunt's ball. It was a magnificent monochrome creation of translucent gold tissue and lace with a white lining, low cut in the bodice and with puffed sleeves that ended just above her long, satiny-white gloves. It would make a perfect frame for the Darcy diamonds, which she wore again around her neck and on her ears, with one brooch to embellish her hair. After Georgiana was ready, Elizabeth hurriedly dressed in her wedding gown and her sapphires and they were both ready by the time the carriage pulled up to the door.

They arrived at Longford House a half hour before the ball was to start so they could take their places in the reception line when the guests began arriving. Lady Whitwell informed them that she had sent a routine invitation to the prince regent for the ball, and had been surprised when she received an acknowledgement informing her that His Majesty would pay a call during the ball.

"His Majesty will give our ball significant *cachet*, but we must now delegate one of the servants to watch for his carriage so we can greet him properly." She added dryly, "I cannot imagine that our little ball would hold much interest for His Majesty, so most likely he will only stay a few minutes." Turning to her niece, she added, "Georgiana, my dear, you look lovely. It will be a long night for you, so let us go into the library; a very small glass of wine will fortify you for the tasks ahead of you."

After a few minutes, Lord St. George appeared from upstairs and joined Georgiana at the wine decanter while the rest talked in the hall about the arrangements for the ball and Lady Whitwell instructed them in their roles.

"My dear cousin Georgiana," St. George said suavely, "I am happy to be able to spend a few minutes alone with you. I have wanted to talk to you for some time."

"Really?" she asked, raising her brows slightly.

He did not appear to notice her repressive tone, and continued with an affectionate smile, "Yes, my dear, I have been quite overcome since seeing you again after our long separation. You are a beautiful woman, Georgiana, and I am deeply in love with you. I hope that you will consent to be my wife."

He looked at her longingly and awaited her answer.

"I am sorry, Cousin, but I cannot," she said quietly.

He started and stared at her. "What?" He made a motion with his hand as if he wished to recall his exclamation.

"I said that I will not marry you," she enunciated slowly.

"And why not, may I ask?" he said, his voice rising.

"I do not think that we are compatible, Cousin," she said, looking at him calmly.

"What are you waiting for, a duke?" he said with a curl of his lip. "I cannot imagine why else you would reject my suit."

"No, I do not imagine that you can," she said coldly.

"Well I hope you are not, because, my *dear* cousin, you are neither rich enough nor beautiful enough to capture a duke," he hissed.

Georgiana looked at him with a steely eye that caused him to momentarily quail, then she said, very quietly, "I fear, Cousin, that you have forgotten how you treated me when I was a child; however I have *not* forgotten any of the times that you pushed me, or pulled my hair, or maliciously broke my toys. I also suspect that you now find my company acceptable only because my husband will be the recipient of £30,000 when I marry. I, on the other hand, have no desire to marry a spoiled child who will throw away his patrimony and my dowry on gambling and dissipation."

Lord St. George glared at her, speechless for a moment, then attempted to gather the shreds of his dignity and said distantly, "Well, I would not want to pressure you into a marriage that was distasteful to you, Cousin."

"Excellent," she said, and immediately set down her wine glass and left the library.

When the first carriage pulled up, Georgiana had rejoined her family in the hall and appeared to be ready to greet their guests, but Elizabeth was surprised to see that her eyes glittered darkly and her mouth was compressed. She did not have time to talk to her before the first couple appeared, but she watched her covertly during the long reception line. Whatever had upset Georgiana, she did her part correctly, if not with perfect ease, introducing Elizabeth to those guests who had not met her previously. Elizabeth turned from making conversation with an arriving family she had met at an earlier party and realised that the colonel had also arrived, and appeared to have been there for some while. She was diverted to see that he had taken a place at one side of Georgiana, while Lord St. George stood stiffly at her other side.

As the first of the guests had arrived, Elizabeth saw Lady Whitwell signal the orchestra to start the dancing. Lord St. George came to claim the first dance with Georgiana, bowing very formally to her. After a preliminary short number while the dancers sorted themselves into lines, with Lord St. George and Georgiana at the head, they struck up a lively dance. Elizabeth and Darcy had been placed within sight of the refreshment table where they could inform Lady Whitwell if it needed attention, and Elizabeth watched Georgiana with veiled apprehension. Her eyes were again glittering above her noncommittal smile, while her partner's face was an unreadable mask, his feelings betrayed only by the narrow line of his mouth.

"I think Georgiana and Lord St. George must have quarreled," Elizabeth whispered to Darcy.

He turned his attention to the dancers and, after watching them for a few moments, nodded. "I think you must be right. What do you suppose they are quarreling about?"

"I do not know," she said vaguely as she stared at them, and then added to herself, "but I could make an educated guess."

The first dances finished. Lord St. George bowed stiffly again to Georgiana after leading her from the floor, while she returned the bare minimum of a curtsey. Colonel Fitzwilliam came to claim the two dances for which he had engaged her, and she turned to him with a slow smile, which continued to play about her lips all during their dances. She again lifted her eyes to his each time they faced each other in the figure. The colonel seemed pleased with his partner but glanced frequently at his brother, who was partnering Miss Bingley. Caroline, at any rate, seemed very happy with the attention and her face was wreathed in smiles during the dances.

Whatever was ailing Georgiana and Lord St. George, neither seemed to let it ruin their evening and they both danced every dance—but they seemed to manage to avoid meeting each other off the dance floor. St. George and the colonel did their duties as the sons of the house and made sure that every young woman had her share of partners, but Elizabeth was relieved when the colonel managed a second pair of dances with Georgiana.

Late in the evening, Elizabeth happened to glance over at Lady Whitwell at the moment when a footman approached and whispered in her ear. She quietly signaled the orchestra leader and they struck up "God Save the King" just as the prince regent and several of his retinue entered the ballroom. The family all greeted him very formally, and he spoke with each of them for a moment. When he got to Darcy and Elizabeth, he raised her from her curtsey and said:

"Ah, dear lady, I believe that we met not two days ago." He glanced at Darcy with a rather mischievous look in his eye. "I hope that your esteemed husband will forgive me if I beg for your hand for the next dance."

Elizabeth raised one brow slightly, but consented with a graceful curtsey. She could not imagine why the prince regent would be interested in dancing with her. She knew that there must be many women in the highest circles who would be far lovelier and much more polished than herself. Darcy bowed to his ruler to indicate his approval of the invitation, but his face was a polite mask. Elizabeth advanced to the dance floor, her hand on the prince regent's arm and, as they stood at the head of the line for the start of the dance, felt an astonishment superior to any she had experienced before.

The prince regent was a personable man and, in spite of his corpulence, his smile was attractive; and he put himself out to be agreeable to Elizabeth. She answered his conversation politely but rather warily, not wanting to step out of correct protocol, and schooled her face to show nothing but calm interest in her partner's conversation. In spite of all her efforts, she was unable to completely contain her marvel at her current situation.

She glanced over at the family group and saw Miss Bingley standing with Viscount St. George. Miss Bingley's eyes were narrowed and she whispered rapidly in the viscount's ear. Georgiana was standing with her arm through her brother's, and was smiling at her.

The prince regent began asking courteous questions about where she was from, and where she had met Darcy. She glanced at Darcy at this question and found that he was watching the prince regent without expression. She smiled at him and his face relaxed; the corners of his lips turned up slightly, and he sketched a small bow in her direction. When the dance finished the prince regent escorted her off the floor to where Darcy was standing and thanked her for the pleasure of dancing with her. She gave him a reserved smile, and curtseyed as she said:

"I thank you, Your Majesty, for the great honour."

After a few more minutes of conversation with the guests, the prince and his entourage left and the ball went on, unchanged except for the murmurs of wonder around the room over the honour conferred by the appearance of the prince regent, and the fact that he had danced with Mrs. Darcy.

When the dancing had continued, and the guests' attention had turned away for a moment, Elizabeth whispered to Darcy:

"And what am I to make of that situation? I am perplexed as to why the prince regent chose to ask me to dance."

Darcy smiled wryly. "I think that His Majesty was curious about you. He also likes to occasionally show his power as an arbiter of fashion and has apparently decided that he endorses your entrance into the *beau monde*. His approval will give you and Georgiana *entré* into all levels of society, should you wish it."

Elizabeth gave a small shrug and went back to watching the dancers.

After the prince regent's visit a number of the guests who had merely acknowledged Elizabeth when they arrived came over to talk to her: the obvious result of the prince's favour shown her. Several of the women proffered invitations to tea to Elizabeth, and some of the gentlemen suddenly seemed to recognise Darcy, inviting him to ride or to meet them at their club for a glass of wine. Both Darcys responded with all the courtesy required, but noncommittally, and eventually the sycophants faded away again.

Elizabeth was having a glass of punch late in the evening when she felt a hand on her arm. She turned to see Georgiana, who look perplexed.

"Have you seen Colonel Fitzwilliam, Elizabeth?"

Elizabeth glanced around the room but did not see the colonel. "I am sorry, Georgiana, I have not seen him in quite some time."

Georgiana looked disappointed, although she tried to hide her chagrin. "I was hoping to dance with him again tonight."

Elizabeth was about to reassure her sister when a sudden wave of dizziness overcame her. Georgiana saw the colour drain out of her face, and said in alarm: "Are you well, Elizabeth?"

Darcy turned from where he had been talking to a group of gentlemen when he heard his sister's voice. "Elizabeth? Are you ill?"

Elizabeth tried to subdue the dizziness, but finally said in a whisper, "My dear, could you please help me out of the room?"

He took her arm and they left unobtrusively, with Georgiana behind them. As soon as they reached the hall Elizabeth could no longer hold herself up and she sagged on Darcy's arm. He lifted her and carried her upstairs to one of the sitting-rooms and gently set her down on the sofa. As he put a throw pillow under her head he said firmly:

"Elizabeth, I am calling the doctor."

She protested weakly, "No, I am feeling better. If I just lie here a few minutes I will be fine."

Lady Whitwell entered the room. "One of the footmen told me that you were feeling faint. I have sent for the doctor and he will be here soon."

Darcy thanked his aunt while she put her hand on Elizabeth's forehead. "She does not seem to have a fever. Are you still feeling unwell, my dear?"

"I am better, thank you," Elizabeth said as she tried to sit up. "It was just a momentary dizziness."

Darcy and Lady Whitwell both said, "No" firmly and she was unable to oppose their combined wills; she reclined again.

The doctor arrived in a quarter hour and the others left the room while he examined Elizabeth. When he came out of the room Darcy said anxiously:

"How is she, Doctor?"

The doctor smiled wryly, "She is fine. She needs to rest."

When Darcy looked a little confused the doctor added, with a slightly ironic smile, "Go in and see your wife, sir."

Darcy entered the room and sat at Elizabeth's side.

"The doctor says that you need to rest, my love."

She smiled beatifically at him and took his hand.

"I am going to have a baby."

His eyes opened wide in surprise, and then he put his arms around her and kissed her tenderly on the forehead. "You are? When?"

"In about five months."

He kissed her again, and they both forgot about the ball in their happiness, and in his relief that she was not ill. After a few minutes, Darcy suddenly sat back and chuckled.

"What are you laughing about, my dear?" Elizabeth said with a quizzical smile.

"It just occurred to me that I should have been prepared for this. It was very unlikely that you would let your sister Jane perform an act as significant as having a child without you joining her."

She laughed with him and admitted the truth of his observation.

Later at home he told her what the prince regent had said concerning her when Darcy had met with him in March, which he had forgotten until the ball. She was amused that their marriage could have an effect so opposite to Lady Catherine's dire predictions.

"Did you have time to talk to Georgiana and find out why she and St. George are not speaking?"

"No, I am afraid that I forgot," she said.

"Well," he commented philosophically, "if it is important, I am sure we will eventually find out." The matter was dropped.

Chapter 27

To sanction Vice, and hunt Decorum down.
Lord Byron, "English Bards and Scotch Reviewers"

The next day found a great increase in the number of invitations that were received at Ashbourne House. Darcy cynically discarded most of them as bids to gain their favour after the prince regent's actions the night before. One of them, however, he held for a moment, his lips pursed.

Elizabeth was writing a letter to her friend Charlotte and telling her about her expectations, but she looked up at him and asked curiously, "What is it, my dear?"

"An invitation to a party at Lord Rathburn's this evening. He is a member of the prince's coterie and was with him when he came to the ball last night. My initial impulse is to discard it with the others, but Rathburn was at Cambridge with me and was not a bad fellow. We have not kept in contact, but perhaps we should attend; it might be interesting for you to see how the highest circles entertain. I would not want to take Georgiana into those circles until I see how they behave these days, but she has a party this evening with my aunt and uncle. Some of the *haut ton* affairs can be rather decadent but we can always leave if it is too warm for our taste."

"I am almost afraid to ask what sorts of things go on at these affairs," Elizabeth said dryly.

"I would not even mention some of the things in the presence of a lady; however, Rathburn's invitation says that it is 'an evening with a few friends.'"

"I have no objections if you wish to go, dear," said Elizabeth, and she continued to sort the visiting cards that had been received the day before.

They arrived at Lord Rathburn's residence a half hour after the start of the party and were greeted by their host before entering the drawing-room. Lord Rathburn was unmarried and a cousin did the honors as hostess. He received his introduction to Elizabeth with slightly blurred courtesy and, in turn, introduced the Darcys to his cousin, Miss Foster, before handing them over to a footman, who bowed them into the salon. The crush of people in the room made movement difficult, but they managed to slowly make their way to the refreshment table, hampered by frequent stops to greet Darcy's acquaintances and to introduce Elizabeth. She could hear music in the adjoining room and presumed that there was dancing, but could not see over the sea of heads between her and the door. The refreshments were piled high on the table, an extravagant display of delicacies of every sort, and champagne was flowing freely.

After obtaining a cup of punch for each of them, Darcy led the way to the inner room in search of breathing space.

"So much for 'a few friends,'" he murmured in Elizabeth's ear, and she nodded.

The dance floor was sparsely filled as a cotillion began. They managed to find two seats near a window where they could observe the dancers and find some relief from the suffocating heat. Elizabeth did not recognise any of the people in the two rooms through which they had passed, and Darcy did not stop except to briefly introduce her, so she assumed that he had not found any acquaintances to his taste. It would have been difficult to converse in either of the rooms in any case because of the terrific clamour of voices and music.

After watching the dancers and greeting the occasional associate or old schoolfellow for about half an hour, Darcy, looking bored, offered to fetch Elizabeth another drink. She accepted gratefully; she was very warm and was happy to cool herself with her fan and look out the window at the full moon, which glazed the tops of the trees with silver.

He had not been gone long when the string quartet struck up a different sort of tune than those that had preceded it. Elizabeth looked around at the dance floor and her eyes widened as she saw the dancers pair off in couples. Although she had never seen it danced, she suddenly realised that they were starting a waltz. She was nonplussed and debated with herself whether it would be preferable to remain where she was and have it thought that she condoned such activities, or to try to make her way quietly towards the salon and risk losing Darcy in the crowd. As she hesitated, trying to appear unconcerned, she saw a movement to her right from the corner of her eye and turned to find herself confronted with—not her husband as she had expected, but Lord Rathburn. Her host bowed unsteadily and requested her hand for the dance. As she paused, too shocked to immediately answer, Rathburn slurred, "C'mon, Mrs. Darcy. I'm sure your husband wouldn't mind you dancing with an' ol' schoolfellow." His had stumbled over the final word but managed another wobbly bow.

"I … I am sorry, I do not waltz, my lord," she finally exerted herself to say.

She was frantically racking her mind to find a way of extricating herself without causing an unpleasant scene, when relief came from an unexpected quarter. A voice behind her, filled with disgust, said sharply:

"Rathburn, you are disgracefully drunk or you would not even consider insulting a lady such as Mrs. Darcy with your offensive suggestion."

Rathburn attempted to draw himself up in affronted dignity, but only succeeded in throwing off whatever precarious balance he still possessed and was forced to lean on the back of a chair to remain upright.

"I say, Byron, you've no right ..."

"I have the right of any man of culture and manners to prevent an insult to a lady."

Lord Byron stopped a young woman in a scandalously diaphanous gown who was passing and said heartily:

"Mrs. Carleton, our host desires to waltz with you but is too modest to ask. I beg you to indulge him."

The woman smiled and eyed Rathburn. "I am not sure that Lord Rathburn is up to the waltz at this moment, my lord."

"Do try, please, for my sake. He will be desolated if he does not waltz tonight." He gave her an intimate smile, and she agreed, taking her partner's hand and steering him carefully onto the dance floor.

"I apologise for Rathburn's behaviour, Mrs. Darcy. I am sure that if he was not in a drunken stupor, he would not behave like such an idiot ..." Lord Byron began, when Darcy suddenly reappeared behind his left shoulder, to Elizabeth's relief. Following her eyes, Lord Byron looked around at Darcy, who towered over him, and greeted him coolly. Darcy bowed courteously enough, but Elizabeth caught a quickly quenched blaze of anger in his eyes before he did so, and she knew that he had seen her predicament. She stood abruptly and turned to her rescuer.

"I hope that you will excuse me, my lord, but I am not feeling very well. The heat is stifling and I was only waiting for his return to ask my husband to take me home."

"I am desolated, Mrs. Darcy, but I hope that you will feel better with some fresh air. Perhaps we will meet another time under more auspicious circumstances."

"Perhaps. I thank you for your assistance," she managed to say with finality.

She curtseyed, and they left the room as quickly as they could through the salon, which seemed even more crowded than when they had arrived. Their host was still struggling through the waltz with his partner, and his cousin was hidden somewhere in the crowd, obviating the need to say good night. Neither Darcy nor Elizabeth spoke until they were safely in their carriage and on their way home.

"I am absolutely livid that that disgraceful rake had the audacity to ask you to waltz with him," Darcy began to whisper angrily. "How dare he insult you with his disgusting attentions!"

Elizabeth tried to calm him by patting his arm and saying:

"It is over, my dear. I really do not think that he was trying to offer me an insult. I suspect that Lord Rathburn thinks that any woman would be eager to waltz with him. After all, his patron, the prince, has given the dance his tacit approval by not speaking out against it. I told Lord Rathburn very clearly that I did not waltz, so it is not likely to happen again. In his state, he will probably not even remember the incident in the morning. I have to say, however, that I was delighted that you appeared when you did. I was not sure how to extricate myself from my rescuer, and I did not like to be rude when he had aided me." Darcy shook his head, the heat of his anger beginning to subside, and after a moment, she added archly, "Well, I certainly learned how the *haut ton* enjoy themselves, did I not?"

This drew a small smile from him and the dry comment, "Indeed, yes. Now you also know why I don't associate a great deal with that crowd. If I had realised that this would happen, and how pervasive was the debauchery of the royal following, I would never have taken you there, and I apologise. I thought that Rathburn would have more sense."

"Fortunately, no real harm was done, so we might as well forget it," she said in a soothing voice. "Lord Byron was able to deflect our host before he became obstreperous."

"I am not at all pleased that Lord Byron was the one who rescued you, either. He is not a man to whom I wish to have an obligation. I am surprised that he does not approve of the waltz."

Elizabeth hesitated a moment, then said gently, "He is probably making a virtue of necessity, my love. He is most likely not able to dance well with his deformity."

Darcy looked a little chagrined, but his eyes sparked. "You are probably right. I find it a bit hypocritical of him to condemn it, however, when he has performed many acts far worse than dancing the waltz."

"Mmm. I am just glad that Georgiana was not with us."

"I would most certainly agree with that sentiment."

She rested her hand affectionately in his, and they made the rest of the ride home in silence.

The next morning, Elizabeth told Georgiana about the incident and she was shocked.

"Do you mean that he thought that you would allow a stranger to touch your … your *person* while you danced? That is unbelievable."

"It is. There were, however, plenty of couples who were waltzing, so there are obviously some who think that it is acceptable. And truthfully, it would not really be shocking if all of the couples were married."

Georgiana lowered her voice and glanced around. "What does the waltz look like?"

Elizabeth peeked out of the door to make sure that there was no one to see them, then took Georgiana's right hand in her left and put her right hand at Georgiana's waist, standing about twelve inches from her and facing her. She tried to imitate the steps but they both kept tripping over each other's feet, so Elizabeth tried to show her by herself, turning in graceful circles as she swept around the room.

"I am not sure if I have the footwork down, but this gives you an idea. It actually would be quite beautiful to watch, if it were not so scandalous to see unmarried couples dancing that way. And ... Georgiana?"

"Yes?"

"Please do not tell your brother that I told you about last evening or showed you the dance—I believe that he would not approve of this conversation. However, I feel that it is better to know how to avoid society's pitfalls rather than to pretend that they do not exist."

Georgiana smiled impishly and said, "Of course, Elizabeth, I would not *dream* of mentioning this to him."

Chapter 28

So he passed over, and the
Trumpets sounded for him on the other side.
John Bunyan, "The Pilgrim's Progress"

Early in the afternoon, Georgiana was sitting alone in the drawing-room again working on her new sonata. Elizabeth had retired upstairs to rest, and Darcy had gone to his library to meet with his man of business. The house was quiet. Georgiana was surprised when Burton announced Colonel Fitzwilliam. She blushed slightly but greeted him politely and asked Burton to bring them some coffee. But when she started to move away from the instrument he exclaimed:

"No, do not move. I'll pull a chair up next to you."

She sat back down on the bench, but picked up Lucky, who had been sitting beside her, and put him on her lap with her fingers entwined in his hair to conceal their trembling. She stared at the keys, feeling as if a hand was twisting her stomach into several knots. The colonel asked her how Elizabeth was feeling and she was about to answer when the coffee arrived. She thanked the footman breathlessly, following him with her eyes as he departed and closed the door. The colonel cleared his throat as she turned back to stare again at the pianoforte keys and, after a pause, said:

"Georgiana ... I am relieved that you are alone this afternoon because I wanted to talk to you."

He seemed to lose his voice momentarily, and Georgiana glanced up at him quickly and then back down at the keys. His face was flushed. He pulled at his collar, cleared his throat again, and finally said:

"I want to tell you that, well, that I ... I love you." He took a deep breath and hurried on "I mean, I, of course, have always loved you as a little sister, but now, in the last few weeks, I have come to realise that you are the most important person in the world to me, and I wanted to know if you would consider ... if-you-would-do-me-the-honor-of-becoming-my-wife ..."

He stopped in confusion and then leapt to his feet as her face blanched white and she closed her eyes.

"Are you all right, Georgiana? I am sorry; I did not mean to upset you ..."

Her face suffused with colour again, and she opened her eyes and turned to him. She took his hand with a smile of such happiness on her face that he was unable to support himself; he sank back down onto his chair as she whispered:

"I thought that you would never ask."

Interpreting this correctly as an assent, Colonel Fitzwilliam took her hand, placed it gently against his heart and said:

"Georgiana, my darling, I have been in agony for, oh, I do not know how long—it seems like an eternity—trying to decide if I dared tell you how I feel. I was so afraid that you would say no, or, worse yet, say yes only because you felt an obligation to me."

They talked for some minutes, he of how he had gradually come to realise that his feelings for her were not those of merely a cousin or a guardian, and she of how she had grown to love him over the years and how she had struggled to try to make him see that she was no longer a child. The colonel finally said, still rather diffidently:

"I have been walking around the last few weeks feeling very strange. When I see myself in a mirror, I look exactly the same on the outside as I ever have, but inside I feel rather like the vase over there would look," he pointed to a bouquet on the table in a crystal vase, "if you struck it with a hammer."

"Shattered?" she whispered with a small smile.

"Indeed yes, shattered is the perfect description of my state. I wondered that it was not visible to everyone I met. I left the ball early last night, risking my mother's displeasure, because I could no longer bear to see you dancing with so many men who were younger, richer, and more handsome than I…. I have so little to offer you beyond my devotion, and you deserve everything good in the world."

"I do not care about anyone else but you, dearest Edward, and I never have."

He kissed her hands affectionately and softly continued:

"I was particularly afraid that my brother would make you an offer and that you would accept him," he said. "He has so much more to offer you in the way of fortune, but it would be unbearable to me to see you married to him when I would meet you frequently as a close relative—and you would be the wife of another man." He added grimly, "As your guardian, I also felt that you could do so much better than a soldier with no patrimony."

Georgiana turned to him with a small smile. "Lord St. George did make me an offer: last night before the ball." Fitzwilliam sat up straighter in surprise. "I turned him down. Your brother seems to think that I am unable to remember how badly he treated me when I was a child," she said tartly. "It was understandable that a young man of more than twenty years would not be interested in spending time with a little girl thirteen years younger than he, but he was always scornful of me when you and my brother were not present. I am afraid that I do not believe his character has undergone any revolution since then, in spite of his compliments and attention." She added in a softer tone, "You, on the other hand, dear Edward, were invariably kind to me."

"I hope that you have not agreed to marry me merely because I was not unkind to you when you were six years old."

"I am afraid my gratitude to you for teaching me to ride my pony does not extend that far!" she exclaimed.

He kissed her hands again and then went on to tell her:

"I felt for a long time that I would rather risk losing you than to take the chance of putting a wall between us forever; but I finally realised that the years would stretch out in an eternity of regret if I did not at least try."

They soon agreed that he would go speak to her brother immediately and ask for his consent. He left the room just as Elizabeth was entering, and bowed to her with a bewildered expression on his face. She turned to Georgiana with a questioning look when he had shut the door. Georgiana promptly threw herself into her sister's arms and burst into tears.

When the colonel appeared quietly at the library door, Darcy was reading some documents but was alone at his desk, his man of business having left some minutes before.

"Darcy," he said, and his cousin looked up, startled. "Darcy," he said again, his voice tight and strained, "I have asked Georgiana to marry me and she has accepted me. I hope that you will give your consent."

Darcy rolled his eyes heavenward and closed them briefly before saying in a pained voice:

"Good God, man, what took you so long?"

He opened his eyes, laughed briefly at the sheepish look on his cousin's face, and added more seriously, "I will most happily give my consent, Fitzwilliam."

The colonel began to say, not very fluently, that he knew that he had nothing to offer Georgiana in the way of fortune, but Darcy stopped him with an upraised hand, saying quietly:

"Except yourself, Edward, except yourself. If marriage with you is what Georgiana wants, then it is enough."

They shook hands with all the warmth of their many years of mutual regard and respect, then returned together to the drawing-room where Georgiana was sitting silently, holding tightly to Elizabeth's hand and waiting for them. When she saw their faces, she ran to her brother and embraced him, shedding a few more joyous tears, while Elizabeth warmly shook the colonel's hand and wished him joy. When the congratulations were finished and everyone had expressed their pleasure in the prospect of the cousins' marriage several times, the colonel finally recollected himself and said:

"I had best go to Longford House and tell my parents. They will be very happy to finally have one of their sons bring home a bride, especially one with such an irreproachable family background." He grinned at Georgiana.

They all repeated their congratulations and, after extracting a promise to join them for dinner that night, sent him away.

Georgiana spent the rest of the day in a state of happy distraction and seemed unable to quite believe that all her hopes had been realised. Even Lucky had to resort to barking at her several times to get her attention when she was staring into space instead of rolling his ball for him to chase. Elizabeth left her sister to her enjoyment of her happy prospects, and sat with Darcy in the library for an hour in the afternoon.

"Do you think that the colonel will continue with his regiment after he and Georgiana marry?" Elizabeth asked him.

"I don't know; even with Georgiana's fortune he will be hard pressed to afford to live in London with any comfort. We will have to see what he plans and how soon they want to marry."

"I am just happy for Georgiana; I think that she would approve me revealing to you now that she told me in January that she has loved him since she was six years old—as a brother, she thought. She did not know the true nature of her feelings until after the situation with Wickham when she was shocked into the realisation that Wickham meant nothing to her and that it was the colonel she has always loved."

"It is good to know that Wickham has performed one positive service in his life," Darcy said dryly.

She laughed and said, "Indeed," before sending François to get her shawl, for the day was somewhat cool and she and Georgiana were expected at the Bingley's for the afternoon; there was much to tell them.

Jane was surprised and delighted at Georgiana's news, and Miss Bingley was warmly congratulatory to "dear Georgiana," although she had a rather speculative look on her face as she wished her joy.

That evening Colonel Fitzwilliam came early while the ladies were dressing for dinner, and drew Darcy into the library. Darcy looked at the expression on his face and said:

"What in the world is the matter, Fitzwilliam?"

"I just wanted to let you know," he said uncomfortably, "that I went home this afternoon to tell my parents that Georgiana and I were engaged." He clasped his hands behind his back and stared over Darcy's head at the books behind him. "They, of course, were very pleased with the news—however, my brother was also there. He was astounded when I told my news and said 'I do not believe it!' So I asked him to what he was referring. He said that he did not believe that Georgiana could be so stupid that she would marry me."

"And what did you say?" Darcy asked quietly.

"I foolishly said, 'Do you mean because she would turn you down for me?'"

"Did she?" Darcy said, glancing up in surprise.

"Yes, she told me this afternoon. He asked her to marry him last night before the ball, and was sure that she would not turn down the Viscount St. George, future Earl of Whitwell," Fitzwilliam said bitterly, starting to pace around the room. He suddenly stopped and looked at Darcy with a ghost of his usual mischievous grin. "Actually, I gather from the little that Georgiana said, and from his reaction, that she gave him quite a dressing down. I wish that I could have seen it. Seeing my dear brother receive such a set-down would have been salutary."

"Elizabeth noticed that she looked fairly grim when they rejoined us before the ball, but she did not have a chance to talk to her before the guests arrived. Georgiana seemed to be fine after greeting the guests so Elizabeth did not pursue the subject. So, what did you do after St. George's comments?"

The colonel stopped pacing and stared up at the ceiling, looking embarrassed. "I asked him to go outside with me for a private conversation. I then told him that I did not ever want to hear him say such a thing about my fiancée, or any other respectable young woman, again. He sneered at me and asked me what I was going to do to enforce that demand—so I hit him."

"You what?!" Darcy sat up in his chair.

"You heard me. I am deeply sorry that Georgiana's name should become involved in such a sordid display, but I can at least say that there were no witnesses to it." His lip curled as he added, "My brother, however, will not be partaking of the gaieties of the season for the next week or so, until the black eye that I gave him fades. My parents are absolutely furious with him. My mother is not speaking to him and my father took him into the library while St. George was still holding a wet cloth to his eye and told him (in a booming voice that I am sure all of the servants heard) that he was ashamed to call him his son and that if he could prevent him from inheriting the estate and title he would do so. He also cut off his allowance, which he *does* have the discretion to do. St. George is furious but unrepentant, and you know how stubborn he is." He sighed deeply. "What a mess it is. How did he get to be like this?"

"I do not know, but I know that your mother and father have always seemed to be excellent parents and have tried to make him be a responsible adult. Still, if you recall, he was always very self-centred. I think he must have been born that way. The two of you have always looked very much alike and been the total opposite in temper. Do you remember when we found him throwing rocks at the barn cat at Whitwell Abbey? He just shrugged when we yelled at him and asked why we were so angry: 'it was just an old cat.'"

"Yes, I remember that and a thousand other things. What upsets me the most right now, however, is that I will have to tell Georgiana something about it; she will wonder why St. George is not at any parties over the next week or so."

Darcy drummed his fingers on the desk. "Very true. You will have to tell her. She will probably be embarrassed that you were fighting over her, but on the other hand, you can't leave her in ignorance; she may have more embarrassment having people asking her where he is, or saying something inadvertently." After a moment of silence, he gave his cousin a sly smile. "Besides, what woman would not be secretly happy to have her fiancé proved to be a knight in shining armour, willing to battle for her honour?"

Colonel Fitzwilliam blushed and then grimaced. "I will talk to her this evening and tell her something."

"I suggest that you tell her *everything*. As Elizabeth once pointed out to your father, my sister is not one to be overcome by the truth, even if it is unpalatable, Fitzwilliam. She would not thank you for trying to 'protect' her from reality to that extent."

Fitzwilliam nodded his agreement.

The ladies came downstairs for dinner, and Jane and Bingley and the Gardiners arrived. Elizabeth had invited them to dine a few days before, and now there was a particularly happy reason to have the family gathered. Georgiana was wearing the green gown she had worn to the Elliots' ball, but with her pearl necklace and earrings and the bracelet the colonel had given her for her birthday, and she was flushed with happiness as she accepted their congratulations.

Colonel Fitzwilliam smiled and kissed Georgiana's hand before leading her into the dining-room at the head of the line, a position of importance that pleased Elizabeth greatly.

Later, after the gentlemen had rejoined the ladies in the drawing-room, the colonel took Georgiana to the far end of the room and began talking earnestly to her. While the Gardiners and the Bingleys sat and drank their tea and coffee, Darcy asked Elizabeth to play for them and he sat next to her at the pianoforte so that the two lovers could speak in privacy. Elizabeth was halfway through a sonata when Georgiana burst out giggling. She and Darcy both looked over; Georgiana had her fingers delicately covering her mouth and Fitzwilliam had a self-conscious expression on his face. Then Georgiana took his hand and said something very quietly in his ear, which made him smile foolishly at her.

Later, when they went upstairs, Darcy explained to Elizabeth what had happened at his uncle's house, and she also laughed.

"It serves St. George right!" she exclaimed.

"It does indeed. I cannot believe that my cousin would behave in such an ill-bred fashion, particularly saying such things about his own cousin. I have half a mind to blacken his other eye!" he said scornfully.

Elizabeth laughed again. "That would be very satisfying, no doubt; however, it might be difficult to keep it hushed up if everyone in the family takes a turn at blackening his eyes."

"Unfortunately," Darcy said seriously, "there has always been a great deal of competition between my two cousins, on St. George's side at least. It is rather odd, since he is the one who will inherit everything, including the title and all the entailed property, while Fitzwilliam will get little or nothing. I suspect St. George realises that, for all his wealth and prospects, Fitzwilliam has always been the one whom everyone likes. When we were young boys, Fitzwilliam and I always went off to play without him, because even then he was an arrogant braggart who always wanted to rub our noses in the fact that he would one day be an earl. It probably bothered him very much that neither of us seemed much impressed by him."

"I had wondered why you never mentioned your elder cousin when you are such good friends with the colonel. It is very surprising to me that the colonel is as happy and easy as he is after having to deal with that treatment from his brother for his entire life."

"Well, his parents have always tried to improve St. George's temper and make him face the responsibilities that go along with his status, and Fitzwilliam has always been relaxed and easy; it is just his temper to be contented. My aunt must be very happy that he is marrying Georgiana."

"I am sure she is. She sent her a long note this afternoon telling her so. She wants us all to dine with them tomorrow night, if you have not made other plans."

Darcy chuckled suddenly.

"I wonder if St. George will dine with us."

They both laughed heartily.

The next evening the Darcys arrived at Longford House for dinner, and Georgiana was embraced and kissed by her future mother- and father-in-law.

Darcy and Elizabeth were told how happy they were that they would be even more closely related. They had a very enjoyable dinner and Georgiana was bubbly and talkative in her happiness. Lord St. George did not put in an appearance and was not mentioned by the family.

When they had a moment of privacy in the drawing-room, Lady Whitwell told Elizabeth how pleased she was about the engagement.

"Edward has always been my favourite son, although as a mother I should probably not admit it. I have been worried about his future, since almost the entire estate is entailed; his marriage to Georgiana answers all of my concerns and, of course, makes me very happy for them both. I wish I could feel as sanguine about my eldest son's future," she said, looking rather sadly towards the staircase that led to the upper floors.

Elizabeth took her hand and patted it reassuringly. Lady Whitwell sighed for a moment and then seemed to pull herself up, smiling at Elizabeth.

"Thank you, my dear. I might as well not discuss it. I do not want to put a damper on Georgiana and Edward's happiness tonight, so we will just let the future take care of itself, shall we?"

Elizabeth agreed, and they quietly listened to Georgiana playing the pianoforte.

After they dined, they were all to go to the Bingleys for the party that Jane had been planning. It would be Jane's first foray into entertaining during the London season and Elizabeth hoped that all would go well and help establish her sister in her rightful place in society. It was to be a small party, with friends and relatives, and they would have dancing and cards and would conclude with a late supper. They hurried over their coffee and tea so that they would not be late, and then left for Berkeley Square.

Chapter 29

This man of clay, son of despite.
John Milton, "Paradise Lost"

Jane's party was an unqualified success. The guests included Bingley's relatives—the Hursts and Miss Bingley—as well as a number of friends of Bingley's. The Comte de Tournay was there as well, at Caroline's request, Elizabeth presumed. When the Darcy party entered, Miss Bingley asked whether Lord St. George was with them and Lady Whitwell calmly told her:

"I am so sorry, Miss Bingley, my eldest son is not feeling well tonight and so could not come. However, I am sure that he will be better soon."

Miss Bingley quickly covered her disappointment and spent the evening being charming to the comte. The Blake family and Jonathan Walker were at the party and Kitty was kept happy dancing and, in the intervals, talking with Edward Blake. Georgiana's friend Catherine was also there, as she and Jane had become well acquainted during the season, and she spent the evening conversing with Sir Robert Blake when she was not with Georgiana. A whist table was set up in the parlour adjoining the salon for those guests who could not, or would not, dance, and the dining-parlour offered a variety of refreshments. Jane had been fortunate enough to find a housekeeper for the town house who was highly respectable and very competent, and the arrangements for the party were most elegant.

Elizabeth and Darcy spent the evening talking with their friends and helping to ensure the enjoyment of their brother and sister's guests. Elizabeth took a moment to rest her feet halfway through the evening; she entertained herself by watching her husband as he had a lively conversation with two of Bingley's friends whom she had not yet met. She tried to remember his forbidding appearance when she had first seen him, but the memories were fading, more happily replaced by the amiable countenance that truly reflected his character.

The guests finally trickled out of the door at around one o'clock, leaving the host to relax with one last glass of wine in the company of his nearest relations while Jane rested her feet on a footstool. She looked modestly pleased with the success of her little entertainment, and Elizabeth bolstered her feelings with her own compliments.

"I had a delightful time, my dear sister. Now you can relax for the remaining days of the season and let other hostesses work to entertain you, although your triumph sets a rather high standard for them to maintain."

"Dearest Lizzy! You are always so good to me!"

"Indeed I am not! I am only stating the plain truth of the matter," Elizabeth returned with spirit as she gathered her things for the ride home.

The next morning Darcy went to his club, and when he came home he told Elizabeth the news with a bleak face.

"I saw the colonel while I was at my club. He says that his brother left town this morning and would not say where he was going. He merely told his father that, since he no longer had an allowance to enable him to live like a gentleman in London he was going into the country." After a moment he added, "I wonder what his creditors will think of this turn."

"At least Georgiana will not have to meet him in public."

"Fitzwilliam and I are both concerned about what he is up to, as are his parents, obviously. I hope that he does not do anything to discredit the family name."

"I think that Lord St. George thinks *too* much of the family name, but it is difficult to predict what a man will do when he is angry," Elizabeth said grimly.

"Well, there is, unfortunately, not much we can do about it, whatever it is, but I am sure that my aunt and uncle are going to have a disagreeable time until he reappears."

Elizabeth agreed that this was likely, but could see no hope of improving the situation except to be a support to Lord St. George's parents. Darcy agreed, and decided to visit his uncle that afternoon.

Several days went by without news of Lord St. George. The colonel was divided between his happiness with his engagement and concern over his brother and what he might do in the heat of his anger and resentment. Georgiana tried to keep his spirits up and his mind off Lord St. George, with some success, and they both basked in the good wishes of all of their friends.

Catherine Freemont called on Georgiana often, and showed a lively interest in her friend's situation and happiness. And as always, Georgiana took delight in her company. Miss Freemont, Elizabeth noted with pleasure, took great care to include Kitty in all of their conversations, which was very kind of her and a credit to her good breeding. As usual, Georgiana had shown good sense in her choice of friends, notwithstanding the episode with Wickham.

Georgiana even received a letter of congratulations from Lady Catherine after the engagement was published in the papers, which she showed to Elizabeth:

MY DEAR NIECE,—

Congratulations on your engagement to Colonel Fitzwilliam. The match is highly suitable and I am very happy that you, unlike some people, are willing to do your duty to the family. Give my regards to the colonel and his family.—Sincerely,

LADY CATHERINE DE BOURGH

"My aunt would not be quite so pleased had she known that I turned down Lord St. George to marry the younger son of the family," Georgiana stated smugly.

"I am surprised that she is not angry because she might have gotten the colonel for her daughter. After all, a younger son and an heiress with no brothers or sisters: what could be better?" Elizabeth smiled mischievously at her.

Georgiana responded with a delicate snort, and they moved on to more agreeable topics.

The next day the Darcys were at breakfast when Burton announced Charles Bingley. They all looked up in surprise at this early call. Bingley's eyes were sparkling as he, at Darcy's invitation, sat down at the table. After the footman had laid his place and retired from the breakfast parlour, Bingley burst out with:

"I thank you. I ran over without breakfasting in order to bring you the big news. I wanted to let you know that Caroline accepted a proposal of marriage from the Comte de Tournay."

They all exclaimed over this and demanded further details.

"He came to me this morning and asked for my permission. He apparently asked her during a party they both attended last night. She must have given up on Lord St. George when he disappeared from London. I feel very odd, by the bye, giving permission, as the head of the household, for my sister to marry someone old enough to be my father," he said in some embarrassment.

They all laughed at him and gave him their congratulations, and Elizabeth added that she and Georgiana would call on Miss Bingley later in the day to convey their felicitations to her in person.

As Darcy was seeing him out after breakfast, Bingley added quietly, "Caroline is absolutely indecently happy about her engagement. I am sure that she has never forgiven you for marrying Elizabeth instead of her, and she is gloating over the fact that she will be a *comtesse* while Elizabeth is a commoner. Oh, she hasn't been so vulgar as to say it aloud, but I can see it by the look in her eyes."

Darcy smiled and answered formally, "Well, I sincerely hope that Miss Bingley has all the enjoyment of her title that she deserves," and, after Bingley gave him an ironic glance, sent him on his way.

That afternoon, Elizabeth and Georgiana called on the Bingleys and gave Miss Bingley their best wishes. She was very condescendingly gracious to both of them and Elizabeth later told Darcy:

"I felt rather like a peasant who was noticed by a royal personage—far more so than when I danced with a true royal personage."

She was very amused by Caroline's preening during the visit and had difficulty keeping her countenance serious and sincere, but Georgiana, noticing the look in her eyes, squeezed her arm under the cover of her shawl. That captured her attention, and she was able to sip her tea and control herself, although she was unable to look at Georgiana for fear of losing her composure again. The visit finished and, when they were safely in the carriage, both of them relieved their feelings by giggling uncontrollably for several minutes.

"I must thank you, my dear sister, for pinching my arm," Elizabeth said as she dabbed at her eyes with her handkerchief. "I needed something to draw my attention. I am afraid that you will think me very ill-bred for being unable to keep my composure; however, Miss Bingley and I have a long history. I fear that her pride and condescension will be boundless now that she will have a title." She sighed and shook her head.

"Yes, I expect that it will. Well, I hope that a title is enough to ensure her enjoyment of a life encompassed by marriage to a man who is twice as old as she and who has not a sou." She coloured suddenly in confusion, realising that some ill-natured gossips might make similar comments about her engagement. She finally said, with downcast eyes, "I hope, at least, that there is some affection between them. They have not known each other long."

Elizabeth took her hand. "I hope so, too, my dear."

They finished their ride home in silence and spent the rest of the day quietly reading; they had another ball to attend that night as the season wound down to its finish. There would be only a week until they would leave town and return to Pemberley. Elizabeth was looking forward to returning to the retirement and serenity of the country, where they could relax and rest and get away from the soot of London.

Georgiana enjoyed the ball and Elizabeth thought that she could detect not-too-well-concealed relief on the faces of some of the debutantes; her sister-in-law was no longer competing with them for a husband and had, in addition, not taken one of the available older sons. On the way home Elizabeth commented on this, but Georgiana serenely shrugged off the lesser feelings of her acquaintances:

"They, of course, do not realise that I was never competing with them in the first place, and that they are welcome to any future lord or landholder that they can enchant, with my blessings."

Elizabeth patted her hand fondly.

Lord Whitwell came to see Darcy the next morning, and was closeted with him for about an hour in his library. Later, Darcy told Elizabeth about the meeting.

"We discussed what we wanted to do for Georgiana and the colonel. My uncle would like to give them Longford House. I had not realised that it is not included in the entail, but he purchased it himself years ago and held it out of the entail because of his concerns about his eldest son's behaviour. My aunt and uncle prefer to spend most of their time in the country, and Longford House is large enough to accommodate them as guests when they come to town. They have a smaller house near Berkeley Square, just around the corner from Bingley's house, which is leased out and is in the entail and will go to St. George when he inherits. I thought that I would see if I can find a small estate near Pemberley to give them for a wedding present, so we could see them often and so Georgiana can benefit from your society when the colonel must be in town."

"That will be lovely! I am sure that they will not want to be near Whitwell Abbey when your cousin inherits."

"No, my uncle felt, as I did, that it would be better for them to be in another part of the county, and settling near Pemberley would solve that difficulty. My uncle is trying to decide what to do about St. George. They have still not heard from him since he left town. My uncle is quite exercised in his mind, as he is struggling to determine how to be fair to both of his sons. He is hoping that St. George is somewhere quietly thinking about his iniquities and resolving to change, but fears that it is not so."

"Well, however the problem of St. George resolves itself it will not affect Georgiana's happiness. She tells me that they want to wait until next spring to get married, soon after she turns eighteen. Lady Whitwell would like them to have the wedding at St. George's in Hanover Square, but Georgiana and the colonel have not yet decided if that is what they desire."

"Hopefully, Fitzwilliam will be able to get to Pemberley often this summer, once the season is over and the turmoil from Napoleon's defeat dies down. Now that Napoleon is on Elba, the situation in Europe should stabilise."

Chapter 30

... virtue solely is the sum of glory,
And fashions men with true nobility.
Christopher Marlowe, "Tamburlaine the Great"

As the week neared its end, they were beginning to prepare for their return to Pemberley. There was much to do in the way of packing and planning after such a long stay in town and Elizabeth was kept busy supervising the servants. After several days of bustle they were finally ready to depart and planned to leave early the next morning. Georgiana was rather downcast to be leaving her fiancé, but was trying to keep her spirits up by anticipating how beautiful it would be in Darbyshire at this time of year. On their last evening in town they were engaged to dine with the Bingleys, who would also be leaving in the next day or two and taking Kitty with them to Netherfield. The colonel was also invited to dine and arrived at Ashbourne House early. He was announced to Darcy, who was in his library reading, and said:

"I am sorry to interrupt your plans to leave, Darcy, but the prince regent wants to meet with you tomorrow at one o'clock."

"Whatever for? We have no further business to conduct since I last saw him," Darcy said shortly.

"I know only what I have told you, Cousin," he said, holding up his hands in submission. "I am, once again, merely acting as a messenger."

Darcy sighed and said, "All right, I will be there. I can hardly refuse, can I?"

Elizabeth was disappointed that they were to put off their departure, but they would have an enjoyable dinner with the Bingleys that evening, and then she and Jane could use this unforeseen opportunity to see each other again the next day. They then would all leave London on the same morning.

Georgiana was rather quiet all evening, as was the colonel, but they spent every moment possible with their heads together, talking. Miss Bingley, on the other hand, was a picture of vivacity as she fawned over her fiancé, who was also present, until even Elizabeth's amusement at her behaviour began to wear thin.

The next day was spent in waiting. All of their things were packed and ready to go in the carriages, but they must await the pleasure of the prince regent. Elizabeth was hard put to not comment on his rudeness in waiting until they were almost in the carriage before he demanded to see her husband.

Darcy left the house in good time for his appointment at the palace and was gone for more than three hours. When he returned to Park Street, the door was opened by Burton himself instead of one of the footmen.

"Welcome home, my lord."

Darcy stopped in astonishment and stared at the old butler.

"How did you know, Burton?"

Burton just smiled smugly.

"Does everyone in the household know?"

"No, my lord! Of course not!" he said, shocked, "Mr. Oliver and I would not say anything until we had your permission!"

Elizabeth and Georgiana were in the music room practicing a duet when Darcy came in. Elizabeth saw that he was holding a piece of paper in his hand and had a rather odd look on his face: a combination of amusement and chagrin.

"What in the world is the matter?" she asked in surprise.

He merely handed them the paper, which was a letter of patent renewing the title of Earl of Winslow and bestowing it upon Fitzwilliam Edward George Darcy, "for his support and assistance to the Crown." Elizabeth's mouth dropped open for a moment and she was unable to speak; while Georgiana stared at the letter in confusion. Darcy obviously noted the rapidly changing expressions on their faces as they comprehended all of the ramifications of his title, for he started laughing, but soon controlled himself and gave them the details of his afternoon.

"The prince regent evidently felt that he owed me a debt after this spring, and this particular gift costs him nothing. There are no lands with it or other benefits beyond the title because they all devolved to the king when the title fell out of usage."

He paused for a moment, looking at the letter and then added with a sardonic smile, "In fact, I am sure that he particularly enjoyed giving me this, since he knows that it means that I will have the duty to become a member of the House of Lords and come to London when Parliament meets. He knows me well enough to know that I will not shirk my responsibility, however repugnant it is. I believe he also means it as a snub to my aunt, Lady Catherine, since she will be absolutely livid to find that, instead of being ostracized by society, we are moving up to the nobility: particularly so since the title was originally her father's. Fitzwilliam tells me that the prince regent is not very fond of my aunt's domineering nature. He knew her husband well and always felt pity for the poor man being attached to her, however noble her birth. Because of her respect for his title, the prince regent has, fortunately for him, been relatively safe from her personal criticism of his behaviour, but he nonetheless finds her a trial."

"But why did he give the title to you, Brother?" Georgiana asked, a frown creasing her brow.

"I am afraid, my dear, that I cannot tell you that."

"It has something to do with that time you were gone, before my presentation, does it not?"

He kissed her on the top of her head, but did not answer.

Elizabeth finally overcame her shock and breathed, "I am … absolutely astounded."

"There is more. Georgiana, this concerns you. He made the colonel a baron and gave him an estate not five miles from Pemberley."

"Truly? That is wonderful! Where is it?"

"It is the Walker estate."

She looked startled. "What?"

"Yes. This is, I am afraid, very shocking," he said, his face grave. "As you both know, young Walker has mortgaged the entire family estate in order to keep up with his debts while he looks for a rich wife. Apparently, things came to such a difficult pass that he decided to take more direct action to relieve his financial distress, and he joined a group which was smuggling English arms to the Americans and their supporters. When the government agents caught them, his estate was confiscated."

"But it did not really belong to him yet … his father was merely letting him run the estate," Elizabeth protested.

"I presume that, since the charge in this case was treason, they had the powers necessary to take it. It is possible that the elder Walkers could make a claim to have it returned to them, but they are absolutely destroyed by their son's actions and have retired to a small cottage near Derby, where they can hide their shame in anonymity and still see their daughters and their grandchildren. They will have to disown their only son to save some semblance of their good name and a future for their grandchildren in even a modest level of gentle society. It is a tragedy." He shook his head sadly.

Elizabeth shivered and said, "Those poor people. I never did like their son; he reminded me too much of another worthless young man of our acquaintance, although Master Walker was less bad in a way. His face smiled, but his eyes were cold and calculating—unlike Wickham, he was unable to dissemble well enough to hide his true nature, which was beneficial to the rest of us since it allowed us to detect his schemes more easily. The elder Walkers, however, always seemed very friendly and forthright."

She suddenly realised that she had not related the incidents that had occurred with regard to Jonathan Walker before Darcy's aunt and uncle arrived at Pemberley, other events having pushed it out of her mind once the threat was over. So, after a glance at Georgiana, she told him now. His eyes glittered in anger as she told the tale.

"I do not feel such compassion towards the Walker family now. Master Jonathan is very lucky that he did not attempt to force a marriage with Georgiana, or he would have found himself at the wrong end of my pistol when I returned, and my sister would have been left a widow. At any rate, my cousin is now Baron Lambton, and the estate was given to him. I will have to think what I should do about his creditors and about the elder Walkers. I will not now need to look for a country house for Fitzwilliam and Georgiana. The house could, I believe, be made very charming with some modernisation and, of course, the location could not be better." He walked around the room, tapping his leg with the beaver hat which he still held in his hand, having forgotten in his astonishment at Burton's greeting to give it to a footman when he came in.

Georgiana spoke again, sadly, "I feel very sad that my good fortune is at the squire's expense." She paused, then her eyes opened wide and she said, "What about Miss Blake?"

"I do not know what will happen to her. Presumably she will break the engagement. Thank God they had not yet married. They seemed to be in a hurry when they became engaged, but perhaps Sir Robert discouraged too precipitous a marriage after our conversation. Do not worry, my dear, I will do what I can to assist the elder Walkers without offending their pride, but if the colonel refused the estate it would merely go to someone else, and you and Fitzwilliam would have no income to support the responsibilities that come with his title. Also, even if the Walkers applied to the Crown for the return of their property, it was mortgaged for its entire value, and they would never be able to pay it off."

"I suppose that is true, but I still do not feel quite right about it."

"Perhaps if I approached them and said that I know that they could probably obtain the return of their property—but that I would like to buy it, not wanting my sister to be uncomfortable in her home—they would sell it to me. I will want to pay off those that hold the mortgage, at any rate, so you do not have any problems with them in the future and can enjoy your home in good conscience."

"You are so good, my dear brother!" she said, embracing him, "I would feel much better about it if you could try to do that. Elizabeth, could we go see Miss

Blake as soon as we get back to Derbyshire? I assume that they will be home soon."

"Of course, Georgiana, we will go as soon as we can."

Darcy kissed Georgiana on the forehead and escorted the two ladies upstairs so that they could all dress for dinner. Jane and Bingley were coming tonight with Kitty, so they would have one last evening together before both parties left town. The colonel would also be joining them for dinner, and would travel north with them as well, delaying as long as possible his separation from Georgiana. They would have an early evening since everyone was traveling at dawn the next morning. When Burton announced the Bingley party in the drawing-room, Bingley burst out as soon as the door had closed:

"So it *is* true, Darcy! I heard just before we left the house that you had received a title this afternoon! Burton looked as if he could die from happiness when he said 'I will announce you to his lordship and her ladyship.'"

The Darcys and the colonel joined them in their laughter, and they spent the rest of the evening telling them that part of the story which was open for discussion. Their enjoyment was tempered by the sad tale of the Walkers and their son, but Georgiana confessed that she was becoming interested to see the house and what work would need to be done on it.

"I already know one thing that absolutely must be done; we must get rid of those horrible yews that are overwhelming what might otherwise be an attractive house. They are so dark and dank looking! I suppose we shall have to find another name for it once the yews are gone, however."

Darcy and Elizabeth both laughed, but agreed that cutting them down was a good first step towards making the house their own. They stayed up later talking than any of them had planned since this news did not wear out its interest quickly, but eventually their guests left and the inhabitants of Ashbourne House went to bed for what rest they could get before they must rise and travel.

As they were about to part in their sitting-room to go to their dressing-rooms, Darcy suddenly stopped Elizabeth with a touch on her arm and said quietly:

"I had forgotten in the turmoil of the day; I saw that scoundrel Lord Byron today as I entered the palace. He apparently enjoyed the little time he spent with you at Lord Cranton's dinner and Rathburn's party, in spite of your lack of interest in his company, because he asked me to give you his regards. Perhaps it is *because* of your cool reception of his attentions that he realises that you are unique in his experience of London society. There are some men who find a situation such as this a challenge to their charms rather than a damper upon their enthusiasm. I apologise for being remiss in delivering the message, but I must admit that I agreed to give you it without a great deal of enthusiasm." He smiled at her, one brow lifted sardonically.

"Well, I thank you for the message. You have now done your duty by his lordship by delivering it. I believe that our best course against his importunities is indifference. Shall we retire?"

"Indeed, yes, my lady," he said with a courtly bow.

They made the trip to Pemberley in three days, traveling at an easy pace. The weather was warm but not too uncomfortable, and Elizabeth could feel the tension of the last months gradually leaving her as they got closer and closer to home. They arrived in the early afternoon of the third day and were greeted enthusiastically by the staff, who had already heard from Burton of their master's elevation to the peerage. Smithfield was smiling proudly as Darcy and Elizabeth led the way into the hall, while Georgiana and the colonel paused to speak with Mrs. Reynolds and receive her congratulations on their engagement and his new title and estate. Elizabeth gave a sigh of relief as they all entered Pemberley House. They were home.

Chapter 31

How sharper than a serpent's tooth it is
To have a thankless child.
William Shakespeare, "King Lear"

The summer was in full bloom in Derbyshire, and they were all happy to breathe the fresh country air after the coal smoke that hung like an eternal fog over London. The first two days they were home Darcy needed to catch up on the estate business, so Georgiana and the colonel rode over to Coldstream Manor with Elizabeth to see Miss Blake. In the carriage, Georgiana said to the colonel:

"I would like you to take Sir Robert out of the room if I am able to see Miss Blake. I hope that it will not embarrass you if I tell her about my stupidity with Wickham, if I think that it will help her."

He smiled at her. "You may do as you see fit. I trust your judgment, my love."

"Thank you," she returned with an affectionate smile.

When they arrived, the butler told them that Miss Blake was out, so the colonel asked for Sir Robert. They were shown into the drawing-room and Sir Robert came almost immediately. After greeting them he started to apologise for his sister's absence, but Georgiana gently held up her hand.

"We came, Sir Robert, to give Miss Blake our sympathy for the distress which she must be going through. If there is some way that we can help her, I hope that you will please tell us."

He smiled bleakly. "I am most grateful for the friendship that you have shown to my sister, Miss Darcy, but she has refused to see anyone since we returned." He thought for a moment, and then said hesitantly, "I believe, however, that if you do not mind waiting, I will take advantage of your visit and see if I can coax her downstairs."

"We would be most happy to wait," Georgiana said kindly.

Sir Robert left the room, and was gone about fifteen minutes. When he returned he gently supported his sister on his arm. Her face was pale and thin, and a few tendrils of hair had escaped untidily from her chignon. She sat on the sofa next to Georgiana and looked down at her hands in her lap. Sir Robert looked at them in mute appeal, and the colonel said:

"Sir Robert, perhaps you could offer me a glass of wine."

"Of course, of course." He escorted the colonel from the room with patent relief.

Georgiana took Miss Blake's hand and softly said:

"We are most concerned about you, Miss Blake, and we hoped that we could bring you some comfort in your hour of distress."

Miss Blake abruptly put her hands over her face and began sobbing. Georgiana put her arms around her and let her cry, patting her shoulder and crooning soothingly. When the young woman's tears had abated somewhat Georgiana said:

"You must not let this overcome you, my dear. In time, the pain will fade a little and you can go on with your life."

Miss Blake said, with a voice that was harsh with emotion and tears, "I suppose so. I am so humiliated to have not seen what kind of man he was. I did not know about his criminal activities, of course, but I find now that he probably only wanted my dowry to pay off his debts. It is very unlikely that he cared about me at all, and I did not see it. I was so eager to have a husband that I blinded myself to his character." She sobbed again, and Georgiana looked at her keenly for a moment and then said:

"You are not the first woman who has been taken in by a scoundrel, my dear. I myself almost made the same mistake two years ago, except my fault was much worse than yours. I actually considered eloping with him, as he wanted me to do. Fortunately, my brother saved me from myself. I can look back now with amazement that I ever thought that I loved that blackguard."

Miss Blake looked up, surprised. "Does the colonel know about this?"

"Oh yes. He has been my guardian along with my brother since my father died. He knows every detail, as does Elizabeth." She nodded at her sister-in-law. "It was that episode that opened my eyes and made me realise that I loved Colonel Fitzwilliam; so, you see, the pain I endured served a useful purpose."

She smiled at Miss Blake, who gave her a watery smile in return.

"Thank you. Thank you for coming and thank you for telling me this." She looked back down at her hands. "It is good to know that I have some true friends."

Georgiana patted her hand and stood up. "You probably have more than you realise. I will leave you now, but I will come see you again in a few days if you will allow me. My dear sister has acted as my confidante on many occasions, and you may trust her absolutely, as you may trust me, if you wish to speak confidentially with either of us."

"Oh yes, please do come, and thank you again." Her smile was a bit brighter as Georgiana and Elizabeth left her.

While they were riding back to Pemberley the colonel put Georgiana's arm through his and patted her hand.

"So what was the result of your *tête-a-tête?*"

"I told her about my sordid past." She smiled ruefully at him, and then added, "I believe that she felt somewhat better when I left. I certainly feel better now about owning the Walker estate."

"Shall we go this afternoon and look it over?"

"I would love to. Would you like to join us, Elizabeth?"

"Thank you, but I believe that I will rest this afternoon. Perhaps Mrs. Annesley could go with you."

"That is an excellent idea; she and Lucky can chaperone." She smiled at her fiancé.

"The house seems in very good condition, but I would like to have you look at it with me," the colonel said to Darcy after he and Georgiana had examined the house from attic to cellar. "Perhaps you could recommend a builder who could check its structural integrity for us."

"Of course, Cousin, I would be happy to. I know a builder in Kympton who is a capable fellow and, just as importantly, is reasonably honest, and who could inspect it with us. I will send him a note to meet us there tomorrow."

Elizabeth spent the time while the others were engaged with planning the alterations to The Yews resting on a *chaise-longue* in the cool shade of the folly with a book and with Pilot lying at her feet, a deep lassitude having overtaken her now that the season was over. The Gardiners were expected the next day for a two-week visit, and Elizabeth was hoping to recruit enough energy to entertain them properly. Although she knew that her aunt and uncle would forgive her any deficiencies in her arrangements, she did not want the hospitality at Pemberley to be compromised under her stewardship.

The Gardiners arrived in time for a late breakfast the next morning, making good time on their travels with the excellent roads and balmy weather, and the fortnight that they were at Pemberley was among the most relaxed two weeks that Elizabeth had experienced in the past six months. They had no other guests, the colonel hardly counting under that category any longer, and the weather was uniformly fine and not too hot. Elizabeth took her aunt, and sometimes Georgiana, around the park nearly every day in her little phaeton and Georgiana enjoyed showing both the Gardiners her future home.

Mr. Gardiner was of significant assistance in helping to plan the changes to The Yews because of his experience, through his business contacts, with purchasing the commodities necessary to refurbish the inside of a house, and was able to suggest a number of sources to them. It was Mrs. Gardiner, however, who came up with the new name for their manor, The Yews no longer being an appropriate appellation now that all of the huge, dark evergreens had been removed. After seeing the many climbing roses and other flowers that Georgiana had planted in front of the rosy bricks and half-timbered walls that had been exposed after the yews were sacrificed, giving the house a warm, comfortable air, she suggested:

"My own taste would probably avoid something alliterative, such as Lambton Lodge, and it is neither an abbey nor a castle. I would suggest something warm, such as 'Belle Fleur' or 'Bellamy,' or something of that sort for the centre-piece of your demesne, Lord Lambton." Her eyes twinkled at Georgiana and the colonel.

"I believe you are right, my dear Mrs. Gardiner," the colonel said. "I think that Bellamy would be a perfect name for our home. What do you say *ma belle amie?*

Georgiana blushed a bright red at his words, but, after a moment's embarrassment, agreed with tolerable calmness that it was a delightful name.

The others laughed at her and agreed that Bellamy was a suitably beautiful name for their home.

The two weeks of the Gardiners' visit passed very quickly for Elizabeth and all too soon it was time for them to return to London. Elizabeth felt rejuvenated after the relaxed days and early nights, and thanked her aunt and uncle when they were taking their leave.

"It has been wonderful to have you here; I feel like my old self again. I do not think that I had appreciated how tired I was after Georgiana's season until now. Give the children my love when you get back to London."

They agreed and, after taking leave of the others, climbed into their carriage and drove off.

On the third day after their departure, Elizabeth looked up from a light doze in her *chaise-longue* in the late afternoon to see her husband approaching with two unopened letters in his hand.

"It looks as if you have received a letter from your friend Charlotte, my dear."

"Oh, how nice. You did not need to bring it yourself, my darling," she smiled up at him.

"It was my pleasure, my lady."

She was still amused at his use of that title which was so prophetic the previous fall.

"Do you feel up to a walk after you read your letter?"

"Yes, my lord, I should be delighted." She tipped her head modestly and looked up at him through her lashes coyly, then opened her letter while he settled himself on the bench next to her chair and began his own. She looked up in surprise when her husband gave an abrupt snort.

"What is it?"

"It is from that wretched Lord Byron. He says:

> *LORD WINSLOW,*—
>
> *I am sending this to you so that you may decide whether to give it to your lovely wife or to discard it into the fire. I finished this poem early this summer and it will be published within the next year. It was initially inspired by a cousin of mine, but I soon realised that Lady Winslow was much on my mind when writing it. It is yours to do with as you wish.—Your humble servant, etc.*

Darcy silently handed her the enclosed sheet. Elizabeth was astonished that the few minutes that she had spent talking with him during the season would be enough to so influence Lord Byron, or to make him defy propriety to such an extent, but she was curious and opened the neatly handwritten sheet, reading:

She Walks in Beauty

She walks in beauty, like the night
    Of cloudless climes and starry skies;
And all that's best of dark and bright
    Meet in her aspect and her eyes:
Thus mellow'd to that tender light
    Which heaven to gaudy day denies.
One shade the more, one ray the less,
    Had half impair'd the nameless grace
Which waves in every raven tress,
    Or softly lightens o'er her face;
Where thoughts serenely sweet express
    How pure, how dear their dwelling-place.

And on that cheek, and o'er that brow,
    So soft, so calm, yet eloquent,
The smiles that win, the tints that glow,
    But tell of days in goodness spent,
A mind at peace with all below,
    A heart whose love is innocent!

She read the poem silently and then returned it to her husband, saying:

"Well—Lord Byron may be a menace to society, but you cannot deny that he *is* a poet. It is lovely, and I really cannot be insulted by the sentiments expressed, however impudent the author. What a pity that it was written for another woman," she concluded dryly.

Darcy gave her a small smile and she turned back to her letter, but after a few moments reading she made a little gasp.

"What is it?" Darcy asked, sitting up abruptly.

"Charlotte writes her congratulations to us and says that they are all well and little Catherine is now six months old." She looked up at him and added, "I will not sport with your intelligence by explaining why she is named Catherine." Darcy rolled his eyes and she continued, "She then goes on:

> *We have been rather lively in Kent in the last few weeks as Mr. Darcy's cousin, Lord St. George, has been visiting his aunt, Lady Catherine. He is very pleasant and seems to be much taken with his cousin, Miss de Bourgh. We have been called to make up the tables at cards several times since his arrival (as you are aware, Miss de Bourgh does not play whist) and we have found his lordship most amiable.... etc.*

"So ... Lord St. George is in Kent, happily ensconced at Rosings and playing up to Lady Catherine for all he is worth while his relations are all worrying themselves sick about him. I hope that my suspicions about his motives in going to Rosings are incorrect," she said with a frown.

Darcy looked very grim. "I am very much afraid that my suspicions echo yours. He must be making a play for my Cousin Anne's hand so that he can obtain the Rosings estate."

"Poor Anne. Do you think that he would go that far?"

"I would not be at all surprised. Lady Catherine is probably not aware of what went on in London this spring, since my aunt and uncle would not want to have the news of their son's ill-behaviour bandied about. And even if she was aware she might overlook it for the chance of a titled husband for Anne."

"I pray that we are wrong," she said softly.

"So do I, my dear, so do I. But I must give the colonel this news as soon as possible, so that he may inform his parents. He and Georgiana are still in town with Mrs. Annesley. I think that I should postpone our walk, my love, and ride into town and see if I can catch up with him."

"Yes, my dear, go and find them. This is a very unpleasant reflection on your cousin's character, and I dread to think of the distress that he will cause his entire family!"

He kissed her hand briefly and hurried to the stables to order his horse, then ran into the house to change into riding clothes. By the time he was back downstairs his horse was ready, and he sprang into the saddle and rode off at a brisk trot. Elizabeth was left to her book but it could no longer hold her attention. As the day warmed, she moved into the drawing-room, while Pilot retired to his usual spot in the library to continue his nap. The time seemed to creep by interminably as she awaited Darcy's return.

Finally, after two hours had slowly ticked by and she had reread the same passages at least three times, the entire party returned together. The colonel was in a state of barely controlled agitation when he came in and immediately ran upstairs to have his man pack his things. Darcy informed her that his cousin had decided to carry the news to his parents himself, and discuss with them what recourse they might have in this situation.

"Perhaps you should go with him, my dear, so that you may offer your thoughts on the matter. They will need as many clear heads as possible if they are to think of a way to avert this misuse of their niece."

Darcy sighed. "Perhaps I should. I cannot say that I am eager to leave you again, just as we have arrived home." She put her hand to his cheek and he turned his head and kissed her palm.

In the end, Darcy did go with his cousin. After a rather tense evening in which they could find little to talk about in front of the servants, they all retired early and the gentlemen rode out first thing the next morning. Elizabeth received a letter the next day assuring her that they had arrived in safety, but with no further news.

He wrote her one other time during the week he was absent. He shared his disappointment that they had been unable to find a way of preventing St. George from following through on his presumed plan without offering Anne and Lady Catherine a grave insult, which would only further estrange them from the family. Lord Whitwell had at first been inclined to think that his eldest son was finally showing a sense of responsibility, but when Darcy and Fitzwilliam gave him the full particulars of his niece's state of health, he was shocked and dismayed. He could not convince himself that his wayward son would marry a woman who was a complete invalid, except for the most venal reasons. They had still heard no word from St. George or Lady Catherine regarding the viscount's presence in Kent, and Lord Whitwell had finally, reluctantly, decided that they must do nothing at present for fear that they would precipitate events. It was his hope that

Lord St. George would reconsider his actions before offering for his cousin's hand. Darcy and the colonel finally acquiesced, and at length left for Pemberley.

While Darcy and the colonel were at Whitwell Abbey, Elizabeth and Georgiana attempted to keep to their usual routine of walks, music, and needlework; but in actuality they spent most of their time together revisiting the problem of Lord St. George, with nothing but discouragement to reward their time.

A few days after the gentlemen had departed Elizabeth received a letter from her sister Jane. She had not heard from her since they had left London, and she eagerly opened the envelope and read:

> DEAREST LIZZY,—
>
> I am sorry to be so dilatory in my correspondence; I know that you will understand how busy we are reopening Netherfield after the season and your generous heart will forgive me. It has taken longer than I would have liked to have the household functioning properly as the Wickhams joined us unexpectedly not long after our return. Lydia is feeling well and her confinement is due in a few weeks and so wished to be near family. I myself am beginning to feel rather like that elephant that we used to look at in Papa's African animal book when we were children, so I am sure that it was a long trip from Newcastle for our sister. I am becoming more and more nervous about my confinement, but will be glad to have the ordeal over. Bingley assures me that I am as beautiful as ever, but I do not feel beautiful in the least. I do, however, appreciate his tact.
>
> I must tell you, my dearest sister, that returning to Hertfordshire after this extended absence has made it very clear to both of us that we cannot stay at Netherfield permanently. After the superior company of yourself and all the Darcy family, it is difficult to tolerate the excesses of our own family. I know that you will forgive me for speaking so plainly, but I find myself blushing constantly over the manners and attitudes of many of our relations. You will not be surprised to hear that Lydia is unchanged after a year of marriage and talks only of parties and schemes when she is not complaining about how poor they are. Because of all these things, we have decided to quit Netherfield as soon as we find a suitable estate to purchase, and we are hoping to find one near enough to Pemberley so that we can see you and Darcy, and Georgiana and the colonel, frequently. I must go now and visit our parents; our father has missed both of us

very much and I feel rather guilty to be contemplating a move, but
we feel that it will be for the best. Give my best regards to ... etc.

Elizabeth shook her head over this epistle's reflections upon her family, and Georgiana asked her what the news was. She read the relevant parts of the letter to her, and Georgiana was very pleased that the Bingleys were, hopefully, to move closer to Pemberley. This topic gave them something more enjoyable to converse about than the sins of their cousin, and they spent many hours in pleasant speculation over where the Bingleys might find an estate in Derbyshire, temporarily at least forgetting Lord St. George.

Chapter 32

... there's nothing in the whole universe that perishes, believe me;
Rather it renews and varies its substance.
Ovid, "Metamorphoses"

After Darcy and the colonel returned from Whitwell Abbey, they told Elizabeth and Georgiana about their discussions with Lord and Lady Whitwell. They were all dismayed and shocked by the situation, but in spite of numerous talks, they—none of them—could construct a solution that would solve the problem without causing many others. It consumed the thoughts and devoured the sleep of them all, and only the need to appear as usual in front of the servants forced them to give up their interminable rounds of talk. But finally, as the days of summer advanced, they began, slowly and reluctantly, to let go of the problem and to wait, as Lord Whitwell had recommended. The beautiful park at Pemberley was of great service in this regard, as the sunshine and warm breezes tempted them out-of-doors most days, and their difficulties diminished in the beauties of nature.

The colonel had finally to return to London and his duty, and Darcy spent a great deal of time after his cousin's departure riding hard over the estate and working himself into a state of exhaustion so that he could forget St. George's questionable behaviour. Elizabeth knew that he was frustrated over his inability to help his cousin Anne, and she suspected that he felt particularly responsible for her welfare because he had rejected the long-standing plans made by his mother and Lady Catherine for a marriage between Darcy and Anne in order to marry Elizabeth. She pitied him but felt that she could best help him by standing silently by in case he needed her, and quietly ensuring his physical comfort with food and fires, even if she could not comfort his mind. She went about her daily duties with only half her attention, however, and frequently walked the paths along the stream aimlessly as she tried to find some solution to the problem that filled her thoughts again now that Darcy was returned to Pemberley. Georgiana had reacted to the news of her cousin's sordid plans by clinging tightly to her family for comfort and solace, often silently joining Elizabeth in her walks. They reassured her that she did not have any fault in the aftermath of her dispute with St. George, but she felt guilty nonetheless.

Eventually, Elizabeth found herself, after many days had passed, able to attend to the sermons of the parson of Lambton church. Instead of being caught in an endless cycle of dismay and concern for the anguish that Lord St. George might introduce to his family, she could listen to and comprehend the message and confine her internal thoughts to a small prayer at the end of the service for the protection of her Cousin Anne, still at the mercy of her mother's matrimonial ambitions. Georgiana, too, began again to show an interest in the summer and in her future home in Lambton, discussing Bellamy with her sister and brother with the appearance of as much enjoyment as before.

They were temporarily distracted from their preoccupation by the news from Jane that Lydia had borne a beautiful, healthy daughter the first week of July:

> ... *Both Lydia and little Juliet are very well and are spending her confinement at Netherfield with us. Mr. Wickham left for Bath the day after Juliet's birth to take the waters for a rheumatic complaint which he developed in the cold North, or so he says. Lydia is nursing her child as she hopes to avoid having another very soon, in which I encouraged her.... etc.*

Elizabeth shook her head at the news that Lydia was now a mother, but she was happy that they were well. The Wickham's must have greatly overstayed their welcome if even dear Jane was showing signs of cynicism. At least with mother and child at Netherfield Lydia's family could be sure she would receive excellent care. She wondered if her younger sister had given any thought to the tragic associations of her daughter's name. Of course she had not. The real romantic tragedy was Lydia's marriage to Wickham, and if her sister did not yet see *that* she would be impervious to the implications of naming her daughter Juliet.

The news was only a temporary respite from the recurring discussions of St. George's plans, and those concerns quickly resurfaced, but finally, one Sunday in August, the parson, Mr. Woodson, preached a sermon on the acceptance of God's will. He was a rather small and timid-appearing man who was hampered in village society by extreme shyness. He appeared to best advantage when speaking from the pulpit, putting on the ancient dignity and authority of the Church when he donned his surplice. His message that day was a simple one: "Find God's will and, when you do, accept it as your own." Elizabeth heard a small sigh escape from her husband next to her, and she slipped her hand through his arm. He did not move, except to cover her hand with his. Later, not long after they had returned to Pemberley, he appeared in the doorway of Elizabeth's morning room and stood there irresolutely, watching as she finished writing a letter to her sister Lydia, congratulating her on the birth of her new daughter and expressing her pleasure that they were both well. When he did not speak, she looked up.

"Elizabeth?"

"Yes, my love?"

"Georgiana and Mrs. Annesley are off to the new house. Do you feel up to a walk this morning, before the day gets too hot?"

"I should adore a walk!"

She gathered her notepaper, put it in a drawer of the desk, and sent François upstairs for her bonnet. As they left the house through the conservatory, they turned together towards the path leading over the ridge. They slowly wound their way up the path, now covered with boughs of green leaves and cool after the sunny lawn. They had not returned to the waterfall since leaving London, and Elizabeth breathed in the summer smells and felt the breeze on her cheek with pleasure. She had completely recovered from the torpor which had overcome her when they first returned to Pemberley from town, and now felt eager to reach the top of the ridge.

When they reached the crest she was panting and so rested a moment before following the winding trail downwards. Darcy expressed concern over whether she was overexerting herself in her delicate condition, but she reassured him that she felt very well. She turned to look towards Pemberley House, but could only see a corner of the stonework through the trees. She turned back, and the trail was an inviting green bower leading to the stream, which could now be heard as it murmured invisibly far below. When she had caught her breath, they continued down until the path ended above the waterfall.

They sat under the same tree where they had picnicked the previous fall, Darcy's arm around her and her head on his shoulder as before. Elizabeth gazed upward at the green roof over their heads and at the glimpses of sunlit sky she could see between the leaves as they danced in the breeze. She was relaxed almost to the point of somnolence, when she had a sudden thought and sat up abruptly, turning eagerly to Darcy.

"I do not know why I did not think of this before! I do have one suggestion that might be of service to your cousin Anne."

"Please tell me; I could use some good news, my dear," he said, raising his brows questioningly.

"I do not know if you will be entirely pleased with this idea, but do you not think that you should write to your aunt, Lady Catherine, and try to reestablish cordial relations with her?"

He frowned. "I am not sure that I want to do that after her entirely uncalled-for comments about you, my love."

"I believe that you should give her another chance, if only for Anne's sake, dearest. You do not need to apologise for your actions—I, for one do not repent of them at all," she said with a brief smile, "but if you can merely open the door slightly it may allow you to be of some use to your family in their concerns, whereas now you are *persona non grata* to Lady Catherine and have not the smallest influence over her."

"My aunt has always been a woman to give advice rather than accept it, but you are right: I should try to recover my status as her nephew, if only for the comfort of the rest of the family." He sighed and rested his head on top of hers; thus they remained for many minutes, each contemplating the letter he would send.

When they returned to the house, Darcy shut himself in his library to compose the letter. After more than an hour he had finally finished and he brought it to Elizabeth to read:

> DEAR LADY CATHERINE,—
>
> *I am writing to let you know that Lady Winslow and I are well, and she is expecting our first child in November. As you are, I believe, aware, Georgiana's presentation and debut went very well this spring, thanks to the efforts of Lady Whitwell and Lady Winslow, and she is engaged to Colonel Fitzwilliam, now Lord Lambton. They are planning to marry in the spring. She is very happy preparing the house on the estate given the colonel by His Majesty along with his title and it should be ready to live in by the time they marry. Lord Whitwell is giving them Longford House for a wedding present, so they will also have a house in town. If you are able, in the future, to visit Pemberley, you and Cousin Anne are always welcome.—Sincerely,*
>
> FITZWILLIAM DARCY, LORD WINSLOW

"It is not the most gracious letter I have ever written, but it was the best that I could do under the circumstances, unrepentant as I am," he said sheepishly. "I decided that pompous and formal, with emphasis upon our new titles, was the best tone to take with my aunt."

"It will do; she will either accept it or not, and I doubt if she would respect you if you groveled. She is the one who must decide how important her family is to her own happiness and whether she will reach out and grasp the proffered olive branch."

"Well, I will send it off and we will see how she responds. I have also written to Lord and Lady Whitwell to inform them of our actions."

The letters went out the next morning, and since they could take no further action until they received a response (if any), they returned to their accustomed activities. Elizabeth spent hours advising Georgiana on the decorating of her future home. The structure had been found to be sound, but most of the house needed a great deal of updating, so they had an enjoyable time picking out papers, carpets, and furniture. Darcy had paid off the mortgage so the creditors had dispersed; but the senior Walkers had refused any recompense for the estate, telling him with dignity that it would not be right for him to pay for the unconscionable acts of their son and wishing Georgiana and the colonel every happiness in their new home. As they were very firm in their decision, he was compelled to accept their word, however reluctantly.

As September approached with the anticipation of slightly cooler temperatures, Elizabeth received a letter from Jane inviting them to Miss Bingley's wedding to the Comte de Tournay:

> *DEAREST LIZZY,—*
>
> *Caroline has asked me to assist her in writing the invitations for her wedding, so I am writing to you first of all. They will be married on September first at St. George's Hanover Square, at ten o'clock in the morning. If you feel well enough to travel, we would very much like you all to stay with us until we travel to London for the wedding. Mr. Wickham returned from Bath and took Lydia and little Juliet home to Newcastle a few days ago. Both Lydia and the baby were doing very well.... etc.*

Elizabeth discussed traveling with Darcy and with the doctor in Lambton, and they felt that she could safely go, as long as the trip was taken in easy steps and she was not overtired. Her own confinement was not expected until November, so, although she was beginning to feel rather ungainly, she thought that she could travel in reasonable comfort; Darcy would go with her and make everything easy. She was relieved that the Wickhams had finally left Netherfield after a nearly two month's visit. Elizabeth would not ask Darcy to visit the Bingleys if Wickham was present and she wanted to see her sister Jane. Poor Jane, to have to put up with the Wickhams for two months in her condition! She wrote to let her know that they would be arriving in a few days, and the servants spent the day packing for the trip.

Georgiana was delighted to have an opportunity to see her fiancé for the first time in several weeks. They had been corresponding almost daily as the work on the house progressed, discussing changes to their plans and how quickly (or not) the work was finished. Georgiana had not said anything to Elizabeth about her feelings in the matter, but Elizabeth could tell that she was already getting impatient for the wedding. Next spring, Elizabeth thought, seemed very far away as they looked at it from the middle of August.

They left for Netherfield the day after Jane's invitation arrived and spent three nights on the road, as the coachman kept the horses to a sedate trot. Elizabeth felt very well and was amused that her husband and all of his servants treated her like a piece of precious and delicate porcelain; it was really not her temper to be an invalid. They drove decorously up to the front door of Netherfield in the late afternoon of the fourth day and Elizabeth and Georgiana embraced Jane. Her slender figure was swollen by the life within her, and she led them to the drawing-room and immediately sat down, breathing heavily. Elizabeth noticed that she had dark circles under her eyes and her face appeared strained as she said:

"Please pardon me, my dears. I do not have much energy at the moment, but I am truly happy to see you!" She burst into tears and clung to Elizabeth. Her sister patted her back and soothed her, but caught Darcy's startled eyes over Jane's head and jerked her chin toward the door. The two gentlemen arose with alacrity and disappeared into the billiard-room, Bingley peering back through the doorway for a moment in concern.

After they had started the game, Bingley leaned on his cue. He glanced back towards the drawing-room, then cleared his throat and said, with an attempt at his usual good humour:

"Your visit was very timely—I thought that I would need to move to Derbyshire before our previous guests would depart! I finally mentioned that we expected you for my sister's wedding and Wickham suddenly remembered that he needed to be back in Newcastle immediately!"

He grinned knowingly at Darcy. Although he was unaware of all the details of Darcy's history with Wickham, he knew that his friend had good reason to detest his brother-in-law.

"I have wanted to tell you that Caroline was absolutely livid when she heard that you received a title. I really thought for a few moments that she was going to have an apoplectic attack, Darcy—or would you prefer that I call you Lord Winslow now?"

Darcy snorted derisively, and Bingley grinned and went on:

"I believe that is why Caroline is hurrying her wedding, so that she can be addressed as 'my lady' as soon as possible."

Darcy shook his head in mock reproach at his friend's levity, and they continued their game.

In the drawing-room, Jane had dried her tears and was telling her sisters that she was really feeling very well, just tired, but she would be happy when the baby arrived.

"I am very happy that you felt well enough to come Lizzy, because, as I think I told you, I am getting rather nervous as my confinement approaches. Mamma has daily been filling my head with all the terrifying occurrences that she has seen or heard of when women have babies. I try to reassure myself that she had five children without any difficulties, but I am unable to ignore the tales. I am not sleeping much because I am not very comfortable, so it does not take much unease of mind to keep me awake all night. It also does not help that my poor husband is very worried about me; this is all new for him too, after all. I feel better already having you here to keep me sensible, Lizzy," she finished as she dashed a remaining tear impatiently from her eye.

Elizabeth patted her hand and reassured her as well as she could with her little experience of childbirth; and she was determined to prevent her thoughtless mother from frightening Jane further, if at all possible. They had two days in Hertfordshire before they would go to town, and, hopefully, much could be done in that time to divert her mother. She would speak to her father about the matter.

As the evening wore on, however, she could not help but be concerned about Jane traveling to London in her condition. She discussed this with Darcy when they retired and he agreed that, as short as the drive to town was, it was probably not wise for Jane to travel. Elizabeth thought about this, and the next morning, when she had a chance to see Jane alone, she put her opinion before her sister—offering to stay with her while Bingley, Darcy, and Georgiana went to London for the wedding. Jane considered very briefly before she agreed to the idea.

"Yes, I am sure you are right, Lizzy, that I probably should not travel. I just hate to let Caroline down on her wedding day."

"I am sure she will understand, Jane," she said. Then she added tartly, "Consider this: if she really wanted for you to be there, she could have put off the wedding for a couple of months, now could she not? Bingley will be there to give her away and she will be happy as can be with her society friends around her to give their congratulations."

Jane smiled her agreement and went to tell Bingley their plan. Later in the day, while Jane was resting, Bingley sought Elizabeth out in the music room and sat next to her, saying:

"Thank you, my dear sister, for staying with Jane while we go to London. I was very worried about her traveling, but I did not want to leave her here without a family member to take care of her, either. You have eased my mind greatly."

"I am happy to be of assistance, although I hate to forgo Caroline's society wedding." She smiled at him and he laughed.

"Yes, I hope everything goes as she plans it, or she will be fit to be tied. I have already begged Darcy to allow me to stay at Ashbourne House so that I do not have to live through Caroline's wedding-day nerves. I am not sure that I am strong enough to survive it."

"What are their plans for their honeymoon? Will they stay in London, or travel?" Elizabeth inquired politely.

"They are planning on driving directly to the comte's estate, which is near Oxford, so it is not far from town."

"Has Caroline seen the house yet?"

"I don't believe so, but the comte has described it to us. It is a small manor house that is about seventy years old. He told me that he wants to use Caroline's dowry to buy more land to add to his estate and provide steady income."

"That sounds very sensible. Well, I hope they will be very happy. Make sure that you convey our best wishes." Elizabeth's eyes twinkled and Bingley smiled back at her; then his brow furrowed.

"I will, but please send an express if anything should happen while we are gone. I can be here in three hours on a fast horse."

"Do not worry, I will send for you immediately after I send for the doctor."

When Elizabeth told Darcy of her plan, he approved it immediately.

"I think it is an excellent plan, my dear. Is she still nervous about her confinement?"

"Yes; and my dear mamma has been filling her head with lurid tales of death and disaster."

"Do you, perhaps, want to stay until Jane is over at least part of her confinement? I am sure that she would feel better with you here, and Georgiana and I could stay in London so that she could see the colonel for a couple of weeks."

"That would probably be a good idea. If nothing else, I can keep Mamma from terrifying her. It would be nice to see Papa a little longer, as well."

"We will plan on staying in town for about a fortnight, then, until you write us that Jane is well enough for us to take you home."

"Thank you, my love. I will miss you. At least I have the consolation at this separation that I will know where you are!" She smiled impishly at him.

He responded with a cocked eyebrow and a kiss on her forehead before he joined Bingley for a ride over his temporary demesne. Elizabeth rejoined Jane and

Georgiana and told them of the completed plan. Georgiana's eyes glowed when she realised that she would be able to spend an entire fortnight with her future husband. They spent the afternoon trying to relax and make Jane as much at ease as possible, but she was too uncomfortable to sit still for long. The tedium was broken when Doctor Porter called to see Jane late in the day. After he had examined her in her room he came to Elizabeth, who was waiting in the drawing-room, and told her that all was well, and that the baby could come at any time.

"It is well, then, that she is not going to her sister-in-law's wedding in London the day after tomorrow."

"Oh no, my lady, that would not do at all; she must certainly stay home!"

"She will, and I am planning on staying until she has her lying-in and feels better."

"That will be of very great assistance to your sister, I am sure, my lady."

"Thank you, Doctor."

The Bennets came to dinner that evening and Jane felt well enough after a long afternoon rest to join them at the table. Mrs. Bennet's eyes glittered brightly all evening as she carried on about her pleasure at becoming a grandmother.

"I am so excited! By the end of the year I will have three grandchildren! I hope that everything goes well, Jane, my love. Mrs. Long's eldest niece just had her lying-in, but, poor thing, the baby died a few hours later." She conveyed this news with ghoulish satisfaction, oblivious to Jane's ghastly pallor. "And her lying-in was more than thirty hours! They almost despaired of the mother's life, too."

Knowing that Georgiana was now becoming acquainted with all of her mother's weaknesses, Elizabeth felt herself blush several times, and for Jane's sake was desperate to stop her mother's flow of talk. Darcy finally saw her worried looks and engaged Georgiana and Kitty in talking about London, including Bingley and Jane. Elizabeth was able to turn to her father, plunging into the first topic that came to her mind.

"Papa, have you heard from Mr. Collins lately?

"No, my dear, I have heard nothing from him. What are your plans for the time you are here?"

She glanced down the table to make sure that they were not overheard. "I am hoping to keep Mamma from scaring Jane to death with her talk," she said quietly, "and to keep Jane quiet and as rested as may be until her confinement."

"That is an admirable plan, if you can carry it out, my love," he returned wryly.

The next afternoon Bingley, Darcy, and Georgiana left for London after Bingley had spent the morning hovering over his wife in poorly concealed concern. Elizabeth spent the rest of the day attending to Jane, who seemed relieved after her husband's departure.

"I love Mr. Bingley with all my heart, as you know, dear Lizzy, but his agitation over my condition is not conducive to rest," she admitted with a blush.

When their mother came to call in the early afternoon, Elizabeth determinedly kept the conversation to the latest news from London and what fashions they had seen during the season. Jane seconded her efforts gamely, and they were able to keep their mother on trivial topics for the entire visit.

Elizabeth received a letter the following day from Darcy telling of their safe arrival, but it was not until two days later that she received an account of the wedding from Georgiana.

> DEAREST ELIZABETH,—
>
> Well, my dear sister, the wedding is over and the newlyweds are now at the comte's estate near Oxford. The day was sunny and rather warm for the season, but not unpleasantly so, and we arrived at the church early as Mr. Bingley was, of course, to give away the bride. Miss Bingley was dressed in a beautiful gown of cream silk, with yards and yards of Belgian lace. Her bonnet was of cream, with ribbons of silver, and her bouquet was of cream hothouse roses surrounded by small fern leaves. The church was about a quarter full of friends and family of the happy couple, and Miss Bingley was very gratified by the number who attended, in spite of the unfashionable date. Everything went off very smoothly, and Mr. Bingley was smiling and gracious, as always, when he handed his sister off to her husband-to-be. The Hursts held a wedding breakfast for the newlyweds and they stayed for about an hour before retiring to change into their travel clothes. They left for Oxford immediately after, and we visited with the other wedding guests and were back at Ashbourne House in time for dinner. Colonel Fitzwilliam joined us for the wedding and reception (looking very handsome in his uniform, I might add!), but his duty required him to return to the palace afterwards, so we did not have much time to talk. I would tell you who was at the wedding, but I am afraid that I did not notice once my dear Edward arrived. He will join us for dinner here today. My dearest sister, I don't know how I will bear waiting until the spring for our wedding. It seemed like a sensible plan two months ago, but now the spring seems an eternity away. I will not complain any further, however! My best love to Jane and I hope that she feels very well.—Love, etc.

Elizabeth was entertained by Georgiana's letter, and read it to Jane.

The heat was abominable for the rest of the week, with storm clouds piling up in the west but no rain to give them relief. Jane spent a good deal of the day in her room, where Elizabeth would read to her or quietly do her needlework while her sister slept. Bingley had returned to Netherfield the day after the wedding, explaining that his anxiety about his wife prevented him from staying longer in town. Elizabeth tried to reassure him whenever possible, but there was not much that she could say to lessen his fears, and he was clearly very worried; wandering about the house restlessly all day and checking on Jane every half hour. Now that Elizabeth was at Netherfield, Jane seemed to have recovered from her nerves and frequently thanked her sister for coming to be with her.

A few days after the wedding, Elizabeth received another letter from Georgiana:

> MY DEAR SISTER,—
>
> We are having an enjoyable time in town, and have found sev-
> eral concerts and plays to attend. Every day, however, my heart sinks
> lower at the thought of leaving Edward. We have talked it over, and
> I have decided to speak to my brother about marrying sooner than
> the spring. Do you think that we could make arrangements sooner,
> or do you think that we are being too precipitous? Please write and
> advise me, and give your family our best.—Your loving sister,
>
> GEORGIANA

Elizabeth wrote her by return post:

> MY DEAREST GIRL,—
>
> Talk to your brother and order your wedding gown as soon as
> may be. The only arrangements that are of importance are yours and
> the colonel's.—With all my love, etc.

About a week before Jane's expected confinement, Elizabeth was reading to her while she rested on the couch in the drawing-room when Jane suddenly pushed herself to a sitting position.

"What is the matter, my dear?" she asked solicitously.

"I have just had a rather bad pain. I have been having them on and off all day, but never this severe."

"I will have Bingley notify the doctor."

"Yes, please." Her face tightened as another pain came.

Elizabeth hurried to Bingley's library, where he was trying to do some estate business, and asked him to summon the doctor. He jumped up from his chair in alarm and called for the butler to bring Dr. Porter. They returned to the drawing-room, and he supported Jane as she walked up to her room. Her maid summoned one of the older housemaids who had some experience with childbirth and together they settled their patient in her bed. While Bingley waited anxiously in their sitting-room, Elizabeth sat down next to Jane's bed and took her hand.

When the contractions came Jane squeezed her hand until it was over; they were coming about every ten minutes. It seemed a very long time until the doctor arrived, but it was most likely less than half an hour. After examining her, he stated that she was, indeed, in labour and that the baby was in the correct position. He gave her a small amount of laudanum to help with the pain, and they all prepared for a long vigil. Elizabeth cooled her sister's face with a damp cloth periodically as the afternoon wore on. She tried to be calm for Jane's sake, but her inexperience in these matters gave her much concern and she felt her heart beating very fast every time her sister had a pain.

"Jane, dearest," Elizabeth asked after an hour, "would you like for me to send for Mamma?"

"Do not worry her, Lizzy, all I need is you to comfort me."

Elizabeth smiled and patted her hand weakly. Jane's maid and the housemaid bustled around the room, gathering towels and adjusting the bedclothes, but they spared reassuring smiles for the patient and her sister. Elizabeth, at least, was comforted by their presence.

Several hours passed before Jane's pains finally began coming closer together. When they persisted, Elizabeth went for the doctor, who had stepped into the sitting-room for a cup of tea. He examined his patient and gave her a little more laudanum.

"The baby will come very soon, now. You are doing very well, Mrs. Bingley."

After a very long half hour in which Elizabeth tried to overcome her distress and follow the doctor's directions with alacrity, she finally heard a cry and looked up to see the doctor holding her new niece. She sat down in relief and wiped her brow with her handkerchief, then remembered her sister and sponged Jane's face with a cool cloth, her hand trembling. The housemaid took the baby to the other side of the room to wash and dress her, and Elizabeth watched silently while the doctor dealt with the remaining unpleasant details of the process. When he finished, and Elizabeth had helped the maids to make Jane clean and comfortable in her bed, the doctor stepped over to the sitting-room door and beckoned to Bingley with a reassuring smile.

"You may come in, sir, and see your new daughter. She and your wife are both doing very well."

Bingley was as white as a ghost when he first entered the room, but quickly recovered when he realised that Jane truly was well. He rushed to her bedside, hesitantly took her hand, and kissed it tenderly. Jane smiled, and then looked up at her sister and said:

"Let me hold her."

They placed her cleaned and gowned baby in her arms, and she and Bingley stared at her in awe. Elizabeth watched them and suddenly felt dampness on her cheeks. She put her hand up to her face in confusion and then realised that she was crying as she watched Bingley gently kiss his wife on her forehead. The doctor congratulated him on having a healthy child and took his leave.

When Jane dropped off to sleep, Elizabeth crept out of the room, surprised to see that it was barely dusk. She felt light-headed and remembered that she had not eaten since breakfast and it was now long after the dinner hour, so she wandered downstairs, where the housekeeper met her and bustled her into the small dining-room.

"My lady, you must not overtire yourself. I have some nice cold roast beef and salad for you. You will feel much better after you eat."

Elizabeth dutifully ate the food the housekeeper placed in front of her and let the comforting words wash over her, until the housekeeper finally bustled back out to make trays for the nurses upstairs. Bingley came in and joined her at her meal, but they ate mechanically and did not speak much. Afterwards, Elizabeth congratulated her brother-in-law and went upstairs to check on Jane. Her sister was sound asleep, so she went to her room to lie down, exhausted by Jane's pain and her own fears about *her* upcoming confinement. She fell asleep instantly and slept until morning.

When she awoke, she dressed and hurried to Jane's room. The nurse the doctor had found for them had arrived the evening before and taken over the baby's care, and Jane had slept well for the first time in weeks. When Elizabeth saw her sister, she already looked more like her usual self. She stayed with Jane for much of the day, entertaining her mother and sisters when they came to call, and writing the news to Darcy and Georgiana when her sister dozed off. Bingley had his dinner upstairs with his wife and Elizabeth dined alone in the small dining-parlour to give them some time together. The doctor had checked on Jane during the day and said that both she and the baby were doing well.

After dinner, she returned upstairs to see how Jane was feeling and sat on her bedside for a while until she was ready to sleep.

"Lizzy, I wanted to tell you that we have decided to name her after you. We will call her Elizabeth Anne. I hope that will please you, my dearest sister."

"I am very honoured to have little Lizzy named after me," she said in surprise, and embraced her sister, tears again starting to her eyes.

When she had been at Netherfield for nearly two weeks, and Jane was recovered enough that Elizabeth no longer had any fears about her health, she received two letters. The first, from Darcy, said that they would return from London the next day:

> MY DEAREST WIFE,—
>
> I am happy to hear that Jane is feeling so well and that the baby is healthy. It seems an age since we left Netherfield and I can hardly wait to see you. I know that Georgiana has been corresponding with you, so this will come as no surprise, but she and the colonel have decided to marry as soon as possible. They will both return to Netherfield with me tomorrow and I am hoping that we can return to Pemberley within the week. They will be married in the Pemberley chapel, probably a week after we return. I hope that you are feeling well, and that your nursing duties with your sister have not tired you, my darling.—With all my love, etc.

The second letter was from Georgiana:

> DEAREST ELIZABETH,—
>
> We have talked with my brother and our wishes have prevailed (not that there was much opposition in the case!). My gown is not quite finished, but the seamstress will bring it to Pemberley within a few days of our return for the final fitting. I will describe it to you when we get to Netherfield, which will be in the early afternoon tomorrow, and a week after our return to Pemberley we will have Mr. Woodson marry us in the Pemberley chapel. I did not expect a year ago that I would be married so soon, and I must confess that I feel rather giddy! I will see you very soon.—Love, etc.

Chapter 33

She is your treasure, she must have a husband.
William Shakespeare, "The Taming of the Shrew"

Within a week and a half they were back at Pemberley. Both Jane and little Lizzy were doing very well when they left and Elizabeth had regained her equanimity, refusing to allow herself to worry about her own confinement. This resolution was the more easily kept since the plans for the upcoming wedding gave them all much to talk about during the long drive home. The air when they reached Derbyshire was noticeably cooler and more comfortable than that in Hertfordshire, and Elizabeth could already see a few yellow leaves peeping out from amongst the green along the highway.

After they had climbed with relief from the carriage and greeted Reynolds and Smithfield, the housekeeper handed them a letter. It was from Lady Catherine and had arrived while they were still in Hertfordshire and held at Pemberley, since Reynolds knew that they would be home within a day or two. Darcy read it and handed it silently to Elizabeth, his face a cipher. Lady Catherine mentioned none of the previous unpleasantness, but her tone was as militant as always:

> LORD WINSLOW,—
> *I thank you for your letter and will wait upon you at Pemberley on the second of October. Anne will accompany me and we expect to stay a fortnight. I am sorry that we cannot make a longer stay, but you may not be aware that your Cousin Anne just became engaged to Viscount St. George and we must hurry back to Kent to make the arrangements for the wedding, which will be quite soon.—I am yours sincerely, etc.*

Elizabeth, startled, looked up at him as he stood over her while she read. "The second of October. That is today!"

"Indeed it is," he said with a sigh, and then added acerbically, "We are fortunate that we arrived at Pemberley before she did. It would not have improved our relationship if she visited and we were not at home!"

Georgiana's eyes looked rather wary, but the colonel's only response was to say with a sigh:

"I had better warn my parents about my brother's engagement."

Lady Catherine and her daughter arrived just before they were about to have a cup of tea, so Elizabeth had the tea things to occupy her when their guests came down from their rooms after changing from their travel clothes. Mrs. Jenkinson and Miss de Bourgh arrived first and, as usual, Miss de Bourgh sat mutely on the couch while Mrs. Jenkinson fluttered around her. Lady Catherine seemed surprised to be the last to arrive in the drawing-room and, as soon as the courtesies had been performed, resentfully carped:

"How did you and Anne get down before me, Mrs. Jenkinson? I came down almost immediately."

Mrs. Jenkinson seemed to quail before her, and stammered that it did not seem as if they had hurried. Georgiana turned to Anne and said:

"I understand that you are engaged to be married, Cousin Anne. I congratulate you."

Anne thanked her quietly and resumed her mute posture.

Georgiana turned to Lady Catherine and added:

"It is very fortunate that you have come at this time, Lady Catherine. The colonel and I are to be married next week. I was afraid that our plans would not allow all of our family to be present at the ceremony, so I am very pleased that you are here."

Lady Catherine launched into a harangue on the preparations that were necessary for a proper nuptial and firmly pointed out that they must not have their wedding until after Anne and Lord St. George were married as the date was already set. Georgiana and the colonel both nodded gravely at each point she made until she finally ran down and sipped the tea Elizabeth had poured her.

Elizabeth gave a slightly desperate look at Darcy and he took up the thread of the conversation.

"I am happy to see you Lady Catherine. It is quite some years since you were at Pemberley, is it not?"

"I was last here in the year before your father died. This tea is too weak, Lady Winslow. You should tell your cook to steep it longer."

Elizabeth nodded with as much graciousness as she could muster and passed a cup to Mrs. Jenkinson. Those were the only words Lady Catherine addressed to her the entire evening. Georgiana tried to engage her aunt in conversation again by telling her about the colonel's estate in Lambton. This diverted her attention for about half an hour while she told Georgiana how many servants to hire, what kind of paper to put on the walls, and how the gardeners should arrange the shrubbery. They all listened attentively (or at least with the air of attentiveness), although Elizabeth soon felt as if her eyes were glazing over.

Eventually Lady Catherine gathered up her daughter and Mrs. Jenkinson and they went upstairs so Anne could rest for an hour before it was time to dress for dinner. Elizabeth sighed with relief and went to her own room, followed by Georgiana.

"What are we going to do, Elizabeth?" she whispered furiously. "She is going to make our lives a misery if we try to marry next week."

"Calm down, my dear." She put her arm around her sister's shoulder. "We need to talk to your brother and the colonel. Let us go back downstairs and find them while Lady Catherine is still in her room."

They found the gentlemen collapsed in comfortable chairs in the library. They had already begun discussing the wedding problem.

"Georgiana, my dear," the colonel said ruefully, "I do not see that we have any alternative but to put the wedding off until after my brother's wedding. I really care not what Lady Catherine's opinion is, but it would be unfair to force my parents to choose between us."

Angry tears welled up in Georgiana's eyes but she forced them down and answered, "I do not see any alternative, either, but I just want you all to know that I am going to be *seething* inside the entire time that my aunt is here."

The colonel took her hand, kissed it, and said, "When the disaster that is my brother's marriage rites is finished, I will marry the bravest, strongest, most understanding woman on earth as soon as can possibly be managed." His eyes twinkled at her until a reluctant smile appeared on her face.

When the crisis was over, Elizabeth dragged herself back upstairs to lie down. Even though the date her baby was due was more than a month in the future, she felt enormous and her ankles were swelling after sitting up for too long. It was clear that Lady Catherine's visit was to be a great challenge to her amiability and she tried to prepare herself. She dozed off in spite of her tension and did not awaken until François entered to help her dress. Elizabeth looked in the mirror while François rearranged her hair, which had been disordered by her nap, and saw her pale face looking like Ophelia's floating in a dark pool staring back at her. It took all of her fortitude to draw herself up and glide down the marble staircase with a pleasant smile upon her face, but she was determined to do it for Darcy's sake, and for the sake of Georgiana and the colonel and his family.

When she reached the bottom of the stairs, Darcy stepped forward from the doorway of the drawing-room to kiss her hand and offer her his arm solicitously, a sardonic tilt to his lips, which he smoothed into a bland smile as they turned to enter the room. They survived the evening by sitting mutely while Lady Catherine held forth on various topics, nodding at the appropriate times in the conversation. At the end of the evening when they had retired upstairs, Darcy put his arms around his wife and said:

"I find it incredible that I tolerated that woman for all those years. I hope that this attempt to ease my family's relationships bears fruit because we are making a great sacrifice having Lady Catherine here. You, especially, are sacrificing the serenity of your home and I want you to know that I appreciate your efforts." He kissed her a little awkwardly over her rounded form.

"I can only blame myself, since it was, after all, my idea to invite her. I have to say that I am happy she does not really want to talk to me; it at least relieves me from too much of her intrusive attention. Georgiana and the colonel will probably receive most of it because there are an *infinite* number of items of advice that Lady Catherine can give about their wedding and new house."

As she had expected, the fortnight of Lady Catherine's visit made perpetual demands on Elizabeth's good nature, but they finally reached the end of it. Darcy dealt with it by staying continuously at Elizabeth's side, offering her every courtesy and keeping her arm through his, mute testament to Lady Catherine of how excessively happy they were. Georgiana bore up under her invasive scrutiny courageously, inviting Lady Catherine to see her house and garden so that her aunt could have ample scope for her forthright advice. In addition, she attempted to converse with her cousin Anne about her wedding when Lady Catherine went upstairs for a few minutes, but it was uphill work. The only real comment that she received in response to her questions was:

"It doesn't matter; I will still be living at Rosings."

This was given in such a flat tone that Elizabeth was unable to determine if her cousin considered staying at Rosings as a benefit or otherwise. At any rate, Anne did not complain of ill-usage in the arrangement of her marriage. Georgiana played the pianoforte and the harp, at Elizabeth's suggestion, as much as possible so that there would be less time available to converse with Lady Catherine. Her aunt praised her playing and admired her drawings excessively, and also spent a great deal of time talking about Anne's wedding, which was to be the first week after their return, in Kent. One morning, before Lady Catherine had appeared for breakfast, Georgiana commented to Elizabeth:

"I would be much more elevated by her praise if I did not realise that she is trying to disparage your accomplishments by excessive praise of mine, my dear sister. She is really very much like Miss Bingley—pardon me, the Comtesse de Tournay—in that respect. My aunt at least confines herself to giving instruction rather than whispering sarcastic comments behind ones back, so I suppose that I should be grateful for her attention," she finished with unusual acidity.

Elizabeth had to smile at this assessment but added, "At least she is correct that your musical accomplishments are excellent, my dear."

Georgiana just smiled and shook her head pityingly at her sister.

When the day came for the Rosings party to leave, Lady Catherine condescended to acknowledge Elizabeth with a brief curtsey as they made their farewells.

"You will be coming to Anne's wedding next week, I am sure," she said abruptly to Darcy.

"I doubt if my *wife*," he said, stressing the word slightly, "will be well enough to travel that far in her delicate condition, and I would not want to leave her at this important time, but perhaps Georgiana could come with Lord and Lady Whitwell." Georgiana nodded agreeably to this, as if she and her brother and sister had not discussed it the night before with the colonel.

The required farewells finally completed, the Darcys and the colonel waved them off from the front terrace with artificial smiles and then returned to the breakfast-parlour to enjoy their morning tea in unbroken silence.

Chapter 34

Far from the madding crowd ...
Thomas Gray, "Elegy Written in a Country Churchyard"

With the departure of Lady Catherine, life at Pemberley returned to its usual peaceful tenor. The fair, cool weather of early October was exchanged for days of cold, sleety rain in the middle of the month. Darcy had arranged for Georgiana and Mrs. Annesley to travel to Whitwell Abbey with the colonel before they were to go into Kent for the wedding at Rosings Park. According to Georgiana's letters, Lord and Lady Whitwell continued to look very grim when the subject of the wedding came up, so they all avoided speaking about it as much as possible. She also wrote Elizabeth:

> *... We will be leaving tomorrow morning for Kent. I must admit that I am apprehensive about this wedding, not only because of my cousin St. George's underhanded pursuit of my Cousin Anne's fortune, but because of the strain it is putting on my aunt and uncle. They have still not heard from St. George; all of their information about him has been received from Lady Catherine, and that of only the most general sort. Colonel Fitzwilliam has already left for Kent in the hope that he can find an opportunity to talk seriously with his brother: not, of course, to dissuade him from the wedding, for it is obvious that it is too late for that, but to attempt to make him acknowledge the seriousness of his responsibility for Cousin Anne's health and happiness. Well, we will see how the situation lies when we get there. I will write when we arrive safely.—With much affection, etc.*

Elizabeth sighed when she read this epistle and handed it to Darcy. He read it silently, then refolded it and left the room. She shook her head sadly, a small crease between her brows, as she listened to his footsteps fade away and heard the tiny click of the door of his library. The next few days he was very tender and gentle to Elizabeth, but quiet and abstracted. At the end of three days, they received two letters from Kent: one to the both of them from Georgiana, and one for Darcy from the colonel. They opened Georgiana's first:

DEAREST SISTER AND BROTHER,—

> *The wedding went off very calmly at eleven o'clock yesterday morning, without any demonstrations of acrimony but also without any great joy, excepting that of Lady Catherine. Cousin Anne wore a magnificent cream-coloured satin dress covered with Venetian lace and with a matching bonnet and veil. Although her gown fitted her well, she seemed to disappear into all of that elaborate lace and become almost invisible. She stood up next to Lord St. George and looked like a child playing at dress-up, or possibly a doll. Lord St. George had a smug but defiant look on his face as he watched his bride walk up the aisle on the arm of Lord Whitwell, who gave her away. His eyes met those of his father, and they briefly locked in a visible struggle until St. George dropped his gaze. The other guests, of whom there were few, naturally did not realise that this was occurring, as my aunt and uncle and the colonel all maintained a dignified façade in front of them. Lady Catherine had a wedding breakfast for the newlyweds after the ceremony so that the guests could congratulate the couple and, although St. George took Anne around on his arm to accept the best wishes of the guests, not once did I see Anne smile. St. George's friends looked rather shocked when they saw how tiny and ill-looking the bride was, and most gave their muted congratulations and faded away. The breakfast was over in a little less than an hour. Lady Catherine had a lavish supper laid on for the family that evening, but Lady Anne left halfway through the meal, as she was exhausted by the exertions of the day. St. George stayed until we were finished, drinking a great deal of wine and talking to his mother-in-law with determined jollity while she preened herself over capturing a lord for her daughter. The gentlemen spent very little time over their port, as you might imagine, and they rejoined us in the drawing-room with faces like stone. We all retired very soon after they came in. I pray that Lady Anne will be well taken care of by her husband, but I continue to have grave doubts. The one minuscule piece of good news is that with all of St. George's greater sins to think about, I completely forgot to feel conscious in his presence, although this was the first time that I had seen him since we had our argument before the ball.—With my dearest affection, etc.*

Darcy sat for a moment staring at the rain beating on the long windows of the salon, then seemed to shake himself and opened the colonel's letter. After he read it he handed it to Elizabeth, saying:

"I am not sure that I should let you read this, since I would like to preserve some sense of dignity for my family. However, you already know so much of it that I suppose it cannot be made any worse."

She took the letter curiously and read:

> *Darcy,—*
>
> *Well, the wedding farce has concluded and St. George and Anne are married. As you know, I arrived in Kent two days before the wedding in the hope that I could drive some sense into my dear brother. He managed to evade me until the day of the wedding, when I bearded him in his lair before he was dressed. He continues to be as intransigent and defiant as ever and, although I spoke to him very calmly (much more calmly than I felt, I am sure you can believe), he would not listen. He admits that having an invalid wife will be a bore, but says that he will not need to spend much time in Kent. He scorns Anne's weakness and frailty and does not respect his mother-in-law. I am ashamed to be associated with this deed, but we all held up our heads and behaved with as much honour as the situation would allow us. We are leaving this morning after breakfast, and will be back at Pemberley as soon as we are able. Lady Catherine will be coming with us, as well as my parents, so tell Mr. Woodson to have his surplice at hand, because Georgiana and I are not waiting any longer. To my happiness at marrying Georgiana is added the immeasurable bliss of having an irrefutable excuse for leaving the presence of Lady Catherine as soon as we are married.—FITZWILLIAM*

These communications left them both subdued and thoughtful, and they did not discuss them but quietly went about their business, making sure that all the wedding preparations were finished by the time Georgiana and their guests returned.

The wedding took place two days later, but it was not until late in the afternoon of the wedding day that Elizabeth had time to sit down and write to Jane about it:

DEAREST JANE,—

Well, this morning Georgiana and the colonel were married in the Pemberley chapel. Lord and Lady Whitwell and Lady Catherine came directly to Pemberley after the wedding in Kent, so all of the closest family members on both sides were present, excepting only Lord and Lady St. George. François and I helped Georgiana dress, as we did in London. Her maid is coming along very well, but she did not feel that she could take all of the responsibility for such an important occasion. Georgiana told me that she would have liked to be married in her sea-green or her gold gown, since she feels that the occasions on which she previously wore those gowns were the turning points in her (as she puts it) "pursuit of the colonel's heart." Since those gowns would be somewhat unconventional and she does not want to give Lady Catherine anything more to talk about, she chose instead to wear a beautiful creamy white silk gown with no lace or other adornment. The skirt was made of several layers of the sheerest silk that you can imagine, and it floated around her like gossamer as she came down the aisle. Her hair was curled around her face, and she wore a white bonnet with a short veil, and her pearls and the bracelet that the colonel had given her for her birthday. After she was dressed, I went down to the chapel and found that Lady Catherine had planted herself in the first pew. Since there was not room for the entire family in front I sat in the second pew, and when Lord and Lady Whitwell came in a moment later they sat with me. Reynolds and Smithfield, and a few of the other upper servants, sat in the back pew. When the organist started the processional, Lady Whitwell reached over and took my hand. I looked up at her and she smiled at me, but she had tears in her eyes, as did I. Georgiana glided down the aisle like a ship with all her flags flying and her face beaming. I have never seen a bride more unwavering than Georgiana. Although she never showed the slightest loss of temper after the initial upset of their plans, when they returned from Kent I believe that any difficulties put in her way would have fallen before her determination like straw before a flame. Mr. Darcy tells me that the colonel was fidgeting in the library all morning until it was time for him to dress for the wedding—he almost drove my poor husband mad—for fear that the wedding would be put off again, but of course it was not. We had a lovely wedding breakfast, and the bride and groom left at one o'clock for Bellamy. The colonel was able to push the workmen *to make the house livable for them by finishing enough rooms for the comfort of themselves and their few servants. They will stay only a few days and then travel back to London, where they will stay at Longford House; the colonel will finish turning over his duties in the next few weeks and then resign his commission. They plan to remain in London for a few weeks, since Georgiana wishes to be there when my lying-in occurs, and we will leave for town the first week of November and stay until I am able to travel back to Pemberley.*

Our guests left not long ago and already the house seems empty without Georgiana. I am glad that she will be close once they have settled into Bellamy. I hope that your search for an estate near Pemberley goes well, my dear sister, for I long to have you near me as well. I must go now; Mr. Darcy and I are going for a short walk— the weather has finally cleared after almost two weeks of rain and we both feel the need to breathe some fresh air out-of-doors (and breathing is about the only part of a walk that I can manage at the moment!). Love to Mr. Bingley and my dear little Lizzy; and, of course, to you, my dearest Jane.—Your Loving Sister,

ELIZABETH

She folded her letter and sealed it with a melancholy sigh.

At Bellamy Georgiana was at the pianoforte, her husband sitting in a chair next to her, while she played the Italian love songs that she had performed for Elizabeth in London the previous year. The colonel watched her hands as they moved over the keys, her long fingers stroking the keys tenderly or pounding them passionately. Her hands fascinated him. They looked slender and delicate at rest, yet strong and sure when she played her instruments. When she neared the finale of the piece, Fitzwilliam noticed the ringlets at the side of her hair dancing as she reached a *crescendo*, and suddenly felt the desire to keep them dancing. He softly blew on them, pleased with their swaying. When she finished, Georgiana turned on her bench to face him.

"Is there some reason that you are blowing on my neck, Cousin?" she asked dryly, "Are you bored with the music?"

"Not at all, but I confess that I am more interested in the musician at the moment." A mischievous grin spread over his face. "And I suddenly recall that you had an extremely ticklish neck as a child."

"Oh no … do not even think about tickling my neck," she said warningly.

"Why not, little cousin? Do you not want to play?" he asked ingenuously, but she was stern:

"I commented to Elizabeth at one time that I desired to slap your face when you called me 'little cousin.'"

Fitzwilliam smiled blandly for a moment, in apparent surrender, then suddenly grabbed her waist and swung her around onto his lap, cradling her like a baby. He offered his cheek to her and said:

"Here it is, little cousin, do with it what you will."

She reached up and ran her fingers through his hair, then grasped his head and turned it to face her.

"I can see that I must do some educating of my husband in the properly respectful manner to treat his wife."

Still holding her, he put his hand on his heart and declaimed, "If I may paraphrase, my lady: 'Georgiana, love on, and I will tame my wild heart to thy loving hand.'" In his normal voice, he added, "And you thought that I had wasted my youth tormenting my tutor instead of studying my books." He offered his cheek to her again. "So what is your verdict, little cousin?"

"Perhaps, Cousin, I have changed my mind," she said softly, then tugged his head down and kissed him.

Darcy came into her morning-room just as Elizabeth was putting away her writing materials, and she looked up at him, smiling.

"Are you ready for a walk now, my love?" he asked softly.

"I will be in a moment, if you will just call François to help me change my shoes."

They walked slowly towards the trout stream and crossed the little bridge so that they could sit on a bench in a sheltered nook. After a few minutes Darcy said:

"I received a letter from Bingley this morning."

"Really? What news did he have?"

"He is going to look at an estate in Staffordshire that sounds promising. The house is rather small and in an insalubrious location, but he thinks that it might do until they could build another; and there is an inviting hill overlooking the river that would be a fine location for the new house. The property is on the border of the county, not thirty miles from here, just across the River Dove."

"That would be lovely!"

"He would like me to look at it with him the day after tomorrow. Is that acceptable to you?" He looked at her searchingly.

"Of course it is," she said in surprise.

"I do not want you to feel bored and lonely. I know that you will miss Georgiana terribly."

"Like a piece of my heart is missing," she said with a sigh. "But I will not allow myself to be sad when she is so happy. And we will soon be together again." She watched a leaf swirling by in the stream, and then smiled. "After surviving my first London season and all of the subsequent events, I confess that I could use a day or two of boredom."

Darcy laughed and squeezed the hand that was resting in his. "I am not at all surprised." He mused for a moment and then said, "I thought that the season went very well, all things considered."

"Yes. It was a little peculiar veering from being snubbed to being groveled over, but I am sure that next year no one will give me any particular notice. We will spend our time with our friends, and those who snubbed us and those who groveled after I danced with the prince regent will have forgotten that there was anything at all unusual in our marriage."

"I am sure that you are right." He smiled at her and added, "Perhaps we shall have other things to think about than the whims of London society."

She glanced down at her swelling form and smiled back at him. "Perhaps we shall."

Historical Notes

Although Mr. Darcy's adventure in Paris rescuing the prince regent's letters is fiction, the secret marriage of the Prince of Wales to Mrs. Fitzherbert is fact. As Prince of Wales, Prince George was subject to the Acts of Settlement of 1701 and the Royal Marriages Act of 1772, which required that he obtain the approval of his father, King George III, to marry. For Prince George to marry without his permission would make him ineligible to inherit the throne, and the king would never consent to his marrying a Catholic. This was a prejudice that was codified in the law and was the result of a long history of strained relations between Catholic and Protestant Christians in England that began with Henry VIII and his break with the Pope over his divorce of Catherine of Aragon in 1532.

Mrs. Maria Anne Fitzherbert was a young woman of ancient Catholic lineage who, in 1784 when she was first introduced to Prince George, had been twice widowed and lost her only child. The prince was immediately transfixed by her attractive face and demure nature, which contrasted greatly with the sophisticated ladies of the court. Her refusal to bow to his wishes and become his mistress or, later, his wife inflamed the desire of the prince and he pressured her indefatigably until she finally decided to flee to the Continent to escape his importunities. The prince fought this move, even up to the point of stabbing himself in the leg and claiming that he had attempted suicide over his despair at her pending departure. In order to calm him, she agreed to marry him, but instead left for the Continent at daylight the next morning.

The prince was kept informed of Mrs. Fitzherbert's location by her traveling companion and he sent numerous letters trying to convince her to return and marry him. When she would not respond to his letters he decided to follow her and put forward his suit in person. This required the permission of the king for him to leave the country, which was refused. After several angry letters back and forth, the prince was obliged to give up the scheme or risk a final breach with the king. After almost a year and a half of the prince's passionate urging, Mrs. Fitzherbert finally agreed to marry him and they were wed with the utmost secrecy on December 15, 1785, by a Church of England minister who had been languishing in debtors prison and was willing to commit a felony (for the illegal marriage was considered such under the law) for financial relief.

Unfortunately for the cause of true love, the prince continued his dissolute lifestyle and frequent philandering after his marriage and finally, in 1793, their relationship had deteriorated seriously. The prince's advisors strongly urged him to take a royal Protestant wife to quiet the rumours about his marriage to Mrs. Fitzherbert, in hopes that this would convince Parliament of his desire to do his duty to his country so that they would then vote to give him some relief from his debts. He finally agreed, broke off with Mrs. Fitzherbert in 1794, and in April 1795 married his cousin, Princess Caroline of Brunswick. The prince was repulsed by the princess's looks and personal hygiene when they met and he lived with her for only a very short period before he could tolerate her no longer. The princess conceived during this brief period and bore the prince a daughter, Charlotte, who lived twenty-one years before dying in childbirth, leaving the prince without a legitimate heir. The Prince and Princess of Wales spent the greater part of their married life separated.

Prince George became prince regent of England in 1811 when King George III was declared permanently insane. The king had suffered from a similar fit of madness in 1788 to 89—most likely, according to modern medical historians, the effect of porphyria, an inherited disorder of haemoglobin metabolism—and Parliament had subsequently passed laws allowing for a regency in case of a recurrence of his disorder. This indeed did recur in late 1810 and the prince was declared regent in early 1811. The Prince of Wales continued as regent until his father's death in 1820, when he became King George IV, ruling until his death in 1830.

During the Regency period and the years preceding it, England was a member of various European coalitions formed to oppose Napoleon's efforts to conquer most of the countries of Europe and bring them into his empire. On March 31, 1814, the Sixth Coalition forces occupied Paris and on April 6 Napoleon abdicated in favor of his son; then, at the insistence of the Coalition, he unconditionally surrendered on April 11, 1814. He was exiled to Elba, an island off the west coast of Italy, and remained there until February 26, 1815, when he escaped and rejoined what remained of his army. He was finally defeated by the Duke of Wellington at Waterloo on June, 18, 1815, and was exiled to the remote island of St. Helena in the southern Atlantic Ocean until his death six years later.

George Gordon Byron, Sixth Baron Byron, was one of the major poets of the Romantic period, which included the years of the Regency, and from his name is coined the phrase "the Byronic hero," of which he was the epitome. In spite of his slight stature and a limp caused by a birth defect, he was notorious for his dissolute lifestyle and numerous affairs; some historians number them in the hundreds, and many were the wives of prominent men. One of these well-known affairs was with Lady Caroline Lamb in 1812, who famously described him after their breakup as "mad, bad and dangerous to know." His poetry was popular during his life, but he was compelled to flee England in 1816 after the breakup of his marriage because of rampant rumours of incest and homosexuality, rumours assisted by the jealous Lady Caroline Lamb. "She Walks in Beauty" was written in 1814 and published in early 1815 and describes the beauty of a cousin of Byron's whom he saw when she was in mourning, her pale skin a vivid contrast to the deep black of her mourning clothes.

The presentation at court of young men and women of the nobility and upper gentry as they reached adulthood was fraught with strict tradition and protocol. The young women were presented at court Drawing Rooms and the young men at Levees. A woman who had not been presented at court before her marriage and who qualified for presentation because of her husband's status would be presented as well, since protocol required presentation before she could attend any court social functions. The dress for a man when presented at court was not significantly different from his typical formal wear, except that he was required to wear a sword. The ladies, however, had an elaborate set of instructions for their dress, and until the prince regent became king and changed the requirements they were required to wear clothing much like what we normally picture Marie Antoinette and her French court wearing. This included a tight, fitted, low-cut bodice over a corset, with the mantua, or wide hoops, which had been fashionable in the mid-eighteenth century. They must also wear a train exactly three yards in length and an ostrich feather plume in the back of their hair. Married women added a tiara to this costume. When the prince regent became King George IV, he changed the court dress requirements to fit more into the then-current fashion (except for the requirement for an ostrich feather plume in the hair, which remained). This trend of having court dress reflect contemporary fashions continued until the mid-twentieth century, when Queen Elizabeth II dropped the court presentation ritual and substituted a less formal and rigid Garden Party, which relieved much stress for the young ladies of the gentry and nobility.

For further reading I would recommend:
1. David, Saul. *Prince of Pleasure.* New York: Grove Press, 1998. (A biography of the life and regency of Prince George.)
2. McGann, Jerome J. *Lord Byron: The Major Works.* Oxford: Oxford University Press, 1986. (The introduction includes an extensive biography of Lord Byron.)
3. Orczy, Baroness Emmuska. *The Scarlet Pimpernel.* Simon and Schuster, Inc., New York, 2004. (The classic story, first published in 1905.)

978-0-595-44844-9
0-595-44844-5

Printed in the United States
126703LV00003B/80/P